The Closer You Get

THE CLOSER YOU GET

MARY TORJUSSEN

CANELO

First published in the USA in 2020 by Berkley, an imprint of Penguin Random House LLC

This edition published in the United Kingdom in 2020 by

Canelo Digital Publishing Limited
Third Floor, 20 Mortimer Street
London W1T 3JW
United Kingdom

A CIP catalogue record for this book is available from the British Library.

Print ISBN 978 1 78863 393 2
Ebook ISBN 978 1 78863 115 0

Look for more great books at www.canelo.co

Printed and bound in Great Britain by Clays Ltd, Elcograf S.p.A.

For Fiona Collins and Caz Finlay,
the best friends a writer could wish for.

And for Rosie and Louis, love always.

Prologue

That last walk down the stairs seemed to be in slow motion. The carpet was soft and yielding beneath her feet, and she could feel the fresh gloss paint of the handrail as she clutched it for balance. The late-evening sun shone through the glass door panels, lighting the hallway in a kaleidoscope of colours, and the heavy, sweet scent of roses in the vase on the console table would stay with her forever.

Her head buzzed with pressure and for a moment there on the last few steps her vision blurred and she felt she might fall. But then the sun shifted and everything sharpened into super focus.

The body — for then she knew it was a body, and no longer alive — was twisted and lay at an awkward angle. The giveaway was the blood, though. It was coming from the ear. That's never a good thing, is it?

Gently, she knelt and put her index and middle fingers on the carotid artery, just to the side of the windpipe. She couldn't feel anything at all except warm, damp skin. There was no pulse of blood, no sensation of life. Again and again she pressed her fingers down, hardly knowing what she hoped for, but still there was nothing.

Her legs shaking, she scrambled to her feet, unsure what to do, when the room darkened momentarily.

Startled, she looked up.

In the hall mirror she saw the reflection of someone staring through the window at her.

She knew then they had seen everything.

Chapter 1

Ruby

The journey home seemed to take forever. I'd left the office early for a change, determined to get ahead of the evening rush, but still the traffic snarled to a halt within minutes. That's not uncommon on a Friday evening, but it was usually a relief; this was the first time in years that I was impatient to be home.

It was a hot and humid summer afternoon in late June. The sky was overcast and showers threatened. The car's air con was on full blast but my skin still prickled with sweat. The radio was on and I flicked from news channel to music as I waited for the cars ahead to move. I couldn't find anything to focus on. My phone beeped and I glanced at the screen. It was a text from my husband, Tom.

Just left London. Back at 7 x

I read it and replied OK, then added X. I muted my phone and slid it into my handbag. I didn't want to be disturbed: I needed to think.

Eventually the traffic started up again, with no indication of what had happened. There was no broken-down vehicle, no police cars or ambulance. Nothing but stationary traffic then a sudden release. I put my foot down on the accelerator, glad to be moving, to be on my way.

-

The railway station is a couple of miles from our house and on impulse I turned into its car park instead of carrying straight on home. I needed to check. I had to be certain.

As I drove in, I gave each car I passed a furtive glance. There was just the smallest chance I'd meet him on his way out; I wouldn't have put it past him to have said he was on the train when he was actually in his car coming home from the station. I had no reason to be there and, if he saw me, he'd assume I was going somewhere or returning. The suspicion would always be there, no matter what I said. But maybe that didn't matter now. The die was almost cast.

Still, when I finally saw his car I breathed a huge sigh of relief. He'd parked quite a way from the station entrance, and I remembered that morning, when he'd left the house at six for the early train. He'd been annoyed as he couldn't find his wallet and would have to hurry. I was in bed, feigning sleep, my ears straining to hear what he was doing. Now I could see he hadn't straightened the wheels before getting out of the car and pictured him braking sharply, reaching for his briefcase on the backseat, and then jumping out and slamming the door after him. I could see his expression, knew his face would be grim, his mouth narrow.

My stomach tightened at the thought, and I quickly left the car park. I needed to get home.

–

Our house looked dim and unwelcoming under the cloudy sky. Automatically, I parked in my regular spot on the road outside the house and quickly looked around. There was no sign of anyone. I'd made sure I was home before my neighbour Oliver arrived. Usually, he and I got back from work just after six and we'd have a chat there on the path between our houses before Tom came home. I was glad he wasn't there that afternoon, but worried he might turn up at any time. I didn't want anyone to witness this.

I reversed my car up the driveway to the garage, then went through the garden gate at the back of the house. I opened the kitchen door and listened, but the air was still and all was quiet. I took the key to the shed from its hook and went back outside.

For just a second, when I was unlocking the shed, I held my breath, my stomach tilting at the thought of what I was about to do.

Two large suitcases stood there, just where I'd put them at eight o'clock that morning. Quickly I moved them into the boot of my car, checking the driveway each time in case I was disturbed. Another bag followed: my cabin bag that I'd bought for my last trip abroad. I hadn't thought then that I'd use it for this journey, too. Then there were other bags that I'd put in the shed that morning containing towels, bed linen, my hair dryer and toiletries. My laptop. None of my books were there; I didn't have room in my car to take them. I'd pick them up another day. Last to go into the boot was a box file with all my documents: my birth certificate, our marriage certificate. Deeds to the house. Insurance. Bank statements. My passport. It had surprised me how much I'd had to take and how much I'd been able to leave. Each time I put a bag into the boot, I closed it afterwards, just in case. I was being paranoid, I knew. Tom wouldn't be here just yet. I had more than an hour to go.

When everything was in my car, I rearranged the shed so that it didn't look as though the bags had been there and quickly swept the tiled floor, in case there were tracks in the dust. Then I moved my car. There was space for a couple of vehicles on our driveway, but one had to park behind the other and it could be a nuisance trying to get out in the morning. Long ago I'd got used to Tom's having priority. Now when I parked back on the road outside our house, I noted the irony that by doing something that he'd told me to do, I was able to easily escape.

Back in the house, I put the shed key on the hook by the back door, and stilled it with my hand. I didn't want anything to give me away.

The kitchen was clean and tidy. It was a large room with French doors that looked out onto the garden. The patio was a sun-trap and a riot of colour with all the flowering plants I'd put into pots and hanging baskets. When we first moved in, this room and the garden had been my pride and joy. Back then I'd had fantasies of long lazy Sunday lunches with children running around on the lawn afterwards, of Saturday-night dinners with friends, of late weekend breakfasts reading the newspapers in our dressing gowns and planning our day. Things hadn't exactly worked out like that.

Gradually, insidiously, the kitchen had become the only room in the house that was truly mine. Even my books had been relegated to the spare room. But here I could do what I wanted, decorate it however I liked. Over the years, though, cooking changed from a pleasure to a chore, something I really enjoyed only when Josh, my teenage stepson, came to stay.

Standing in the kitchen for what might be the last time, I panicked and for one mad moment I wondered whether I should cook something for Tom's dinner. He probably would have eaten it, too. Of course, I didn't. It would be too weird. What would I cook, anyway? An everyday dish to remind him what he wouldn't have again? Something special for a momentous occasion?

What I should have been cooking was written on a notepad on the fridge door. Every week Tom put together a list of meals. Tonight's was Thai curry. My hands were damp with stress as I opened the fridge door and saw all the ingredients there, waiting. That curry hadn't a chance of being made now. There was plenty of food, though; it wasn't as though he'd starve, and the wine rack held dozens of bottles. There would be fewer tomorrow morning, I knew.

I walked from room to room, running through my mental checklist, double-checking I'd taken everything I needed. It was as though I was leaving a holiday home, a place I'd always known I would leave one day. Though I'd lived here for nearly twelve years, now I could see how little space I'd taken up.

6

On the mantelpiece in the living room was a recent photo of Josh; his expression made it clear he hadn't wanted his dad to photograph him. Another was of the three of us, taken at Disney World on our first holiday together when Josh was seven. I'd been with Tom for two years then. Josh was beaming at the camera in this earlier photo and I looked happy, too. Well, I was, then. I reached out to touch it. My face in the photo was unlined, free from worry. I couldn't remember the last time I'd felt like that. A couple of days before, when Tom was in the shower, I photographed the recent photo, then zoomed in on Josh's face in the earlier one and clicked. I planned to get copies printed as soon as I could.

I looked around for my iPad. It had been my thirty-sixth birthday a few months before and Tom had bought it as a surprise. It was a newer version than his, though, and he used it more than I did. I remembered he'd charged it up the night before; he must have taken it on the train to London with him. It didn't matter. He could have it. My pulse quickened. None of this mattered now.

I checked that the driveway was still clear and quickly ran upstairs. The bathroom looked just as it always did; I'd left everything that we both used. My toothbrush and toiletries were gone from their cabinet. I knew he'd note their absence. The linen cupboard was still full; I'd taken some of the bed linen and towels we used in the spare room, but intended to start afresh as soon as I could.

Our bedroom looked just the same, though of course as soon as Tom opened the drawers and wardrobes he'd see the gaps. I couldn't take everything, but it was pretty clear that things were missing. My heart thumped at the thought of Tom searching this room later, opening doors and drawers to check what I'd taken, furious that I'd gone, that he hadn't realised I was preparing to run. That morning I'd had only an hour or so to pack and of course I couldn't make lists in case they were found, so for the last couple of weeks I'd been memorising items like in a children's memory game. I'd lie in bed each night going through the lists in my head. When I drove to work I'd test myself, saying the items out loud, frustrated when I couldn't remember something.

On the landing outside the spare room was a plastic bag that Tom had filled for the charity shop several months earlier. It had been his birthday and I had bought him some presents. He'd hinted at these for a long time, a book on a photographer he loved, a new camera case, and a Paul Smith shirt he'd bookmarked online.

"Interesting choices," he'd said, and set them to one side. My stomach had dropped. I should have known not to buy anything without his agreement. Permission, even.

He thanked me for the gifts, but something about his expression had made me say, "What? What is it?"

He'd just shaken his head and said, "Nothing. I was just thinking how it's a shame that when you're an adult you don't enjoy birthdays anymore."

I'd spent a fortune on Tom that day, on a whisky-tasting session for him and his friends in the daytime and a meal for us in Liverpool in the evening. I hadn't wanted to and I couldn't really afford it, but I'd done what I thought would please him. It wasn't enough. Of course it wasn't enough. And just a few days later the plastic bag had appeared on the landing. "Drop that off at the charity shop for me, will you?" he'd asked. When I'd looked inside, my gifts were there and I'd wanted to cry. I hadn't touched it and the bag remained there, a symbol of everything that was wrong with us. Now I felt like kicking it out of the way but knew he'd see that as a sign of victory, so I stepped past it and went into the room.

I looked around. Apart from the books on the bookcase there was nothing here that I wanted. I'd come back for them later. Next to the bookcase was a wardrobe for our winter jackets. I hadn't packed mine as I wouldn't need them for a few months. And then I realised I'd forgotten to pack something on my list and grimaced. I thought I'd remembered everything. There was a box on the shelf in the wardrobe, squashed behind the spare pillows. I hadn't seen it for a long time; I'd never felt strong enough. How could I have forgotten it?

Just as I reached for it, I heard Oliver's car pull up into his driveway next door. His car door slammed and I pushed the box back behind the pillows, so that it was out of sight again. If Oliver saw me go down the drive to my car, he might see me and come out to chat. If he saw my car, full to the brim of my belongings, he'd want to know what I was doing, where I was going. I couldn't risk that. I'd come back for the box another day.

Downstairs I paced the living room as I waited for Tom to come home. My heart thumped at what lay ahead but I had to do it. Now that I'd found the courage to go, I just wanted to get it over with.

I checked the clock. Where was he? I pulled my phone from my bag. There were no messages. I looked up the live departures page of the railway website; his train had arrived on time. He would be here soon. I tried to do some deep breathing, to count my breaths, but it just didn't work. My breathing was too shallow; I could hear myself pant.

And then he was here, driving up the road, past my car, and turning into our driveway.

My knees buckled and I sat down suddenly. All of my senses seemed heightened with stress and my skin prickled furiously as I heard the bang of the back door, his voice as he called my name, his hesitation as he realised dinner wasn't cooked.

And then the living room door opened.

Chapter 2

Ruby

Tom stood in the doorway, his tall, solid body almost filling the frame. His dark hair was damp with the heat of the day, his shirt crumpled now after the journey home. He could tell that something was up the moment he saw me. I was sitting on the sofa, frozen. His eyes darted around the room, but I was the only thing that was out of place.

"Ruby?" He sounded concerned and despite everything my eyes prickled. "Is everything all right?"

My throat was tight and I could hardly speak, but eventually I said, "Yes. Everything's fine."

He came farther into the room and instinctively I shrank away from him. He glanced at me and I knew he'd noticed that. Not much gets past him.

"What are you doing, sitting here in the dark? Are you ill?"

I shook my head.

"Your mum and dad? Are they okay?"

"They're fine," I said. I hoped they were, anyway. I hadn't spoken to them for a few days. All I'd been able to think about was this moment; it wasn't exactly something I could share with them.

He walked slowly around the room, his eyes on me, then sat on the sofa opposite me. I couldn't pretend everything was normal. At this time on a Friday night I'd always be in the kitchen, cooking dinner. Right now I should be chopping lemongrass, garlic, and chillies, not sitting in a darkening room with my jacket and shoes still on and my handbag dangling from my shoulder.

I screwed up my courage. "Tom." My tongue felt thick and dry in my mouth. "This isn't working for me." I wasn't looking at him — I couldn't — but I could sense he'd turned to stare at me. There was a heavy silence that I just had to break. "I need to go."

"Go? What do you mean?"

"I need to leave. To move out."

He was silent but he didn't look furious, the way I'd imagined he would when I'd had practice runs of this, night after night while he lay sprawled beside me in bed, deep in sleep. When he reached out to me, I had to stop myself flinching, though I knew he'd never touch me now.

"I thought something was wrong, sweetie," he said. "You've not been the same lately."

My throat swelled with tears, both at the endearment and because I hadn't thought he'd noticed. He'd been nicer than usual recently. For more than a year. But once some things are said, they can't be taken back and no amount of being nice will ever make them right.

"Where are you going to?" His voice was steady and calm, so unlike what I'd expected.

I didn't know what to say. I hadn't planned to tell him anything more than the fact that I was going, but I could see now that that wasn't going to work. And he knew I wouldn't want to stay with my family; my mother in particular would be horrified. As for friends — well, there was no one I could have gone to and he knew that as well as I did.

"It's okay," I said eventually. "I've got something sorted."

"What about your bags?"

"They're in my car. I couldn't take everything, obviously. Don't throw anything away; I'll be back to pick up the rest."

He continued to stare at me and I felt myself shrivel under his gaze.

"And I'll call Josh," I said.

"You will not." For the first time that evening his voice was harsh and unrelenting, and I shrank back. "I'll tell him."

I had to accept what he said. I didn't know what he'd tell him. This was the second time Josh had had to deal with a separation; I only hoped that now that he was seventeen he'd be able to cope with it.

I stood up. I needed to leave. What was the etiquette when you left your husband? Did you kiss? Shake hands? Glare at each other? Shout, *See you at the solicitor's*? My hand reached automatically for my bag still slung across my shoulders, and I took my car keys from it. On the key ring were my house keys.

I hesitated. Should I leave them behind? The house was in my name, too, though, of course. In fact, more of it was mine than his, but as we were married that wouldn't make any difference. My aunt had died not long after I met Tom; she'd left my sister, Fiona, and me enough money to put a good deposit on a house. Tom and Belinda had just divorced and she'd kept the house. He was broke and wouldn't have been able to buy on his own. There was no mortgage on our house now; we owned it together. I had a right to those keys. I'd have to speak to him later about what to do about selling it, but for now I just wanted to get out of there. So I kept hold of my keys, said nothing about returning them, and walked toward the door.

"Is that it?" Now he was angry and that all-familiar panic flared in my belly. "You're just leaving without any explanation?"

For a second I considered telling him exactly why I was going, but I stopped myself in time. My keys squeezed so tightly in my hand they nearly broke the skin. "I'm sorry. We've talked about this so many times over the years. I just can't do it anymore."

I'd just reached the front door when I remembered. "Oh," I said, taking off my Fitbit. The skin on my wrist looked tender and pale without it. "I won't be needing this." I put it on the hall table and noticed the green cover of my iPad sticking out of his briefcase. "And it was nice of you to buy me the iPad, but you use it more than I do, so you can keep it."

I didn't dare look at him as I left. He didn't follow me out to my car, but as I walked down the driveway I knew he was staring at me. When I started the car and sneaked a glance back at the house, he'd gone.

Chapter 3

Ruby

I drove as quickly as I could until I was a mile away from home, then stopped the car in a quiet street. My heart was pounding so hard that I had to close my eyes and breathe deeply, counting my breaths, until I started to feel more calm. I was hot and red and my palms were sweating, but all I could feel was relief. It was as though a huge weight had lifted from my shoulders. I'd thought it would be worse than that. Much worse. I'd envisaged a row, with me pleading, him blocking my path, berating me. Then his pièce de résistance: he would cry. He knew how much I hated that.

He's let me go, I thought. *He must have been as unhappy as I was.*

Suddenly my face was drenched with tears and I pulled some tissues out of my bag to scrub myself dry. I'd been prepared for this. All those nights I'd spent rehearsing today, and now that the performance was over, I was exhausted. My phone beeped and I leaped to check it. It was a message from Tom.

I'm sorry if I've done anything to upset you. I didn't mean to hurt you. x

I blinked. I wasn't expecting that. Then another message came through:

I'm worried about you, Ruby. Where will you stay tonight? I'm happy to sleep in the spare room if you want to come home. x

I knew how much that would have cost him to write. He'd never been one to apologise first or to admit he was wrong at all. I didn't know whether to reply; I hadn't factored this into my rehearsals.

Don't worry about me, I replied. I'll be fine. I'll be in touch.

I hesitated, not knowing whether to put a kiss at the end. I don't think I'd ever sent him a message without a kiss, whether I'd meant it or not. It wouldn't have been worth my while. And then I thought no, of course I shouldn't put a kiss on the message; I was leaving him.

I looked at my watch. It was time to go. Butterflies fluttered in my stomach as I thought of what lay ahead. I started the car and at the next turning headed south.

–

As I approached the hotel, I checked my rearview mirror. Nothing was behind me. I turned quickly and drove through to the car park at the back. I glanced round, just to make sure, but I didn't recognise any cars. I parked in the corner, almost out of sight. The first spots of rain were beginning to fall as I took my overnight bag from the boot of the car and I hurried through the car park to the front of the hotel. The receptionist looked up as I entered the lobby.

"Good evening," she said.

"Hi. I've a room booked for a few nights."

"What name is it?"

I hesitated. "Sheridan."

She scrolled down her computer screen and at first I thought she couldn't find it, but then she said, "Oh yes, here we are." She took a plastic key card from a drawer and programmed it. "Room 201. We have room service until midnight and breakfast is between six and ten every morning." She smiled brightly at me. "Would you like a hand with your bag?"

"No, no, thanks." I took the card from her. "I can manage."

I stood by the lift, shaking. This was the most daring thing I'd done in my entire life and now that the moment had come it was as though I was watching myself from outside my own body. The lift pinged and opened. I walked in, gripping my bag. My finger slid over the button for the second floor. The lift suddenly seemed claustrophobic and by the time its doors opened I felt light-headed. I dragged my bag down the corridor toward the room, my heart beating fast. Outside the door I stood for a second, hardly able to breathe. This was it. Once I went in, there was no going back.

Chapter 4

Ruby

It was only when I was safely in the hotel room that I could let myself relax. I kicked off my shoes and quickly unpacked my bag. I hung up my clothes and when I lined up my toiletries at the side of the bathroom sink, I caught sight of myself in the mirror. My makeup was a mess from crying and my face was flushed with relief and excitement. I started to smile and found I couldn't stop.

Quickly I cleaned my face. My eyes were still swollen and my cheeks were pink, so I reapplied my makeup, then added a dab of perfume to my throat and wrists. The sweet familiar smell always calmed me. I looked at my phone. No messages, but I wasn't really expecting one. My stomach rumbled and I realised I was starving. I couldn't face going downstairs to the restaurant, so I rang room service and ordered wine and sandwiches.

It was strange to be alone in a hotel room, propped up on pillows, with only the television for company. The usual Friday-night programmes were on, ones that I'd watch with Tom. He and I would have a drink and sometimes we'd chat, but often we'd watch in silence. It took a lot to make us laugh; if he was the wrong side of the bottle, I'd always let him go first. That night I couldn't concentrate long enough to focus on anything. I kept thinking of the conversation I'd had with him that evening. I'd expected insults to be hurled at me, recriminations to be shouted, his face close to mine, his spittle showering my mouth. I thought I'd be made to feel bad, no matter what that took. The longer I held out, the harder he'd try. I used to cave in, but over the last year or two I'd started to retreat into myself, distancing myself from what he was saying, as though he was talking to someone else. He'd noticed, of course he had, and he'd ramped up his efforts. It wasn't a game; it was more like war.

I'd anticipated having trouble getting out of the house, not because he was violent – he'd never touched me when we were arguing and would stay at least an inch away – but because he hated not to have the last word. It was wearing, to say the least. Sometimes he'd bring up an argument he'd lost years before and try to win it afresh. I'd thought that might happen tonight, too, and frowned. I'd been let off lightly. Why was that? I felt a pang of guilt as I thought of the messages he'd sent since I left the house. He wasn't always horrible, I knew. He could be kind and generous, too. Those messages reminded me of the man he'd been when we first got together.

Just then I heard a noise in the corridor and leaned forward, straining my ears. I could hear the fire door that split the corridor slowly shut, and then a thud. I jumped to my feet and threw open the door.

A porter was pushing a drinks trolley along to the next room. "Sorry!" he said. "That door's a nuisance. I hope I didn't disturb you."

"No," I said, disappointed. "No, it's okay. I thought you were bringing me something to eat."

I went back to the television and started to flick through channels again. Soaps. Game shows. The news. Nothing that could interest me now. I hadn't thought of bringing a book to read and wished I'd brought my iPad with me. Out of habit I got up and started to pace the floor but that made me even more anxious and I quickly got back onto the bed. I pulled out my phone and looked at some news sites and at a forum I liked, but I couldn't think straight. That conversation with Tom had exhausted me. Confused me, too.

There was a clink of dishes and a rap at the door. Room service had arrived.

As soon as the porter had gone, I poured a large glass of wine. Rain was coming down now, lashing against the window. It was comforting, somehow, like a rainy Saturday when you wake up and realise you don't have to go to work. I stood at the window for a long time, watching the lights of the cars, blurred through the rain-splattered window, as they drove along the road. None came into the hotel car park.

Where was he?

—

It took a while for me to realise that Harry wouldn't arrive that night. At ten I had a bath. I propped my phone on the basin beside the bath with a towel under it so that I could grab it to read any message as soon as it came through. The phone remained silent. No calls from Tom, luckily. None from my parents or from my friend Sarah, from work. She and I often chatted in the evening if we'd been too busy to talk at work. I was glad she hadn't called me; I had no idea what I'd say to her. And I couldn't risk Harry calling and having to leave a voicemail message. He might need to speak to me urgently and I wouldn't know until I'd finished my call. I drummed my fingers on the side of the bath. All I wanted was to talk to him.

I knew where he was. He was in the same position I'd been in that night, telling his wife, Emma, that he was leaving her. We'd planned it all, synchronised timings. Now all I had to do was to wait for him.

Chapter 5

Ruby

Harry and I met when I started working for him just over eighteen months ago. The company I was working for had relocated to Edinburgh and I'd been made redundant. I'd spent a while looking for permanent jobs when an agency got in touch just before Christmas to say there was a vacancy at Sheridan's, a company based five miles from home. The PA to the managing director had left and her replacement had just let them down. The MD, Harry Sheridan, was looking for someone who would work there for a month on a temporary basis with a view to a permanent job. He'd felt that was a more reliable way of judging whether someone was a good fit.

He'd asked the agency if I could come in for a couple of days, just after Christmas, while it was quiet. That first morning I arrived, he and I were the only two in the office. The receptionist had sent me up to the third floor and Harry was waiting for me as I exited the lift. He was tall with cropped fair hair, and dressed casually in jeans and sweater. He looked nice enough, pretty ordinary really, until he smiled. Then everything changed.

"Hi." He shook my hand. "I'm Harry Sheridan."

"Ruby Dean."

"Thanks for coming in. I thought it would be better to bring you in this week while it's quiet, so that I can go through some things with you. I hope it's not spoiled your Christmas break."

"Not at all." Actually I was happy to be up and out of the house; the atmosphere had been toxic for days. Tom and I had had an argument, one that left me hot with shame and embarrassment afterwards. We hadn't spoken to each other for several days and when I got up to go to work, I could see he was dying to know where I was going. He wouldn't ask, though, and I wasn't going to tell him until he did.

Harry took me into his office suite and showed me around. His office overlooked fields at the back of the building and there was a window between his room and the outer office where I learned I would sit with a woman called Sarah, who worked for another director. It was two days after Christmas and the office was full of Christmas lights and half-empty tins of chocolates.

We sat in his room drinking coffee while he talked about the business and how it had started up.

"I was working in an office on a big industrial estate, similar to this," he said, "miles from any shops. There was a staff canteen, but it didn't sell anything healthy, and the vending machines just sold sugar and salt, in one form or another. And all the people in the office would complain about it, that they were putting on weight. They'd forget to bring in something from home and there were no shops nearby, so they'd end up eating junk food. And I just thought, what if you could get healthy snacks delivered to you at work? It's worked out really well. Some people have something delivered every day, others once a week, usually on a Monday morning or a Friday afternoon. We're doing pretty well." He laughed. "It's amazing what people will buy if it's in small enough quantities and cute enough packaging."

"Interesting," I said. "But to judge whether it's a really good idea, I'd have to sample them, of course."

He laughed again. "I'll arrange that."

I'd given him my CV when I met him and now he pulled it out of the envelope.

"So you were made redundant from Jackson and Greene?"

"Yes, they closed their offices here and moved up to Edinburgh," I said. "I was PA to the MD, Leo Jackson."

"And you didn't want to move up there? It's a beautiful city."

"My husband's doing well in his job here," I said. "He didn't want to move." I didn't tell him that as Tom earned more, he had the final say. "His son's here, too, so he wants to stay close. And Edinburgh's much more expensive." We were just about to make the final payments on our mortgage; as Tom had said, it didn't make sense to start borrowing again.

Harry was quiet, reading through my CV. "Oh, you went to Liverpool University?" he asked. "I did, too, a few years before you, though." For the next couple of hours I don't think we said another word about work. We found we had so much in common; we'd both lived in the Penny Lane area, had gone to the same bars, spent the summer evenings in Sefton Park.

For those two days we were alone and by the time I left the office on Friday evening, I felt as though I'd known him for months. That night, we went down in the lift together and there was a moment where we both reached out to press the button for the ground floor and our hands touched.

We both felt that spark. For a split second I thought I'd got a shock off the panel on the lift wall, but then it registered that I'd touched his hand, not the panel. I jumped back and pushed my hands into my coat pockets. I didn't dare look at him. We both stood in silence, then realised the lift hadn't moved. Neither of us had pressed the button.

He gave a nervous laugh and when I looked furtively at him his face was scarlet.

"The office is shut for New Year's, so I'll see you on Wednesday," he said formally as we exited the building.

"Okay. Happy New Year."

"Happy New Year," he said, and there was another moment, then, when we stood looking at each other. "Let's hope it's a good one."

I felt so tender toward Harry as I remembered our first meeting. I picked up my phone to send him a message to tell him I understood if he couldn't get away that night, but managed to stop myself. We'd agreed right from the start that we would never do that. We used only the office messenger system to communicate, never our own phones, though Harry would call the office landline if he was driving and wanted to chat at the end of the day. It would have been too easy to be discovered if we contacted each other at home. And I knew that if Harry was likely to get in touch in the evening, I'd sit there waiting for his message, yearning for it. I wouldn't be able to have my phone out of my sight. He'd be the same, he'd said. I didn't even have his number on my phone; I couldn't bear the thought of Tom finding a text or a voicemail message there, of thinking – knowing – something was going on.

So in all that time we didn't swap numbers. We would talk on the office phone, send internal messages throughout the day, but most of all we'd just talk face-to-face. His office was next to mine; we could see each other through the glass. That afternoon, though, we'd entered each other's numbers onto our phones and he made us memorise them, too, just in case.

"In case of what?" I'd asked.

"In case I'm so eager to get to the hotel that I crash the car," he'd said. "Think of it – the car crashes, the phone's destroyed. I'll need to get the ambulance guys to call you."

I'd gone back to my desk to do some work, and he called me on the office phone several times over the next few hours, just to tell me my own mobile number. I was no better; I did the same. We were both giddy with excitement. Apprehension, too.

That afternoon, as soon as Sarah had left work for the weekend, I'd tapped at his office door and said, "Tonight?"

His face had lit up and I knew that he loved me. "Tonight."

"You're sure? It's not too late to back out."

He nodded. "I'm absolutely sure," he said. "I promise."

An hour later my skin was pink and soggy with the heat of the water and I hauled myself out of the bath. I knew he wouldn't come that night, but I thought of the next morning, of him arriving at the hotel while I slept, coming into my room and kissing me awake. As I smoothed body lotion into my skin and brushed my teeth, ready for sleep, I thought of him at home right then, thought of them arguing, him telling his wife he loved me. His wife crying. I caught my eye in the mirror and looked away. *It was his suggestion we got together*, I reminded myself. *He said it would all work out, that he and Emma were unhappy together. That he loved me and wanted to be with me.*

Still, though, when I put on moisturiser I didn't look at my reflection in the mirror, and when I turned off the lamps and lay in the darkness, my face was hot with shame.

Chapter 6

Ruby

I woke with a jolt at seven the next morning. The curtains in the hotel room were thick and the room was dark. For a moment I thought I was in my bedroom at home with Tom beside me, but when I stretched out my leg and found nothing but the cool sheets, I remembered everything.

Last night I was awake until the early hours thinking of all possible scenarios: maybe Emma had clung to him, shrieking, unable to cope with him leaving. My stomach dropped. Did that mean he'd feel he could never leave? Maybe he'd had an accident on his way home. I'd checked and checked the local news and travel sites on my phone and there was nothing reported, but then there was only usually a report when a road was blocked or there'd been a fatal accident. Because of his business he was well known enough in the local community for anything like that to be reported. I breathed a sigh of relief; at least there was nothing about that online.

And then another fear hit me. Maybe he'd had a heart attack. He was forty-one. Surely that wasn't a dangerous age? Had the stress been too much? But he seemed healthy enough, an advertisement for his own products, and he hadn't seemed stressed when I left work the evening before. He was nervous, of course, but he was happy. Vibrant. He was about to have a final meeting with Jane, Emma's sister, who was working for Sheridan's as their chief accountant. Jane was leaving work that weekend to go back to university to study for an MBA. We'd based the date we'd leave home on her departure date as neither of us wanted to work with her once she knew Harry was leaving her sister for me.

I bumped into her by the lifts as I was about to head off home.

"Sorry I'm so late to see Harry," she'd said. "I've been rushing around all day. I need to hand over all my work. Is he in his office?"

"He's still in a meeting with Rick Brown. He shouldn't be long."

I felt so awkward as I took her to my office and made her some coffee. She told me about her new course and her hopes for job opportunities afterwards, and I felt like the worst kind of woman, chatting to her when her brother-in-law was planning to leave her sister to be with me.

"You go off, Ruby," she said after a few minutes. "Sorry to have kept you." She took her coffee into Harry's office. "I'll wait here for him." She pulled her phone out of her bag and I could see that I was dismissed. "I've got some calls to make before I go."

–

I stayed in the hotel room all day, calling for room service, waiting for Harry to show up. I was still expecting him to come flying through the door, apologising like crazy, kissing me and hugging me and wanting reassurance that I hadn't changed my mind. The room was reasonably big, but I felt confined. I hated sitting still all the time and found myself pacing, walking around the two armchairs and coffee table, around the desk and leather chair, just walking and walking around the room, counting each step I took to try to stop myself obsessing about where on earth he was.

Social media was not my friend that day. I stared obsessively at his photo on Facebook. It was one from a couple of years ago, before I'd known him. He was on holiday, sitting at a bar in Jamaica, drinking a cold beer. He was smiling and raising a glass in celebration; I'd always hated that photo, because I'd known he was smiling at Emma. Just as a stopped clock is right twice a day, a marriage is never completely unhappy. There will be days – or moments, even – when everything's fine and you remember why you're with that person. That photo seemed to have caught one of those moments in their marriage.

He and I had never been friends on Facebook. I rarely used it; it just seemed to magnify the faults in my life.

"Emma uses my phone sometimes," he said when I asked him about it. "I don't want to have to worry about whether she's going to see messages we've sent each other. It's not fair to her. And I don't want to see what you're up to with your husband. I don't want to see photos of you both and see what a great time you're having."

I didn't know exactly which recent photos of us would show that, but I knew what he meant. "What about Twitter?"

"I hardly use it unless it's for work. I don't use social media that much, really. Emma does, much more than I do. She loves Instagram."

I wished he hadn't told me that. As soon as he went into a meeting I turned my screen so that Sarah couldn't see it and signed up to Instagram, using an alias. There was Emma, with gleaming blond hair and a huge smile. Her eyes were blue, her skin tanned, and she looked so confident, so feisty, that immediately I knew why Harry was with her. I felt sick with jealousy. I closed the screen and carried on with my work, but all I could think about was the way she looked at the camera straight on, her chin tilted upward, her gaze direct. She wasn't someone I wanted to get on the wrong side of.

I hadn't looked at Instagram since. I hadn't wanted to think about Emma, to see what I was up against. But that day, on my own at the hotel, I went through every single post she'd made on there. I looked at the photos she'd taken, the comments she made, the people she followed. I watched the clips she'd posted and made a mental note of all the movies and television programmes she liked. She hadn't posted anything for a few weeks, I noticed, and briefly wondered why, but then I scrolled through her history and saw she'd have a spurt of posts, then nothing for a while. Luckily there weren't many photos of Harry on there; while I wanted to see him, I didn't want to look at him through her eyes.

At home I'd made a point to not look at either Harry or Emma online. I knew Tom would be all over it if he'd noticed. And to be honest, I wanted to pretend she didn't exist. I didn't want to think of Harry at home, chatting to her, watching those movies with her. I felt sick at the thought of catching him out in a lie, where he told me he'd had an early night, only to see her post that they'd been out for a meal with friends. It's a head-in-the-sand approach, I think, which you need to have if you're having an affair with someone who's married. You can't let yourself think about the reality, that they are living a life separately from you, and that is not only their real life, it's their choice. You don't tend to find photos of married men in handcuffs or chained to walls in cellars with their wives standing guard over them. Or not on the sites I go to, anyway.

When evening came and darkness fell, I knew he wouldn't be coming. I felt so hemmed in, in that hotel room. I had to get out, to get some air. And of course, though I told myself I was just going for a drive around, I knew where I was going. I went out to my car, where I'd hidden it away the night before. It was still packed full of bags and boxes. As I said, sometimes it's best to avoid reality, so I angled my rearview mirror so that I couldn't see any of my things, and set off.

I'd never been to Harry's house before, never driven past it, even in the early days. I'd been too scared, for one thing, worried I'd be seen and he'd think I was stalking him. And then after I knew I loved him, I didn't want to go near, to see the life he lived with another woman. Now I was nervous but determined to take the risk. I glanced around. The road was lined with chestnut trees and his house was large, about thirty years old, and separated from the pavement by a large lawn.

When I saw there was a light in their hallway, I put my foot down and drove quickly to the end of the road. I stopped there for a while, my heart beating fast. He was inside; I could knock if I wanted to, and I'd see him. I'd be able to ask him what had happened, where he'd gone to. And then I thought of his wife, Emma, standing behind him. I could picture her now, giving me that sassy stare. My stomach clenched as I thought of her saying, *Who is it, darling?* What would he reply? Suddenly I realised I didn't know what he'd say. What he'd do. Would he embrace me or deny he knew who I was?

It was a quiet neighbourhood and no one was around. I started my car and slowly drove past their house again. And then I realised. Her car was there: a little red Mini that I'd seen her in one day when she picked him up from work. His wasn't there. I knew it wouldn't be in their garage; we'd talked one day about how everyone just filled their garages with junk.

I turned the car round and stopped just short of his house. It looked as though she was at home, perhaps in the kitchen at the back. Then it dawned on me. She was at home. He was out. Had he come to see me? Had he left her?

Quickly I drove to the end of his street and turned onto the main road. My heart was almost in my mouth as I raced back to the hotel. I parked in the first space I saw and ran into the lobby. The receptionist looked up at me and smiled. She started to greet me, but I dashed into the lift. I hadn't a moment to spare. I grabbed my key card from my pocket and swiped it until I could open the door.

No one was there. I stood in the room, sweating and panting, my heart racing and my mind in a whirl. Where was he?

I looked everywhere for a message, some sign he'd been there, but there was nothing.

I collapsed onto the armchair. Had he only just left when I got to his house? Would he turn up here soon? I went to the bathroom and saw myself in the mirror, my hair damp and wild, my face red. If he arrived now, he'd recoil, I thought, and held a cold, wet washcloth to my face until I calmed down.

He didn't arrive that night and for the rest of the weekend I waited there, too nervous to go out in case I missed him. I paced the room, counting my steps, wishing almost for the reassurance of my Fitbit. And then I'd shake myself and sit down again, try to watch a movie or a game show, anything to take my mind off the fact that Harry hadn't shown up.

Of course I still felt the pressure to look good when he did get here, so though I was staying in, my face was made up, my hair brushed, and I wore my nicest clothes. But deep inside I think I knew by then that he wouldn't come, and by Sunday night, my shoulders were slumped and no matter how much makeup I had on, the dejected air I wore took the shine off my face.

Chapter 7

Ruby

By Monday morning I was desperate to see Harry. I still had faith in him, still believed something had happened to prevent him from coming to me. If only I could see him, all would be explained.

I hadn't drawn the curtains the night before in case I overslept, and woke at five o'clock as the first flickers of dawn stole into my room. I leaped out of bed and showered, blow-dried my hair, and ironed my dress for work. By six I was sitting by the window, waiting impatiently for him to arrive. I'd been sure he'd come to the hotel early that morning, to explain what had happened. We'd be interrupted at work, I knew; we wouldn't be able to talk privately until Sarah left to pick up her kids and this sort of conversation was too important for internal messaging. I tried to think of his diary and whether he had any meetings today, but for the last week I'd been working on automatic pilot and now I couldn't remember any of his plans. But at least I'd be able to see him. To know he was all right. And to ask him when we'd be together.

Gradually I realised Harry simply wouldn't have time in rush hour traffic to get here to talk to me and then get back to work, so at seven o'clock I picked up my jacket and handbag and left the room, checking again with reception whether anyone had left a message for me. Nobody had. Of course they hadn't; I had my phone with me, fully charged and silent as the grave. Before I left the room I stuck a note onto the mirror just in case he turned up while I was out. *Call me*, it said. I left my number to remind him, though he'd sworn he'd never forget it. *Call me anytime. I love you x*

–

The car park at Sheridan's was half-full. I couldn't see Harry's car there. I looked at my watch. He was usually here by now. My anxiety ramped up and I drove around a couple more times. He definitely wasn't here. I parked away from the rest of the staff; I didn't want anyone to notice that my car was crammed full of bags and cases.

I saw my friend Sarah in the distance and hurried toward her. We walked into the building together.

"Good weekend?" she asked. She knew nothing of my affair with Harry, of course. Nobody did.

"It was okay." I tried to keep my voice bright. I thought of the hours and hours I'd spent staring into space, waiting for the click of the door, for my phone to ring. For anything, really, to tell me what the hell was going on. "I was a bit bored, actually."

She looked at me as though I were mad. "Bored?"

I forced myself to laugh. It felt odd talking to her; the only person I'd spoken to since Friday night had been the receptionist at the hotel. There was so much to say, but nothing I could tell her.

I fumbled in my bag for my lanyard and hooked it around my neck. I followed Sarah as she walked through the security turnstile. She flashed her card, waited for the green light, and went through. Then I flashed my card. Except when I did it, the light shone red instead of green. I flashed it again. And again. It was still red.

"Danny?" I called to the security guard. "There must be something wrong with my card. Can you let me through? I'll get a new one when I'm upstairs."

Danny came over to me, his expression as polite as usual, but without his customary smile. "Step aside, will you, Mrs. Dean?"

I frowned. *Mrs. Dean?* We were all on first-name terms at work. Without thinking, I stepped aside and immediately the crowd behind me formed a queue for the turnstile.

He went over to the chairs that were for visitors, next to the entrance. "Take a seat here, will you?"

Sarah was waiting for me on the other side of the reception area. "You go on," I said to her. "I'll get this sorted out and see you up there."

She nodded. "I'll make coffee."

I sat and waited, though I didn't know what I was waiting for. Danny had disappeared and I had no idea where he'd gone. Perhaps he needed a key to open the gate? And then I saw Mark, one of the guys from the Sales department, come in from the car park, carrying a huge box. Another security guard came over to the turnstiles and flashed his own card so that Mark could pass through.

I walked over to the turnstile. "Can I come through with him?" I asked. "I'll get my card sorted as soon as I get upstairs."

"Sorry, miss." The security guy looked at me, then looked quickly away. "You'd better wait for Danny to come back."

I stared at him, but he walked away. Slowly I went back to my chair. I waited for another five minutes. People filed through from my office and waved hello. A couple of the directors' PAs gave me curious glances but I just smiled and said, "Won't be long."

And then the lift doors opened and our director of Human Resources, Eleanor Jones, got out. A group of young women instantly stood up straight and I saw one check her watch, clearly relieved she was early. Eleanor was a stickler for time-keeping. She was holding a cardboard box that looked like it held reams of photocopier paper. It was only as she looked across at me that I realised she was there to meet me.

My stomach lurched. She came over to me and though I wanted to stand to greet her, I couldn't; my legs were shaking too hard. She sat beside me, pink with embarrassment.

"I'm sorry, Ruby," she said. She passed the box to me. I looked down and saw my things from my desk drawers. My spare cosmetics. My sweater. A hairbrush. Headache pills. I winced. I knew my contraceptive pills would be in there, too. On top was an envelope with my name on it. "Your contract's been terminated."

Chapter 8

Ruby

Eleanor didn't stay long and neither did I. I started to ask why they were letting me go, but she stopped me.

"You haven't been here two years yet," she said. "Legally we're not obliged to give you that information. I'm sure you know the reason why, though. I don't think we need to discuss it here, do you?"

I glanced round at the inquisitive faces that were passing by and flushed. How had she known about our affair?

"But you haven't the right to fire me." My voice rose. "It's not my fault!"

Eleanor looked as though she wanted to say something more, but she merely repeated, "You know that within the first two years we have the right to let you go at any time and for any reason. You've been here eighteen months."

"But…"

She stood up. Clearly our meeting was at an end. She touched the envelope in the box. "I've written you a short reference and there's a cheque for this month's salary, a month's notice, and any outstanding holiday pay, too."

I stood, too, not knowing what to do or say. She passed me the box and ushered me to the door. I saw a couple of friends walking in, hurrying when they saw Eleanor. I could tell she was tempted to chase after them to remind them to be on time, but instead she stood on guard at the door, watching as I walked to my car.

Rage hit me as I drove away. I'd never been fired before; my work was always well done and I hadn't had a day's absence in the eighteen months I'd worked there. I didn't let myself acknowledge that that was because I hadn't wanted to miss a day with Harry. I drove to a supermarket car park a couple of miles away and parked as far as I could from anyone else. My heart pounded as I took out my phone.

I was so filled with shame and rage that although I'd promised I'd never do this while he was still with Emma, I dialled Harry's mobile number. Immediately, his voice boomed out.

"Hi," he said.

My heart banged. "Harry?"

And then he continued. "This is Harry Sheridan. You've reached my voicemail. Please leave a message."

I managed to control myself. I knew I mustn't leave a message. Quickly I ended the call and tapped in Harry's direct number at work. After two rings the call was picked up.

"Good morning, Harry Sheridan's office."

I held my breath for a second. It wasn't him. I recognised the voice; it was Paula, Eleanor's assistant. We weren't exactly friends, but we got along okay.

"Paula? It's me, Ruby."

"Oh," she said, and my heart sank. This wasn't going to be easy. "Did you want something?"

"Can I speak to Harry?" I wasn't even going to pretend that I didn't know why she was odd with me. "Can you put me through?"

She gave a sharp intake of breath, as though this was person-ally affecting her. "I'm sorry. All of Mr. Sheridan's calls are coming through me now." There was a pause and then she said formally, "Would you like to leave a message?"

For a split second I thought of giving her the message I really wanted to pass on and Paula going to the canteen at lunchtime and repeating it to everyone, but I managed to restrain myself.

"That's all right," I said politely. "Don't worry."

I ended the call before she could. It was the only satisfaction I could take.

–

I went back to the hotel then, not sure what to do. I stopped at reception on my way in and asked whether anyone had called, but they hadn't. There was no reason why Harry would have called the hotel, but I always felt I had to ask. I hurried to my room, still hoping he'd be there, and as I turned the corner I saw the door to my room was open. My heart leaped but then the maid came out, pushing a laundry trolley laden with fresh towels and toiletries. We said hello and she left the door open. I could see in an instant that he hadn't been there.

I sat on the bed and opened the envelope, just in case Harry had left a message for me. Of course he hadn't. The reference was signed by Eleanor and was brief enough to make my face smart. It would be clear to anyone that I hadn't left of my own accord. I pulled everything out of the box. It was humiliating to think of someone going through my desk like that, packing up my things, knowing I'd been fired. I wondered how early they'd been in to work, to do that so quickly. When had they been told? *What* had they been told? I sent a quick text to Sarah to ask her to call me.

I took one of the contraceptive pills out of its packet. This was the time of day I'd usually take it. At the weekends, I'd smuggle a couple of pills underneath an eyeshadow palette. I couldn't let Tom find them. Now I held it to my mouth and wondered whether I should take it or not. Was there any point? But I thought of Harry saying "*I promise*" and summoned my faith in him. I slid the pill into my mouth and swallowed it.

My phone rang, startling me. I leaped off the bed thinking it must be Harry but saw Sarah's name on the screen.

"What's going on?" she asked. "When I got here someone from HR was at your desk, emptying the drawers."

"Who was it?"

"That dark-haired guy. The intern. I think his name's Nathan. He wouldn't tell me what's happened. He looked terrified; I think he thought it was my desk. Have they moved you to another department?"

"Not exactly," I said. "I've been fired."

"What? What for?"

I hesitated. "Oh, they didn't say. They just said they'd ended my contract."

"They can't do that!"

"They can," I said. "I've only worked there for eighteen months. They can dismiss staff at any time up to two years."

"What? Just like that?"

"Seems so."

There was a silence then and I knew she was calculating how long she'd been there. "But why?" she asked eventually. "Why would they do that?" I started to speak, but she interrupted me in a low, hurried voice, "Not now. I have to go. I'll call you later." And she was gone.

—

By the early afternoon I felt as though I was going crazy. I'd driven past the offices a couple of times, trying to see whether Harry's car was there. I couldn't see it. He normally parked by the entrance to the building; there were only a few spaces there and it was tacitly understood that they were left for senior management or clients, but sometimes, if he came to work a bit later, he'd just grab any space he could. I didn't want to go onto the car park itself; I'd seen one of the security guys out there and although I doubted they were waiting for me, I wasn't going to take any risks. Even just driving up and down the road was stressful enough — I was lucky that my car was small and black, like thousands of others — but at least they couldn't stop me from driving on a public road. By five o'clock, I was parked farther up the hill, able to see the cars as they formed a line

38

to leave the car park. There was no sign of Harry's car. Again I drove up and down, feeling like a fool. By six thirty the car park was empty except for the cars belonging to the security guards and cleaners, and I knew there was no point hanging around.

And then I thought, *Maybe he's left early and gone to the hotel!* I raced back, my heart pounding, but knew as soon as I opened the door and called his name that he wasn't there. My message was still there, though, stuck to the mirror: a pathetic reminder to a man who clearly didn't love me that I wasn't about to give up on him.

–

That evening I made inroads into the minibar and dialled Harry's number again and again, though it was still switched off. I just wanted to hear him say his name. Love was now mixed with utter rage and I was just sane enough to not leave a message. My phone rang as I was reaching for a can of tonic water. My glass toppled and gin spilled onto the bed as I grabbed my phone. When I saw the caller's name on the screen, my heart sank. It was Tom. I hesitated, then answered it.

"Hi, Ruby. How are you?"

"I'm okay, thanks." Try as I might, I knew I didn't sound convincing. "How are you?"

"Oh." He laughed nervously. "I'm missing you, actually. The house seems really empty without you."

Tears prickled the back of my eyes. If he wanted to know what loneliness felt like, he should try being in my position. I coughed and said, "You'll be fine, Tom." I knew he would be. He'd always make sure he was.

"I just wondered… Do you want a divorce? You didn't say."

The odd thing was that although I'd thought of this since long before Harry and I decided to live together, Tom's question now was like a punch in the stomach. I had enough to deal with, without having that as well. "Oh. I hadn't thought of that. I suppose so."

"Well, if we're living separately it seems the obvious thing to do. It's pretty clear you don't want to be with me anymore." There was a long pause and I had to stop myself from saying I didn't know what I wanted. "Do you want me to file? I think you're meant to be living apart for two years first, but people seem to move much faster than that."

Panic flared in my stomach. "I don't have any money for a solicitor. Can't we sell the house first?"

There was silence and I looked at the phone screen to check we were still connected. "I could get a couple of estate agents to call round and give quotes if you want? It would make it clearer when we divide everything up, I suppose. It's up to you, Ruby."

I looked around the hotel room, at the pile of empty minia-tures that lay on the bedside table, at the box I'd been given by Eleanor. It was so pathetic. I'd made such a mess of my life.

"What is it?" he said softly. "Hey, don't cry, babe."

Babe? I couldn't remember the last time he'd called me that. At the beginning it had been his pet name for me and each time he said it I'd melted inside. It had been a long time since I'd reacted like that but that day somehow those old feelings came back. His voice sounded so kind and it reminded me of when we first got together, when he'd been gentle and loving. When I thought I was special.

"Talk to me," he said, his voice low and urgent.

I couldn't. I couldn't say anything.

"Have you changed your mind? Do you want to come back?" He made it sound so easy. So enticing. "We can talk things through, Ruby. Just come home."

"No," I said quickly, before I could tell him to come and pick me up and never let me go again. "No. Sorry, I have to go."

I ended the call but sat on the bed holding my phone tightly, my face wet with tears. Just for a moment I couldn't remember why I'd left and why I couldn't return.

Chapter 9

Ruby

Later that evening Sarah called me again.

"How're things, Ruby?"

"Oh, you know. Couldn't be worse, really."

"Have you been drinking?"

"I've just been fired," I said. "I've got the right to have a drink."

"You're right. I'm sorry. And I'm sorry I didn't call earlier. It was hectic all day and then I was busy with the kids. This is the first chance I've had to talk to you. How are you feeling?"

I longed to talk to her about what had happened but I couldn't. "Oh, okay. It was a shock, though."

"I bet. You've been there for ages."

"Eighteen months." *Long enough to think you know someone*, I wanted to say. *Long enough to trust him. To love him.*

"What did Tom say?"

I hesitated. Of course Sarah didn't know I'd left home. "Oh, not much. There are plenty more jobs out there."

"He's right." She chatted about her day; clearly they hadn't got anyone to replace me yet, so a lot of the work I would normally do had landed on her shoulders.

"Not the phone calls, though," she said. "They're going through to Paula. I don't know why they're not coming to me."

"What do you mean? Why isn't Harry answering his own phone?"

"Oh, he wasn't there. Didn't I tell you? He won't be in this week."

I felt a huge sense of relief. There was an explanation for this after all. "What? Has he had an accident?"

"An accident?" She laughed. "Oh no, nothing like that. He's gone on holiday."

"What?"

"Yes. Jane came in this morning to thank us for her leaving present. She didn't have the chance to speak to everyone on Friday. She said Harry was going on a lovely romantic holiday with his wife."

I could hardly believe what I was hearing. "But he didn't say anything about that to me."

"That's exactly what I said to Jane. I told her we knew nothing about it, and she said he'd kept it quiet because he wanted it to be a surprise for Emma. Apparently they left on Friday night and they're away for a week."

I was about to interrupt, to say that they couldn't have gone away because I'd seen lights on in their house when I was parked there on Saturday night, watching, but stopped myself. She'd think I was a stalker. And then it registered: he must have set up the lights to come on automatically. His car wasn't there. They'd gone off in that, together. I knew he hadn't left home – obviously – but to think he was on holiday with her instead, while I was driving myself crazy on my own in the hotel, was like a punch in the gut.

"It must be great to be able to take off whenever you want, mustn't it?" said Sarah.

My mind was racing. "Yes. That must be nice," I said through gritted teeth, when it was clear a response was expected.

"It's lovely. So romantic. It's to celebrate his wife being pregnant."

Chapter 10

Ruby

I don't know how I got through the rest of the phone call. I knew I couldn't call again to ask Sarah about Harry: Why would I? I doubted I would see much of her; we didn't meet that often outside of work, though we'd been good friends in the office. And she and her husband were very hospitable, always having friends around for dinner and for parties, though Tom rarely wanted to go. How could she introduce me? *Oh, this is my friend Ruby. She dumped her husband to be with a married man, who in turn dumped her! Now, who shall I sit her next to?* I could just imagine the way they'd look at me. They'd think I was the enemy of civilised society. So this was my only chance to find out about Harry and Emma.

"I didn't realise they were having a baby," I said, trying to keep my voice under control. I forced myself to add, "How lovely. He'll be a great father."

"He will." I could almost hear her settling down for a good gossip. She'd kill me if she knew I was keeping such a huge secret from her. "There's always been talk about children."

"There has?" I managed to say. "I hadn't heard anything."

"It was probably before your time. You weren't at the last Christmas party, were you? She was there and she wasn't drinking. We all assumed she was pregnant, but didn't hear anything more about it."

I hadn't gone to the party. We'd agreed we'd never manage to keep our affair secret if I had. I'd given my excuses, saying that we had a prior engagement. Harry told me after the holidays that he'd been bored and miserable without me that Christmas. He told me he'd rushed back to work.

"I didn't realise," I said. The strain of trying to sound normal was immense and my head was throbbing already. "But then, why would I? I've never even met her."

"Yeah, she doesn't come to the office as much nowadays. I think her business is doing well, so I suppose she's too busy. Haven't you seen a photo of her, though? She's very attractive. Stunning, really."

I knew that already from seeing her on social media. I caught a glimpse of myself in the long mirror on the wall of the hotel room; *stunning* wasn't the word I'd use to describe myself right now. I was a mess.

I made some excuse and got off the phone. It was almost dark now and I sat by the window in the armchair and looked out at the road that ran along the front of the hotel. It had been raining earlier and drops still ran down the windows and the lights of the cars were blurred, though that could have been my tears. I brought my knees up to my chest, hugging them tight. So Emma was pregnant. That had been my dream for so many years and I'd almost accepted that it would never come true for me. Now she didn't just have the man I wanted, she was having his child, too.

Harry hadn't tried to contact me. He hadn't even thought of me. He'd just discarded me like I was nothing to him.

My body was tight with panic. What had I done? I'd lost my past when I walked out on Tom. I'd lost my future, too; I had no job, no partner. No money. Tom earned a lot more than I did; we had separate bank accounts but a shared one for bills. We paid half each, which didn't leave me much for savings. And now I was going to have no money coming in.

"Don't worry about money," Harry had said when we talked about living together. "I'll look after you."

"I don't need looking after," I'd said. "It's just that I'll be broke until the house is sold. After that I'll be fine."

44

He kissed me. "Ruby, don't even give it a second thought."

I really shouldn't have listened to a word he said. I called him again. Straight to voicemail and yes, despite everything his voice still made me weak, though furious, too. I jabbed my phone to end the call before I said something I'd regret and just then my phone beeped. It was Tom. As I read the message I felt a moment of panic that he was psychic.

Just spoken to Henry at work who's trying to sell his house. He said the market's slow at the moment. He was told it could be months before it sells x

I could feel my blood pressure rise at the thought of not having a home or a job. I needed somewhere to live. I couldn't stay in the hotel for much longer. When he booked it, Harry had paid for a week and I couldn't afford to stay there much longer once that time was up.

"I'll book it for the week and then see how it goes," he'd said. "We'll look out for an flat straightaway. We can rent while we're deciding where to buy." He'd sent me some links to huge riverside flats in Liverpool, others with views over the River Dee. "What do you think of these? They're all available immediately."

I thought of them now, those split-level warehouse lofts with their Scandinavian lighting and on-site gyms and twenty-four-hour concierges. What was all that about, tempting me with luxury living then dumping me without warning? That was another thought to add to the burning sense of injustice I'd felt over the last few days. Then my phone beeped again with another message from Tom.

We didn't have the chance to talk about money before you left. I've transferred some to your savings account. Let me know if you need more x

I frowned. He knew my savings account was in name only. I'd had to borrow from him in the past, so he'd known I didn't have a stash of money. Then my phone beeped with yet another message from him. He was messaging me more now than when we were together. It surprised me; I'd thought he'd ignore me.

I hope you're OK x

I sat back on the armchair and held a cushion to my chest, watching the cars passing by. I started to think about Tom and where it had all gone wrong. It was hard to reconcile the man I'd met with the man I'd left, but now I saw the man I'd loved and married emerge again. But then those thoughts disappeared as I remembered the last time I'd seen Harry. Was he just stringing me along? Had he sent me those flat links knowing we'd never live there and that I would have burned my bridges at home? He *knew* I had no money! He had to know I'd be homeless. I thought of him coming back from his holiday, of his face falling when he saw someone else at my desk. He'd be furious when he realised I'd been fired.

I tried his number again but stopped when I heard him say, "Hi." I didn't leave a message. I wouldn't do that. I wouldn't give him the satisfaction.

Later, I realised that Tom's messages were on WhatsApp and he would have seen that I'd read them. I sent him a brief message:

Thanks.

He must have been watching out for my reply, because his came immediately.

Any time. Take care, babe x

I stared down at the message. He was calling me *babe* again? Despite myself I felt that familiar feeling of pleasure that I always had when Tom was nice to me. I'd felt it all the time in the early days, but much less often toward the end. Hardly ever, really. Yet each time he was nice, I felt that warm glow of approval and just wanted more of it. I shook my head. I had to stop thinking like that. I'd moved away; there was no way I should move back. I wanted to challenge him, to ask him what he was playing at, but then I thought of the way he could be if I did that and decided to leave it. I could hardly complain that he was being too nice to me.

The evening was still warm outside. The bedroom window would open only a couple of inches, so I dragged the table to the window and got out my laptop. I spent a couple of hours sending my CV to employers in the area. I was just about to find something to watch on Netflix when my phone pinged. I jumped at the sound. It was Tom again.

Ruby, your mum's just called on the landline. Thought I'd warn you – she's calling you in a minute x

Oh no.

Exactly one minute later my phone rang and I winced. When I reluctantly accepted the call, all I could hear was the sound of sobbing. I sighed and went to flick the kettle on. I was in for a long call. I put the phone on loudspeaker, made some coffee, and opened a packet of biscuits.

"Hi, Mum." More sobbing. I stirred the coffee and chose one of the biscuits. Mmm, shortbread. My favourite. I ate it before saying anything more. "Are you okay? Have you fallen? Do you need me to get help?"

She gave a loud sniff that put me right off my coffee, then said, "I have never been so ashamed."

If I'd been at her house right now, I would've tiptoed around her trying to make everything all right, but I was broke and alone and homeless, and suddenly I thought, *Hang on, I am the one with the problem here, not her!*

So I said, "Oh no, what have you done?"

"It's not what I've done, it's what you've done. I've just had that poor man on the phone. Crying, he was. Said you'd left him and he didn't know why. I couldn't believe it! I only saw you a month ago and you said nothing to me."

Funny, that. I wondered for a second about Tom. He hadn't wasted much time getting sympathy from her. Had he really been upset? For the first time I thought of him in the house on his own, sitting there in the evenings without anyone to talk to. He didn't have many friends, just colleagues he'd sometimes go for a drink with. He'd never lived alone; it must have seemed very strange. Lonely. I knew he'd be drinking more than he should, then stopped myself. What he did now had nothing to do with me.

47

"And that poor son of his." She gave a heavy sigh. "Having another broken home."

I wanted to tell her there was a common denominator involved here and it wasn't me, but there was no point. Women didn't leave men. That was the rule my mother lived by. They should not just abandon their husbands. They should forgive and forget and maybe encourage the man into a hobby that took him out of the house, preferably every evening and weekend.

"How's Dad?" I asked, interrupting my mother's prophecy that Josh would end up on the streets, a drug addict, unemployed: helpless and hopeless because I'd walked out on his father. She hadn't asked how I was or even where I was. This was her problem, not mine.

"He's devastated," she said. She started to cry again. "We both are. I don't know how you could do this to us."

In the background I could hear my dad asking where all the chocolate biscuits had gone to. Like me, he was clearly finding food a comfort in his hour of need.

"At least we'll be spared the shame for a while," my mother continued. "Your sister's invited us to stay. We're leaving next week, on Monday. 'Get an open return,' she said. 'Stay as long as you like.'"

My sister, Fiona, lived in Australia now. That invitation must have been ripped out of her. I knew she would have told them to get an open ticket because she wanted the chance to tell our mother to leave at a moment's notice.

"Mum, would you mind if I stayed at your house while you're away? I could look after your plants and keep the house safe."

"Keep the house safe! I couldn't trust you with a key. Not after what happened last time."

"Last time" was twenty years ago when I'd been mugged in broad daylight and their house keys were in my purse.

"It would make things so much easier for me." I thought of looking for a flat, of spending money I didn't have. I didn't feel particularly at home at my parents' house now, but it would be a lot better than a rental. "I'll be careful, I promise."

"No, you won't," she said. "We'll lock up ourselves, thank you. We might be away months. I know Fiona misses us. And anyway, what would I tell the neighbours?"

"What's it got to do with them?"

"Well, I wouldn't want you bumping into Mrs. Jennings. Telling her all your business. None of hers have given her any trouble. And here you are, about to be divorced and not even any children to show for it."

Tears stung my eyes then, as she surely knew they would, at the thought of those nights I'd spent each month, hoping and praying that I'd get pregnant. She knew about that; I'd been stupid enough to confide in her. She'd told me that some women weren't made to be mothers. It had taken a long time to forgive that.

"I have to go," I said.

She started to remonstrate but I pressed the End button and, as if by magic, she disappeared.

Later when I'd calmed down, a message came through from my dad.

I'm sorry, pet. You know what your mum's like x

I did, and I knew what he was like, too. I loved him, but he let her get away with such bad behaviour. He pacified her, as though his role in life was to smooth things over when she rode roughshod over other people. It had taken me so long to realise that I was like him. I didn't reply to my dad's message. I didn't know what to say to him.

Just as I was getting ready for bed another message came through. It was Tom.

Hope you're feeling OK now. Don't let her get you down x

And despite everything, for a moment I was comforted. Tom was the only person who knew what my mum was really like. She put on a convincing act for my friends who'd met her and I'd never said anything different to them, knowing they'd

49

believe what they saw first-hand rather than what they heard from me. Though I'd talked to Harry about her, he didn't know her, had never seen the look of frustration and hurt on my face when I was with her.

I looked at my watch. It was after eleven o'clock. I thought of Tom in our bed, lying on goose-down pillows and covered with a quilt as light as a cloud. I thought of the grey silk throw that was draped on the bedpost and the soft lights and the woollen rugs, and the en suite with its power shower for two. And then I looked around my hotel room. It was nice enough, but I was alone here. Not just alone. Homeless. Jobless.

I couldn't help thinking I'd made the biggest mistake in the world.

Chapter 11

Ruby

The next morning I was up early. I had two goals: to find somewhere to live and to get another job. By nine o'clock I was back at Mersey Recruitment, the agency that had found me the job at Sheridan's.

When I walked in, every eye was on me and instantly I realised they all knew why I was there. My face flamed. I walked up to the manager's desk. Kourtney O'Dwyer was a Canadian woman who'd married an Englishman and had settled here with him. She was the owner and manager of the agency; everything had to go through her.

"Ruby," said Kourtney. She was pouring a cup of coffee from the machine at the back of the room. "What a nice surprise." When I'd first approached the agency after I was made redundant she was newly pregnant. She'd found me the job at Sheridan's within a day, and I hadn't seen her since. Now she was back off maternity leave, her body softer than before, but her eyes held the same hard, determined glint. I could only hope she didn't look at her baby like that.

I sat down opposite her. She ignored me for a few minutes, doing that thing people do when they want to show you exactly who's more powerful in the conversation. It did the trick; I felt like I was shrinking in front of her.

She didn't offer me any coffee, but lifted her own cup and sipped. "What can I do for you?"

"I'm looking for work." I stumbled over my words. The office was silent and I knew everyone was listening to me. "I've left Sheridan's now."

"Yes," said Kourtney. "We know."

My face was hot and damp with perspiration. "I wondered whether you had anything else available."

There was a silence, then she slammed her mug down. I jumped and knocked the table. Coffee spilled out onto papers she had laid out there. She swore under her breath and one of her minions came rushing over with a cloth.

She leaned over the table and I thought for a moment she was going to grab me. "Are you serious?" she hissed. "You had an affair with a married man. A married man with a pregnant wife. At Sheridan's, our *best client*! During working hours! And, now you've been fired, you want us to find you somewhere else?"

"What? How did you know that?"

"It's a small town," she said. "I know everyone."

I got to my feet. I wasn't going to argue that nothing had happened in working hours, that I hadn't known his wife was pregnant. I'd been a good employee, I'd never been late, and I'd always worked overtime whenever he'd asked me to. I didn't mention that I'd set up systems that streamlined their administration, that Harry had said I was ten times better than Clare, his previous PA. I could tell, though, from looking at Kourtney's furious face that nothing I said would make a difference.

I picked up my bag and turned away.

The other staff were staring at me, agog, but lowered their eyes when they saw me glaring at them. The office was hushed as I walked through, my face burning, my heart pounding. As I shut the door behind me I heard an explosion of angry voices.

So, it might be better to look somewhere else for a job.

Chapter 12

Ruby

My mistake was going from the recruitment agency straight to the letting agency, where with increasing desperation I was taken to view a number of flats.

My home with Tom had been lovely, even if it didn't always feel like mine. I'd lived there with him for twelve years and in that time we'd worked hard on it. Every room was freshly decorated. Paintings hung on the walls, soft rugs lay on the oak floors, and everything was clean and comfortable and warm. Josh came to visit a couple of times a week, but even he didn't make much mess. Before I married Tom I'd lived in my own flat, a stylish minimalist place whose huge windows overlooked the skyline of Liverpool. I'd loved living there; there was a crowd of us in our twenties who had flats in the area and there was always someone to go out for drinks or a lazy Sunday brunch with. Those friends were long gone. Some had moved abroad and it was inevitable we'd lose touch, but others had disappeared after I married Tom.

Before I went to the letting agency, I bought coffee in a small café, hoping I wouldn't bump into anyone I knew. I was still humiliated from the conversation with Kourtney. I knew she must have had a complaint from Sheridan's, but had they really told her about our affair?

I desperately wanted to talk to Harry, but I forced myself not to call him. He was the one person whose advice I valued, yet he had let me down so badly.

When I'd finished my coffee I checked my bank balance on my phone. I needed to know how much I could spend on rent. Without a job I'd struggle to get somewhere anyway. I was close to tears at that thought. I opened my banking app and my jaw dropped. Tom had put £5,000 in my account. It made me realise that I'd had no idea how much he had in savings. Was this a lot to him? It was to me; I had virtually nothing in the bank. How much did he have?

I sent Tom a message:

Thanks for putting that money in my account.

Immediately he responded.

That's fine. Let me know if you get stuck. Come round to the house when you can; we need to talk about the sale x

I slid my phone into my pocket. I had a horrible feeling that if I had to go back to my house, I'd want to stay there.

–

I couldn't believe how expensive it was to rent. I hadn't rented since my early twenties and then I lived in house shares. I wasn't going to do that now; I needed my own space.

Pretty quickly I remembered why I used to share a house; it's so much cheaper than having your own place. The rental prices anywhere decent were high. I needed to get a job and a new home fast. I couldn't live in the hotel for much longer. I had to get something, no matter what it was like.

For the first time in years, money was absolutely the priority. The cheaper, the better, I thought, until I saw what cheaper would get me. I flinched at the photos of some of the flats, at the flimsy front doors; the cheap, unstable furniture; the stained and worn carpets.

I didn't know what to do. Should I buy furniture? Surely I could have some from the house. When it was sold, Tom would move into a smaller place. He wouldn't need all of the furniture. And some of it was mine, too. I wondered whether he'd let me have that back.

I decided to look only at furnished flats; I needed to move in immediately. And of course, just as I expected, the issue of my not having a job came up.

"Name of employer?" Gill, the woman at the letting agency, asked. I froze. She saw me hesitate and added grimly, "So that we can write to them to ask them to confirm your employment."

Frustrated, I said, "I've just finished a long-term contract. I'm looking around for work now." I crossed my fingers. "It won't take long."

"I'm sorry. Most of these landlords will only let to employed tenants."

I stared at her. "That's disgraceful!"

"Not really. They need to be sure you can pay the rent."

I thought of the money Tom had put into my bank. "I can pay the rent. That's not a problem."

"Very well," she said coolly. "You'll have to pay six months' rent in advance and a deposit against damages."

"How much do you think I'll have to pay per month?"

She shrugged. "Most of the one-beds go for around six or seven hundred a month. Before bills, of course."

Frantically I made calculations in my head. "I can put six months' rent down now, but I want a monthly contract. I don't want to pay rent if I've got somewhere else to live."

"There's no point in you trying to write your own rules. The courts have no power to make a tenant leave until six months are up, so you won't find a landlord who'll give you a contract for less than that." Gill must have seen the wave of panic that flooded me then, because she softened and spoke more kindly. "Look, if you sell your house and want to move out of the flat early, I'll put in a good word for you. You'd lose your deposit, but they'd probably let you go."

By the time we reached the fifth flat I was ready to take anything. Gill parked her car just off the main road. I got out and looked around. There was a row of a dozen or so shops and the area was tidy and well kept.

"The flat's up above the florist's shop on the corner," said Gill. "I've placed people there before and everything's been fine."

"Is it safe around here?"

"As safe as anywhere," she said. "In the daytime all these shops are open, of course, but it's a quiet enough place at night. It's not the sort of place where you'll have trouble with people hanging around."

"Are there other flats in the building?"

"No, these shops have just one flat above each of them." The front door was on the side road, around the corner from the shop entrance, and Gill pulled out a key ring and opened the door. Inside there was a small hallway and a set of stairs leading up to the flat. An unadorned lightbulb hung from the ceiling and she flicked the switch before we both went upstairs. In the dim light the stairs looked gloomy and the thick carpet was covered in a fine layer of dust.

Once we were upstairs, though, things looked a bit better. The stairs went up to a small landing with doors going off it. The living room was large and light, with a bird's-eye view of the street. It was furnished with a mishmash of furniture, as though everyone who'd lived there over the years had left one item behind; nothing matched in style, era, or colour. There was a large wooden table and a couple of chairs in the window overlooking the street. Outside, at the end of the street, schoolchildren waited at the bus stop and a couple of old ladies stood chatting outside the greengrocer's shop, their shopping bags by their sides. Below the window was the awning covering the florist's shop below. I pulled up the sash window. The air was warm and a light breeze floated in from the river, carrying with it the scent of flowers from the display below.

I turned to Gill. "This is better than the others, isn't it?"

She said, "Yeah, it is," but her eyes were fixed on her phone and I could tell her mind was on something else. My gaze flitted over the sofa that had seen better days and the marks on the paintwork. I could sort that out. I went through to the bedroom; it overlooked the narrower side road and was big enough for all the bags and boxes I had. I breathed a sigh of relief as I saw the bed was new and still in its plastic cover.

"Is it free to move into immediately?"

"You can move in on Thursday, if you like. I'll get back to the office now and contact the landlady. I'll draw up a contract and e-mail it to you later today. If your payment clears tomorrow, then you can move in the next day."

"I'll take it," I said.

Chapter 13

Ruby

Early on Thursday morning I went down to the hotel reception with my bags to settle the bill. I wanted to pick up the keys to my flat as soon as the agency opened.

I handed over my credit card.

"That's okay, Mrs. Sheridan." When the receptionist called me by that name, it was as though she was rubbing salt into my wounds. "Mr. Sheridan has paid for the room."

My heart thumped. "Is he here?"

She looked surprised. "No. The payment was made in advance. Haven't you seen him?"

I flushed and muttered something about him being delayed. "I'll pay for room service separately." I handed over my card. The last thing I needed was for Harry to receive the bill for all the alcohol and snacks I'd had. I pictured him casting an eye over the list, judging me.

I thought back to the day when Harry had booked the room online for a week. "Are you sure about this, Ruby? Dead certain?"

My stomach had tightened with nerves as I said, "Yes. Yes, of course!"

"Promise?"

"Yes! I promise."

He'd beamed at me and entered his card details. "Me, too," he'd said, and then he'd kissed me.

I was deep in thought as I drove from the letting agency to my new flat. I couldn't stop thinking about that Friday evening when I left work, believing that Harry and I would be together that night. It tormented me. He'd grinned at me as I left. Who would do that to someone they were going to let down? He knew I was going to leave my marriage for him and he knew he wouldn't be there for me. I couldn't forgive him. And I thought of Emma, at home with her pregnancy, knowing nothing of this, not realising the man she'd chosen to be the father of her child was promising to move out to be with another woman. How had we both got it so wrong?

I managed to find a parking space outside my new home. Seeing it afresh didn't exactly make my heart sing. It was scruffier than I'd remembered, with peeling paint and bare wooden window frames. Inside, the hallway floor was littered with junk mail. I picked it up and separated out a couple of bills for the previous tenant. There was nothing for me, of course.

I jammed the front door open and carried everything from my car into the empty hallway, then made several long slow journeys up to my flat, dragging my bags and boxes with me. The first thing I did was to open all the windows. I could hear the sound of customers chatting on the pavement below. It was comforting, somehow. As though I had company. I planned to go down to the florist's later to introduce myself and buy some flowers for my living room. It had been so long since I'd had to consider close neighbours; my house with Tom was detached and although Oliver lived only a short distance from us, we never had to worry about disturbing him. It would be different here, I knew.

Looking around the flat, I realised I should have brought more things with me. But Harry and I had decided on a new life together. We'd said we wanted to choose everything together, to start again, without reminders from our previous lives. I could see now how stupid that had been, as though a lamp or a bookcase would remind us of our spouses, when our own thoughts didn't.

Without thinking, I went into the kitchen to make myself a cup of tea before I unpacked. Of course there wasn't anything there. I'd have to start again and buy a kettle and some mugs. Even teaspoons. I thought of my kitchen at home, crammed with food processors and three sets of cutlery, the cleaners and scrubbers under the sink, the tea towels neatly arranged in the cupboards, the copper-bottomed pans that hung from the hooks on the wall, the knife sets, the recipe books, and the china, the lovely china I'd collected over the years. The happiest days of my marriage had been spent in that room, alone.

This small grubby flat was so far from where I thought I'd be living that I could hardly make sense of it. I should be with Harry today, looking at flats with him. Moving in with him, christening our new bed. We'd even chosen the bed we'd buy, had looked at tons of them and had made a decision on one. He'd bookmarked it online and said that ordering the bed would be the first thing we'd do when we were together. My mouth tightened. He'd be okay, I knew that, wherever he was. Sarah had said he was on holiday for a week. Were they on a beach somewhere right now as though all was well in the world? Would he leave Emma lying on a recliner in the sun and go down to swim in the sea, thinking about me and the narrow escape he'd had? Perhaps he'd run back up the beach toward her and shake cold water over her hot tanned body so that she'd shriek, then take her hand and chase her back to their room.

I shuddered. He'd told me they hadn't slept together for a long time and I'd believed him. I was such an idiot. I knew if I told a friend about our affair, they'd say he was having his cake and eating it, that faced with the reality of leaving his lovely home, he'd chosen the easy way out. And I knew that was true – I was almost sure of it – but when I thought of his face that Friday evening, just when I said good-bye, he looked so happy and smiling and… well, I was going to say *trustworthy* but that probably isn't the right word, given he was cheating on his wife.

I went to the bathroom and splashed water on my face. I couldn't afford to get upset now. I'd wanted to leave Tom; I'd thought of it for years. And now I'd left him. I needed to cope with that, rather than thinking about what might have been.

–

The first thing I did once I'd carried everything up to the flat was to go to a supermarket and buy a load of cleaning products and some cheap kitchenware so that I didn't have to eat out. I had no intention of taking those things with me to my new house, so I just bought a fork, a knife, a spoon. One plate, one pan, one bowl. I felt a bit like Jack Reacher, as though I should keep my toothbrush in my pocket.

I was okay until I started to buy some food. Automatically I picked up a box of muesli and put it into my trolley. It was as though something pinged in my brain and I couldn't stop staring at it. People pushed past me and I moved to a quieter aisle. I realised I'd been eating that cereal for years and years. It was a muesli with all sorts of things in it, nuts, raisins, the lot, and though the packaging was impressive, I'd never liked it. It tasted dusty and too sweet. Yet I'd eaten it every weekday for years. Tom liked it and used to say there was no point in getting two different cereals, that they'd go stale. Whenever I suggested trying something else he'd go quiet and moody. It was crazy, really, how much his mood could affect me. Why had I put up with that? I went back to the cereal aisle and looked at the range on offer. Which should I buy? What did I actually like? My head started to hurt. I didn't know. I just didn't know what I liked. It hadn't mattered what I liked.

Tom chose everything. And, to be fair, he did usually make the right decision. He had good taste – I knew that. It's just that… well, sometimes you want to choose something yourself, don't you? When I was living at home my mum decided everything. We either did things her way or we suffered; my sister and I learned that lesson pretty early on. And Fiona got away from it by emigrating when she was eighteen. As for me, I had a few years of freedom and then just when I was really enjoying my life, I met Tom.

I put the box back on the shelf and moved away. I wouldn't buy any cereal at all. I'd have something else. But the same thing happened in the other aisles. I didn't know which bread to buy, which cheese I liked. All I knew was which cleaning materials I liked, which washing powder was best. Even the soap confused me. Should I buy the one we always used? Did I actually like it? I didn't know anymore. I could feel my throat swelling with tears and knew I had to get out of there. I hurried around the store, throwing things into the trolley. The only criteria was that I hadn't had it at home. If it looked familiar, I didn't want it.

There was a woman in the supermarket who was buying cushions and blankets; she looked like she had good taste so I watched her and just bought what she did. This was a tip my mother had passed on to me. Not that she did it herself, of course, but she told me my taste was a bit odd. Unreliable, she said. She told me the best thing to do was to copy someone else who seemed to know what she was doing.

As soon as I was home, I unpacked my shopping. Already I knew I'd made some bad decisions. I didn't care; I stuffed the cupboards and the fridge full of food. I threw the cushions and blankets onto the sofa, scattered a couple of magazines on the coffee table, and placed a plant from the florist's shop downstairs on the windowsill.

When I'd finished I realised the room was arranged just as ours had been at home. It was like a poor man's version of our living room. I stood for a while, unable to decide what to do. Tom had always been the one who decided how the living room would look. I knew I had to change things around; it would bring back too many memories otherwise, so I dragged the sofa into another position and put the table and chairs by the window. The furniture was heavy and I was hot and sweating by the time I finished, but I didn't stop until it didn't resemble home at all.

I hadn't bought alcohol. At home we'd have wine delivered from the local wine merchant and Tom would stock up the drinks cupboard with whisky and gin and liqueurs. I don't think he'd had a day without a drink in all the time I'd known him. Usually I'd join him, to blur the edges of my life. I didn't want anything like that here, though. I'd drunk enough at the hotel to last me a good while. I didn't want to drink myself into a stupor now. Not now. I'd escaped that life. I needed to be wide-awake for my new life.

I packed up all the empty bags and packaging and went out to the alley at the back of the shops where all the bins were kept. I found mine with my flat number painted on it and was just about to open it when something brushed past me. I screamed, thinking of mice and rats and foxes.

When I stepped back from the bin and looked around I saw a cat was hiding between two bins, watching me. It had a coat of matted black fur and as I turned toward it, it ran down the alley to where a bin had overflowed. It started to scratch and pull at a bag of food there and I realised it was starving.

I thought of the cat that Fiona and I had had when we were growing up and how spoiled and loved he was. "Haven't you got a home to go to?" I asked gently. I stooped to see whether it wore a collar. It didn't, just a scratch on its ear that looked as though it wasn't healing properly. "Are you hungry?"

Slowly it came toward me and sniffed. I held my hand out and felt its tongue flick out to lick me. It turned then and started to root in the bag of rubbish, found a piece of meat, and shot away into its place between the bins to eat it. I watched for a while, wanting to stroke its fur, to give it food and water, but I shook myself. It was clearly living on the streets.

Reluctantly I left it alone but when I went for a walk that evening, I found the cat in the street, roaming around, sniffing in the gutters for food. On impulse I bought a few packets of cat food from the corner shop. I took a couple of foil containers from my kitchen and filled one with water, the other with food. I knew I shouldn't feed a stray cat; it would think it belonged to me, but I couldn't bear to think of it hungry. I took the containers down to the lamp post outside my house and watched from the doorway as the cat devoured the food.

It looked desperate. I recognised that look. It was how I felt, too.

Chapter 14

Ruby

Back in the flat, I charged my phone and put on one of my favourite playlists. I dragged my suitcases into the bedroom and started to unpack. I had to shut out the memories of packing the week before, hastily cramming clothes into my bags, muttering my memorised list as I raced around gathering everything together. I remembered sitting on my cases to zip them shut, so excited for my future. That excitement had vanished now, oddly enough. I tried to forget my imagined future as I organised my clothes in piles on my bed: jumpers, shirts, jeans, dresses. There were hangers in the wardrobe and I was just about to hang the dresses up when the music stopped and my phone beeped.

Immediately I thought of Harry. Like a fool, I hurried over to check. Of course it wasn't him. At that moment, though, it was the next-best thing: an e-mail about a job.

> Dear Mrs. Dean,
>
> Thanks for completing our online application form. Apologies for the e-mail rather than a phone call but I'm in a meeting and can't talk at the moment.
>
> I'm looking for a PA for the next few months and haven't found anyone suitable through the agencies. I'm returning to my office in Boston in the New Year so I'm just looking for temporary cover until then.

I've got a busy week ahead and won't be in my office until next Monday. I'm in Manchester at a conference today and wonder whether you could meet me there for a chat about the job? Details are below. I'll book a meeting room but perhaps we could meet in the café at the front of the building at 2 p.m.?

Kind regards

Alan Walker

Managing Director

Immediately I brightened up. At last, a response and it was for a PA role, too. I replied at once, saying I'd be happy to meet him.

–

I drove to the conference centre, panicking in case I was late. It was on the other side of Manchester and it took longer than I'd estimated to drive through the city traffic, but still I managed to get to the car park in good time. I had to park on the top floor. I hated multistorey car parks, with their tight bends and tighter spaces to park, and I could feel the perspiration trickling down the back of my neck by the time I parked in an empty space.

As I arrived at the café, I looked at my watch. There was plenty of time; I was fifteen minutes early. I ordered coffee and sat in the window, just as we'd arranged, and took out my copy of the *Times*, so that he'd know it was me. I sent him an e-mail to say I was there. I felt like I was going on a blind date and for the first time I felt a bit uneasy.

I'd already checked the links he'd sent me but now I Googled his name. He was on LinkedIn and all his work and educational history were laid out in front of me. There was a photo, too; he was in his late fifties, quite attractive, with an engaging smile. He'd owned a small company for ten years, according to the bio there. I wondered why he was looking for a PA now, then remembered what he'd said about going back to the States. What would happen to his business then?

After half an hour, I was bored and starting to get a bit edgy. I forced myself to relax. I didn't want to look annoyed when he did turn up. I spent a few minutes rereading my research into his company, then bought a copy of the *Manchester Echo* from a stand outside and started to look at jobs advertised in the Manchester area. It was forty miles from home and a much bigger city than I was used to. I could live here, I mused. I could live wherever I wanted to. I was ready for a change.

I waited until just before four o'clock, feeling increasingly irritated. Surely he should have the courtesy to call me? I stood to go and a group of businesspeople standing nearby pushed through and took over my table.

I asked for help at the reception desk but the guy working there didn't have details of any individuals, just organisations who'd booked in. Given that Alan Walker's business was so small, I wasn't surprised that the name wasn't on his list. He checked the meeting rooms, but there wasn't anything booked in Walker's name.

"Sometimes people book a room at the last minute," he said. "It's first come, first served. Maybe he thought he'd wait until you met up?"

"I suppose so." But he'd said he would book it in advance. Why hadn't he done that?

Now the large reception area was full of people coming down from their meetings. I stood by the desk, holding my newspaper and feeling like a fool, but didn't see him among the crowds. Certainly nobody was lingering; they were all chatting and hurrying for the exits.

Just then my phone beeped. I sighed with relief. It wasn't the guy about the interview, though; it was Oliver, my neighbour from home.

Hey, Ruby, how're things? Haven't seen you for a while. Are you at your mum's? x

All I wanted right then was someone to talk to. A friend. I called Oliver's number but it rang out. Within seconds I got another text: Sorry, just waiting for a client and can't speak just now. Are you OK?

I realised he didn't know I'd left home. I wasn't going to tell him just now. I had to focus on this interview. I'm OK, I replied. Turned up for a job interview but it looks like the guy hasn't shown up.

It was a few minutes before he replied and I thought his client must have appeared, but then a message came through:

That's terrible. Sounds like someone you wouldn't want to work for anyway. Have to run, will be in touch soon x

He was right, I thought. I'd waited well over an hour for him and he hadn't even had the decency to call me. Did I really want to work for someone like that? I sent Alan Walker an e-mail:

> Is our meeting still on? Happy to wait if you're running late.

There was no reply and five minutes later, I called his number. I had no idea what I would say. I was raging, but knew I'd have to keep calm. The call rang out but didn't go to voicemail. I frowned. Why hadn't he got voicemail? How was anyone supposed to get in touch with him? I tried again a couple more times, but still no one answered. I sent another text saying that I'd have to leave soon, but again there was no reply.

By then the place was almost empty and the guy on reception kept staring at me. It was obvious I was wasting my time. Slowly I headed back to the car park. On the ground floor I scrabbled in my bag for the parking ticket and fed it into the machine. The fee was fifteen pounds. Furiously I looked through my purse; I hadn't enough cash. I took out my credit card, completely fed up.

When I got back to my car I saw I had a missed call. My phone had been in my bag since I left the conference centre and the call was made ten or fifteen minutes before. The number wasn't the one I'd been calling but I assumed it was Alan. I returned the call immediately, but as soon as I said, "Hello?" I was cut off.

I thought maybe I'd caught him in a meeting and he couldn't talk freely. I wondered whether to wait, but knew I had to leave the car park within five minutes or pay for another ticket, so I sent him a text:

Sorry to have missed you. Looking forward to talking later.

Just as I approached the motorway, I heard the beep of a message from deep inside my bag. I took the first exit and parked on an industrial estate to check my phone. The message was from the number I'd called in the car park. It said:

If you call me again you'll be sorry.

Chapter 15

Ruby

I drove back to the flat in a fury. As soon as I was in my living room I opened my laptop and looked at the e-mails Alan Walker had sent me. He was the one who'd suggested I drive forty miles to meet him and then hadn't shown up. I'd heard of guys doing that on dates, but for an interview? And had he sent me that text? I was going to let this guy know what I thought of him.

I looked him up again on LinkedIn. He was beaming away in the photo, looking so happy with himself. It was just after five o'clock now. I opened my e-mail and started to write a message, but after a few lines I guessed he'd just ignore it and I couldn't hang around waiting for his reply. I saved it as a draft just in case I needed it later and tried the number that he'd given me. As soon as it rang, the call was cut off. Furious now, I called his office's direct line instead.

"Good afternoon, Alan Walker's office," said a young woman.

"I'd like to speak to Mr. Walker. It's a private matter."

"Who's speaking?"

"Ruby Dean."

She went away for a moment, then came back. "Could you tell me what it's about? I'm his personal assistant."

"I think he would prefer it if I didn't." It didn't sound as though she knew she was about to be replaced and I didn't want to be the one to tell her.

A minute or two later, a man spoke. "Alan Walker here. Who's calling?"

"It's Ruby Dean."

There was a pause, then he said, "Sorry, have we met?"

"Good question. We should have met but we haven't."

He sounded confused. "I'm sorry?"

"We were supposed to meet today in Manchester. I wondered whether you wanted to reconvene."

Now he sounded bewildered. "A meeting? Who *are* you?"

I said again, "I'm Ruby Dean. You invited me to interview at the North West Conference Centre today."

"What?" There was no mistaking his confusion. "I haven't a clue what you're talking about."

"You e-mailed me earlier today. You said you were looking for a PA."

"Not me," he said firmly. "I've got a PA. You've just spoken to her. What was the sender's e-mail address?"

I found it on my laptop and read it out to him.

"That's not mine. It doesn't belong to anyone in this company." His voice softened slightly. "I think you've been the victim of a hoax. If you hear anything more from them, get back in touch, will you?"

Hot with embarrassment and anger, I thanked him again and ended the call, really glad I hadn't asked him whether he'd sent me a text from a different phone telling me I'd be sorry if I contacted him again. Then he really would have thought I was mad.

Once again I looked at the e-mail. The e-mail address had Alan's name and then the company name. I frowned. How could someone create that? It wasn't as though it was a random Gmail address. So I went online and searched for that company's website. A white screen appeared, telling me the site couldn't be reached.

Frustrated, I shut my laptop. Why would someone ask me to interview if they weren't going to turn up? Why would they use Alan's name? Was he lying about the e-mail?

I stomped into the kitchen. By now I was starving. In the fridge was a lasagne I'd bought that morning. It didn't look tempting but I was too hungry to cook something from scratch. I put it into the oven and while I waited, I opened all the windows to let some air in and went back to the unpacking I'd started earlier that day.

The bathroom wasn't big enough to hold all my toiletries and I took the bulk of them into the bedroom to put into a drawer there. On the bed lay my clothes in piles, just as I'd left them before I went to Manchester, and I started to put them away. When I'd put my T-shirts into the chest of drawers I turned to the bed. Where were my dresses? I closed my eyes and thought of that morning, how I'd laid everything out in piles. I'd put my dresses one on top of the other, straightening out creases as I went in the hope that I wouldn't have to iron them. I shook my head. I was sure I'd done that. I could remember the feel of the fabric as I stroked the wrinkles away.

I wondered whether I'd taken them into the living room, though couldn't think why I would have done that. I turned at the doorway to check the bed again, to see if they'd fallen onto the floor. The wardrobe door was standing slightly ajar. Slowly I reached out and opened it wide. All of my dresses were there on hangers, just as I'd planned, swaying in the evening breeze.

Chapter 16

Ruby

I woke at five the next morning, hardly knowing where I was. The early-morning sun crept through the thin curtains, lighting up the bedroom. In that light every single blemish could be seen, from the cracked plaster on the ceiling to the little rips in the wallpaper. A small silver cobweb hung in the corner of the room. My eyes fixed on the wardrobe. I could not remember hanging up those dresses. Then I thought of a movie I'd seen, *Still Alice*, about a woman suffering from early-onset dementia. I shuddered. That couldn't be happening to me. I was just tired. I had too much on my mind. Too many worries. I must have hung up the dresses while I was thinking about the interview and that's why I couldn't remember doing it.

That made me think of the interview the previous day. Why had I been set up like that? I wondered whether it had been Kourtney O'Dwyer at the employment agency, making me suffer for my sins. Or Eleanor at Sheridan's. The thought flashed through my mind that it might be Harry, punishing me. I pushed hard against that thought. He wouldn't do that. Why would he? I hadn't done anything to harm him. But my eyes drifted up to the cobweb; I was unemployed and living in a run-down flat because of him. He'd had no reason to do that to me, but he'd still done it. Could he have taken it further? I jumped out of bed to stop myself thinking about it. It couldn't have been Harry. He loved me. Or at least he had. I couldn't bear to think he no longer did.

Last night had been the first night in a long time that I'd gone to bed stone-cold sober. Tom and I were more at ease with each other if we were tipsy and then at the hotel I'd had to drink so that I could sleep. But now it was time to change.

My running shoes lay on the floor in the corner of the bedroom. Harry and I had planned to run together in the park that summer and I'd packed them into my car, eager for my new life with him. As soon as I saw them I knew what I was going to do. I was going to go back to being the woman I was more than thirteen years ago, before I met Tom. Before I met Harry.

–

My street was quiet when I left the flat. I'd thought the shop on the corner would be open, the owner getting newspapers ready for the day ahead, but it was in darkness and all was still.

I took a deep breath and focused on the middle distance, and then I started to run. I hadn't run for years and years, since the days I'd lived in Liverpool. A couple of friends and I would run along the dockside there in the early morning, and now more than ten years later I was doing the same, though on the other side of the river.

Predictably, within a few hundred yards I was winded. I sat on a bench by the river wall and waited a few minutes, my chest heaving and my face burning and damp. In the distance I saw a group of runners, a club, maybe, graceful and fast, scattered along the skyline. They came toward me like a flock of seabirds and passed me, nodding acknowledgment, but still in their own worlds. It was as though I was looking at my earlier self. My earlier life. I wanted to be like them again, carefree and strong.

I stood up, full of renewed determination. I could do this. It might take a while, but I could do it.

–

Later that morning I sent off more CVs to the larger companies in the North West and filled in dozens of application forms for jobs that were advertised in the local newspaper. I felt full of energy, as though nothing could bother me now. I'd run for an hour and though I was aching, my mind had cleared. I didn't care what kind of work I got now; I just needed something to help pay the bills. There were a couple of small local agencies advertising for temporary staff and I sent them an e-mail, attaching my CV. Temporary work was exactly what I wanted. I wasn't going to hang around once my house was sold. Within an hour both agencies had responded with an almost identical e-mail:

> We're sorry, we don't have any work available for someone of your calibre.

I stared at the screen. What? What did they mean? I sent a text to Sarah, telling her about the meeting with Kourtney at Mersey Recruitment and quoting the messages from the other agencies.

How would you take this? I asked.

Sorry, Ruby, she replied. I don't think that's a compliment. It sounds more like an insult. Who's it from?

A couple of agencies. Lansdowne and Hill Street.

She replied within minutes.

They all know each other. You can't get away with anything. And they swap jobs all the time. Years back when I was temping, I was talking to a woman from one agency; when I went to another agency the next day, she was working there! They all meet up every Friday night at the pub in the square. Cross one and you cross them all.

My stomach dropped. Kourtney must have been talking about me. If I didn't get any work through the agencies, I'd be stuck. Another message came through. It was Sarah again.

Eleanor Jones used to work with them, too.

Was that how Kourtney had known about Harry and me? I'd suspected everyone at work, and now I knew who it was. Sarah sent another text:

Adam's got some friends coming round tonight. Fancy meeting up for wine and a chat? I can come to yours if you like or we could go out.

Of course Sarah thought I was still living with Tom. I looked around my new living room. Sarah and her husband, Adam, had been to my old house a few times and we'd been to their house. She'd loved my home and was polite about Tom, but I wasn't sure she'd really warmed to him. She didn't know where I was now, was completely unaware I'd left home. The thought of bringing her here horrified me. I sent a quick message:

I fancy going out. McCullough's at 8?

–

McCullough's was a bar just over a couple of miles away from each of our houses. It was a lovely warm night and I walked there. I arrived first but I'd been eager to leave the flat. That summer, gin was everywhere, and when I saw the cocktails on offer I abandoned my good intentions about alcohol and ordered a strawberry gin. Sarah came running in twenty minutes later, full of apologies, just as the place was getting crowded.

"So sorry! Lovely to see you." She kissed my cheek and sank into a chair. "Oh, that looks good. I'll have the same." When her drink arrived she sipped it and leaned back with a sigh. "God, I needed that. It's been a horrible week."

"For me, too."

"Of course, sorry, I wasn't thinking. What on earth's been going on, Ruby? I've missed you so much at work. Are you okay?"

Immediately my eyes prickled with tears. "Yeah, I'm fine, thanks."

"I can't believe they let you go," she said. "Do you know why? Nobody's said a word." She gave me a sympathetic look.

"You were a great worker. They couldn't deny that. You had that office running like clockwork. I hope they put that on the reference."

"They forgot to put that on," I said. "My reference was insultingly short."

"What? That's outrageous! I'll ask Harry to write you one. He's back at work on Monday."

"No, don't," I said quickly. "Don't ask him."

She stared at me. "Whyever not?" she said. "It's the least he can do."

I took a gulp of my cocktail and thought, *Why not? Why shouldn't I tell her? Why should I protect him when he's treated me like this?*

"We were having an affair," I said. "That's why I got sacked."

Chapter 17

Ruby

I couldn't have got a better reaction if I'd tried. As I spoke, Sarah was sipping her gin and when she heard what I said she started to cough, then choke. Her face scarlet, she stood, brushing off my attempts to help her, and rushed to the ladies'. I sat back and wondered whether I should have told her.

When she returned, her face was still hot and pink. "Sorry," she said. "I wasn't expecting that. My drink went down the wrong way."

"Are you all right?" I passed her the glass of water the barman had brought over for her. "Here, drink some of this. I'm sorry I gave you a shock."

"You really did," she said. She drank the water, then started to look better. "I wonder why I haven't heard anything at work. I haven't heard even a hint of a rumour."

"Thank God for that." It would happen, though, I knew that. I looked at her, wondering whether I could trust her. "Don't tell anyone any of this, will you?"

"Of course I won't," she said, and reached out to touch my hand. "We're friends. But tell me everything. When did you meet up?" She lowered her voice. "Did you go to hotels?"

Suddenly I didn't want to tell her the details. I didn't want it to sound tawdry, as though we'd been constantly, furtively looking for the opportunity to have sex. And we hardly ever booked into a hotel for the afternoon. Just a few times. Once a month or so. I held my face really still, the way I used to at home, so that she didn't see a telltale flush, a giveaway smile. "We never spent the night together," I said. "Not until Paris. Tom's home every night. I would never have got away with that."

Sarah looked disappointed. I think she wanted stories of glamour and hotels and jewellery. It felt ridiculous to tell her that our affair had consisted mostly of snatched moments together that had meant more than any time in a hotel. Every week or so I'd travel to meetings with Harry and those hours spent in the car together had been like little holidays: something to look forward to and to treasure afterwards. I'd keep quiet when Tom asked about work and always made sure to include Sarah or another woman if I told him I'd been anywhere. He'd usually switch off if I said too much, anyway; his eyes would glaze over and he'd turn on the television or open a book.

"And nobody found out? Tom didn't suspect?"

"No, he didn't suspect a thing," I said. I didn't say that I was so used to watching what I said, in case Tom was annoyed, that lying came really easily to me now. "I was home every night. He had no reason to be suspicious."

I remember the first time I lied to him. An actual full-on lie. There wasn't an ounce of truth in it. It was ten at night and Tom had just arrived home. He'd had a meeting with clients in Glasgow that day and, knowing he'd be late, I'd spent some time with Harry in his office after hours. I'd got home at eight, so that when Tom touched the bonnet of my car, the engine would be cold, and I'd called him from the landline, as he liked me to do, but he hadn't answered his phone. Before he'd even taken off his jacket he'd said, "What did you do this evening?"

I panicked for a split second but remembered that as soon as I'd got home I'd dialled the house phone to check the time of the last call, but he hadn't called me. Without a pause, without even thinking about it, I'd said, "Oh, today was a really horrible day at work. It was so busy and Sarah just wasn't pulling her weight." *Sorry, Sarah.* "And I was listening to the radio on the way home and someone was talking about meditation and how it helps if you're stressed, so when I got in I put some on YouTube and had a go." I laughed. "I was really bad at it, but it did the trick. I've just had a nap."

Tom picked up the remote and flicked the television on then, and went to YouTube. He still had his jacket on, his car keys in his hand. He looked at the sites last viewed; there was no mention of meditation. He looked back at me, his face still.

"I wouldn't do it in here where anyone could look in the window! You had my iPad, didn't you, so I took my phone upstairs and did it there." I smiled at him. "We could do it together, if you like, when you're ready for bed? I promise you'll sleep like a baby." I knew there wasn't a chance in hell that Tom would meditate. I quickly added, "I've made you some supper. Fancy a glass of wine with it?"

Now Sarah said, "Typical of me not to notice what was going on. So that trip to Paris. The conference. You were together then?"

My face flamed. "Yes."

She ordered more drinks and I thought that after that one I wouldn't have any more. I'd tell her too much. "But you were risking everything," she said. "Your marriage. His marriage."

I could tell she thought I was crazy. "I loved him." I couldn't say whether I did now or not, and hoped she wouldn't ask me. "And I thought he loved me."

"But why were you fired?" she asked. "I don't understand."

"Yeah, that wasn't exactly what I thought would happen." My throat clenched up and I took a long slug of my drink for courage. "Harry and I decided we wanted to be together. It was all agreed. I was going to leave Tom. He was going to leave Emma. It was all arranged."

"What? You were leaving home to live with Harry?" *And you didn't tell me?* rang in the air. "When?"

"Last Friday."

"But Jane said he went on holiday on Friday night. She said it was all planned." She looked confused. "I wondered why he hadn't said anything about it. You know how he'd normally look forward to his holidays and talk about them. He never even said he'd be off work."

"He wasn't meant to be," I said. "He was meant to be leaving home. To be with me. We'd booked a hotel and were supposed to meet up there."

She was quiet for a minute and I could tell her mind was racing. "When I left the office at three o'clock, you didn't say a word. I asked what you were doing at the weekend and you said, '*Nothing much*.' Remember, I asked if you fancied going to see a movie that night? You said you were tired and just wanted to watch television."

"I'm sorry. I felt horrible about that. I would have told you on Monday. We'd planned that I'd tell Tom and he'd tell Emma, then we'd meet in the hotel afterwards." I could feel my throat tighten. "And then he didn't turn up."

"But you did?"

"Yes."

"And you'd already told Tom it was over?"

"Yes."

She took a deep breath. "Oh no. I don't think I could have done that. I would have wanted him to leave home first, I think."

I winced. "That was the thing. I thought I could trust him."

"I wouldn't trust anyone that much." We sat in silence for a while, then she said, "So you got to the hotel and Harry wasn't there?"

I nodded, still furious at his betrayal. "I waited all night. All weekend." I thought of how I'd sat there so excited at first, before I started to worry. I remembered calling the hospitals and felt such a fool. All that time he was on holiday, having a romantic break with his wife.

Sarah looked shell-shocked. "Didn't he call you?"

"Nope."

"Did you call him?"

"A couple of times." Or a couple of hundred times. "His phone went straight to voicemail."

"He might have switched it off. It wouldn't even register you'd called unless you'd left a message. We were told he wasn't taking messages. They needed a break."

"But I didn't know that. I didn't know anything. He just didn't turn up and then I went to work on Monday, thinking he'd be able to explain himself, but I couldn't get in. My pass wouldn't work. And then Eleanor came down to reception and gave me my things from my desk." I was hot with embarrassment at the memory. "She knew I'd been seeing Harry. She made that pretty obvious."

"But how would she know? Did Harry tell anyone?"

"No. He didn't tell anyone about us, not even his best friend. Nobody knew."

"Isn't that discrimination? I'm sure it doesn't matter how long you've worked there if you're discriminated against. Maybe you could appeal?"

I shook my head. "There's no way I'm going to do that. I've looked it up and I could appeal, but what's the point? I don't want to work there now, not after all that."

"No, I wouldn't, either," she said. "But how did Eleanor know? She didn't know about it all along, did she?"

I paused. I hadn't thought of that. "I don't think so. She came in to talk to Harry on Friday morning and I made her some coffee. She was fine. Told me about her holiday to Japan last month. In any case, I can't see Harry telling her anything personal." My head ached with worry. Had someone overheard me talking privately to Harry? Had they seen us? I winced at the thought. We thought we'd been so careful. "I tried to call him at work but his phone was redirected to Paula. And then you told me he'd gone on holiday with his pregnant wife." I tried to laugh but I really couldn't. "While I'm living in a crappy flat on my own. And he's not even here to yell at."

Now it was my turn to stumble toward the bathrooms and stand in the privacy of the cubicle, tissues pressed hard against my eyes to stop myself breaking down. If I'd had my phone with me just then I would have called Harry and told him exactly what I thought of him. When I returned to the bar I saw Sarah sitting and staring into the log fire, her expression unreadable. I wondered whether this was going to change how she saw me, whether I'd lose the only friend I seemed to have now.

She jumped up when I reached our table. "I'll get us another drink."

"Just water for me, thanks. The last thing I need tomorrow is a hangover."

When she came back from the bar with a glass of white wine for her, water for me, she asked, "So where are you living?"

"I've got a flat above a florist's on Nelson Street. It's all right, but I haven't lived in that kind of place since I was a student. Hopefully, it won't be for long. Tom's going to sell the house, so I'll get half of that and I'll be able to buy something small."

"You could have come to stay with us," she said. "We've got a spare room."

I thought of her lovely husband and her two small boisterous children. That was the family I'd wanted for myself. I couldn't put myself through it. I tried to smile. "Thanks, but I needed to be on my own."

"Still, I wish you'd called me. I hate to think of you in the hotel, waiting for him. And then his wife's pregnant, too." She was quiet for a minute, then said, "I bet he was telling you that he and Emma weren't sleeping together, wasn't he? Did you really believe him?"

I flushed. "It wasn't something we talked about."

"But were you…" She hesitated. "You and Tom. Were you still sleeping together?"

I shook my head. I didn't want to think about that. The few times we'd had sex over the last eighteen months I'd felt sick with guilt, as though I was unfaithful to Harry. I realised then that Sarah thought I was saying we weren't, because she touched my arm and looked sympathetic.

She took a long drink of wine. Clearly it was Dutch courage, for she said, "Do you think this was the only time Harry slept with someone else?"

Chapter 18

Ruby

I stared at her. Not once in the last eighteen months had I thought of this. "What?"

"I mean, do you think he makes a habit of it?"

"No! No, of course he doesn't."

"So he's never had an affair before? Or a one-night stand? A fling when he's been away from home?"

"No!"

"Are you sure? Has he told you that?"

I wanted to say that of course I was sure, that before he met me he'd always been faithful, but how did I know? It had never come up in our conversations. I assumed he hadn't played the field while he was married, but could I swear to it? I shelved that thought; it was something I needed to think about when I was alone.

So instead of talking about Harry and other women, I asked, "Do you know when the baby's due?"

That was my way of trying to figure out when it was conceived, of course. If I knew the due date I'd be able to work out when he'd slept with Emma. There were apps that would tell me that. Not the exact date, of course, but the week, at least. I'd read that five days before ovulation was the fertile window. Five days. A working week. A very long weekend. The thought of finding out when she'd got pregnant made me feel ill. I knew I'd go back in my mind to that week and think about how he'd acted toward me. Had he hesitated as I'd come into the office one morning? Had he felt a surge of guilt? Was he about to tell me that all this wasn't a good idea and that I should look for another job? Or had he given a self-congratulatory secret smile, knowing he'd got away with it, sleeping with two women? I felt sick at the thought of that.

"No idea," said Sarah. "Jane came in to tell us about it; she was very excited about becoming an aunt. Her own children are in their teens now; she was looking forward to holding a new baby again." She paused for a few minutes, then said, "I still can't believe you were having an affair. You don't seem the type, somehow."

"I'm not the type, whatever that is. I just loved him." I softened as I remembered. "And he loved me."

Sarah looked at me as though I was the most naive person she'd met. "He was married, Ruby. And so were you. It was never going to end well."

"I know, I know," I said. "It's unforgivable. But what he did to me, encouraging me to leave home to be with him and not turning up, well, that was the greatest betrayal."

"I think his wife might disagree with you," said Sarah quietly. "And Tom, too."

I winced, wishing I'd stayed in that night. Why was I putting myself through this?

"What about Tom?" she continued. "Did you tell him you were leaving to be with Harry?"

"No," I said quickly. "No, I didn't tell him anything. If you see him, don't mention it, will you?"

"Of course not. I doubt I'd see him anyway. But why did he think you were leaving him?"

"We hadn't been getting on well," I said. "Or rather, we only got on well because I did whatever he wanted. I wasn't happy at home." I hesitated before going on. Some people just don't get it and I had a horrible feeling Sarah was going to be one of them. "Tom's hard to live with. He's controlling. Possessive. I've wanted to leave for a long time."

Sarah seemed confused. "That's not how he came across when I met him."

"No, he could put on a great mask."

"Yeah, they're never the same in company as they are when you're on your own with them. But are you sure it wasn't just because you were in love with Harry and you were comparing them?"

I shook my head. "I almost left a couple of years ago, before I even started working with Harry. I'd just about had enough. And then my mum fell over and broke her arm, so that took me out of the house some, and things were a bit easier. But then a couple of Christmases ago it was awful."

"What happened?"

"Just an argument," I said. It had been more than that, though. You know when someone says something and it cuts you to the quick? I was naked at the time and Tom was clothed, which made me feel so much more vulnerable. It wasn't something I was going to talk to Sarah about.

She reached out and touched my wrist. "Don't you wear your Fitbit now?"

We both looked down at my wrist. I was wearing a bangle instead; it felt too odd to have nothing there.

"I've never seen you without it," she said. "Where is it?"

"I gave it back to him. He..." I knew she wouldn't understand me, but I'd had enough gin to keep going. "He tracked me all the time."

"What, where you were?"

"No, it didn't do that, thank God. He tracked my footsteps."

She frowned. "What?"

"He would check it, see how many steps I'd taken."

"Oh, Adam does that," she said. "We both wear one at the weekend and he's always checking his against mine. When we went to New York in the summer I did twice as many steps as he did, even though we were together all the time." She laughed. "That's the advantage of being so much shorter than him. He never got over it. Said it was much easier for me to do ten thousand steps."

I knew this story. She'd told me about it ten times. "It isn't like that, though. He's always trying to catch me out. Let's say I go to the shops one Saturday. I walk there, buy the newspaper, walk back again. Then the next Saturday I'll do it again and he'll check the steps against the first trip. And then he'll cause a fight, saying I didn't go to the shop I said I'd gone to. And one day I didn't wear it to work. He was convinced I hadn't gone to work at all. He kept a check of everything I did, Sarah. Every step I took. I couldn't bear it."

I didn't tell her about the times I'd try to fool him. I always parked in different spots in the office car park, to confuse him. He seemed to think I should be doing roughly the same steps each day. I could tell he was comforted if the figures matched his expectations. A few weeks ago I gave the Fitbit to Harry, who put it in his pocket when he was going to a meeting in Manchester; he knew he'd walk for a couple of miles. He told me he'd gone up and down the stairs several times instead of using the lift, just so that the figures would be skewed. That was after I'd told him about it, of course. When I knew I was leaving. He'd been horrified and wanted me to throw it away, but by then I just wanted to hand it back to Tom when I left. He'd know what I meant.

"Honestly," said Sarah, "you're reading too much into that. He's just trying to keep you healthy. Anything else he's supposed to have done?"

I bristled. "It would take too long to tell you. Maybe another time." I couldn't have coped if she'd told me that she thought his behaviour was normal. I'd spent years being told one thing but believing another. I couldn't bear her telling me that Tom was right all along.

"Okay," she said. She reached out and touched my arm. "Things will be all right. Once there's a buyer for your house, I'll come with you and look for somewhere of your own."

I smiled, relieved. "I'd love that. I'm not sure where I'm going to move to, though."

"It doesn't matter. I'll help you."

"Sarah," I said. "I hate to ask you this, but will you give Harry a letter from me? Or ask him to call me?"

From her expression I could tell she really didn't want to. "Can't you send him an e-mail?"

"I'm worried one of the tech guys might see it. And I don't want to text in case Emma sees it."

She hesitated. "I don't really want to get involved, but yes, okay. Send it to me and I'll make sure he gets it. He's back at work on Monday."

"And you'll ask him to call me?"

"Yes." She drank some wine, then leaned forward and gave me a hug. "Of course I will."

Chapter 19

Ruby

I spent most of the weekend alone, just me and a notepad and pen, trying to write a letter to Harry. It was hard to write, imagining his expression as he read it.

He and I had talked all the time. We worked hard, too, but between us was the ease of age-old friends. It had been like that since I first met him. It was as though I'd been existing in some sort of half-life, living the smallest possible version of myself. When I met him I could feel myself growing, blossoming. I could say anything to him and he'd understand. Not that we sat debating serious topics all the time, of course. We talked about anything and everything. Our favourite wine. The first person we kissed. The books we couldn't be without. The songs of our youth. Our conversations would be piecemeal throughout the day, then at the end of the day we'd almost always have time for a proper talk. And the more we talked the harder we worked; Sheridan's had done really well in the last year and Harry had told me again and again it was because he was invigorated by me. Revitalised.

And now Emma was having his child. I couldn't let myself think about how that had come about. I thought of his face as he found out. I could only guess at his expression. Had he given me a second thought? Had he just forgotten about me in the joy of discovering they would have a child together? In the pit of my belly was a growing fury that he thought so little of me that he couldn't even be bothered to tell me it was over.

On Saturday afternoon it was windy and raining outdoors, and I stayed in my flat, looking out of the living room window at the river beyond. And I thought of Harry on his sofa right now, his hand stroking Emma's belly, making plans together, thinking of names and their baby's future. They might go out later and look at paint for the nursery, at cots and cute little outfits. Any day now, they'd go out for the afternoon and come back laden with bags and wallpaper and furniture, all for the new life they were sharing.

I had no plans like that, or not for a long time. When I'd married Tom, I was still young and children weren't something I'd really thought about. Having Josh around seemed to fulfil whatever maternal desire I had, though really he and I were more like friends. I had learned early on not to take on a maternal role. Josh was Tom's child, not mine. After a while I was worried about being tied to Tom for life; I'd seen the bitterness between him and Belinda, and I'd slowly realised that at least half of the time their animosity was down to him. I knew that if he and I split up, it would be unbearable if we shared a child.

"I don't think we should go down the IVF route," Tom had said, when I'd suggested it after a couple of years of trying for a baby. "It can do so much damage to marriages. People tend to get obsessed with it; it's all they can think about."

It was all I could think about anyway. I knew he was right, though. If I'd had hospital appointments and treatment and so on, I knew what I'd be like. I'd be totally obsessed.

"And we know we can have children," he said. "I have Josh. *We* have Josh. You know he sees you as family." He gave me a sympathetic smile. "And, well, you were pregnant, too."

I winced, hating to think of that time in my life. When I was eighteen and about to go to university, I discovered I was pregnant by a boy from school that I'd been seeing for a few months. I hadn't known whether to go through with it or not, but decided to go ahead, to defer university for a year, and to have the baby. A couple of days after the twelve-week scan, the baby clearly thought otherwise.

"If we just keep on trying, we'll be lucky. They'll come one day."

But they hadn't. It wasn't for want of trying, though. Soon Tom was waiting with me, month after month, buying me pregnancy tests, holding me as I sobbed each time the words *Not pregnant* were revealed. I thought of the soft toy he'd bought me right at the start, the first time we tried to get pregnant. He'd come home with it, a long, soft, furry dog, the colour of caramel with treacle toffee eyes and the floppiest ears. When you squeezed its ear it made a barking noise and Tom nick-named him Captain Barker, saying it was clear that the dog should be a higher rank than a mere mister. When he gave it to me that first night, we were so full of hope and promise for the future and we'd laughed so much I'd cried with happiness. Over the months and years the dog moved from the armchair in our room to the wardrobe in the spare room and eventually, just before I moved out, I took it to a charity shop for another baby to have. A real baby.

I thought of the dog's new owner that afternoon in my flat, sitting at the window not knowing whether it was my tears or the rain that blurred my vision, and wondered whether they could smell my perfume, feel the hope that clung to the dog for all those years. I hoped they could, hoped they never felt the despair that led me to give it away.

–

Eventually, I grew sick of feeling so bad and forced myself out into the rain. There was a cinema nearby and I booked myself in for a movie that was so loud and action-packed that I didn't have time to think. The cinema was nearly full and just seeing other people nearby gave me the illusion of company. Though

I wanted someone to talk to, when my phone buzzed at the end of the movie and I saw it was Oliver, I felt too fragile to see him just then.

Ruby, I've just spoken to Tom. He said you've left home. Is everything OK?

I winced. I knew I was going to have to face this with everyone. I kept my reply short.

All OK, thanks.

His reply came within seconds. Fancy meeting up to talk about it? I'd invite you round but Tom's at home so I doubt you'd want to call here. Just say where and when and I'll be there.

I thought about the day I'd had, with no human interaction, and the day ahead – Sunday – always the most miserable of days.

Meet me for brunch at the Marino Lounge at 11 tomorrow?

He replied immediately. I'll be there x

Chapter 20

Ruby

It was odd sitting in the bistro having brunch with Oliver. He'd been to our house tons of times, for meals and barbecues and drinks. One year he'd even had Christmas lunch with us, because his fiancée had just left him. We'd bumped into him in the supermarket, looking forlorn, and when I heard he was going to be alone, I invited him to our house. He'd brought the makings of cocktails and I'd been plastered by the end of the night. And we'd been to his house, too, when he got promoted, when he got engaged. I'd never been out with him on my own, though. Why would I?

But most of the times Oliver and I talked, I realised now, we were on our own. And I grew used to not telling Tom about it; I knew he wouldn't like it.

I remembered the first time I kept quiet. A couple of years ago, Oliver and I were sitting on the garden wall, chatting. Tom was working late and Oliver was telling me that he'd been promoted at work. He told me all about the interview and the other candidates and what the panel had said to him when they offered him the job. We'd been interrupted as usual by Tom calling me on the house phone, to check I was there. A few days later Oliver was around at our house for a drink and when Tom asked how his job was, Oliver said, "Oh, well, I've been promoted at work. I'm their marketing director now."

There was a split second where I could've said, "Oh yes, of course!" but I didn't. I knew it would lead to endless questions from Tom about when we'd spoken, what was said, and why I hadn't told him. I just couldn't do it anymore. So instead I said, "Wow, congratulations! When did that happen?" And there was the slightest hesitation on Oliver's part as he answered me, as though he hadn't told me about it in great detail just days before.

I knew it was wrong of me. There was a complicity between us, that we knew something that my husband didn't. It's not right. I know that. But sometimes, well… sometimes you just want to keep things to yourself. And that's what it was with Oliver; it wasn't that I was colluding with him, more that I was keeping just a fraction of myself to myself. I was allowing myself a private life.

And that was the start of it really; it wasn't long after that that I started to work with Harry, and by then I was skilled at deception, adept at keeping my thoughts and, later, my actions to myself.

–

"So," said Oliver, after we'd finished eating. We'd just ordered coffee and I'd thought I was going to get away without having to answer anything personal. We'd covered his job and his upcoming holiday to Ibiza. "Why did you and Tom split up?"

I flushed. "Have you spoken to him?"

"Yes. It was a bit strange, really. I noticed your car wasn't there for a few days and when I saw him bring Josh home I asked him whether you were at your mum's. I was really shocked when he said that you'd left. He said he didn't really understand why you'd gone."

Now I really was embarrassed. "He did understand. I've been telling him for a long time that it's not working."

"Maybe he didn't want to tell me. He seems the sort of guy who's quite proud. I can't imagine him telling me anything private, really."

I nodded. "He hates anyone to know anything about him."

"So you're really not going back?"

"No," I said firmly. "That's not going to happen. I'm just waiting until my house sells."

"So are you staying with your parents?"

"No. They're going to Australia tomorrow to see my sister. They plan to stay there for months."

He laughed. "Have they told her that?" He'd been to my house on Tom's birthday when my parents and sister were there and he'd seen Fiona's exasperation with my mum.

I grinned. "She's told them to get an open return but my mum's interpreted that as Fiona wanting her to stay there for a long time. But in any case I can't stay there. I might embarrass them in front of the neighbours. Apparently I'm killing my mother. She says she can't stop crying."

"Really? I saw her in a café in Liverpool on Friday afternoon. She was having a cream tea with a friend and looked pretty happy."

I laughed, feeling lighter for the first time in ages.

"Put it this way, she hasn't lost her appetite as a result of you leaving Tom. That cake stand was empty."

"You should've sent a message," I said. "I could have phoned her, just as she was tucking in. It would have been funny to see how her expression changed."

"I will do if I see her again."

The waitress approached us and left the bill on our table. Oliver took out his wallet and smiled at me. "I'll get this. So was it just that you were unhappy with Tom? I wondered whether you might be interested in someone else."

I was startled. Had he seen me change as I grew involved with Harry? I knew Tom hadn't noticed – he would have said if he had – and even Sarah had been astonished at my revelations. Oliver and I had always got on really well. Had he noticed what nobody else had?

"Tom had changed over the years," I said, careful not to actually answer his question. "He always wanted to know what I was doing, where I was. It was suffocating at times. And things had to be done his way or I'd pay the price afterwards."

Oliver looked shocked. "He'd hurt you?"

"No, nothing like that. He just had these moods and I never knew what to expect. He'd ignore me. Blank me. He could go on for weeks, acting normal with everyone else, but not speaking to me at all."

"I'd never noticed," said Oliver. "How often would that happen?"

"It wasn't often at the beginning. He could go months when everything was great. When he was moody then, I could get past it. But it's been more and more often. For the last few years I've been living on my nerves, worrying about when it would happen again. Do you remember the Christmas before last? He didn't speak to me for the whole of the holiday period."

Oliver frowned. "I was at your house for New Year's for drinks that year, wasn't I? Josh was there, too. Everything seemed normal."

"Tom hadn't spoken to me for five days at that point. He used to behave normally while other people were around, but if you watched carefully you'd see he never spoke directly to me. He'd be quiet if I spoke, but never reply. Even Josh didn't always notice. Tom only started talking to me again because I went to work at Sheridan's after Christmas and he wanted to know where I was going each day." I laughed at the memory, though it hadn't been funny at all. "The curiosity near enough killed him."

"Why would he do that?"

I shrugged. "I don't really know. It didn't have to be anything I did. It could be something I didn't do. Something I didn't know I was meant to do. He was always careful not to let anyone else know, though. And I was so stupid. I went along with it." I stretched my arms behind my back, trying to get rid of the tension. "It doesn't matter now."

"But why didn't you leave before?"

That question really irritated me, but it confused me, too. I didn't know why I hadn't left. It's so hard to leave a marriage, to walk away from everything. It's like leaving your family. I knew I was weak, knew I hadn't had the courage to leave, to take that leap into the unknown. And I was always broke, too. I'd known that if I'd left I'd struggle to manage financially. I had a sick feeling that I'd only managed it this time because I had Harry to go to. I wished I was stronger, wished I was the sort of person who could just think, *I've had enough* and end it. "I kept hoping it would get better, I suppose. And then I reached a tipping point a while ago and knew I had to leave."

"What happened?"

I shook my head. I wasn't going to answer that. "I just knew I couldn't live like that anymore." I sat quietly for a while. "Then I met someone. Someone special." A familiar flare of anger shot through me. "Or so I thought. It turned out he wasn't special at all."

Oliver sat back, staring at me. "You were seeing someone else?"

I shrugged. "Nothing came of it."

I wasn't going to tell him about my affair with Harry. That was private, something I held to myself even now, when I was in bed in the dark. No matter what had happened between Harry and me, nobody could take that time away from me. And I knew that wherever Harry was, whatever he was up to now, it would be the same for him.

Chapter 21

Ruby

On Monday morning I got up early and drove to Sarah's house to put my letter to Harry through her door before she left for work.

She lived on a quiet street a couple of miles from my flat. As I approached her house I could see it was in darkness with the curtains drawn, and, like her neighbours, it seemed that she and her family were still sleeping. As quietly as I could I pushed the envelope through her letterbox and slid away in the early-morning mist back to my car.

I started to drive toward my flat, but when I turned on the radio and heard the six o'clock news bulletin, I thought of Harry and what he'd said to me one day.

"I wake every morning just before the alarm at six thirty," he'd said. "Isn't it odd how that happens? Every single day I wonder what's woken me. And I lie there and my mind seems to scan through everything that might have happened. Was it my phone? Someone at the door? A car engine starting? And then, always, within a second or two, my alarm will go off. And that happens no matter what time it's set for."

"Is it an alarm clock?" I'd asked. "Does it make a slight sound, just before it rings?"

"No, it's my phone. Hold on, though, let's check."

And he set his alarm for a minute's time and we sat in silence, the two of us, leaning forward to listen, to check whether we could hear something, a sign that the alarm was going to go off.

And then when it did, with a blast of "You Can't Always Get What You Want," I shrieked and jumped.

That evening I'd set my own alarm for the same time the next morning and I'd woken a few seconds beforehand, just as he did, and lay there in the soft darkness of my bed, with Tom lying beside me, still in a deep sleep. I thought of Harry in his own bed, lying next to Emma. I wondered whether they were lying close together, whether his arm had snaked around her waist in the night, or her legs were entangled with his. I turned to look at Tom, at his dark wavy hair, tousled on the pillow. He was lying as far from me as he could, and I'd been clinging to the edge of our bed in my sleep.

I'd felt a familiar stab of jealousy, deep inside, and wished I wasn't here in this bed with Tom. I wished I was anywhere else. I'd known Harry for only a few weeks at that point and already I longed to go into work. On Saturdays and Sundays I found the time dragged, and when Tom suggested a long weekend away, I turned it down. I didn't want to be alone with him. I needed the distractions of everyday life to cope with living with the wrong man.

-

Now it was as though I was operating on automatic pilot as I drove down Sarah's street and took a left turn, knowing that this would eventually take me to Harry's house. I was last here the day after he was meant to leave home, when I still thought he'd come to me.

I sat in my car a few doors down from his house, on the other side of the street. The curtains were closed and the house was dark. His car was parked at the front, next to Emma's red Mini, and I knew he was home, back from his holiday from real life.

And then dead-on six thirty, just as he'd told me, the light went on in one of the bedrooms and then another light lit up a small window at the side of the house. For a second my heart leaped, thinking that he and Emma were in separate bedrooms, but I realised the smaller room was a bathroom. Then the hall light went on and I knew he'd gone downstairs to make coffee. I could picture him there, waiting for it to brew.

I sat and watched for several minutes, my heart beating fast. Then the light went off in the bathroom. When the curtains in the living room at the front of the house were drawn back, I ducked down in my seat, though I knew I couldn't be seen. My eyes were fixed on their house.

As the minutes passed, the bedroom light was turned off and I saw a blond woman at the window, drawing the curtains back. I couldn't see her face, but I knew who she was. I'd seen her on enough Instagram posts. She didn't look up and down the street. Why should she? When his car lights flashed, dead-on seven o'clock, I turned the key in my car's ignition. I needed to get away, fast.

I got as far as the corner and stopped the car. I couldn't resist taking one last look.

There on the step was Harry, his back to the street, completely unaware of me. His wife, Emma, stood in the doorway. He was wearing a suit; she was still in a robe.

As I watched from a safe distance, I saw him reach out and cup her face, then kiss her. Her arms came up around his neck and they stayed like that, their bodies close, for a few moments.

I put my foot on the accelerator and drove slowly away, but by the time I reached the end of the road, the impression of that tender embrace was emblazoned on my mind.

Chapter 22

Emma

Of course I knew Harry was carrying on with Ruby. Of *course* I did. What, do you think I'm nuts?

It had been obvious for ages. He would come home with a little pink glow on his face and a skip in his step, and for a while he suffered from that well-known disease that affects adulterers: mentionitis.

Every time he opened his mouth he'd tell me something about Ruby. That she was so clever. So funny. They'd been laughing all day. Great, just what you want to hear. She was married, he told me, and I shut him up a few times by asking him questions about her husband, a guy called Tom who worked in Sales. He sounded as bad as his clown of a wife, to be honest, but Harry was never interested in talking about him. Once, I asked whether he wanted to invite Ruby and Tom to our house for dinner. I thought I'd like to see what I was up against. He refused so quickly that I became even more suspicious.

At first I treated it as a bit of a crush. I remembered feeling like that when I was in school; there was always someone I'd had my eye on. I found my old school diaries when my parents moved from our family home into a bungalow, and quite honestly, it was as though I was permanently in heat during my teenage years. So after twenty years together, I wasn't *that* surprised that Harry had had his head turned a bit. I put it down to the stress we'd been under, running two businesses and trying to get pregnant. I never thought he'd actually have an affair, though.

And then I missed the biggest signal of all. It was a rookie error on my part and I've been kicking myself for it ever since. You see, he just stopped talking about her. Her name was never spoken; it was as though she'd been spirited away and he'd had his memory wiped. And I fell for it. I almost forgot about her.

I should have known.

–

One Friday night in May, Harry came home from work later than usual. I'd already showered and changed into a dress and heels; we were going out for dinner that night. I went out into the hallway when I heard his car draw up outside.

"Hi," I said when he came into the house. And it was so odd. He smiled at me but he looked different, somehow. His smile was just too polite and he didn't quite meet my eyes. Now, we've been together through thick and thin, but he's never done that before. Immediately I was on high alert.

He dumped his bag down on the hall table. "Hi."

"Did you remember we're going out with Annie and Patrick tonight?"

"Yeah, sorry I'm late."

Still odd. Still no eye contact. My skin started to prickle. I went up to him and kissed him on his cheek. He stood still to let me, not responding with a return kiss. With a jolt I remembered his crush on Ruby and realised that that fear had never really gone away. I quickly glanced at his face for signs of lipstick, took an inward breath to detect a hint of perfume. There was nothing; this did confuse me, I admit. I have a pretty good sense both for perfume and for danger – or I thought I had – and I could have sworn there'd be something there. But no, all I could smell were the traces of his cologne from that morning, and his shirt was still crisp and uncreased.

He pulled away from me. "I'd better get a shower."

I followed him upstairs, telling him about my day and noting he wasn't saying much about his own. I knew he had something on his mind. Something that I wouldn't want to hear.

He waited until he was in the shower before he told me.

"Oh, by the way," he said.

I steeled myself. Something was coming. Whenever someone tells you something you really don't want to hear, they do it with their face covered, either in the shower, while taking off a sweater, or in the pitch-dark of a bedroom. It's Psychology 101, isn't it?

So, he said, "By the way, you know that trip to Paris?"

"No." I knew perfectly well which one he meant. It was the following weekend. He'd put it on the kitchen calendar. Now I wondered whether this would be our own personal Armageddon. I felt my body, taut and wired, and didn't know whether I wanted to run away or to fight. "Which trip is that?"

"It's in a few days' time." From the careful way he spoke, I realised he knew exactly how many days it was. He probably had a little calendar he ticked off every day, like a child's Advent calendar, though with a bigger incentive than a sliver of choco-late. "A week from today, I think. There's a conference and I'm going to see about getting some French suppliers on board. We're giving a presentation, too. Remember?"

My throat was dry but I forced myself to act normally. "Oh, I remember now," I said. "That sounds interesting. Paris should be fun, too. Will you meet Ben there?" Ben was a friend of ours from university; he'd been living in Paris since we all left Manchester almost twenty years ago. "It would be good for you to meet up."

The pause was three seconds; I counted.

"I'm not sure," he said. "There'll be a few of us going so I probably won't have time."

If I could have pointed a torch beam in his eyes to get the truth out of him just then, I would have. "Oh? Who's going?"

"Nobody interesting." He reeled off the names of a few of the younger guys who I knew would be off looking for a bar as soon as they landed. I waited. Here it came. "And Ruby's coming. We need someone to help with the presentation." Another pause. "We won't see much of her, though. She'll be off sightseeing as soon as she gets the chance."

"That sounds like fun!" I said, in dutiful-wife mode. "You'll have a great time."

He switched off the shower and grabbed a towel. When he spoke, his voice was light with relief. "Oh, it won't be fun," he said. "You know that sort of thing; it can get boring at times. I'll book into a hotel with a gym, I think. It'll give me something to do in the evenings."

Somehow I didn't think he was going to be at a loss for something to do. I waited until he was back in the bedroom, flushed with heat and duplicity, before I said, "Oh well, why don't I come with you? I'd love a weekend in Paris."

He almost fell over himself to tell me that no, actually, that wasn't a good idea. "Well, you can come if you like," he said, "but I won't be able to spend any time with you. I'll be in meetings all the time. Why don't we go together, later in the year? We could stay for a week and meet up with Ben. Perhaps take a trip to Versailles while we're there – what do you think?"

I wanted to ask him why he needed a hotel with a gym if he was going to be so damn busy. "I don't mind," I said. "I can go to the galleries and do some shopping."

He turned his back and towel-dried his hair so that I couldn't see his expression. "Well…" he said, "it would be nice if you came. Only if you're sure, though."

–

The next day, my dreams of scuppering his adventures came to an end as I received a call from my business partner, Annie, telling me that she needed to take some time off work because her mother had fallen and broken her leg. I would have to work flat out over the next week so that our project was delivered on time. While I commiserated with her, part of me wanted to kick her mother's other leg because I knew that had been my chance to put a stop to Harry's shenanigans.

"Don't worry, darling," Harry said when I told him. "It's just a work trip. I'll be too busy to spend any time with you."

And when he returned from Paris on Sunday evening, he certainly looked exhausted.

But then, so was I.

Chapter 23

Emma

Harry was flying out to Paris on the eight p.m. flight, which meant he had to be at the airport at six. All week I'd been trying to get bits of information from him. I learned that the other guys would be there from Thursday night as there were people there they needed to speak to. Ruby would be travelling with him, because – oh, who knows, he gave some convoluted reason about her having to be at work on Friday to take minutes at a meeting.

That Friday he was up earlier than usual and spent more time in the shower. Getting himself Ruby-ready, I suspected, but a huge part of me hoped like crazy that I had the wrong end of the stick. He hadn't mentioned her for a while, and only then when I asked him a direct question. He wasn't a good liar, but he was consistent.

"You're pretty quiet this morning," I said as he drank coffee in the kitchen.

He looked at me, startled. He seemed so preoccupied I think he'd forgotten I was there. "I am? I'm just thinking about the meeting we're having this morning about the new selection of snacks we're planning. I'm anticipating problems with Production."

"I thought you hadn't made a final decision about them. Wasn't that what you were going to Paris for?"

He was like a rabbit caught in the headlights. "I am. Yes. That's what the meeting's about."

"Wouldn't it make more sense to have the meeting after you'd been there?"

Now he was back to his old self. "Emma, don't tell me what to do at work, will you?"

"No, but it's just…"

"Stop it. I know what I'm doing." He must have seen my face fall. "Sorry, sweetheart. I'm just preoccupied with it all at the moment."

"That's okay. Your flight's at eight, right?"

"Yes."

"The others went yesterday?"

He nodded.

"So it's just you and Ruby going tonight?"

His face became still and his eyes flickered away from mine. "Yes, I think so," he said. "But I'm not sure whether we're flying together. I'll have to check her flight time."

I think that was the first time Harry had ever told me a direct lie. Though how would I know? But this *was* a lie; I knew it.

–

I worked hard all day but I couldn't stop thinking about Harry. Why was I just lying down and taking this? I was his wife and I didn't want to lose him. I looked up at the clock. It was nearly four. Time to act. I would go to Paris, too. If I did that, nothing could happen between Harry and Ruby. I knew I'd feel a fool, gate-crashing their little party, but what was the alternative?

I took my laptop from the office; I would work in the hotel room. I drove home and quickly packed an overnight bag. Minutes later I was in my car, heading toward Manchester airport.

I hurried from the car park to the terminal building. The check-in line was pretty long and I stood against a wall, away from the crowd, waiting for Harry to arrive. I didn't want to buy a ticket until I was certain he was definitely taking that flight. I knew he wouldn't have arrived before me; he was never early for anything.

I waited and waited, scouring the crowds for Harry. I didn't want to send him a message, I wanted to surprise him. Deep down I knew he'd be shocked, rather than surprised, but I'd gone past caring about that. The line at the check-in grew shorter. I looked at my watch impatiently. It was now after seven o'clock, prime time for traffic problems around Manchester. He needed to get a move on. I took my passport and credit card out of my bag, realising I should get a ticket now rather than wait for Harry to turn up. If he only just got there on time I might be too late to buy one. I went over to the ticket office and stood in the short queue there. The woman in front of me had emptied her handbag onto the desk in an effort to find her passport and I turned away, exasperated.

Then I saw him. He sauntered through the departures concourse carrying his bag as though he had all the time in the world. He looked much more relaxed than I would be if I was arriving that late for a flight. He reached the stand for Air France and stood at the back of the queue. I thought he must be taking a different flight from Ruby's and my heart lifted with relief. He took off his jacket and rolled up his shirtsleeves, revealing his forearms. They were tanned and muscular and even at that distance made me weak at the knees. His hair was tousled and when his face broke out into a huge grin I felt myself respond. I smiled back and was just about to wave, when I realised he wasn't smiling at me. He hadn't even seen me.

Just when I'd taken a few steps toward him a woman brushed past me, darting through the crowds. She was tall and slender, with dark brown hair and that pink complexion that blushes easily. She was blushing now and laughing, too. She went up behind Harry and did that thing where you tap on one shoulder but stand on the other side. He swung one way and didn't see anyone, then turned the other way and saw her. His face lit up in a huge smile. He reached out and put his arms around her, hugging her so hard he almost lifted her from the ground.

And still I was persuading myself, well, okay, they are friends and he's hugging her. He can have a female friend, right? I can be a cool wife. I took another step toward him. But then he cupped her face in his hands and gave her the sweetest, most gentle kiss on her mouth. She was wearing a little silk vest and blue jeans and as she raised her arms to wrap them around his neck, I saw her back, pale and soft, and watched his hands slide around her waist, under her vest, to stroke her skin. A woman nudged Harry to indicate the queue was moving on. He and Ruby blushed and I saw them apologise. He took Ruby's passport from her and opened it. I saw him smile and say something to her, then she reached up to whisper in his ear. He kissed her hair and pulled her to him.

I couldn't take my eyes from them.

They were called up to the desk and one by one they showed their passports, had their bags weighed, and were given boarding passes. They turned away from the desk and I saw her touch his arm and ask him something. He pointed down the concourse to the security exit and, hand in hand, they walked off toward it.

My face was stinging as though I'd been slapped. I took out my phone and called Harry. I had no idea what I would say to him. It rang three times. He pulled his phone from his pocket and looked at it. I was about fifty yards behind him, now, following them. The ringing stopped. He'd cut me off! He didn't say anything to Ruby – if he had I wouldn't have been responsible for my actions – but put his phone back into his pocket. I don't know whether I imagined that slight hesitation before he put his arm around her shoulder.

I looked from him to her, at the way she reached up to touch his hand, the way she nestled against him, and I thought, *Enjoy it while you can, Ruby Dean. I am going to blow up your life.*

Chapter 24

Emma

I have never been the kind of person who'll just sit and take whatever someone chooses to dole out. Why would I do that? No. No. Better to pre-empt them. Get in first. Fire the first bullet. That's more what I'm like.

And Harry should have known that.

So that night I went straight from the airport to Ruby's house, to tell her husband that my husband was having an affair with his wife.

—

By the time I parked on the road by their house, ready for a quick getaway, I was feeling pretty nervous. I looked at the house; it was a good size. Well kept. A large magnolia tree sat in the corner of the garden, still in bloom, its graceful fragrant flowers just starting to shed. Everything here seemed so respectable, so normal, that I had a moment of panic in case I'd got it wrong and Ruby answered the door. What would I say? And then I pulled myself together. She wouldn't be here. That was definitely her at the airport. I recognised her from the Sheridan's website, though there her face was pale and serious. There was clearly more to her than you might assume from that photo. No, she wasn't here. She was boarding her flight around about now, snuggling up to my husband. I'm sure they'd had a quick celebratory drink while they were waiting, clinking glasses at the prospect of a naughty weekend away, thinking they'd fooled everyone. Well, not me.

I walked up their driveway. It was nearly dusk and lamps were lit in their living room. I could hear the faint sound of a television. Someone was home. My stomach clenched with stress but I knew I had to go through with this. I took a deep breath and rang the bell. Through the coloured glass panels in the front door I could see someone moving in the hallway. He came closer, his body blocking the light, and I took a step back and braced myself. The front door opened.

A man stood on the doorstep. He was tall and dark, about my age. He was wearing a grey T-shirt and soft denim jeans. Nice-looking, really. Put it this way: he didn't look like a good-enough reason for Ruby to be sleeping with my husband. Not that you can always tell, but still.

He stared at me. "Yes?"

"Hi." I started to speak but my throat felt raw. I know I'm all for bravado, but this was taking its toll on me. "Are you Tom? Tom Dean?"

He nodded and made to shut the door. "I don't want to buy anything, thanks."

I bristled. "I'm not selling you anything!" I took a deep breath. "Is Ruby here?" I knew she wouldn't be, but I had to double-check.

He shook his head. I could see he wasn't going to give away a damn thing.

"I'm Emma Sheridan," I said. "Ruby works for my husband."

"You're Harry's wife? Is everything okay? Nothing went wrong with their flight, did it?"

"I doubt it," I said with confidence, because I always think that bastards get away with everything. "Can I come in? I need to talk to you."

He looked behind me, as though I might have a posse with me, and automatically I looked, too. His house is on a corner and he has only one neighbour; that house was in darkness and its driveway was empty. Then he remembered his manners. "Yes, of course. Come on in."

He ushered me through the hall and into the living room, then switched off the television.

"Would you like a drink?" he offered. There was a bottle of red wine open on the coffee table and a glass stood beside it, half-full.

Right then I would've done anything for a glass of something even stronger, but I answered, "I'd better not. I'm driving."

"Sparkling water? Orange juice?"

"Water would be great, thanks."

He disappeared into the kitchen and came back with a tall glass of icy sparkling water. He set it down on the table beside me. "Let me take your jacket," he said. "Have a seat."

He was nervous, I could tell. I gave him my jacket and sat down on the sofa. I felt like I was going to be sick. The room was lovely, actually, much nicer than I'd expected. The colours were soft and relaxing, and a bowl of pink summer roses on the table made the room warm and welcoming. On the mantelpiece were a couple of photos in silver frames. I saw a teenage boy with a direct gaze and hair down to his shoulders: he looked like he wouldn't take any crap. Then there was a photo of the same boy aged about seven with a smile that would break your heart. Next to him was Tom, looking tanned and relaxed, and on the other side was a woman in her thirties with dark glossy hair and sharp cheekbones. I'd last seen her an hour or two before, kissing my husband. She had her arm slung around the boy in a casual hug and I wondered what on earth she was doing, having an affair when she had so much to lose.

"What did you want, Emma?" Tom said. He was clearly trying to act nonchalant, as though your wife's boss's wife came calling uninvited every Friday evening, but his back was stiff, I noticed, and his hand gripped his wineglass. He took a long drink – I knew exactly how he felt – and put the glass down on the coffee table.

"I wanted to talk to you," I said. "I think my husband is having an affair with your wife."

He stared at me, then laughed. "What?"

"Your wife works for my husband," I said. "They're away in Paris this weekend."

"Yes. They're at a conference. She's his PA."

"That's not all she is." I hated that, no matter how I tried, I sounded bitter. As though I cared.

He stared at me for ages. I met his eyes straight on. I knew I'd sounded like a bitch, but I had nothing to be ashamed of.

"Tell me everything," he said.

And so I did.

Chapter 25

Emma

We hadn't talked for long before I caved in and let Tom pour me a glass of wine, and then when he asked if I'd like another, I decided that I'd take a taxi home. Soon the bottle was empty.

Tom stood. "I'll get some more wine."

While he was out of the room, I called, "Mind if I use your bathroom?"

"Of course not. It's out here, off the hallway."

In the bathroom I looked around furtively, trying to get a sense of the woman who had attracted my husband. Everything looked clean and freshly painted, but there was nothing personal there. No photos, no cosmetics, just soap and hand cream and a mirror on the wall. I took one glance at myself, at my face, flushed pink with alcohol, my hair awry, and thought of Ruby standing there every day, looking at herself, standing just where I stood right now. I thought of her looking pleased with herself, smug with her double life. I shuddered and quickly left the room.

Tom passed me another glass of wine.

"Are you absolutely sure about them? You couldn't be imagining things?"

"No. I've wondered about it, whether something was going on, but now I know there is. I saw them at the airport just now." I'd already told him that; I guessed it was taking a while for it to sink in.

He flinched. "I took her there this evening. Dropped her off. I thought there would be a few of them there. That's what she told me."

I shook my head. "The other guys went yesterday. It was just Ruby and Harry today."

"When you say 'guys,' are you including women, too?"

"She's the only woman going," I said.

His mouth tightened and I guessed then that Ruby had been economical with the truth about this visit. There was a long silence where we sat without looking at each other, clutching our glasses for comfort.

"They'll be arriving now," he said.

We both looked at the clock on the mantelpiece. It was nine thirty here, ten thirty in Paris. I thought of them walking through the airport, hand in hand. They'd get a taxi to the hotel and sit for a while, ordering drinks in the hotel bar. Maybe they'd have dinner. After a while they'd say it was time to call it a night, knowing, *knowing* what would happen. Then not long after they'd find themselves in the lift, crushed together with a party of people, aware of each other's bodies, deliberately not looking at each other. I remembered that feeling from when I first met Harry and felt a stab of jealousy that he was experiencing it again with someone new.

I wondered who would turn to whom, who would be the first to suggest that they have a nightcap in one of their rooms. Would it be her? It's so easy to blame the other woman, but the picture Harry had painted of her when she started working for him was hardly one of a confident woman. Yet there she was, on a little trip with my husband. Confident enough for that.

And that's how it had begun with Harry and me, years ago, though neither of us was involved with anyone else at the time. I was in my first year at university; he was in his last. I'd noticed him for a long time and one summer night we were at a party in his student house and we sat on the porch steps and talked for hours. When it was late and most people had gone home, he hesitated, bit his lip, then said, "I don't suppose you fancy one last drink, do you? I've got some Jack Daniel's upstairs," and I'd sighed with relief that he'd acknowledged something was going on. I remember going up to his room, giddy with excitement. He shut the door behind me and kissed me there, so that I was pressed up against the wall, his hands in my hair, his mouth on mine. "I've wanted to do that since the moment I saw you," he said as he came up for air, and I had flushed with pleasure.

I thought of him saying that to Ruby and felt sick. And yet, why wouldn't he? He'd known it had worked with me. Maybe it was his party piece, something he said to all the women he'd been with.

I looked at Tom and wondered whether he was going through the same thing.

"Are you going to confront him?" he asked. "Now that you know for certain."

"I don't know." I desperately wanted Harry to stay with me. To choose me. I knew that if Tom and I challenged them both now, there was a huge chance they'd run off into the sunset together. I couldn't cope with that. "I think I'll bide my time. How about you?"

He looked unsure. "I don't know. I want to call her now. I won't, though."

"No," I agreed. "Don't do anything just yet."

He got up and went into the kitchen. I heard a tap running and when he came back in, his face was damp and there were splashes on his T-shirt. "I think you're right," he said. "We should bide our time."

"See what happens."

He hesitated, then shrugged. "I don't want to think about this now." He poured me another drink. "Tell me about yourself. What do you do?"

And so I curled my feet up on their soft velvet sofa and I had another sip of wine and started to talk to Tom about my life. What it was like to be me. It was more intoxicating than the wine, I have to admit. For a while there'd been a barrier between Harry and me; I knew now he'd created that. I realised when I spoke to him nowadays it was as though there was a brief pause where he had to stop thinking his own thoughts and acknowledge mine, but then he'd forget mine immediately afterwards and go back to his own. It was more than that, though. It was as though I was speaking another language and he needed time to translate. And the distance had grown greater as time went by. So that night it was the first time in months that I felt someone was really listening to me. Speaking my language.

And then it was quiet and when I looked at Tom, I saw he was looking at me, too. His expression was serious, as though there was something he had to say.

"What?" I said. My mouth was suddenly dry. "I'm sorry. I've been talking too much."

He shook his head. "You haven't. I just wanted to say…" He sat up, put his glass on the coffee table. "You're really lovely." His gaze was so intense and I just couldn't look away. "I don't know how Harry could do that to you."

I swallowed, suddenly close to tears. He leaned forward and put his hands in my hair, just as I imagined Harry was doing to Ruby, probably right at that moment.

And then he kissed me.

Chapter 26

Emma

I know, I know. I shouldn't have done it. *We* shouldn't have done it. There's no excuse. None at all.

Except I wasn't the only one behaving badly, was I?

I woke before dawn the next morning, my eyes snapping open to see the fluorescent digits of a bedside clock blinking at me. My head banged with a red wine headache and my mouth tasted foul. I must have been asleep for three hours, I reckoned. The room was dark, but light spilled in from the lamp on the landing, and I could see Tom, sprawled out on the bed beside me. His face was in the pillow, his breathing deep and regular. He'd drunk as much as I had. More, perhaps. I think he'd had a few drinks before I got there. It's no excuse, but there it is.

I lay as still as I could, letting my eyes scrutinise the room. We were in their spare room; I don't think either of us had had the stomach or the sheer gall to sleep together in their marital bed. The bed was large and comfortable, with deep pillows and a huge feathery quilt that he'd pulled up over us just before we slept. It wasn't that that made me feel uncomfortable, obviously. His clothes were on the floor, where I'd thrown them the night before. I winced and looked away. There were pictures on the wall – I wished they were generic, so that I could feel superior – God knows I needed to claw back some self-respect – but they weren't. They were clearly chosen by someone who was interested in art, who loved the pictures and had spent ages deciding on frames and positioning and the way the light would shine on them. The huge bookcase held so many books that were in my house, too, and I knew, I just knew that they were Ruby's.

I closed my eyes. What an absolute bitch I was. In that moment I hoped that Harry *was* in bed with Ruby. I hoped he was having a good time and wasn't giving me a second thought. I felt grubby and tawdry and just like the most anti-feminist person I could imagine. I was in another woman's house and in her bed with her husband. I hadn't thought I could sink so low.

I needed to get out, to go back home. I cringed as I realised I'd be leaving Ruby's house where I'd betrayed her so absolutely, to go back to Harry's where I'd done the same thing to him. I felt ashamed of myself.

The last thing I wanted to do was to talk to Tom, so inch by inch I slid silently out of the bed. I was naked and couldn't see any of my clothes in that room. I made sure I didn't open the door any farther – I didn't want the light to waken Tom – and found my underwear on the landing floor. Quickly I scrambled into it.

Down in the living room the lamps were still lit and two wineglasses stood on the coffee table, one half-full, the other empty. I looked away, disgusted. My dress lay crumpled on the sofa, just where Tom had removed it, and I put it on, trying to ignore the scratches on my back and the soft, tender bruises that were starting to bloom on my wrists and thighs. My shoes were just where I'd left them; I'd kicked them off before I curled up on his sofa.

I swallowed. *Their* sofa.

When I was dressed, I grabbed my bag and put my jacket on. The night was still warm but my body felt chilled to the bone. My car keys were next to my handbag on the table in the hall; when I put them there the night before, I thought I'd be staying for only a few minutes. I picked them up without making a sound, then let myself out of the house, closing the door quietly behind me.

I crept down the driveway, glad that there was no automatic lighting that would have exposed me. The night was still, the sky the darkest blue. Nobody was around. All the lights in the houses nearby were off, the cars safely parked in their driveways. It was as though I was the only person awake.

My car was parked on the road next to their house. I left my lights off when I started the engine and only put them on when I drove around the corner and onto the main road.

The car was cold and I rubbed my arms to warm up. As I did so I realised I'd left something behind. Harry had given me a heavy silver bracelet for my last birthday and I'd been wearing it the day before. For a second I didn't know what to do. I couldn't go back into the house to ask for it back, yet Harry would notice if it was missing. Then I shrugged and carried on driving. I knew Tom would see it, would hide it from Ruby. I'd tell Harry I'd lost it. I'd feign innocence. Shock, even.

I drove in silence, not wanting to hear music that would make me think of this night again. When I drew up at my house half an hour later, I breathed a sigh of relief to see Harry's car wasn't there. Of course it wouldn't be; it would be at the airport, left happily there while he went off to have fun with Ruby.

My stomach was clenched so tightly I had to squeeze my arms around myself. What a mess.

Even though I knew he wasn't there, I still tiptoed into our house and furtively checked each room was empty before I could relax. Then I ran a deep, scented bath and while I waited for it to fill, I scrubbed my teeth again and again to get rid of the smell and taste of wine. The taste of Tom. I closed my eyes and vowed I wouldn't drink again. I couldn't be trusted.

I lay for nearly an hour in that bath and felt just as bad when I got out as I had when I got in. Harry had broken his promises to me by sleeping with Ruby. I'd felt released from my own promises to him, then, but still my head thumped at the knowledge I'd broken my own moral code by sleeping with another woman's husband. Each time I remembered Tom kissing me, touching me, I recalled the look on Harry's face as he kissed Ruby.

In bed I clutched my phone, wanting to talk to Harry, to ask him how we got to this place. I started to type a message: I wish we could go back to the way we were but I thought of him reading it with Ruby by his side and I just couldn't do it. Tears blurred my vision and I deleted the message and switched the phone off.

By the time I fell asleep it was nearly seven and sunlight flooded the room. I slept until noon, then woke, my mouth dry and my head aching. There was a message from Harry on my phone, apologising for not picking up my call the evening before. He said he'd been just about to board and couldn't talk. I switched off my phone. My eyes focused on our wedding photo on the bedside table. Harry stood behind me, his arms around my waist. I leaned back against him, my eyes glazed with happiness and desire.

I could hardly recognise us now.

Chapter 27

Eighteen months earlier

Ruby

I could hardly wait to go back to work after New Year's, after meeting Harry the week before. Tom was waiting for me when I came home on Friday night. He was still on his Christmas break. He had a glass of wine in his hand and I could tell from his flushed face that he'd started early that day. It was a bitterly cold day and I ran from my car up to the house, slipping on the icy patches on the driveway.

"Hi," he said, as though he hadn't been ignoring me for several days. "How's work?"

"Fine." I stamped my boots on the doormat, then sat on the stairs to take them off.

"Where are you working now?" he asked, as friendly as you like.

"Sheridan's," I said. "On the industrial estate. They sell healthy snacks and send them out by post."

Within five seconds Tom was on his phone, looking them up. "Who're you working for?"

"Harry Sheridan. The MD. I'm working with a woman called Sarah. We both work for him." There was always safety in a female companion. I didn't tell him that I hadn't met Sarah yet because she was on holiday that week, or that Harry and I had spent most of the last two days chatting rather than working.

"What's he like?"

I shrugged. "All right. Older than us." I was so used to holding back what I thought, of having an impassive face, that the lie was easy. "I didn't see that much of him. Sarah was showing me how to use their computer system."

He seemed mollified. "Have a drink," he said, and poured me a glass of wine. The bottle was empty now and he went to fetch another. I glanced at the clock. It was barely six. "I thought we'd get a takeaway tonight. What do you fancy?"

I knew his game. He was going to act as though nothing had happened and if I referred to it later, I'd be in the wrong. So I stood in the doorway and stared at him, silent. He realised what was going on then, of course. I could see his feelings flitter across his face, first fear, then anger, then regret.

He walked over to me and touched my cheek with his hand. I flinched.

"I'm sorry, Ruby."

He leaned forward to kiss me. I tried to move back but I was up against the wall by then and couldn't. I started to panic and shoved him away.

He followed me upstairs and in the bedroom he shut the door behind him, but kept his distance. "I'm sorry," he said again. "I lost my temper and said things I shouldn't have said. You know I never want to hurt you."

Part of me wanted to run a mile from him and the rest wanted to believe what he said. I didn't want to think I was married to a man who could be cruel. So I just said, "If you say that sort of thing to me again, it's over," and he agreed, his head bowed, then he went downstairs to order a takeaway from my favourite restaurant, though he didn't like the food there much himself. And for the next few months he was back to his old self: friendly, interesting, happy to see me.

Living with Tom was like walking on eggshells. I lived in constant dread that something would set him off and had to quickly learn how to conceal my opinions. To silence my voice. He could go for ages being completely normal. He'd be friendly, funny, talkative, and kind. And then he'd switch. I'd feel the change coming, like the drop in air pressure just before a storm. Instantly I'd be wary, on guard, and kicking myself for relaxing.

When the New Year was upon us and it was time to go back to work, I made sure I complained, said I wished the holiday was longer, that I didn't want to go to work in a boring office. Tom accepted it to the point where he snapped at me to stop complaining. But in my car on that first day back at work, I had to breathe deeply to control my excitement at the thought of seeing Harry again.

He felt the same. I saw it in his eyes that morning, in the way he greeted me. He changed as soon as Sarah appeared, becoming professional and businesslike. It was as though he'd shown me his true self, the one he kept hidden from others. She seemed okay, but was a bit withdrawn at first. From something Harry had said, I thought she'd wanted my job; it would have been a promotion for her. I kept quiet and focused on my work, but as soon as she'd gone home, mid-afternoon, Harry would find an excuse to come into my office to chat.

–

It was more than two months before he kissed me and for every moment of that time I was aware of him. At times I felt myself relaxing too much, and I had to remind myself that he was my boss, that we were both married.

Since we met, Harry and I had been careful to never touch each other. We'd shaken hands on first meeting and then of course there'd been that moment in the lift when we'd both reached out for the ground floor button and felt the spark. We hadn't admitted to that for a long time. Since then we had been watchful and had made sure we were never physically close. At night I'd lie in bed while Tom slept and think about that, about whether Harry was deliberately avoiding touching me. It seemed pretty clear at times that he made sure he wasn't too close to me. I was glad, because I wasn't sure how I'd respond, but sometimes I'd wonder whether it meant he didn't really like me. And then I'd think maybe he just didn't want a lawsuit, and I'd smile at the thought of myself ever complaining about him, and I'd be able to sleep.

One Tuesday afternoon in early March, Harry came into my office.

"I've just had a call from Paul Heaton," he said. Paul was the chief buyer for a major supermarket chain and Harry was hoping to break into retail rather than relying solely on online sales. "I was supposed to be seeing them on Thursday but they've asked if I can go tomorrow instead."

I winced. "You set aside tomorrow to work on that, didn't you?"

"Yeah. The guy just can't make it on Thursday now. His wife's got a last-minute hospital appointment and he needs to be with her. There isn't another day that we're both free for a few weeks. I said I'd do it, but it'll mean a late night here."

"Want me to stay and help? Tom's away in Berlin at a conference, so I can stay late."

He gave me a relieved smile. "That would be fantastic. Thanks so much."

I took my bag to the bathroom and sent Tom a message.

Going to see a film and go for pizza with some of the women from work tonight. I'll call you when I get in. Hope your trip's going well x

I didn't get a reply.

We worked hard for the next few hours gathering together all of the information that Paul Heaton needed and putting it into a presentation. At eight thirty Harry leaned back in his chair. "I think we're done now. That was quicker than I expected, thanks to you."

I smiled and stood up to fetch my coat and bag from the cupboard. "I'm glad you got it all sorted. It'll be a big deal if they take you on."

"Wish me luck." He smiled at me and my knees weakened. He must have known that that smile would just undo me.

"Fancy getting something to eat?" he said. "You must be starving."

I shook my head. "Better not." He knew exactly what I meant.

We left the office together and went down in the lift. The building was empty and quiet. We said nothing, just stared ahead, but the tension between us was almost overwhelming.

Harry walked me over to my car at the far side of the car park. We hadn't said a word since leaving my office. I fumbled for my car keys and pressed the button on the fob. The lights flashed on. I turned to him to say good-bye.

There was a moment's pause when things could have gone either way. Gently he reached out and touched my face. Our eyes met. His thumb brushed across my mouth and I started to tremble. Tentatively I reached out to stroke his hair and then he kissed me.

Chapter 28

Ruby

Those two nights in Paris were bliss. I felt like a teenager again: full of lust and love and hope for the future.

Harry had offered to give me a lift to the airport, but I'd refused. I didn't want him to drive me back to my house afterwards, either, for Tom to come out and see me saying goodbye. I wanted to keep that weekend to myself as something to cherish. It had taken a lot of persuasion and outright lies to get him to agree to my going on the trip. I'd told him there were other women going and that I'd be with them all the time. But then Tom insisted on taking me, saying I'd never find my car again if I left it in a multistorey car park at the airport. He was probably right about that. At the terminal he kissed me goodbye as though he loved me. I guess he thought someone from work might see us; he'd always put on a good act in public. He told me he'd call me over the weekend; Harry and I had had contingency plans to deal with that.

As soon as I got out of the car, I didn't give him a second thought. I know that's wrong, but by that point I'd mentally separated from him. I knew I'd leave him one day; it was inevitable now. But still, even then, I wasn't dreaming about leaving to be with Harry. I just needed to get out of my marriage.

Harry was so excited to see me. You would have thought we'd been apart for days rather than two or three hours. He was late, of course, so we hurried toward the check-in as soon as he arrived. A few people were ahead of us in the queue. I pulled out my passport and Harry took it from me to look at my photo.

"You don't look very happy there." He grinned at me to take the sting out of his words. "I know they say you mustn't smile, but you didn't have to take it so literally."

Embarrassed, I took my passport from him and kept it closed. I'd renewed it three years before, when Tom and I were going through a bad time. He'd booked a holiday without telling me; two weeks alone with him in a foreign country was the very last thing I'd wanted. I thought I was in luck that my passport had run out, but he made me an emergency appointment with the Passport Office in Liverpool so that I could renew it the same day. My photo showed me looking exactly how I'd felt that day: depressed and fed up.

"Things were bad for me then."

He put his arm around me and pulled me to him and whispered, "I'm sorry. It looks like you were going through a tough time. I shouldn't have laughed at you." I leaned into him and kissed his cheek. The clerk called me forward to weigh my bag and check my documents and by the time Harry had done the same, I felt okay again.

It had been years since I'd travelled with anyone but Tom. It was an adventure, like the start of a holiday, where you think anything can happen.

"He didn't suspect anything, did he?" asked Harry when we were having a quick drink at the bar before boarding the plane.

I shook my head. "I'm so used to hiding things from him now. He didn't suspect a thing."

"Nor did Emma," he said. "Mind you, she's always thinking about work. I doubt she's even noticed I've gone."

I knew Tom would've noticed I'd gone. I knew I'd pay the price when I returned.

Our flight was only ninety minutes long and it seemed by the time we got on and had a drink it was time to get off again.

I was disappointed; I enjoyed sitting with Harry in the cramped cabin. It was good to be able to be with him without worrying about someone seeing us. I'd had a quick look around the cabin as we entered, and I know Harry did, too. When everyone was seated, he walked the length of the plane and I know he was checking to see whether there was anyone he knew. When he came back, he sat down and said, "All safe," and kissed me.

The flight was great, not too crowded and with a smooth takeoff. It seemed to go by in a flash. Landing has always terrified me, though, and as we approached Charles de Gaulle airport, I squeezed my hands tightly to take my mind off what was happening.

Harry looked down at my lap. "Are you okay? Your knuckles are white."

I nodded. "I hate this. I don't mind flying, but this..." We bumped onto the runway and I caught my breath.

"We're here now." He held my hands and gently rubbed them. "You're okay."

I tried to smile. "We're alive!"

He laughed. "That bad, eh? You should have said, honey."

"It's stupid, I know," I said. "I know all about there being more chance of an accident if you're crossing the road, but it still terrifies me every time."

He stroked my face with the back of his hand. I leaned against his hand and kissed it. "Do you remember I told you Tom and I went to New York a couple of years ago?"

He nodded.

"Tom was sulking on the flight and when it was time to land, he deliberately turned to talk to the man sitting next to him, knowing I'd need someone to cling to. It was bad weather, too, windy and pouring with rain, which made it even more scary for me. I was in bits when we got off the plane."

Harry's mouth tightened. "He's a really nice guy, your husband."

I looked away, ashamed suddenly that I was still married to Tom. "Don't let's think about him now. I want it just to be us this weekend."

—

Our hotel was small, with only twenty rooms, and in the Pigalle area in northern Paris, where old-style cabarets mixed with hip new bars and restaurants. The Moulin Rouge was right at the end of the street. The other staff from work who would be at the conference were staying in a different hotel near the Champs-Élysées; there was a casino nearby that they wanted to go to. They'd shown no interest in where we were staying, except to check with me that we weren't staying at their hotel. This was a weekend away for them and they didn't want their boss hanging around with them at night.

"This is so beautiful," I said when we entered the lobby. "The last time I was in Pigalle was when I was eighteen and backpacking. We stayed in dormitories and had to bring our own sleeping bags."

This hotel was as different from that as it could be, with its Moorish tiles and crimson velvet chairs and nineteenth-century oil paintings adorning the walls.

He laughed. "I knew you'd like it." He held me to him and I felt his breath against my cheek, making me shiver with anticipation. "I chose it especially for you."

We had separate rooms, as the booking was made through work, but we had no intention of using one of them. As soon as we were alone he was kissing me, up against the door, as though we'd just met.

When we finally made it back to the bar, I watched him as he spoke to the waiter in French, talking about the wine list. He seemed nervous, on edge, and I panicked in case he was regretting things, but then he turned to me and smiled and said, "I got myself tied up in knots there. I have no idea what I've just ordered," and I relaxed.

We were discussing where to go for dinner when it started to rain and we decided to stay put and order food there. The barman explained they didn't serve dinner, just bar snacks, then brought us an array of delicious tapas: little cubes of Emmental cheese sprinkled with celery salt, polenta cakes garnished with cherry tomatoes and pomegranate seeds, and bruschetta with black olives and roasted red peppers. I was nervous about that; I always found it difficult to eat in front of other people after Tom made a sarcastic comment about the way I ate when we were first together, so I made sure I was really careful. We sat in the window of the hotel with our wine and tapas, looking out at the bustling street and talking about our memories of how we first met. It was one of those moments in my life that was just perfect. And yes, I had to go up to my room half an hour before Harry did, so that I could call Tom and tell him I was okay. He didn't answer, of course. He didn't answer his phone all weekend and I knew he was annoyed with me for going. I was annoyed, too, as I knew if I hadn't answered my phone when he called he'd have been furious, but when I got home he actually apologised and told me he'd been out with work friends and hadn't heard it ring. It was such an unexpected reprieve, I felt light with relief.

–

It was on Saturday night that Harry first suggested we should live together.

We'd had to go to the conference that morning so that he could do his presentation. As usual, everyone was wowed by him. I felt so proud of him as he talked, engaging everyone, making them laugh. He had so many people come up to him afterwards, pressing business cards into his hand, asking to set up meetings with him. The day was a success and he was on a high as a result.

But the reason he'd done so well, he told me, was because of me. I still feel a full-body blush at the thought of the night before. It was the first time we'd had so much time together. Complete privacy. He was so gentle, so lovely. The way he held me, kissed me: I knew that he had feelings for me, that it wasn't just sex. After he slept I lay snuggled up alongside him and felt so sad and low at the thought of going back to Tom, of seeing Harry go home to Emma. I knew that I wanted to leave Tom. I think I'd known for years, but I hadn't felt able to, had thought I wouldn't cope alone.

On Saturday night we walked for miles through the streets of Paris. I don't know whether we thought nobody would recognise us or whether we just didn't care by then, but we were holding hands and it would've been clear to anyone that we were a couple. When we arrived back at our hotel, Harry pulled me to him just before we reached the door.

"Ruby, I've got something to say to you." He kissed me. "I love you."

Just as it had a hundred times since I met him, my stomach flipped. "I know," I said. "You've told me that before."

He laughed. "I tell you every day."

He was right. He did.

"But it's different now. This isn't enough for me, just seeing you at work and whenever Tom goes away. I want us to be together." He looked so serious. "What do you think?"

I felt as though I was taking a huge leap into a void. I took a deep breath. "I want to be with you, too."

"Let's do it," he said. "Let's make it happen."

And that was the night we planned it, that in a month, on the day that Emma's sister, Jane, was leaving work, Harry and I would go to our homes and I'd tell my husband and he'd tell his wife that we were leaving home.

Chapter 29

Emma

Of course, what I hadn't taken into account was that I'd get pregnant.

Harry and I had been together for twenty years, since we met at university. Back in those days I had contraception nailed down tightly. The very last thing I'd wanted was to have a baby. I wanted to work, to have the freedom to travel and see friends. A baby would only get in the way of that and luckily Harry felt exactly the same. Once we hit our mid-twenties and our friends started to have children, we decided to have one ourselves. We thought it would be the easiest thing in the world.

It was such a shock to discover it wasn't. After a couple of years we had fertility tests – those were a joy, I can tell you – and we were both found to be fertile. The doctors called it unexplained infertility; everything was in working order but I just wasn't getting pregnant. We had three attempts at IVF, but nothing happened except bitter disappointment. I think it affected Harry more than me, really. In the early days, whenever those feelings of utter, utter broodiness hit him, he'd get up and do something. He'd run miles in the middle of the night and work fourteen-hour days so that he wouldn't have time to think about it. That's when his business really took off. All of his efforts went into it.

I was working hard, too. I'd trained in web design and after a few years of working in larger companies, my university friend Annie and I decided to go it alone and we formed a small business together. We hired an office in a Victorian school that was converted into small offices and studios. We could have worked from home, but neither of us was good at solitude and having somewhere to go each day helped keep us motivated.

When I was absorbed in my work, I didn't think about getting pregnant. I just took the view that if it happened, it would, but then it didn't and after a while, I forgot all about it. For the last few years I hadn't thought about contraception. It had been well over ten years since we'd decided to try for a baby and by now I hadn't thought there was a chance of pregnancy.

So when I slept with Tom, it really hadn't occurred to me there might be consequences. Not of that kind, anyway. It had literally never crossed my mind, not beforehand or during or afterwards. Not one thought.

I don't know whether it was subliminal or what. Had I had that fling with him knowing I might get pregnant? I was thirty-eight: Was my body thinking I had one last chance? I hated to think I'd do that to any man, to use them to have a baby. I was ashamed I'd done it to another woman. Bad enough to sleep with her husband, but to not protect her – her above everyone – against my getting pregnant? I had never imagined that my overwhelming feeling at finding out I was expecting a baby would be shame.

–

I found out on a Friday, a month after I'd been to Tom's house. Those weeks had been strange at home. It was as though the temperature had changed between Harry and me. I couldn't relax. I kept myself busy at work, arriving early and coming home late. Annie would leave work first and I'd tell her I'd leave soon, but then I'd go to the kitchen and make coffee and hang out there to see who would join me. A lot of the people who worked in our building were young and single; they'd often go out for a drink after working until eight or nine o'clock.

I joined a gym, too, and told Harry I wanted to get fit. *Like Ruby*, I wanted to yell.

I didn't confront him about Ruby. I knew I would have to, but I couldn't bring myself to. I felt embarrassed. Humiliated. And I couldn't work out how I could tell him I knew without him finding out I'd slept with Tom. I was on tenterhooks all that time. I didn't know whether Tom would confront Ruby. If he did, he'd have to tell her how he knew. And she would tell Harry and it would all come out. I wanted to keep the moral high ground as far as fidelity was concerned. Though my nerves were on edge I tried to act the same as usual, but Harry seemed preoccupied with work and I didn't think he'd even noticed the difference in me.

The odd thing was that almost every night since I'd seen him with Ruby, we'd find ourselves in each other's arms, making love as we did in the early days, passionate and uninhibited. It wasn't as though we intended that to happen. It was only when we were in the dark that we'd turn to each other. We didn't say a word, either at the time or later. There was no eye contact, no whispers or shared laughter. I didn't know whether we were trying to make up to each other for what we'd done or whether we were seeking comfort and reassurance. In the mornings, though, I'd feel confused and hurt. I couldn't meet his eyes, not even to see whether he could meet mine.

–

That morning I woke later than usual and felt as though I hadn't slept a wink, though I had no memory of being awake in the night. I sat up and rubbed my eyes, then turned to see Harry was still in bed. He was always the one who woke first, the one who was up as soon as the alarm sounded. Usually he'd fix coffee before my eyes were even open. He'd put a mug on my bedside table and waken me with a quick kiss before jumping into the shower. Mornings were his best time and I'd seen it as a great quality, but now I wondered whether he was just eager to go into work to see Ruby. He was lying on his side, staring at the beam of sunlight that was reflected on the wooden floor. He looked absolutely lost. My stomach tightened. I couldn't live like this.

"You're running late," I said. "I'll make coffee while you have a shower."

"That's okay." He jumped out of bed. "I'll get some at the office."

When I heard the shower stop, I went down to the kitchen and poured a couple of glasses of orange juice and put bread into the toaster.

Harry came down and drank the juice quickly. "I'd better go. Lots on today."

There was no mention of the passion we'd shared the night before. No shared secret smiles or tender touches. As he raced around finding his briefcase and keys, avoiding my eyes, I knew I would have to do something. Annie and I had a solicitor we used when we set up our business. I thought I'd phone her this morning and see if she could recommend someone who could advise me if I decided to leave him.

I'd made toast and though I no longer wanted it now, I took a bite. As soon as the warm, buttered toast was in my mouth, I gagged.

I only just reached the bathroom in time and spat it out. Ugh, it had tasted so weird. Disgusting. I checked the bread and the butter. Both were fine. I drank a glass of water, but could still taste it. It tasted like iron filings. How did I even know what that would taste like?

And then it dawned on me.

Oh no.

I looked at the calendar on the fridge. I knew I'd had my period fairly recently; I'd been to my mum's house, I remembered, and given her a piece of my mind when she gave the last slice of lemon cake to Harry. I'd had to call her the next day to apologise, blaming my hormones. I checked the dates and groaned.

I couldn't be. I *couldn't* be.

Within half an hour I was at the local supermarket, looking at pregnancy tests. I was so familiar with these tests; I'd used them all over the years but for the last few years I hadn't bothered. I'd never got my hopes up, never bought one on the off-chance it would spark a positive result. I'd learned the hard way not to let myself do that.

That day I bought four different tests, then went back for a fifth. I wasn't leaving anything to chance. I went through the self-service checkout and flashed them through, holding them carefully, as though they were unexploded bombs.

Of course, they were positive. All of them were.

My first thought was of Harry. Be careful what you wish for, they say.

No kidding.

Chapter 30

Emma

When I sat down with my diary and worked out the dates, things were even worse than I'd thought. Harry and I had slept together twice in the week before he went to Paris and then almost every day since he came back. I can't even tell you how many times Tom and I had had sex. I haven't been able to bring myself to think about it. There were none of those happy stomach flutters that I used to have after I first got together with Harry. None of those sudden feelings of doubling over with lust. Just a cold dread every time I thought of what I'd done.

And yet I'd still never thought of pregnancy. My mind had been full of shame and betrayal; I'd thought that was the repercussion of sleeping with Tom. And now, looking at the tests, all brightly showing a distinct line or saying *Positive* or *Pregnant*, I didn't know whether to give into the absolute and utter joy of it or to end it immediately. But I knew that was not an option. No matter what happened, I wouldn't do that.

After I'd hidden the tests at the back of my office drawer, I decided to work from home that day. Annie was out of the office visiting a new client for an initial consultation and though I longed to talk to her, I knew I shouldn't. Her husband, Patrick, was great friends with Harry and it just wasn't fair to bring them into this. Though I'd planned to do some work, I couldn't focus and called my sister. Jane was the one I'd always turn to when I was stuck. Right from childhood we'd covered each other's backs, in every possible way. I wanted to confide in her, to ask her what I should do.

I rang her mobile several times that morning, but she didn't answer, so I sent her a message:

Jane, I need to talk to you. Call when you can x

A few minutes later she replied:

It's my last day at Sheridan's. I won't get the chance to talk until later. Are you OK? x

I sighed. I'd forgotten that she was leaving work that day. I didn't want to talk to her and be cut off in the middle, so I replied:

Yes, can you call when you've time to chat? x

Luckily I had tons to do that day as I was finishing a website before handing it over to Annie to test, but though I tried to distract myself, all I could think was, *Who is the father of my child?*

–

And then I had a breakthrough. In between bouts of work, I'd been trying to find out whether a DNA test could be done on a foetus. Just typing that into Google filled me with horror. Years ago, when I'd thought I might get pregnant, I'd had dreams of how I'd tell Harry. I'd thought of us buying a test together, gripping each other's hand as we waited for the results. I hadn't dreamed my baby might not be his. In one night, I'd ruined it. Both of us had ruined it.

At first all I could see were invasive tests. I closed the screen. I couldn't even think of doing that. I wasn't going to put my baby at risk. Yet the thought of waiting for months and months until it was born made me feel dizzy with panic. I wasn't sure I'd survive the wait. And how could I tell Harry he wasn't the father when he was holding the baby in his arms?

I started a different search. And then I discovered that there was another test I could take. It was much more expensive than the last, but I had my own savings account so that wasn't a problem. If I waited until I was eight weeks pregnant, I could have a blood test that would test the baby's DNA against a possible father's. It would take five business days before the results came back and then I would know for certain who the father was.

At the thought of that discovery I had to put my head in my hands and take deep breaths. I realised I had no proof that Harry had actually slept with Ruby. What if he denied it? He might say they were just good friends, that they liked to flirt, but that he would never be unfaithful. I was pregnant; all the proof of infidelity was against me, not him. I was the one with no excuse whatsoever.

When I calmed down, I read further. Not only would I need to give a sample of my own blood, I'd need to supply the DNA of one of the potential fathers for comparison purposes. They talked about mouth swabs. Four were needed. How on earth was I meant to do that? I felt like screaming. Would I have to go round to Tom's house to ask him to do it? I couldn't do that; what if Ruby was there? And on the website it was really clear that a signature was required from each party. How could I ask Harry to do it? I couldn't think of one reason on this earth that would convince him to do that. My marriage would be over immediately. I decided I would sign for Harry. I'd have to.

I knew I needed to test only either Harry or Tom. The other would be ruled out that way. So I searched further, a different clinic, different rules, and found I could send in the nail clippings of the potential father. Nail clippings! I felt like I was on a seedy reality television show and there was an audience hissing at me. It did say that nail clippings might not give a clear result, but it wouldn't give a false positive. A saliva swab was preferable but I wasn't going to be able to get that. I looked further; if I could get a big enough sample of hair, there was a chance they could test that, too, as long as the roots were present. Harry's hair was too short for that, I knew. Unless I pulled it from his head myself – quite a tempting option, actually – I'd never be able to get a sample. Panic surged in my belly. What was I going to do?

Quickly I cleared my search engine history. The very last thing I needed was for Harry to see what I'd been looking at.

I went to the kitchen to make coffee, but as soon as I opened the packet of coffee beans the smell hit me and I had to race to the bathroom again. Afterwards I sat in the living room, my body shaking and sweating, and I wondered how on earth I was going to wait another couple of months before I told Harry I was pregnant.

–

As it turned out, I didn't have to wait at all.

Just before five p.m. my mobile rang. I was wrapped in a blanket on the sofa; all attempts at work were futile as I could hardly move without feeling sick. My mouth tasted of metal, my breasts were sore, and I felt as though I could sleep for a week.

"Hi, Jane."

"Hi." She sounded distracted. "Sorry I didn't call earlier. It's been such a busy day. I can't stay long now actually as I have to go into a meeting soon. We have to do a formal handover. What's up? Is everything okay?"

I suppose it was my hormones messing around, but at the sound of her kind voice, I just burst into tears.

"What is it?" She was panicking now. "Are you okay?"

"You'll never guess," I said. "I've just found out I'm pregnant."

"What?" She sounded as amazed as I felt. "But... how?"

I laughed, then, choking on my tears. "The usual way."

"That's incredible! Congratulations! Oh, Emma, this is the best news ever." I heard her call to someone, "Can I see you before I go?"

"There's something I need to talk to you about." I swallowed. This wasn't going to be easy. "Something I'm really worried about."

"Oh my God," she interrupted. "Pregnant! That means I'm going to be an aunt! Izzy and May will have a cousin! They'll be so excited."

"Listen," I said. "I need to talk to you. Can we meet up tomorrow?"

"Yes, of course," she said. "And then we can... Oh no, hold on a second." I could hear her talking to someone. "I've got to go. Amy needs to talk to me."

"Jane," I said urgently. "Harry doesn't know yet."

But she'd gone.

Chapter 31

Emma

Of course you can guess what happened.

I was sitting in the living room just after seven that night when Harry's car turned into our driveway. My stomach dropped at the thought of the secret I was going to have to keep from him for weeks, if not forever. My skin was clammy and I wasn't sure whether that was from the sickness or from the dread that I felt when his car door slammed. Then I heard the front door open and he called, "Hello?" Usually I would go out to him, greet him with a kiss and a smile, but how could I do that tonight?

And then he appeared in the doorway with the biggest bouquet of flowers I've ever seen. He could hardly fit through the door. They were peonies, my favourite, and their white and pink flowers filled the room with their scent. Just one glance at him and I knew that he knew. I sighed. My sister. She'd never been able to keep anything to herself. Harry's face was flushed and he looked so happy.

"Congratulations!" he said.

I tried to smile. "Congratulations?"

He laughed and put the flowers on the table. "Yes, congratulations! Don't pretend you don't know what I mean!"

"Jane," I said. "You've been talking to Jane."

He came over to hug me. "She thought I knew. But when did you find out?"

"This morning."

"And you didn't call me?"

I winced as I remembered my immediate reaction to my pregnancy was to search for DNA tests, trying desperately to find one that would give a quicker result, and deleting my search history in case he saw it. I'd had no intention of telling him until I knew who the father was. I smiled at him, knowing whatever I did, whatever I said, I was a traitor, and if ever I was found out, he'd remember this conversation for the rest of his life.

"I wanted to tell you face-to-face," I said. "It's... it's such big news. There's a lot to take in."

"Oh, Emma." He held me to him, too tightly really, and it was as though he was saying everything in that hug. "We're going to have a baby!"

How could I possibly tell him that the baby might not be his? Probably wasn't his. Almost certainly wasn't his. His face was flushed with pride, but there was something else there, too. It was guilt.

I recognised it, you see, because I'd seen it on my own face.

–

The flowers were a waste, because the next thing he said was, "Let's get away."

I pulled away from him. "What?"

"Let's just get out of here for a few days. A week or so. Or two, even. Let's just hide ourselves away."

"Two weeks! I can't do that. What about work?"

"One week, then. You haven't got a lot on at the moment, have you?"

"No, but..."

"Tell Annie you need some time off."

I started to laugh. "Just like that?" My mind raced through the projects we had on. We'd just finished a big project and were ahead of schedule; I knew I could afford to take some time off. "And what about your work?"

He hesitated and my stomach dropped. Of course, he'd be thinking about her. And I could hardly criticise him for that, when I might have her husband's baby in my belly.

"Screw it," he said. "I haven't had a break for ages."

I said nothing about his trip to Paris just weeks before. The less I said about that weekend the better.

"Come on, what about going to the Lakes? Or abroad somewhere? Let's find somewhere special with lots of pampering for you. Are you feeling sick yet?"

I nodded. "I feel horrible. Everything tastes of metal; it's disgusting. That's how I realised I was pregnant." I outlined all my symptoms and he listened avidly, just as I'd known he would, when I'd first daydreamed about this moment years before. I felt horrible knowing he probably hadn't caused them, but honestly, I couldn't think of a way out of it. And then I thought of Ruby and Tom, and all I wanted was for us to get as far from them as we could. I looked carefully at him and saw strain in his eyes and knew he wanted to get away, too.

"Okay," I said. "Let's just take off."

"Where do you fancy?"

"I don't care. Let's just get into the car and see where it takes us."

He grinned at me. We'd had that sort of holiday so often when we were young. We'd set off from home not knowing where we'd end up; as long as we were together it hadn't mattered at all. I ran upstairs ahead of him, not wanting him to see the deceit on my face.

It took us ten minutes to pack our bags. I know I felt dreadful lying to him like that and I assumed he felt the same, for when I came out of the bathroom with an armful of toiletries I saw him standing by the window. On his face I saw the expressions that I had felt myself: shame and grief, but joy, too, at being given a second chance.

–

For nine glorious days we stayed away from home and spent every moment together. I'd insisted we fly from Liverpool, not wanting to go to Manchester airport after seeing him there with Ruby, and we'd ended up on a late flight to the South of France. It was like a second honeymoon. We slept in every morning, with no alarm to waken us, and lazed in the sun and swam in the pool. I tried and tried to find something I could eat without feeling ill. When I discovered ginger biscuits did the trick, Harry would call down to reception and ask for them to be delivered to our room, where he'd feed them to me, a tiny piece at a time. I could see how much he loved me, how much he wanted this child, and with each passing day I could see him move closer to me, farther away from Ruby.

Of course I let myself wonder at times what would have happened if I hadn't got pregnant. Of course I did. But then I forced myself to remember the night I'd spent with Tom, too. If Harry had been smitten by Ruby, I think that week away cured him of it. Put it this way: In bed it was as though there'd never been anyone else in our marriage. And now we didn't wait until dark. Afterwards there were whispers and caresses, instead of us turning away and never referring to it again. There were sly smiles the next morning and a race to bed in the afternoon. It was better than it had been for years.

"Let's switch off our phones," he'd said the moment we left our house. "Have a real holiday."

"What? But you never do that."

"I am now. Things are going to change, Emma. I don't want real life to intrude on us. I want to celebrate this baby." His eyes were bright with tears. "I feel as though we've had a new chance."

I leaned over to hug him. I was so relieved that he didn't want to contact Ruby that I accepted what he said at face value, never realising for a minute he had another reason for going off-grid.

"Send Annie a message saying we need a holiday," he said. "I'll e-mail Dave" – Dave was his right-hand guy at work –

"and tell him to take over everything. Let's have a complete break from real life."

So we sat in the car, each sending a message to our business partners, then switched our phones off and put them in the car's glove compartment.

For those days we were away, he never left my side, and, rather than finding that irritating, as I would have done recently, I grew to love it. I felt like we were conjoined twins, that we depended on each other in some kind of essential way. At night in bed he'd lie behind me and stroke my back and we'd suggest baby names to each other for hours.

"Daniel?"

"That's the name of a boy who used to bully me."

"Vanessa?"

"Vanessa was my best friend in elementary school. Until she spat in my dinner."

I was so tempted to say *Ruby*, but I held back, thinking how I'd feel if he said *Tom*. So we ignored certain names, locking them in a room where things from the past lay.

It was one of those times where you immerse yourself in another world, and at the end, it seems as though a year has passed. We came back from France closer to each other than ever, but no closer to resolving the problem that lay between us.

Chapter 32

Emma

Before we had left the house that night, I sent Jane a text to say that we were going away and wanted a bit of time together.

Good idea, she'd replied. Treat it as a fresh start.

I frowned. Had she guessed what I'd been up to? What do you mean? I replied.

I just meant, she sent a couple of minutes later, that this is a blessing for you – a chance at having a family with Harry. Make the most of every minute x

—

A few days after we returned from France, she came round for dinner, full of apologies for telling Harry I was pregnant. "I thought you'd already told him," she said as she hugged me. "I didn't think you'd tell me first!"

"Forget about it," said Harry. I noticed he wasn't looking at her and thought he must be furious with her. He'd waited years for news like that, and I knew he would have wanted to hear it from me first. His voice was cold and I wondered whether this would affect their friendship. "I'll go and sort out dinner. It'll be about twenty minutes." He went off into the kitchen and closed the door. I heard music playing and knew he wouldn't come out until dinner was ready.

"It's all right," I said to Jane, who was now red in the face. "He's so happy. You really shouldn't have told him, but it doesn't matter, not in the long run."

I thought of the alternative: I knew I wouldn't have told Harry by now. I would have pretended the sickness was from food poisoning or a bug, and then he would have panicked and come to the doctor's with me. I knew him; he always wanted to take care of me if I wasn't well. It was a lovely trait, but not really the kind of thing that's useful if you're trying to hide the fact you might be pregnant by another man.

Jane looked at the closed kitchen door then leaned forward and whispered, "Is everything okay?"

"What do you mean?" I stared at her. Had she guessed the baby might not be Harry's? Or did she know about Ruby? Was it known at work that they were a couple?

I felt mortified at the thought of people knowing, but then she said, "Oh, nothing. I just wondered how things were between you," and I realised I needn't worry about that. There's no way she'd keep quiet if she knew he was having an affair. She was my sister. I trusted her.

"They're great," I said. "Really great. It's as though I've got the old Harry back again. And he's so attentive. Honestly, if I make the slightest suggestion that I need something, he's on to it."

"You've got him running around after you?"

"Yes, at night I lie on the sofa and issue commands. He hasn't disobeyed one yet."

She laughed and said again, "So everything's okay?" There was something in her tone then, and I knew she knew something. I just couldn't bear to discuss it with her. I was really comfortable in this position, with my head buried deep in the sand. I didn't want to confront things, didn't want to talk things over with her, to be brave and honest and all of that. Talking is vastly overrated sometimes. All I wanted was a happy pregnancy, whoever the father was. I didn't want to think about whether Harry and Ruby were having an affair and I didn't want to think about sleeping with Tom. I just couldn't face up to things.

So I just said, "Which names do you like?" and within seconds we were laughing and I could nearly – almost – forget what both Harry and I had done.

That night I had the best night's sleep I'd had in months, wrapped in Harry's arms. I felt protected. Safe.

And then Tom found me.

Chapter 33

Emma

The morning after Jane came to dinner, I arrived at my office just after eight, planning to get some work done before Annie arrived. Harry had left at six that morning to fly to Edinburgh for a couple of days of back-to-back meetings. I was prepared for a long day at work and had a bag of ginger biscuits and raspberry tea for emergencies. I'd put on some makeup, but nothing could disguise my pallor. I'd been feeling queasy all night. I was trying to decide whether I'd tell Annie that I was pregnant or whether I'd fudge the issue and say I wasn't well. I knew I wouldn't get away with saying nothing, but didn't want her to worry that I'd pass on a bug. My mind was on the reassurances I would give her for meeting the deadline when, frankly, I looked as though I was on my last legs.

In the office car park I opened the boot to pick up a box of stationery that I'd bought for work. I walked toward the door to the building and saw Tom. I jumped so hard I nearly dropped the box.

He was standing across the road, leaning against his car; I recognised it from the driveway outside his house a few weeks before. He was wearing a leather jacket and jeans, and his dark hair shone in the early-morning sunlight. He was looking pretty good, really. I remained still by my car, unable to think what the etiquette was of bumping into someone who was essentially a one-night stand. Should I wave? Ignore him?

The decision was taken out of my hands then as he crossed the road toward me.

"Hi," he said.

"Hi." I gave him a quick glance and then looked furtively around. Anyone looking at me just then would know immediately that I'd been up to no good. The last thing I wanted was for Annie to see me talking to him; I knew I wouldn't be able to answer her questions. "What are you doing here?"

"I've just had an early appointment with John Holt." He nodded to the building adjacent to ours. "Then I realised you work next door and thought I'd try to see you." He smiled at me. "How are you?"

"Fine, thanks," I said automatically.

"Do you have time for coffee?"

I hesitated. I really didn't want to talk to him but I didn't want to be rude. I glanced at my watch. Annie would be taking her kids to school and wouldn't be at the office just yet. "I have half an hour." I winced. It sounded so miserly, to restrict his time like that. So unfriendly, particularly given the last time we met. "Sorry, you've caught me off guard here. I'm supposed to be meeting a colleague at nine."

"Have you got time to go to one of the cafés down the road?"

I nodded. "Just give me a minute. I need to leave this inside." While Tom stayed outside in the car park, I left the box with the receptionist and went into the bathroom. Luckily nobody else was in there. I ran cold water over my hands and wrists, feeling faint with stress. What did he want? And how had he found me? I hadn't said anything about where I worked. After a few minutes I knew I'd have to face up to him. I sent Annie a quick text to tell her I might be a few minutes late and went outside to Tom.

–

It was an awkward walk to the café. Neither of us said a word, but I was aware of his presence and could feel the tension in him as he walked behind me. It mustn't have been easy for him, either.

"Coffee?" he asked when we were sitting at a table. "How do you like it?"

The thought of coffee was enough to make my stomach turn. Tea, too. I said to the waitress, "I'll have a glass of water, please. Plenty of ice."

Tom looked surprised. "Sure? What about some juice?"

My stomach tilted again. "No, I'm fine, thanks. I've already had coffee," I lied. "I don't want to get too jittery."

"We have decaf," the waitress said.

"No. Water's fine, thanks." I waited until she'd gone, then I leaned forward and said quietly, "I'm sorry I left like that. The other day, I mean." I felt an idiot then. When else could I have meant?

He looked away. "That's okay."

"It's not," I said. "I woke early and couldn't go back to sleep. I didn't know what to do, so I just left. I should have written you a note or something. I'm sorry."

"Don't worry about it," he said. "It never happened."

If only that were true.

Our drinks arrived then and he spent a while opening the little bags of sugar and fiddling around with them. I sat watching him, my stomach clenched as I wondered what he was going to say. I decided to pre-empt him.

"Did you speak to Ruby about Harry?"

"No," he said. "Did you speak to Harry?"

I shook my head. "I haven't said a word. After... after that night at your house, I didn't feel I had a leg to stand on."

"I didn't say anything, either," he said. "I was hoping you were wrong. I couldn't stop thinking about it but I was waiting."

"What for?"

He shrugged. "For any sign there was something going on, I suppose. She was just the same as usual, that was the thing.

I started to think that you'd read more into it than had really been there. But then she left me."

I leaned forward, shocked. "What?"

He nodded, his face flushed.

"Where's she gone to?"

He shrugged. "She didn't say."

I thought of how he must have felt, being told that his marriage was over. Even though we'd spent only that night together, I thought I knew him well enough to know he'd be clinging to his pride. And yet I had to ask.

"Did she say why she was leaving?"

It was clear he didn't want to talk about it. "She just said she wasn't happy."

Impulsively I touched his hand. "You poor thing. Have you been okay?"

"Yes, I'm fine."

"So have you heard from her since she's gone?"

"Not really. Just the odd message. She won't be coming back."

I looked up at him and didn't know whether that was his decision or hers. I squeezed his hand. "When did she go?"

"Two weeks ago. On Friday night. I'd been to London for a meeting and got back around seven. She was waiting for me and said she was leaving."

My mind raced. "On the twenty-first?"

He nodded. "Yes. Why?"

"Oh, nothing." That was the day that I'd discovered I was pregnant. The day that Harry came home with an armful of flowers and a guilty expression on his face. My breath caught in my throat. Had he been going to leave me that day? Were the flowers meant to be compensation? A consolation prize? "Is she still working for Harry?" I asked casually. I could have kicked myself for not checking. But Harry was so involved with the baby and was calling me from work several times a day, often from the office phone. He hadn't sounded furtive as though she might be beside him when he called. I wasn't going to ask him; I didn't want him to see my face if he said she was still there.

"She's not told me anything." He hesitated, then said, "You and Harry... you're getting on all right now?"

I tried to keep my expression blank. I wasn't going to tell him I was pregnant. "Things seem to be okay again. I'm really sorry. I shouldn't have told you anything. It seems to have blown over."

"No, you were right." He pushed his coffee away from him and put his head in his hands. "I hadn't seen any of this coming, that's all."

I leaned back, away from the smell of coffee, but suddenly it seemed so strong, so pungent, that I knew I had only a minute to find a bathroom.

"Won't be long," I managed to say as I leaped to my feet.

When I came back, pale and shaking, my hair damp with perspiration, Tom was sitting back in his chair, looking out of the window. The waitress had cleared away his coffee and juice and there was just a large glass of water waiting for me.

I sat down and apologised.

"So, Emma," he said. "When were you going to tell me you were pregnant?"

Chapter 34

Emma

I stared at Tom. "What? What are you talking about?"

His eyes were cool as they met mine. "You're pregnant," he said. "When were you going to tell me? Or did you think I wouldn't find out?"

"I don't know what you mean."

"Come on, Emma." His voice was calm and steady, just the opposite to how I felt. "Don't even think of denying it. You're what? Mid-thirties? Married a long time with no children? We slept together a few weeks ago." His eyes didn't leave mine and I knew he remembered every moment. "I don't believe in coincidences."

Well, nor do I, I wanted to say.

"What makes you think I'm pregnant?"

He said nothing at first, then leaned toward me and said in a voice so low that I automatically leaned forward to hear him, "Well, I could tell you that there's a look that pregnant women have. You're pale. You have a greenish pallor. That'll be the sickness, right? You should probably try to eat something, even though you don't want to. Perhaps give some plain toast a try?"

My head swirled. Was he threatening me or giving me medical advice?

He smiled then. "Or I could just tell you that I'd seen a book in your bag."

I could've kicked myself. Shoved into my open handbag on the chair beside me was a book called *Pregnancy: Week by Week*.

"It's not yours," I said. "It's Harry's."

"How come you hadn't had children before?"

"Not that it's anything to do with you," I said, "but we decided to wait for a while before having a baby."

"So you're saying that your decision to have a baby coincided with you sleeping with me? I don't buy that." He drummed his fingers on the table. "You know I have a son, don't you?"

"Yes, you told me."

"My ex-wife got pregnant before we married. That was the reason we married, if I'm honest." I flinched. It sounded such a cruel thing to say. He must have noticed my expression, because he went on, "Actually it was the best thing that ever happened to me. I hadn't wanted a baby at that point; I was only twenty-five. But she came off the pill because it was giving her headaches and the next thing we knew, she was pregnant." He smiled at me. "It was wonderful. From the moment he was born I loved him. Before then, even. The intensity" – he laughed – "it's just staggering. Nothing prepares you for it."

I knew exactly how he felt. I was sorry for his ex-wife; I didn't even know her name, but here I was learning all about her private medical history. My mind was racing. She'd got pregnant so easily. Tom had proven he could make a woman pregnant. Wasn't it much more likely that the baby was his? My head pounded. I didn't want his baby. I did want *this* baby, though.

"So who do you think is more likely to be the father?" His voice was soft and persuasive. "Your husband? Really?"

I looked down, feeling sick again. "Yes. Really."

He touched my hand. "Did you think the problem lay with you?" he asked gently. "Is that what's been on your mind all these years?"

I couldn't speak.

"Maybe the two of you together… maybe it was never going to happen that way. That's not uncommon, you know. And now that you're with someone different…"

"I'm not with you!"

"Not now," he said. "But you were. And this is my baby, so who knows what's going to happen?"

He leaned forward and I could smell coffee, sour on his breath. I tried to lean back, to keep my distance, but his eyes were fixed on mine and I didn't seem able to move. "I would have thought," he said, "that a woman of your age who thought there was the slightest chance she might get pregnant would be very sure to use contraception if she slept with another man."

"Do you really think I carry condoms around with me on the off-chance I'm going to sleep with someone?"

He shrugged. "I have no idea. But if I'd been in your position, I would have made sure I didn't get pregnant."

"And vice versa."

He laughed. "You took me by surprise."

I'd had enough. "Do you like black-and-white movies?"

He looked startled at the change of subject. "Yeah, some. Why?"

"Oh, I saw one the other day. It was called *Gaslight*. Have you seen it?"

Slowly he shook his head.

"You remind me of someone in it. But you know what?" I leaned forward and whispered, so that he had to lean forward to hear me. "I can see through you."

He sat back and drank some water. I would have bet my house that he wished it was vodka. "I don't know what you're talking about."

"Really?" I stood up, took some money for my drink out of my purse, and put it on the table. "Maybe you should watch it."

"Don't go yet," he said. "What are we going to do about it? About the baby?"

"*We're* not doing anything about anything." I put my face down close to his. "I am happily married. I love my husband. You and I had one night. *One night!* And you think that's enough to get me pregnant?"

"One night, maybe, but three times."

I flushed. "It makes no difference," I said. "Don't come near me again."

–

I hurried back to my office. Annie was talking to someone in the kitchen at the end of the corridor so I managed to sneak into our office to pick up my emergency toiletry bag from my desk drawer. In the bathroom I brushed my teeth and tried to sort out my hair and face. I still looked shocking, though, and when Annie came back into our office, she took one look at me and said, "Are you okay? You look terrible! You should go home to bed."

"I will, just as soon as we've talked about your meeting in London." She was going there that morning to talk to a couple of fashion designers about their new website, and we needed to go through some figures and dates before she went.

"Don't worry about that," she said. "I can call you from the train. Have you caught a bug?"

I shook my head. I couldn't be bothered trying to fool her; she'd know soon enough. "No, nothing like that."

"What is it? Have you had bad news?"

"Not bad news," I said, though in a way it really, really was. "Most people would see it as good news."

I watched the cogs fall slowly into place. Her eyes opened wide. "You are kidding. Really?"

I nodded and we started to laugh.

"This is wonderful." She hugged me tightly. "Congratulations. How many weeks are you?"

"My last period started on May sixteenth, so that makes it seven weeks. A pregnancy is dated from the first day of my last period, right?"

Annie nodded. "That confused the life out of Patrick when I got pregnant." She laughed. "He was convinced I was wrong and tried to challenge the midwife. She soon set him straight. Have you told your mum yet?"

I tried not to think of how that conversation would go, if Tom was the father. "No, I'm trying not to tell anyone, just for a bit longer."

"Until the scan?"

I wondered how she'd react if I said, *No, until the DNA test results come through to tell me whether the father is my husband or my husband's girlfriend's husband*. I could only imagine the silence that would follow.

Instead, I said, "Just the usual thing to do, isn't it?"

"It's such good news. I won't say a word. Shall we tell people you've got a bug?"

I nodded. "Tell them it's catching; that way I won't have to see anyone."

"How's Harry? He must be over the moon."

I smiled. "He just keeps saying he can't believe it."

"I won't say a word to Patrick," she said. "I'll let Harry tell him when he's ready."

I agreed but as she carried on chatting, so excited by my news, I couldn't help thinking: If the father was Tom, what would happen? I'd have to tell Harry. There was no way I would keep that from him. But what would he do?

At the thought of his reaction, at his disappointment and sadness at not having this chance to be a father, I wanted to put my head down and cry. He would leave me – I knew that. He wouldn't be able to watch me bloom with someone else's child. I couldn't blame him.

Chapter 35

Ruby

When I saw Harry kissing Emma on their doorstep, I knew that it was all over between us. I know it sounds crazy but until that time I'd had daydreams where he'd call me and say he was so sorry. He'd tell me it was all a mistake, that he should never have let me go. In my dreams I'd put up a good resistance, but eventually he'd wear me down and we'd live happily ever after.

But when I thought of the way he leaned toward Emma and cupped her face in his hands and kissed her, just as he had with me the first time he kissed me, I knew that wasn't the sign of a man who was coerced into staying with his wife. My daydreams were just that, an avoidance of real life. I was never going to be with Harry and that was his choice.

I brushed the tears from my face and found some resolve from somewhere. Once the house was sold, I could move away. Far away. That moment couldn't come soon enough, but right now I had to find a job.

So by eight o'clock I was back in my flat, smartly dressed and ready to respond immediately to any job offers. I sat at the table in my living room, looking through the agencies farther afield, given I seemed to be barred from the local ones. I knew from experience that as jobs came in, they'd update their websites, and I was going to be ready for them. I'd spent Sunday honing my CV. I still hadn't heard from the other jobs but knew I had to give them time. It was a numbers game. The more applications I made, the more likely it was I'd get something.

Oliver rang at nine o'clock.

"Ruby, I've been thinking. There might be some jobs at my place," he said. "Shall I put your name forward?"

"That would be great," I said. "Anything will do at the moment. I'm just looking for something to tide me over until the house is sold."

"Great!" He gave me his e-mail address. "Send over your CV and I'll be in touch."

I sent Sarah a text:

Did you give Harry the letter?

She replied after ten minutes, saying:

I've only just got in! I'll put it in his drawer in a minute.

I felt a rage then that he was there in the office as though nothing had happened. He'd just replaced me with Sarah and carried on with his life. It was so hard not to phone him and tell him what I thought of him.

Just then an e-mail came through from a new agency in Liverpool in response to my inquiry, asking whether I could come in to see them. An hour later I walked through their door and was seated at Lesley's desk. She told me that most of the jobs they had were permanent, but I hoped that if I impressed her she'd be able to find me work. As long as she hadn't heard about my reputation, that is.

"So what have you been doing recently?" she asked. "I can see here you worked for Sheridan's in Chester. They're a great employer, aren't they? Did you enjoy it there?"

Interesting question. I felt like telling her just how much I'd enjoyed it but I managed to stay calm and said, "Yes, I was working as PA to Harry Sheridan, the MD."

"And that was a permanent job?"

The only thing I could do was to lie. "It was a long-term temp job. His PA had health problems and needed to be at home for a while."

"For eighteen months?"

I shrugged, desperately trying to think of a reason why someone would need that long off work, but Lesley's phone rang then and when she'd finished with the call it seemed she'd accepted what I had said. "Right, I think we might have something that we could consider you for. Are you sure it's only temporary work you're looking for?"

"Yes. I'm planning to move in a few months and I'm not sure where I'm going to," I said. "I don't want to tie myself down just yet."

Her eyes narrowed and I could see her wondering whether it was going to be worth investing her time in me.

"Of course," I added quickly, "I'm staying in this region, so I hope to keep working with you for longer than that. It's just that I'll be buying a house and want to work nearby, so I'll find a permanent job after that."

I had no intention of staying in this area once my house was sold. I'd be off. I thought of my friends from university who lived in Edinburgh, others in Devon. One lived in the South of France, another worked for the British embassy in Iceland. Suddenly my heart lifted. I would be free to go wherever I wanted to. I had a sudden flashback to something Tom said after a holiday we took. He'd told me he was busy but that I should book something. He said he was happy to go anywhere. I booked us a trip to Italy, to a little place near Sorrento. I thought he'd enjoyed himself, thought we'd had a good time, but right at the end, on the flight back, he said, "*You never quite manage to choose the right place, do you?*" My stomach fluttered with panic at the memory. What if I moved somewhere new and hated it?

My phone started to ring then, deep in my bag. I flushed, knowing I should have turned it off before I spoke to Lesley. "I'm so sorry. I'll just ignore that."

"Don't worry, I was just going to make some more coffee," she said. "Take it if you want."

I took my phone out of my bag and saw that it was from a withheld number. I thought it must be a company, calling about a job application, so I answered the call.

"Hello? Ruby Dean speaking." At first I couldn't hear what he said. "Sorry? Can you say that again?"

"I'm going to do whatever I like to you," a man's voice said. "And you're going to beg me for more."

Chapter 36

Ruby

I pressed the End Call button quickly and switched my phone off, shoving it into my bag. My cheeks were burning and Lesley commented when she came back over, carrying two mugs of coffee.

"Everything all right?"

I laughed, flustered. "You're not going to believe this," I said. "I've just had my first dirty phone call."

"What? Who was it?"

"I don't know. The number was withheld. I thought it might be someone calling about a job."

"What did he say?"

I told her, imitating his deep, rough voice, and she grimaced. "You poor thing. I haven't had one of those calls for years. They seemed to disappear once we had mobiles, didn't they? And if he withheld his number, you can't block him. What a pathetic man he must be, pestering women like that." She settled back at her desk. "I'm afraid there's not much work in at the moment and I have to give priority to my regulars. I'm sure you understand. The longer you work for us the more choice you'll get." My heart sank. This didn't sound good. "The only thing I have available now is to start on Thursday. It's a receptionist job in a small company on the Wirral. Someone's getting married and they're taking three weeks off, so they're looking for a stand-in." She told me the hourly rate and I winced. I'd always earned much more than that.

"I'll do it." I needed something – anything – to get me out of my flat and to help bring some money in.

She typed the details onto an e-mail and sent it to me. "I'll look out for something more suitable for when that job finishes. It's pretty slow this year because of the economy. A lot of companies are making do rather than employing temps. You'll have a lot more luck when you're ready to take on a permanent position."

When I left the agency I walked through the city centre and into a café that I used to go to years ago. I ordered coffee and sat at a table at the back, watching groups of people chatting. Everyone seemed so carefree. I knew that they'd have their own problems, but right at that moment I couldn't see what they were. I straightened my shoulders. I had to stop myself from getting depressed. I'd got myself into this mess and I had to get myself out of it. I sent Tom a text:

What shall we do about putting the house up for sale? Do you think we should do any work on it first?

He replied straightaway. It should be OK as it is. I've painted the hallway and some of the woodwork outside. The rest is fine. I'll get the Molly Maid team to give it a good clean, then get the agents round to value it. Do you want to be there to talk to them? x

While we were together, Tom had often ended his messages with a kiss. I always did, but sometimes he wouldn't, depending on how he felt. I scrolled up and realised that he'd ended every message since I left with a kiss. Was that automatic? Would he realise one day what he'd done and regret it? Or did he mean it: Was he being affectionate?

My stomach clenched at the thought of talking to the estate agents. I knew they'd find out that we were splitting up, because they'd want to know if they could find us something new. And I didn't want to see Tom's face tighten as he'd have to admit we were divorcing. I knew he'd find it hard, especially as it was his second divorce. I didn't want him involved in my life now, to know where I was living or what I was doing. As far as he knew, I was still working for Sheridan's; I certainly hadn't told him I'd been fired. I wondered then where he thought I was living, but shrugged it off. It didn't matter what he thought. I cared for him, but my life was my own now. I think that was the first time that I felt hopeful, as though I had a future that I could control.

And so I replied:

I'd rather not be there if that's OK. Let me know how much the cleaners charge and I'll transfer half to you.

His reply was swift:

Don't be silly, Ruby. I'll sort that out. But how are you? I've been worried about you. Are you OK? x

I almost laughed. I was as far from okay as I'd ever been. I couldn't bear to look round my new home, at its stained carpet, its sofa that made my back ache.

I'm OK. Thanks for dealing with the agents.

I hesitated, but didn't put a kiss at the end. Those days were gone.

He replied instantly. I didn't remember him replying so quickly when we were together.

Fancy coming round for a drink sometime? It would be good to see you again x

I didn't know what to say. I was frightened of saying no outright and I was terrified that if I did accept, I'd find myself moving back in there. I had to force myself to remember what it was like at home and sometimes that was hard to do. I didn't reply. I didn't let myself think about the fact he'd see his message had been read. Quickly I turned off Read Receipts on my phone, though I knew he'd probably already seen that I'd read his message.

I left my phone at the flat so that I wouldn't be tempted to reply. I went out for a walk along the river to the park and took my Kindle with me so that I could read in the sunshine. When I opened it, I saw a new book had been added. It was *The Goldfinch*.

Years ago, before Tom and I got together, we'd both read *The Secret History* by Donna Tartt. On the night we met he walked me miles through the streets of Liverpool, back to my home. One of the many, many things we talked about was that book. We loved it, more so because of that night. I'd been meaning to read *The Goldfinch* for years and just hadn't got round to it. Now it was on my Kindle and the only person who could have sent it was Tom.

Chapter 37

Ruby

That evening, when I was cooking dinner, my phone beeped in the living room. The message was from Josh, my stepson.

Dad's told me you left him. Didn't you even think of saying goodbye to me?

Instantly I felt guilty. Josh had been a constant in my life since I'd met him when he was five. I'd wanted to talk to him, to tell him I was leaving, but Tom had forbidden it. I'd had to give in on that; Josh was his son and it was obvious that Tom would want to tell him first.

Hi Josh, I wrote, my fingers nervous and suddenly slick with sweat. Your dad told me not to contact you until he'd spoken to you. But why would I say goodbye? I assumed we'd still see each other. x

Josh and I had spent a lot of time together, more time than he'd spent with his dad. At times Tom would have to work away when it was his visiting time, so Josh would come over to our house and we'd hang out together. I liked him; even when he was a horrible teen he was still funny and he saved his anger for his dad, not me.

Why would we see each other? he replied. What's the point?

Tears pricked the back of my eyes. I knew he was hurt and I wanted so badly to reassure him.

I love you, Josh. That's the point. Just because I won't be married to your dad doesn't mean I don't want to see you again. x

There was no reply. He'd be mortified, I knew, at my saying I loved him, but it had to be said. His relationship with me was separate from the one I had with his dad. I picked up my phone again and sent him my address.

Come and see me whenever you can. I miss you x

No reply again, of course, which left me plenty of time to worry that he wouldn't want to see me. I was suddenly desperate to talk to Harry, to ask for his advice. We'd spent so much time talking and he'd always been able to calm my nerves.

Sarah would leave the office to pick up her kids from school at three o'clock each day and at five past, Harry would usually appear in the doorway.

"Fancy a coffee?" he'd say.

His smile... there was something about him that drew me to him and when he smiled, it was as though everything lit up in me. I couldn't stop myself. I knew it was wrong but honestly, from the moment I met Harry I felt warm. Loved. I thought we'd known everything about each other and yet I hadn't known that his wife, Emma, was pregnant.

"I don't have any children," I told him, the first time we spoke about our families. "But Tom has a child. He was married before, to Belinda, and they had Josh. He's seventeen now."

"A stepson, eh? What's that like?"

"He's great. We had some difficult times when he was a bit younger." I laughed. "Just the usual teenage angst. But then Tom started to work away some weekends, so Josh would come and stay with me."

Harry had frowned. "Couldn't he stay at home with his mum those weekends and come another time?"

I shook my head. "It wasn't worth the argument. Tom said Belinda wanted time with her new husband, Martin. He said she was struggling to cope with work and taking care of Josh. And Tom and Belinda weren't talking for a long time, so it was easier if Josh just came along at the same time each week. They were both pretty rigid with their arrangements. Well, it's hard to be flexible when you're not talking."

"And didn't you mind?"

"I thought I would," I said, "but I grew to love him. And we got on well, too – better than he did with Tom, really."

I could see Harry hesitate and I knew what he was going to ask me. It's what everyone feels free to ask a woman of my age: *Do you wish you had children of your own?*

I pre-empted him. "I wanted children, but it didn't work out that way. I would have loved to have had them, though."

"There's plenty of time. You're still young."

"I hope I do," I said. "It's just never happened for us." I hesitated, then decided to tell him; there was something about Harry that made me want to tell him everything. "I have been pregnant, though. I had a miscarriage before I met him. When I was eighteen."

He winced. "You poor thing."

I couldn't talk about that. I never had. I think if I'd had a baby since, I would have been okay, but that memory of losing my only child was like having a painful tooth; I couldn't help probing it but each time the pain overcame me.

Harry was quiet then and I wondered about him and his wife, Emma. They had no children but I didn't want to ask him whether that was what they wanted. It seemed intrusive. It was nothing to do with me. I knew how much I would hate it if someone were to ask Tom whether I could have children. I cringed at the thought of that: the way people asked questions as though they deserved an answer, never thinking that their idle curiosity might mean pain for someone else.

My phone rang and I jumped, thinking it was Josh calling for a chat; then when I saw an unfamiliar number, I thought it might be someone responding to my job applications. I put on my best possible telephone voice. "Hello, this is Ruby Dean." There was a muffled noise on the line and I wondered for a moment if someone had misdialled. I said again, "Hello, this is Ruby Dean."

A man spoke. His voice was low and he sounded unsure of himself. "Are you free tonight?"

"What?"

"Tonight. Are you free? Around seven?"

Stupidly, I said, "Free for what?"

"To meet up," he said.

I frowned. That was a pretty odd way of going about an interview.

"Who are you?" I asked, my mind whizzing through all the companies I'd written to. Even at that point in the call I was thinking, *Why didn't you just e-mail?*

He cleared his throat. "Doug," he said, then he coughed. "How much do you charge?"

"What?" Even now I still thought he was an employer; I'd sent my CV out to a hundred companies over the last few days and thought that finally someone was calling about a job.

He told me then what he wanted. He gave me a couple of options, even; he didn't seem bothered either way.

I stared at the phone in horror. "Go away!" I shrieked. "Who do you think you're talking to?"

He started to speak again, but I cut him off and blocked his number.

I wished then I hadn't made that promise to myself about alcohol in the flat. I would have killed for a strong drink. Instead I sent Sarah a message.

Just had a dirty phone call.

Her response wasn't what I'd hoped for. Oooh what did he say?

I sighed. Why did people always think calls like that were funny?

The usual, I replied. I've blocked him now. Unless you'd like me to send him your number?

She sent back a smiley face and I switched off my phone. I was troubled. I'd never had a call like that in my life; now I'd had two in one day. And the bogus interview with Alan Walker still played on my mind. Who had sent the e-mail, inviting me to go there? But the thing that bugged me the most was that memory of my dresses hanging in the wardrobe. When I tried to remember putting them there I felt as though I was grasping at something out of reach. At a memory that wasn't there.

Chapter 38

Ruby

I woke early the next morning with a thumping headache to find forty-seven missed calls on my phone. Eleven of them had left messages on my voicemail. At first I felt a rush of excitement, thinking that I'd soon be offered a job and wouldn't have to take that low-paid receptionist's role. I started to listen to the first message, then hastily pressed the delete key as soon as I heard the guy breathing heavily. With growing trepidation I listened to the second, before cutting it dead as soon as he said what he wanted from me. Feeling sick, I blocked all of the callers without listening to what they had to say.

I sent Sarah another message:

I've had loads of dirty calls, Sarah. I've blocked them but I don't know where they're coming from.

She replied: Sorry, in a rush with the kids. You need to change your number.

But how can I? I said. I've just sent out over 100 CVs to employers and I've registered with all the agencies in the northwest. I could feel myself becoming increasingly upset. I can't just change my number! It would take weeks to tell everyone. I need a job!

My phone rang and I thought it was Sarah, grabbing a moment from work to reassure me. It really wasn't. My hands were shaking when I ended that call and blocked the number.

Google yourself, wrote Sarah. See if your number's anywhere. And buy a whistle. At least nobody will call twice.

There was a hardware shop on my street and I went there immediately. I tested a couple of whistles in the shop and bought the loudest one they had. Back home, I Googled myself, terrified of what I'd find, but nothing was there. I thought of entering the blocked numbers into Facebook, but couldn't bear to put faces to the voices that had called me. I knew I'd never sleep at night if I could picture those men.

All I wanted was to ask Harry what I should do. He was my only confidant over the last year and I missed talking to him so much. I looked up Sheridan's on my phone. On their website were photos of all the people at the top of the company. There at the very top was a photo of Harry. If I half closed my eyes it looked as though he was smiling at me, just as he did day after day when he'd see me at the door to his office.

"Ruby!" he'd say. "Come on in."

He'd stop whatever he was doing and give me all of his attention. Just one look from him and I felt as though I was wrapped in a warm blanket. As though I was home. In Paris he'd told me he loved me. Adored me. He wanted to live with me, to be together forever. And the way he'd looked at me, I'd believed him.

I frowned. Had it just been a ploy to flatter me? Why would he need to do that?

"It's so easy with you," he said. I'd laughed and he quickly apologised. "That came out wrong, didn't it? It's just that I can be myself with you. I don't have to think about things or feel as though you're second-guessing me. I can relax. I haven't been able to do that for a long time."

I'd known exactly what he meant. There was a closeness between us by then that I'd never experienced before. There was a song I remembered from when I was young, and the lyrics were something like *Everything's better when you're around.* That's exactly how I felt. It was as though the world had been sepia and it had suddenly burst into Technicolor and it was all because of him. And I trusted him, pure and simple. I'd known at the time that people would've said I was naive, given he was married and having an affair, but I felt as though I knew the real him. I'd truly believed him when he told me he loved me.

I was so angry then, and I picked up my phone, ready to let him have it. I guessed he'd be at work now and I took the risk that I could call him on his mobile. I hesitated, then withheld my number, before dialling his.

"Hello?" I said when the call went through.

"Hello?" It wasn't Harry; it was a woman. "Who's calling?"

Suddenly my mouth was dry. "Can I speak to Harry Sheridan, please?"

"Yes, of course." She sounded pleasant. Happy. "Who's calling?"

I hesitated. I couldn't give my own name. I didn't know what she knew. "Jenny Leonard," I said then. Jenny was one of my sister's school friends. I've no idea where her name came from right then.

"Just a second, Jenny," she said. "I'll call him." Then I heard her shouting, "Harry? Phone call!"

At the sound of her yelling, I realised that he must be at home. Nobody at work would answer the phone like that. Nobody would shout his name. That must be his wife! Emma. My stomach churned and I thought I was going to be sick. I didn't want to talk to him now. Not with her there.

Then she was back on the phone. "He won't be a minute."

"I'm sorry," I said quickly. "I'll have to ring back. Another call's coming through on my phone. So sorry."

"I'll tell him," she said. "Can he call you back?"

"Thanks," I said, pretending I hadn't heard what she said at the end, and hastily switched the phone off.

My hands were wet with perspiration. What if he'd answered and she was standing next to him? What would he have said? My phone rang then – it was from a local landline number I didn't recognise and my heart leaped.

"Harry?"

"Sorry, darling," a man said. "It's Danny here. Can you fit me in tonight at seven?" And then he told me exactly why he wanted to visit me. I could tell from his voice that he was calling from his house, trying not to be overheard by his wife.

He wasn't Harry but I realised he could have been. If Harry had answered the phone while Emma was in the house, he would've spoken just like that man, in a low, deceitful voice, desperate not to be overheard, but desperate, too, to speak illicitly. Privately. I shuddered. This was the reality. There was little difference in the end, when you boiled it right down, between this tosser who was calling strange women and asking to meet up for sex, and Harry, the man I thought I'd loved. Both were liars and cheats and bastards.

I reached into my bag and brought out the whistle I'd bought. I blew it as loudly as I could, right next to the mouthpiece.

Probably not the answer he was expecting, but hey, you can't always get what you want.

Chapter 39

Emma

It was the hesitation that did it. Who hesitates when they're saying their own name? Harry was in the shower when she called; he was about to drive down to Birmingham for a meeting and I was working from home. When I returned to the phone and realised the caller was in such a hurry to end the call, my sixth sense was on high alert.

Harry came downstairs. "A woman called Jenny Leonard called you," I said. "She'll call back later."

"Who?"

I repeated the name. "Don't you know her?"

"Never heard of her," he said easily. "What did she want?"

"No idea."

He shrugged. "What are you up to today, honey?"

Now it was my turn to hesitate. "I'm not sure. This and that. Plenty of work to be getting on with."

"Don't work too hard," he said, hugging me close. "There are two of you to think of now."

-

The second he left the house, I withheld my phone number and called Harry's office. I hadn't called him on his office number for years; I'd always called him on his mobile when he was at work.

"Hello, Harry Sheridan's office." The woman on the phone sounded young and educated. Cheerful. My stomach tightened with nerves. What was I doing?

"Hello, could I speak to Mr. Sheridan, please?"

"I'm sorry, he's out of the office today on business. Can I take a message for him?"

I thought fast. "Is that Ruby?"

"No, this is Sarah Armstrong."

"Oh, I wondered if Ruby was around. I wanted to ask her something." I had absolutely no idea what I would say to her; I just needed to hear her voice.

"Ruby no longer works here," Sarah said. "I'm Mr. Sheridan's PA now. Can I help?"

Interesting, I thought. *He never told me that.*

"No," I said. "No thanks. I'll call him tomorrow."

She started to say something, but I ended the call and called Human Resources.

"Hello," I said, then lied through my teeth. "I'm Susan Forrest and I've just interviewed Ruby Dean for a job. I forgot to ask her start and end dates with you. Could you let me have them, please?"

The man who answered the phone sounded very young. I knew most of the staff working at Sheridan's and tried to remember what Harry had said about HR. And then I remembered there was an intern who'd started working there in June.

"She's not on our records," he said. "She was employed through an agency. I think it was Mersey Recruitment; that's the agency we usually use. I'd have to ask Finance for the exact dates." He hesitated. "I'm not meant to give out information like that over the phone."

I had a strong suspicion that I'd get more out of this young man if he didn't speak to anyone else first.

"Oh, don't worry about that," I said. "I can call Ruby later, but I know she's driving at the moment. She's on her way to London for a couple of days. I just wondered if you can remember when she actually left so that I can complete this form."

"Oh, I can tell you that. She left on Friday, June twenty-first."

"Okay, that's great. Thanks." I ended the call before he had time to realise he probably shouldn't have told me anything, and sat at my desk thinking things over.

She'd left her job on the day that she left home. The day I'd discovered I was pregnant.

I don't believe in coincidences.

Chapter 40

Ruby

That evening I thought I'd go crazy if I stayed in any longer. All I could think about was hearing Emma calling to Harry in their house. His wife, his home. That was his reality now. It always had been. I should have known that. I needed to do something before I had a drink to forget. I knew that wouldn't work, either. I'd just dwell on it.

I looked out of the open window. The sun was setting and the air was still. I needed to get out. I pulled on my shorts and trainers and ran downstairs. On the floor by the front door was some junk mail and I picked it up to take it out to the recycling bin. I wasn't expecting any mail; in fact, I didn't think I'd get anything there at all, as nobody knew where I was living now and all of my bills were paid online. I riffled through the pile as I walked to the bin in the alley. Among the leaflets and flyers was an envelope with my name typed on it. There was no address or stamp; it must have been hand-delivered.

I opened the envelope, thinking the estate agent must have sent a receipt for the deposit I'd paid, though I couldn't figure out why it had been hand-delivered. Inside the envelope was a card. I pulled it out and frowned.

It was postcard-sized. On one side was a photo. A photo of me. It was taken last summer in my garden at home; I recognised the red halter-neck dress I was wearing. I'd bought it one lunchtime last year for an awards evening for Tom's work and I'd worn it for his birthday. We'd invited some people round and had a barbecue in the garden. I hadn't seen this photo before, but I thought it was taken at that party. I was sitting on my own at a table in the garden, with a glass of white wine in my hand. I could see the bubbles in the wine and the glass was frosted with condensation. It looked as though I was mid-conversation with someone but I couldn't see who. I was smiling and looked happy. Carefree. I couldn't remember feeling like that at home, yet that smile looked genuine.

I was confused. I hadn't realised anyone had taken a photo of me that day. Who had sent me this? I turned over the postcard and saw, written on the back of the card, a message, in a computer font that looked like handwriting. It said, Thinking of you.

—

Though I ran for an hour that evening it didn't do anything to clear my mind. I came home and showered then stayed up late, sitting by the window in my living room, looking down the road at the river. Music was playing on my laptop and I'd lit a few candles as it started to get dark. The curtains were open and outside I could see the lights outlining the banks of the Mersey. In front of me, propped up on a vase of flowers, was the photo. I found a notebook and started to write down a list of everyone who was at our house that afternoon. Oliver was there, as well as a few of our other neighbours. Josh and his girlfriend at the time. They broke up shortly afterwards. Sarah was there with her husband, Adam, and their children. Some of Tom's colleagues and their wives came along for a couple of drinks. My parents were there with my sister, Fiona. She was over from Australia for a holiday. Tom's parents had passed away a few years before; I shuddered to think how they would have reacted to my leaving their son. They really would have wanted revenge.

Who had taken the photo? I thought back to the party. I thought I was the only one taking photos that day. I remembered printing them out later that week and realising I wasn't in any of the shots. And when I looked at that list of people at the party, I knew that only Josh knew my address yet I thought he hadn't arrived at the party until later in the evening; he'd been out for the day with his girlfriend and they turned up when we were all indoors. I just couldn't remember what time they turned up, but who could I ask?

And then I realised it must have been Tom who'd sent this to me. He hadn't taken a photo of me for years, but maybe he had that day and hadn't shown me. I sent him a message:

Did you send me something?

He replied a few minutes later.

You woke me, Ruby. Do you mean The Goldfinch? xx

No, not that, but thanks for buying it, I replied. Something arrived today and I wondered whether it was from you.

In the post? he said. Not me, babe. I don't know where you live. I meant to ask for your address. Can you send it over? x

I didn't reply to that. I ripped up the photo and threw it into the bin. I tried to focus on what I'd be doing this time next year. I needed to get away, I knew that. I found a property website on my laptop and started to search for houses far away from here. I looked at places I loved to visit: Edinburgh and York, London and Brighton. It took about five minutes to realise that I couldn't afford a thing in any of those cities. I started to make a list of cheaper places that I could go to, then started to think about whether I wanted to stay in Britain or whether I should pack up and go abroad. I could wait until my parents came home, then go off to Melbourne. Perhaps I could stay with Fiona until I got myself sorted out.

Or maybe I should go travelling. Set off with no goal in mind, just me and a backpack. The thought flashed into my mind that I struggled to carry a couple of bags of shopping home. I'd go to the gym, then. Run every day instead of just when I felt like it. Become fit. Yes, travelling sounded amazing. Then I panicked. Travelling implied I'd return: What did I have to come back to?

Dave Matthews was singing "Some Devil" from my playlist. No wonder I was feeling depressed. I'd just clicked on Bob Marley's "Everything's Gonna Be Alright" in an attempt to cheer myself up when the phone rang. I swore under my breath when I saw an unfamiliar mobile number. Instead of being scared of it, as I had been, I was suddenly furious.

"Hello?"

"Hello, love," said a man with a strong local accent. "Can you fit me in tonight? I can come round to yours."

I looked at my watch. Tonight? It was already nearly eleven o'clock.

I softened my voice. "Sure, sweetheart," I said. "No problem. But you're new, aren't you? I don't recognise your number."

"Er, yeah." He was clearly trying to keep his voice low and hadn't figured on a long conversation. I wondered for a moment about his situation. Was he at home, telling his wife he was about to walk the dog? In a moment of hysteria I wondered whether he intended to bring the dog along, too. Or was he at the end of a shift at work, trying not to let his boss hear him and thinking his wife would be none the wiser if he was late home, because she'd be asleep anyway? "I haven't been to you before."

"I thought not!" I wished then I had some wine in front of me to give me some courage. Why had I decided not to have anything in the flat? I tried to sound welcoming. "Where did you see my number, darling? I like to keep track of these things."

"I saw it on Sex Works," he said. "Thought I'd give you a try."

I looked around for my whistle, but it was on the other side of the room and I couldn't be bothered to move. "Sorry," I said, though I had no idea why I was apologising. "Wrong number."

I did my usual routine of blocking his number, then pulled my laptop toward me. It was time to see what there was on me online.

Within seconds I'd found Sex Works, with its slogan "Some women are too easy." It was a site for escorts, though it didn't sound as though the women left their own home, so that was a bit of a misnomer. My first name was used – and mine's uncommon enough in women my age around here – and my age was listed as between thirty and forty. They named the area I lived in. My phone number was there with a description of myself and what I would do for money, which made my eyes nearly pop out of my head. Next to my name was a photo of a woman's naked body. Her face was hidden in a pillow. It wasn't me. It wasn't anything like me, apart from her having shoulder-length dark hair.

And you know there were a few comments underneath, where they rated me. They said that I was a slut, that I wanted it but wouldn't deliver, that I messed people around. Yet the calls had continued. What kind of review would there have to be to make someone resist making that call?

My phone started to ring again. It was from a withheld number. It gave me the creeps to think it was someone who was on that site at the same time as me, looking at that photo and my apparent wish list, and ignoring the bad reviews. Maybe it was someone who thought I should be punished for not treating the punters well. Quickly I rejected the call.

I searched on the site and eventually found an e-mail address for the webmaster. It took ten minutes; he really didn't want to be found. I sent a short snappy e-mail promising legal action if my number wasn't deleted immediately.

Then I copied the image next to my name and did a reverse image search on Google, but nothing showed up. I sat back, confused. The men who'd called me were the least of my worries, really. They had no idea where I lived and now that I had the whistle I could get rid of them easily. It was the person who'd posted my details that I was concerned about. Who had done that? Why would anyone do that?

I wondered then whether my name was on other sites. Maybe my address was on them! "*I can come round to yours*," the man had said. Did he know where I lived?

I jumped up and went to the window, pulling the curtains shut. As I did so I could see in the distance two men walking down the road in the direction of my flat.

I froze. Were they coming here?

I had no reason to think they would but the way they walked, with such a determined air, frightened me. As they came near to the edge of the row of shops I reached out and turned the lamp off and, holding a curtain to one side, peeped out. In darkness I watched as they walked past, with no hesitation or glance toward my flat, and continued on down the street.

I breathed a huge sigh of relief. My heart was thudding and I put the lamp back on and slumped onto the sofa.

Who had put my name on that site? I sat in the quiet room thinking who it might be. My age was in the right category. The woman in the photo was a brunette, just as I am. I thought of the calls I'd had – there'd been well over a hundred by now – and shuddered.

Again I regretted not having a bottle of wine in the fridge, but knew it wouldn't really help. This was something I had to do on my own. I poured a glass of water with shaky hands and went back into the living room. I was afraid to play music or watch a movie on my laptop in case I didn't hear someone knock or call my name. Someone wanting to pay me for sex.

I couldn't read. Couldn't focus. I just sat curled up on that sofa, careful to avoid the dip that made my back ache, and tried to think who might have done this to me.

Chapter 41

Ruby

When the agency in Chester had told me the job was basic, they really did mean it. After a few days, I thought I was going mad.

I turned up on Thursday morning, wearing a smart dress, and found the other admin staff looking hostile. They were a lot younger than I was and dressed more casually. One wore shorts and flip-flops and I don't think I saw her do any work in all the time I was there. They eyed me with suspicion from the moment I arrived. I tried to be friendly. I'd brought a big jar of coffee and a tin of biscuits with me and I was happy to talk to anyone, but the thing that ruined it for me was the fact that the manager, Mike, was impressed by me. That meant they couldn't accept me as one of them. They still ate the biscuits, though.

I was there to work on the reception desk but they didn't have many visitors; it was mainly deliveries that had to be redirected to the warehouse. There was a large office for administrators behind the reception area and Mike had a small office off that room. Upstairs were individual offices for other managers. As soon as I got there one of the admin staff hauled a computer into reception for me and they all piled work on my desk. On Friday, an hour before we were due to go home, I'd finished everything that had to be done and went to the bathroom. When I came back I found my in tray was suddenly full to the brim and when I looked into the admin office nobody would meet my eyes. I preferred to be busy but didn't want to do their work as well as my own. I couldn't say anything, though. There were six of them and not one of them had given me a friendly word. The door between reception and their office stood open and as I did their work for them I'd hear them chatting about what they were doing that night. My mind was far away as I typed up their work, daydreaming about what I'd do after my house was sold. I could buy a house here and rent it out, then live off the rental income while I travelled the world. I'd have to stick to cheaper areas, I thought, full of enthusiasm, but then had a sudden vision of myself lying on a beach with a bunch of twenty-year-olds. Just then I heard one of the women in the office say, "I'm going to Thailand in September," and I hastily rearranged my plans.

At 4:30 there was an exodus to the ladies' bathroom, and at 4:50 they all emerged with fresh makeup and straightened hair. The smell of hair spray and entitlement lay heavily in the air. They headed straight for the door without saying good-bye.

–

Just as I got into the car a message came through from Fiona.

They arrived safely. Do you know when they're going back? They are refusing to answer the question and Mum is talking about being here for Christmas. Pray for me.

I laughed. There was no way she'd put up with them for that long. As I drove out of the office car park I decided to stop at the supermarket on my way home for alcoholic reinforcements. I'd changed my mind about staying off the drink; if I was going to work there, I'd need something to help me, at least on weekends. Next to the supermarket was a pizza takeaway and I couldn't resist paying them a visit.

I drove back to my flat, my car smelling of pepperoni and cheese, and couldn't wait until I got inside and could relax. I was facing two days away from those women and I planned to enjoy every moment.

As I scrambled out of the car I struggled to keep my leather shoulder bag away from the greasy box and the bottle of chilled white wine away from the pizza, too. I really wasn't looking where I was going and as I put my key in the front-door lock, I froze.

Someone was behind me.

And then I heard, "Hello, Ruby," and I turned quickly.

It was Tom's son, Josh.

Chapter 42

Ruby

"Josh?" I wanted to kiss him. I always kissed him when I saw him, but my hands were full and he didn't look as though he wanted me near him. "Hi! It's lovely to see you."

"I got your message," he said. "So this is where you live?"

I could see from his face as he looked at the bare dangling lightbulb in the entrance that he wasn't impressed. "Take these, will you?" I handed him the pizza and wine and pushed the front door wide open. "Coming in?"

He grunted and followed me upstairs. "Just dump them in the kitchen," I said. "What can I get you to drink?"

"A large Scotch." He'd been saying that same old joke since I first met him.

I winked at him. "You're not eighteen yet. Fancy a Coke?"

"Yeah, great, thanks. I couldn't have a drink anyway," he added casually. "I'm driving now."

I stopped in my tracks. "Driving? When did you take your test?"

"Just last week. Tuesday. There was a cancellation." He looked at me then and grinned. "Someone had crashed their car so they couldn't take their test."

I laughed.

"Dad bought me a car to celebrate."

"Oh, I wish I'd been there." I was upset at the thought of missing this stage in his life. He'd been working toward his driving test for months; I used to test him on road signs and the rules of the road when he came to our house. "What kind of car have you got?"

"A silver one." He grinned again. He knew I knew nothing about cars.

"Nice," I said, as though he'd told me the make, model, and year. "How was the test?"

"Three minor errors." I could see pride and relief on his face. "And I managed to reverse around the corner without killing someone."

"That's great. I knew you'd crack it."

I passed him a Coke and lit the candles I'd arranged in little coloured-glass holders on top of the mantelpiece.

"What are these?" He picked up one of the photos of him that I'd had printed and put into frames. "Did you bring them from home?"

"No, I took a photo of them and had them printed."

He flushed and rearranged them on the mantelpiece.

"And I light candles and put them next to your photos every night," I said. "It's my shrine."

He turned to look at me and saw I was laughing. "Just as it should be," he said.

I opened the pizza box and offered it to him. "Help yourself, honey." It was so good to have him there. "I've really missed you."

He mumbled something or other and took a slice of pizza.

I went to the kitchen to pour some wine, then realised I didn't want it while Josh was here. I put the bottle into the fridge.

"Josh," I said, coming back into the living room with a glass of water. "I'm really sorry I didn't tell you I was going. Your dad told me not to say anything to you until he'd spoken to you. He insisted on that and I couldn't do anything about it."

He helped himself to another slice and took a huge bite. I knew he was buying time. "It's okay." He shrugged as though it was nothing, but we both knew it wasn't. "No big deal."

"Of course it is. It's a massive deal."

He shook his head and carried on eating. "So," he said in the end, when he'd finished. "You're living here?" He flushed. "Stupid question."

"For a few months," I said. "Not long. When the house has sold I'll get something else."

He looked away. "Around here?"

"I don't know. I think I might go travelling."

He laughed. "What, like a gap year?"

I bristled. "There's no reason why only young people should go travelling." At the same time, I was thinking, *This is what it would be like on the beach in Thailand. Full of young people eating my food and laughing at me.*

"Yeah, well, I didn't have you down as someone who'd go roughing it."

I started to say that I didn't mind where I lived but realised that just wasn't true. I laughed. "You're right. I'd hate it. This is bad enough. A backpackers' hostel would be a nightmare."

He talked for a while then about school and football and his friends. For the first time in ages he didn't mention his ex-girlfriend and I guessed he'd moved on from her now. In September he'd start his last year of secondary school and would be going off to university a year later.

"Still thinking of applying to London?" I asked. He'd talked about nothing else for months.

He nodded. "Though I keep thinking about what you said, about it being a great place to live when you're on a good salary, but not so good if you're broke."

"That's true, but if you really want to go, then you should apply. And you won't be broke," I said. "Your mum and dad will help you. I will, too."

His head swung around. "You?"

"Why not? You're my stepson."

"But you've split up with my dad."

"So? Doesn't take away what we have, does it?"

He coughed with embarrassment then and I took the chance to go into the kitchen to fetch some Ben & Jerry's.

"I thought you'd be living with someone," he said when I passed him a tub. "A guy."

So did I, I wanted to say. "What makes you say that?"

"Oh, you know. It's what always happens. But then Mum talked to me. Said that she hadn't left for anyone. There was no reason why you should have."

"I thought…" I stopped myself.

"You thought she'd left my dad to be with Martin?"

I nodded. "I assumed that's what had happened." In fact I assumed that because Tom had told me that. Several times. He'd told me he'd discovered her having an affair and had ended the marriage immediately.

"No. She didn't meet him until a few months later. My mum and dad separated after Christmas and Martin started teaching at my school the following September. Mum met him at parents' evening and I could tell she really liked him. She couldn't stop smiling. But she didn't date him until I'd gone up a year, into another class."

My head spun. Tom had described it so differently. I'd really felt for him, that he'd found out she was unfaithful. He'd told me about the terrible time he'd had. Now I didn't know whom to believe.

"Did he treat you badly?" Josh asked. "Dad, I mean." He looked away. "Did he hurt you?"

I winced. No child should have to ask that question about their parent.

"No, of course he didn't. We grew apart," I said, trying to be tactful. "I felt as though your dad wanted me to do what he wanted all the time. I couldn't be myself with him."

He nodded. "I'd noticed that. You were always different when he wasn't there. Mum told me he wasn't nice to her at all. She had to get Granny and Granddad to move in before he'd leave." He laughed. "You know what they're like. She said he left straightaway after that."

194

I remembered Belinda's parents from one of Josh's birthday parties. They had a brisk, no-nonsense air about them and I could see why Tom would want to avoid them. "Can you remember that, sweetheart?"

He shook his head. "No, I can't remember him living with us. Not really."

I hated to see him look so down, so I changed the subject and asked what he'd been up to lately. He brightened up and told me about a girl he liked now; a group of his friends were talking about flying to Budapest for a music festival in August and he wanted to ask her if she'd like to come along. Sitting there in my living room talking to Josh as darkness fell, I was the happiest I'd been since I left home. The best times in my marriage were spent with him, when he and I were alone together and we'd talk about books and movies and the girls that he fancied. And then Tom would come in and I'd pretend I was reading and Josh would grunt and we both knew Tom was happier thinking we didn't have much of a relationship without him there.

"You're not wearing your Fitbit," he said.

"No." I rubbed my wrist at the memory of it. "I don't wear it now. It was driving me crazy."

"I'm glad," he said. "I don't know how you stood it, having him check up on you like that."

"He wanted me to be fit and healthy." I spoke automatically and caught myself. Why was I justifying what he'd done? "Anyway, I'm going running now and I'm not drinking. I'm fine."

"Not drinking? You had a bottle of wine in your hand when I got here!"

I laughed. "Work was tough today." I wanted to tell him about the women I was working with, but didn't want to tell him I was fired from Sheridan's. "I broke my own rule."

"Do you have Find My Friends on your phone?" he asked suddenly.

"I've no idea." I swear I never feel as old as I do when I'm talking to Josh. "What is it?"

"It's an app that allows someone to check where you are. Or where your phone is. Same thing, really. It's in case your phone goes missing."

"I don't think so. I didn't put it on."

"Can I check?"

I stared at him. "What for? What makes you think I have it?"

"It was just something Dad said. He knew where you were one day and I couldn't figure out how he knew."

My stomach dropped and I passed over my phone without another word. While he examined it, I took the pizza box and glasses into the kitchen. I stood for a moment with my head bent over the sink. Had Tom known all along where I was? Had he been tracking me? I thought of the photo that had been put through the door, now in pieces in my bin.

When I returned to the living room, I asked casually, "Did you tell your dad where I'm living now?"

"No, of course not. He sent a message the other night, asking me if I knew, but Mum said not to tell him. I just said I had no idea."

"Thanks. Will you tell him you've seen me?"

Slowly he shook his head. "No. Not unless you say it's okay." He handed back my phone. "I can't see anything there. Everything seems fine. I must have been imagining things."

"Are you sure?" I don't know why I didn't feel more relieved. The idea was in my head now and I couldn't shift it. "What about your own? Have you checked?"

He gave me a wry grin. "Are you kidding? I've never let it out of my sight."

"Josh, do you remember your dad's birthday party last year? You were there with Becky, remember?"

"Yeah. I remember. What about it?"

"Did you take any photos?"

He stared at me. "What?"

"Did you take any photos of the party?"

He laughed. "I seriously doubt it. Why would I?"

I shook my head. "Don't worry about it. I was trying to remember who was there, that's all."

"A bunch of old people." He ducked as I reached out to grab him. "I'll have a look if you like but I got rid of a lot of photos after Becky and I finished, and she's the only one I would've taken a photo of that day." He stood up and rubbed his eyes. I knew he still missed his ex-girlfriend. "I'd better go." As he opened the front door he said, "Mind if I come round again sometime?"

"I hope you will." I hugged him. "You know I love you. I think you're great. Getting to know you was the best part of my marriage to Tom."

"Same," he said, then laughed. "You know what I mean."

"I do."

Chapter 43

Ruby

I awoke the next morning to a ping on my phone. Fiona had sent a message from Australia, simply saying:

Please send help.

My parents had been with her only a few days and planned to stay for months. It was winter over there so it wasn't as though she could send them off to the beach all day. She worked from home so she'd struggle to get anything done while they were there. That was the problem with her living so far away; most of the time she was free of them, but every now and then they'd visit for weeks and came back only when she hit her breaking point.

I was just about to reply when an e-mail popped up. It was from Tom, sending a link to the estate agent's site:

> Good morning, Ruby. Hope you're OK. Just to let you know that our house is officially on sale now
> x

Bleary-eyed, I sat up in bed and pulled my laptop toward me so that I could see the photos of my house. I'd asked for them to be sent to me for approval, but obviously they'd taken no notice of me.

My heart ached as I scrolled through the listing. I hadn't been inside our house for weeks and I missed it so much. It was tidy and clean, though I'd put good money on the local Molly Maid being responsible for that. I stared at the picture of my living room. Tom had removed the photos from the mantelpiece and replaced them with a glass bowl from the hall. I zoomed out so that I could see the whole room. He'd moved the sofas, so that they were adjacent to each other instead of facing. I zoomed in on them. The sofas reminded me of the day we bought them. I'd thought I was pregnant that day and hadn't wanted to tell Tom just yet. Every month at that point I'd get so excited and then I'd have that crushing sense of disappointment when my period arrived. At the time we'd bought the sofas, I was obsessed with becoming pregnant and would take test after test each month. It became a joke that really wasn't funny, with Tom coming home saying, "*On my way home from London I just happened to walk past a pharmacy and they had these tests you've never tried! I bought you some for good luck.*"

On that day we bought the sofas, I was two days late and a few tests had proven negative, but I was still sure that my next test would be positive. And while the salesman made his pitch, telling us about the fabric and the size and all the rest of it, all I could think was, *I'll be feeding my baby on this sofa. I'll put my feet up on this footstool and I'll rest my head against these cushions and there'll be a baby lying there on my chest. A little girl, maybe. I'll feel her soft breath against my neck, feel the weight of her sleepy body against mine. Her soft and downy hair will brush against my face as I kiss her gently, secretly hoping she'll waken.* And I was so caught up in this story I was telling myself, that when I sat on the sofa to test it, I closed my eyes and I could almost feel the weight of the baby against me and smell the milkiness of her breath.

"Ruby!" Tom had called. "Don't go to sleep!" He and the salesman had laughed. "Shall we go for this one?"

I'd laughed, too, but for the rest of the afternoon I could feel the sensation of the baby inside me, relaxing into me, and I'd known, I'd just *known* that I was pregnant. Until I got home and found that I wasn't. Of course I wasn't. I never was.

And I looked down at the photos of the living room, with those reminders of my infertility looming so large, and I didn't know whether I wanted to keep them or to never see them again.

My phone beeped again. Tom.

It looks good, doesn't it? x

I replied, Yes, it does. I hate to think of people viewing it though. As I pressed Send I winced. I didn't want him to misinterpret that. All I'd meant was that I couldn't stand to think of people walking around it and judging it, trying to knock the price down. Not that they'd get far with Tom, as far as that was concerned.

He replied immediately. Me too. It was our home for so long xx

I couldn't let myself think about that but as I stood in the tiny shower cubicle, banging my head on the showerhead, then mopping up the suds on the floor afterwards, I thought of Tom and the messages he'd sent since I left him. All of them were nice. Helpful. Sincere. I hadn't thought I'd hurt him so much by leaving.

When I came back from the bathroom there was another message.

I wish you were still here x

—

I had so much on my mind that day. I wanted someone to talk to, who could look at things with fresh eyes. I scrolled through my contacts list. There wasn't anyone there I could trust. I might have called Fiona in Australia, but my parents were there with her and she'd be too wound up to talk.

Outside it was hot and sunny. I sat at the window and saw people in little groups going down to the river and the park. They had picnic bags and strollers with parasols and children with sun hats. Everyone seemed to be with someone. Thoughts were flitting through my mind on a loop. Should I talk to Tom? Should I suggest counselling? I cringed at the thought of hearing what he would have to say about me. Maybe I could go alone? But there was the cost. I looked it up online; I just couldn't afford it if I was living here and on a low wage. And if I went home… I think that was the first day that I seriously considered going back to him. He'd been so kind. He'd had time on his own now; was he regretting the way he'd behaved in the last few years?

The phone was quiet all day. The escort calls had stopped, thank God. I'd checked the site again and couldn't find my number there. The webmaster must have taken my threats seriously. As he should. I couldn't help worry, though, that those guys still had my number on their phone.

By seven o'clock I had read a book and watched two movies. I could hardly remember any of them. There was too much on my mind. I stood up, restless and annoyed with myself for wasting a day. I decided to go for a drive.

It was inevitable that I'd drive past my house. As I drove toward my old neighbourhood, I could feel myself becoming tense. My palms were damp on the steering wheel. I wondered what Tom was doing at this time on a Saturday. Normally we'd be in and Josh would be there. After dinner he'd either go back to his mum's or to a friend's; I'd drive him as Tom would have hit the wine by then and besides, I loved that time alone with Josh.

I drove up the side road next to our house and parked the car. I was worried about Tom looking out of the window and seeing me. I didn't want to see him. I didn't know what I'd say to him. What I'd do. I looked again at the text that he'd sent me.

I wish you were still here x

I thought of parking my car in its usual place, of walking up the driveway and letting myself into the house. I could do that. My house keys were in my bag, still there from the night I'd left. I could walk in and put my bag on the hall table and go into the kitchen and look at the list on the fridge door and see what was for dinner. I could be back in my kitchen with the radio playing, cooking dinner with a glass of wine by my side.

I winced. I used to need that glass of wine. Would I still need it, if I went back?

I don't know why, but I'd assumed Tom would be at home for the evening. His car wasn't there, though, and the house was in darkness. I wondered where he was. Was he on a date? If I stayed there long enough, would he come home with a woman, holding her hand and warning her about the uneven steps in the garden? Would he light the candles in the hearth and pour her a gin and tonic and ask her about herself, just as he'd done with me in the early days? And if I went in there, if I went into my kitchen and made it mine again, would he be glad or sorry when he saw me?

My head was aching and I didn't know what I felt about him now. I was such a bad judge of character. I'd thought Tom was the man for me but I felt like I was stifled and struggling to breathe. Then I thought Harry could help heal me. His relaxed attitude, his affection, and the way he'd treated me as someone precious had drawn me in, but I'd meant nothing to him.

Now I was free, I didn't know who I was or what I was worth.

–

I sat there for ten minutes looking at the side of my house, then started the car and drove round the corner so that I was next to the driveway. If Tom drove past me on his way home I'd just have to deal with it. The *For Sale* sign was placed just where the road turned. That made sense, so that people driving down each road would see it. I knew Tom would have been out there on the lawn, moving it from where the estate agent had placed it to somewhere he deemed right. He had to be right. Even if he moved it only a matter of inches, he'd feel a sense of pride that now it was done properly.

Under the light from the lamp post, I could see the wood-work on the house was freshly painted, the gates, too. There were a couple of new bay trees in huge pots on either side of the front door, and I thought of Tom going to the garden centre on his own one Sunday and struggling to get those pots into the car. He wouldn't have accepted help; I knew that.

I leaned forward and checked the garden. It was tidy and the lawn was neat. It looked as though someone had been busy there. That was usually my job and I wondered who'd been there in my absence. Tom must have paid for a professional; he'd always complained whenever I'd asked him to help me.

Car headlights lit up the road behind me and I swore. Was that Tom coming home? I really didn't want him to see me. Quickly I turned my key in the ignition. At the last minute I realised it was Oliver. His car pulled into his drive and he jumped out and slammed the door. He turned toward me and waved.

Reluctantly I opened my car window and turned off the engine. "Hello, Oliver."

"Hey." He walked down the drive toward me. "What are you doing here? Are you back home now?"

"No, I'd heard that it was up for sale. I thought I'd come and take a look."

"Are you going in?"

Quickly I shook my head. "No. No. I'm not going to do that."

"It's okay, Tom's away for the weekend."

"He is? Where's he gone to?" I caught myself. "Sorry, don't answer that. It's nothing to do with me."

"It's okay. I don't think it's private. He's gone up to Scotland to see his brother. He set off first thing this morning and won't be back for a couple of days. He said something about having a meeting in Glasgow on Monday morning."

"Oh, okay. I know he has a couple of clients there." I smiled at him. "Anyway, nice to see you."

"Wait," he said. "Fancy coming in for a drink?"

"No, thanks." I spoke automatically; it had upset me seeing my house up for sale and knowing how easily I could go back.

I wanted to be alone to think about my response. "I'd better get back."

"Oh, okay." He looked forlorn and tired, and I remembered the times I'd thought of him alone in his house.

"I just feel a bit odd, being back here," I admitted. "I feel uncomfortable, as though the neighbours will notice I'm here and think I've come back." I hesitated. Normally I would have given in and had a drink with him, but I just didn't want to. I've always been a people-pleaser; it was time to change that. I liked Oliver, but I didn't want to start seeing him on my own. "I'd better go."

I had planned to drive home but suddenly I thought of driving to Harry's house, just to sit outside on the off-chance I'd see him. It was like self-harm; I wanted to do it so badly, wanted that moment of release, even knowing the pain I'd feel. I turned the key in the ignition, when Oliver said, "You haven't got over him, have you?"

"I have. I miss him, though."

He hesitated. "I know it's not my business, but he'd probably have you back if you asked him."

I realised that we were completely at cross-purposes. "I meant Harry."

"Who?"

"The guy... The guy I told you about."

Oliver flushed red. "Oh, the *someone special*. Sorry, I thought we were talking about Tom." He took a step back and said, "I'll see you around, eh?"

I nodded and said good-bye. As I drove off I saw him standing watching after me and I thought of the repercussions of my leaving home and how many people had been hurt.

Chapter 44

Ruby

I got through that week at my temp job by daydreaming about my future. I'd scared myself at the weekend, the way I'd almost walked back into my old life with Tom. And then my response to that had been to stalk Harry. I had to stop this. I needed a completely fresh start. So I went onto automatic pilot, working fast while the women piled their filing onto my desk – yes, there's still a way to go before the paperless office hits that particular company – and gave me their audio files to transcribe. As if at a distance, I heard them talk about buttock lifts and implants in their lips – how I *longed* for those procedures to go wrong – and moan about how hard they worked and how tired they were. On Friday they made their way through two tins of Quality Street that one of the managers had brought in without offering me one chocolate and my daydreams were quite violent by the end of the day.

I sent Sarah a message:

It's Friday night and if I don't go out tonight, I'll go mad. Are you free?

It was an hour later and I thought I was going to have to go out on my own, before my phone pinged with a message:

McCullough's at 8?

Before she could change her mind, I replied: I'll be there.

–

Sarah came rushing in late, as I'd known she would. I'd finished a glass of wine by then and was chatting to the Italian barman about the best places to visit in Florence. As I listened to the way he talked about the food there I mentally added it to my list of places to go to live.

"Well, you look happy enough," she said, sounding a bit resentful. She gave my empty glass a pointed look. "You've made good use of your time while you were waiting for me."

I thought of the chances of Sarah getting there early and drinking water while she waited. Neither of those things would ever happen. "Did you think I'd sit and cry?" I beckoned the waiter. "Here, have a glass of wine and cheer up."

She slid off her jacket and climbed up onto the barstool next to me. "I shouldn't really have this," she said. "I'm a bit hungover. It was book group last night."

"Good night?"

"Yeah, it was great. Shame you stopped coming. We were talking about *The Goldfinch*. You would have liked it."

"That's odd, I'm reading that book at the moment." I knew, though, that nothing I thought would add to the conversation. I'd been to the book group a few times and really enjoyed it. We took it in turns to go to one another's houses each month and the hostess would make snacks and provide drinks. After a few months it was my turn to host. I was so excited; ridiculously excited, really. It was only a book group, but I'd seen it as my chance to make new friends. I was starting to feel as though my world was closing in on me. Tom had greeted the women, poured drinks, and I'd thought he'd enjoyed having them there. He wasn't taking part in the discussion, and I hadn't realised he'd been listening in until they'd gone.

When I shut the front door behind them at the end of the night, I was just thinking what a great time I'd had. Tom came up to me and put his arms around me and said, "Did you have a good night?"

I smiled and kissed his cheek and said, "I had a lovely time, thanks." I went into the living room to take the plates and glasses into the kitchen.

He followed me to help, then said, "Ruby, I hate to say this to you, but you should let the other women talk more in the book group."

I stopped dead in my tracks. "What do you mean?"

"It's just something I noticed, sweetheart. You were talking a lot more than they were."

I thought back over the evening. I was sure that for a lot of the time I was sitting quietly, enjoying listening to other people's opinions on the book. "I wasn't! I'm sure I wasn't."

"You were, babe. You were dominating the conversation, and the thing is…" He hesitated, his eyes on mine, then said, "The thing is, they have English degrees, don't they?"

My face was hot and I felt close to tears. "I don't know. Maybe one or two of them do, but I don't think they all have."

"They seemed really smart. And the way they were talking, well, it was proper literary criticism. And you – well, I know you thought you were being funny, with what you said about the protagonist – that means the leading character, by the way – but it was a bit embarrassing."

I turned away and brushed my hand across my eyes. "I didn't realise you were listening."

"I couldn't help it," he said. "The door was closed but I could still hear you." He laughed. "Lucky it wasn't summertime with the windows open. We would've had complaints from the neighbours!"

I walked into the kitchen to get away from him. He was making me relive every moment and see it through a different lens. The thought of him being embarrassed by me was horrifying. On the kitchen counter was a tray of snacks; I'd made far too many. He picked them up and said, "Oh, these didn't go down too well, did they?" and put them into the fridge. "You'll have to take them to work for lunch, to use them up."

So when Sarah said, "You should come to the next one," I said, "Maybe," but I had absolutely no intention of putting myself through that again.

"How's work?" I asked.

"Ugh," she said. "It was horrible today. I was so busy I didn't know whether I was coming or going."

I knew I shouldn't ask her, I knew it would be torture, but I just had to. I said, "What happened?" I steeled myself for the mention of Harry.

"Oh, he wasn't there," she said airily. "He'd taken the day off. He said he'd promised Emma he'd spend more time with her." She drank some of her wine. "I think they were going to choose things for the nursery."

"Really? Isn't that a bit early?"

She shrugged. "Apparently Emma spends all her time looking at baby clothes. Harry says she hasn't bought much yet as she's waiting for the scan results, but he thinks he'll be bankrupt by Christmas." Sarah looked at me out of the corner of her eye and said, "Does it bother you, thinking of Emma being pregnant?"

I'd planned for this. I wasn't going to show weakness. I wasn't going to show just how much I did care. I'd rehearsed this mentally at work while I'd had my headphones in to type up the interminable audio files. "I'm glad he's happy," I said. *At my expense, though*, I thought. *How can he be happy, knowing what he's done to me?*

She laughed. "Liar."

"I am." I thought about it for a few seconds. "Honestly, I am. I needed to leave home. It wasn't good for me. It's a shame it didn't work out with Harry, but in the end, I got out of my marriage. That's what I needed to do."

Most of that was bravado. I didn't want Sarah or anyone else to feel sorry for me, but when I thought of Harry now, it was almost as though he hadn't been real, as though I'd conjured him up so that I could leave home. What was more real was his rejection of me. Memories of him being lovely to me faded as I thought of how he'd let me go home to end my marriage, knowing full well he wouldn't be doing the same.

We sat in silence for a few minutes and then I said, "Did Harry read my letter? Did he say anything?"

She laughed. "I thought you weren't bothered about him?"

"Just tell me whether he read it, will you?"

"I put it in his top drawer. He didn't say anything to me about it." She poured us another drink. "You need to stop obsessing about him, Ruby. He's history now. Move on."

I've always hated that expression. It always seems to be used to shut people up. But I didn't have the courage to say anything to Sarah; I needed her friendship. So I drank some wine and said, "You're right," and she clinked her glass against mine, happy at her success.

Chapter 45

Ruby

We had a great night in the end. We bumped into some people she knew and the night flew by without any further mention of Harry or Emma or that baby of theirs. For a while I was able to forget everything that had happened, though I know the wine helped that along.

At the end of the night we flooded out into the street. Our little town doesn't have Uber yet and a few black cabs were waiting at the end of the street. There was a rush toward them. Sarah lived in the opposite direction from me; one of her friends was going her way and bagged the last cab.

"Will you be okay?" she asked as she stumbled into the taxi.

"I'll be fine," I said. "Speak soon."

"I'll call you."

Pretty soon it became obvious that no more taxis were coming back. The few of us who were left called around the local taxi firms, but we weren't getting any luck. It was late Friday night, the busiest night for pubs and clubs, and it became obvious I'd have a long wait. People started to walk off, deciding to go to taxi ranks in town. I looked around, still half-drunk, and thought I didn't fancy just hanging around waiting there, so I started to walk home.

The route home was along a long road with shops and very few houses. Of course the shops were shut by then and the road was pretty empty. The only people I saw were groups of lads walking in the direction of town, while I was heading away from it. I walked pretty unsteadily along, cursing my shoes. I'd taken a taxi to McCullough's, not thinking I'd be walking home. My heels seemed to catch every gap in the paving stones and I had to watch every step I took so that I didn't twist my ankle. The night was chilly and I pulled my jacket tightly around my chest.

I could see a man coming toward me and moved closer to the edge of the pavement to let him pass. He looked up at me and grinned, then said, "Hello." I didn't respond, but kept my head down and hurried on and I heard his footsteps recede, then the sound of him kicking a plastic bottle from the pavement onto the road.

Then the road was quiet, the streetlights dimmer and more infrequent. There were few houses along this stretch. On one side was a park, quiet now, of course, and pitch-black beyond its railings. On the other were shops and offices, all of them closed. Few had left a light on so I hurried from lamp post to lamp post, realising it had been years since I'd walked home down a dark road on my own. I tried to remember the rules I'd learned as a girl: I didn't walk too close to the buildings, in case someone dragged me down an alley. I didn't walk too close to the parked cars alongside the road in case someone was lurking there. I didn't put my headphones in. I was on high alert. My house key almost scarred the palm of my hand, I was gripping it so tightly.

Then I don't know what happened, but suddenly I felt strange. My skin prickled and my ears strained to pick up cues. I straightened my back and walked a bit faster, while I tried to work out what was happening. And then I realised. I felt someone was there.

The road was quiet and then I heard the soft clink of a car door closing. I turned quickly, but couldn't see anyone. I stood still for a second, focusing on the road behind me, and saw in the distance the guy in the light jacket who'd said hello. He was nearly over the bridge now. I turned and hurried on, but still I felt uneasy pinpricks on the back of my neck.

Cars and vans were parked along the side of the road and the pavement was quite narrow. For a moment I thought of walking in the middle of the road, but then a car drove past and I stayed on the relative safety of the pavement. The car slowed down and took a left turn farther up the road and for a few minutes everything was quiet again. The turning for my road was several hundred yards ahead. Then there was the sound of another car coming up the road behind me.

It was only after it went past that I realised it was the same car that had gone past me just minutes earlier. It was silver, quite big, but I couldn't tell the make or model. I could see it was a five-door and had a dual exhaust. When I saw it drive past the second time I saw the number plate started with *MW*. Once again, it took a left turn farther up the street.

I frowned. Why would the same car come past twice? And then I felt panic rising in my chest. I was walking down this road on my own. There had been no other cars, just this one.

It was as though all my senses were heightened. The sky looked darker; any stars had disappeared. The lights from the shops seemed more sinister, as they cast shadows on the pavements. And my hearing was sharpened: I could hear the sound of the breeze in the trees and the thrum of distant cars. Just then I heard the sound of a car coming up the road again.

And suddenly I was terrified. I couldn't look behind; I didn't want to draw attention to myself. My eyes flickered from right to left and ahead again. There was nobody else around.

I slid my phone out of my bag and held it tightly. When the car went past for the third time I registered the colour: silver, the exhaust: double. The number plate starting with *MW*. And then it slowed down ahead of me. My eyes nearly popped out of my head as I saw it stop in the middle of the narrow road. Its hazard lights started to blink.

I stopped dead in my tracks. There was no way I was going to walk past that car. Both of us were still, like adversaries waiting to see who made the first move. Then the driver's door opened.

I took a huge breath, turned on my heels, and ran back the way I'd come. There was a side street on my left and I raced around the corner and along the quiet street and then turned into a road that was parallel to the one I'd walked down before.

All was quiet. I couldn't hear any car engines or footsteps; nobody was on the streets. Some of the houses had lights on in either the living room or bedrooms at the fronts of the houses and as I ran I made a mental note as to where I could bang on the door.

It was still more than a mile to my house, through all the back streets. I went a zigzag route, always choosing the street with the most lights on downstairs. By the time I reached my street all I could hear was the blood pumping through my veins, the pulse in my ears, my heart beating like a drum.

Holding my keys in position, I raced to my front door. My fingers slipped over the key as I tried to insert it. As the lock turned I thrust the door open and slammed it behind me.

When I was safely upstairs I stood in the hallway, panting. The light from a nearby lamp post shone in through the window. In my bedroom I stood at the edge of the window and looked up and down the yards and the backs of houses on the road parallel to mine. All was still. Slowly I drew the curtains, but I didn't put a lamp on.

The kitchen looked out onto houses on the side street. That, too, was silent, though enough lights were lit to reassure me. Quickly I pulled down the blind. Again I didn't switch the light on in case my shadow could be seen.

In the living room I relied on the hallway light to guide me to the window. I flattened myself against the wall and looked out onto the street.

And then I saw a silver car crawl down the road. There was no reason for it to move that slowly; there was no other traffic about. The driver was on the other side of the road to my house and I couldn't see them at all. At first I thought of using my phone to film it, but I couldn't risk its light being seen. I grabbed a pen and paper to write down the number plate but the street was dark and I couldn't make it out. I stayed hidden and watched as the car turned down the side road, just past my house. A few minutes later it was back.

Someone was watching me.

Chapter 46

Emma

It was so odd living with Harry in those early days of my pregnancy. We both had such huge secrets. He knew nothing about mine and didn't have a clue that I knew his. Whenever I looked at him I would wonder whether he was still involved with Ruby or whether everything had changed for them. He certainly wasn't giving any of the usual signals. He was absolutely present in our marriage and never seemed preoccupied or sad. He was the happiest I'd ever seen him.

And I was happy, too. Of course I was. I was pregnant after thinking it would never happen. But I was furious, too. Harry had caused all this. If he hadn't been having a fling with Ruby, then I wouldn't have gone to Tom's house. I wouldn't have slept with him, I wouldn't have got pregnant, and I certainly wouldn't have to put up with Tom bullying me now.

Even though I hadn't seen Tom again, the threat was still there. Every time Harry was about to leave for work, I ran to the window to check that Tom wasn't waiting for him, ready to spill the beans. Even though the landline was unlisted, whenever it rang I froze in terror and made sure I grabbed it before Harry could reach it. In the end I turned the sound off; Harry wouldn't notice as he rarely used it, but it saved me worrying about him picking it up when I was out. And then I went one step further and cancelled the landline itself, telling Harry we so rarely used it, it was a waste of money. He'd laughed at this unexpected thriftiness and arranged for that money to go into the baby's savings plan. In the evening I'd be back at the window again when he was due home, so that I could be there to divert him if I saw Tom. When I'd hear Harry's car turn into the driveway, I'd check his face, to see whether he looked furious or puzzled or frantic with worry. It was exhausting having to anticipate Tom.

But Harry was always happy now. News of the baby had given him a new lease of life. He'd bound out of bed as soon as the alarm rang every morning, starting the day with a huge smile on his face. He'd kiss me good-bye at the door, holding me tightly and whispering he loved me. It was just like the old days. And at night he'd leap out of his car and run up to the house to find me.

"Hey," he'd say, wrapping me in his arms. "How are you, sweetheart? Feeling okay?"

"I'm fine," I'd reply. Physically I was, after that early bout of morning sickness, but mentally I was a wreck.

"And how's my little one?" He'd stroke my stomach gently. "Is he being good for you?"

"She's been great," I'd say automatically.

He'd grin every time. "Do you think it's a girl, then? I'd love that. She'll be just like you. Perfect."

Usually I'd started cooking dinner by the time Harry came home, but he'd always make me sit down and put my feet up while he carried on with it. He'd put the radio on and I'd hear him singing away, as though he hadn't a care in the world. Well, he hadn't, I suppose. He thought he'd got away with an affair. He also thought he was the father of my baby. He may well be, who knew?

For a few days, I heard nothing from Tom. Gradually I started to calm down. I'd told him that he wasn't the father. I'd told him I was happily married. Even if he did think he was the father, what did he think was going to happen?

I soon found out.

The phone call came just before I was going to bed, a few days after I saw Tom in the café.

Harry and I had had a lovely evening. He'd come home with flowers, and though I knew they were borne out of guilt, they were still nice to have. He was just so happy now; I couldn't remember the last time I'd seen him like that. Whereas before he'd been weary and tired and would be quick to squabble about something or nothing, now he just couldn't do enough for me.

"You look like you could do with an early night." He winked at me. "What about a massage?"

"What do you want in return?" I asked suspiciously.

He laughed. "Nothing, sweetheart. This is just for you."

"Wonderful. Let me have a quick shower first." I poured him another glass of wine and jumped up to go upstairs. Then my mobile rang in my handbag in the hallway. I frowned. "Who on earth's that? It's nearly ten o'clock."

"Just ignore it," he said. "It's too late to take a call."

I scrabbled in my bag for my phone. I didn't recognise the number, but answered the call.

"Hello?"

A man spoke. "I'll say this just once."

Every nerve in my body jumped to attention. I knew that voice. Slowly I moved nearer to the front door, so that Harry couldn't hear me. "What?" I whispered.

"Either you tell him or I will."

Chapter 47

Emma

By the time Harry came up to bed, I was too agitated for a massage. While the shower was running I'd saved Tom's number to my mobile, using the name *Anna*. I was so glad I'd cancelled the landline; I couldn't cope if he called on that when I was out.

"Who was on the phone?" asked Harry when he came into the bedroom minutes later.

"Oh, no one." I smoothed moisturiser over my face, closing my eyes so that I didn't have to look at him. "Just a call centre."

"I didn't think they were allowed to call at this time of night."

I went into the bathroom. "Yeah, well, it might have been one from another country. I didn't stay on long enough to find out." I started to brush my teeth, knowing that conversation would be impossible now, and by the time I went back into the bedroom he seemed to have forgotten all about it.

I turned down the massage in the end, saying I was feeling a bit sick, but Harry then held me for an hour, talking about the baby, what we'd call it, the holidays we'd have, how we'd decorate their bedroom, when I thought she would stop calling him *Daddy* and call him *Dad* instead.

I felt like my heart was breaking.

While he slept quietly by my side, one hand still lightly protecting my stomach, I gently turned away and took out my phone, angling it so that even if he woke, Harry wouldn't see the screen. I went onto private browsing and filled in a form so that I could find out who on earth was my baby's father.

Once my payment was accepted, I was able to access their instructions. I read them religiously. I had to provide a blood sample myself. That was easy enough to arrange through the site. Then I had to collect Harry's DNA and since I couldn't ask him for a swab, the only way I could do that was to collect some of his nail clippings. I guessed that Tom would have happily provided swabs for me, but I didn't want to involve him. And then he'd want the results: What if they weren't what I wanted?

–

So the next day I replaced the bin liner in the bathroom bin and scrubbed the nail clippers. When he had a shower before bedtime, I called through to him, "Harry, you scratched me in bed last night. Cut your nails!"

He came out of the bathroom looking all apologetic and I felt like such a bitch. When he was asleep I crept back into the bathroom and replaced the bag with a new one and hid the evidence in my study. The next morning, after he'd left for work, I put the nails into the bag provided.

The online clinic I'd chosen offered a blood sample collection service, thankfully, given that I hadn't a clue how to find a phlebotomist. I arranged for someone to come to my workplace; it wasn't something I could risk Harry discovering. I arranged an appointment early in the morning, before Annie arrived, and pulled the blinds down in our office so that nobody passing would see what was going on. When the nurse arrived, she was able to take a blood sample without anyone knowing about it.

I felt like a criminal, having it taken so secretly. She was very discreet, though, and was clearly used to this sort of thing. I'd arranged for a courier to pick up the tests immediately afterwards and to take them to the clinic and the whole thing took only an hour or so, but the way I felt now, I knew it would be a long time before I could look at myself without shame.

Later that morning, when I was trying hard to focus on work, a message appeared from Tom:

Do you want me to be with you when you tell Harry? Happy to do it myself if that makes it easier.

I'd had enough. Before I could consider whether I should, I called him.

"Tom? Will you stop sending me messages? You're driving me mad."

"Hello, Emma," he said, as calm as you like.

"I'm not going to tell Harry anything!"

"Then I will," he said. "If you think I'm going to let that man sleep with my wife and bring up my child, then you need to think again."

"You slept with me!" I shouted. I hurried to the office door to shut it tight. "You did the same thing."

"It's not the same at all." The trouble was that I didn't know whether it was or not. I didn't know what I thought about that. "You realise he's getting away scot-free? He's had an affair and you're trying to protect him from knowing about us."

I hesitated. I didn't know why I wasn't confronting Harry about his affair. I couldn't work out whether I was scared in case he left me for Ruby, or whether I wanted to appear the innocent as far as the baby was concerned. I was terrified the baby wasn't his. It was all I could think about. "There is no us."

"Of course there is. We're having a baby. And he needs to know."

"I'll deny it," I said. "I'll tell him I don't know what you're talking about."

"Well, that would be difficult. After all, you left something at my house, didn't you?"

I breathed out. My bracelet. I'd tried to forget about it and luckily Harry hadn't noticed it was missing. I flushed as I remembered him holding my wrists down that night. When I'd wriggled, it had rubbed against my wrist and he'd taken it off and put it on his bedside table. "You have my bracelet?"

"I do. It's perfectly safe."

"Give it back to me, please."

"I will. Of course I will, but not yet." There was a long pause. "How would you explain that?" he asked. "How could it be in my house unless you were there, too?"

I had no answer. I could feel I was about to start crying out of sheer temper and was determined not to let him hear that.

"I'm sure Harry would like to know how willing you were," he said in a soft voice. "You came to my house. You slept with me. I just want to tell him about the baby."

"He knows about the baby!"

"He doesn't know it's *my* baby, though, does he? He doesn't know that you're carrying my baby. That he was cuckolded." He laughed. "I have to tell you I am really looking forward to telling him that."

I ended the call, shaking. When I went to Tom's house that night to tell him about Harry and Ruby, I'd wanted revenge on Ruby. It had backfired on me.

Chapter 48

Emma

Annie called me a few days later, just after Harry left home to go to London. It had rained all night and the sky was still heavy with clouds, but she was as bouncy as ever.

"You sound really tired," she said. "Once you're through the first trimester you'll feel a lot better."

"I hope so. I'm exhausted." I didn't know whether it was my pregnancy that was tiring or the constant thinking and worrying about dates and times and who was more likely to be the father. I'd lie awake most nights now, while Harry slept beside me, chatting to women on online forums, checking figures and charting little graphs. I felt ashamed of myself that I was in this situation; it was something I might expect of a teenager, but I was in my late thirties. The results would take a few days to come through and I felt as though I couldn't relax until then. At least if I knew, I could do something about it, I told myself, but all I could think about was that if it wasn't Harry's baby, our marriage was over.

"Why don't I come to your house now and we can go through everything that needs to be done?" said Annie. "You could work from home today. There are plenty of things you can do there if you're up to it."

I dragged myself out of bed for a shower and dressed, relieved now that I knew I'd be staying home.

When she arrived we sat in the kitchen and worked through our diaries and planned which jobs I could do that day. I wanted to confide in her, but I just couldn't. I couldn't betray Harry like that. Infidelity was one thing – we were both guilty of that now – but if he knew I'd told other people he might not be the father before I told him, it would be all over.

"And we'll have to plan for your maternity leave. There's so much to think about." She didn't know how right she was. If the baby was Tom's, what would Harry do? Would he leave me? And what kind of involvement would Tom want?

"I'm so happy for you," she said. "And for Harry, too." She got up to go. "I've brought you the spare screen. It'll be easier for you than using the one on the laptop. It's in my car; I'll just bring it in now that the rain's stopped." She went out of the front door and I heard her speaking to someone. I thought it would be the old lady who lived next door and I kept out of the way. I didn't want her to come in and start to fuss around me.

Then I heard a male voice talking to Annie. I went to the door to see who it was, and my heart thumped hard in my chest as I saw it was Tom.

"Are you sure you don't want any help?" he asked Annie, who was grappling with a large computer monitor.

"I'm fine, thanks. I've got it." She saw me in the doorway. "Someone to see you, Emma."

I ignored Tom and closed the front door behind Annie. "What's he doing here?"

She turned to face me, surprised. "He said he was a friend of yours. Shall I tell him to go away?"

I nodded. "Tell him I'm not feeling well."

"You do look pale. Don't worry, I'll tell him."

She opened the door and I heard her talking to Tom.

"It's okay, tell her I'll call back one night," he said.

Like a shot I was at the door. There was no way I could risk him calling round when Harry was here. "It's okay, I'll see you now."

"I'll take this up to your study," said Annie, and she disappeared upstairs.

I hissed at Tom, "What do you think you're doing?"

"I just wanted a chat."

"You're not meant to be here!"

I stopped talking as Annie came downstairs and picked up her bag and keys from the hallway console. She gave me a suspicious look and I knew I'd have to fight off some questions later.

"So I'll start work on the Fordham website and be in touch this afternoon." She gave me a hug. "Get some rest."

I kissed her and said good-bye, and then she was off.

Tom watched her drive away, then turned to me and smiled. "I'll be in touch."

"I'm not going to answer any texts, so you needn't bother sending them," I said. "Or answer your calls. I've got nothing to say to you."

"Oh, I think you have. We've got a lot to talk about."

"We don't. I'm going inside now. I'm not well. If you don't go away I'll call the police."

He laughed. "Really? What exactly would you tell them?"

Tears filled my eyes and I brushed them away. "Please." My throat was swollen and my voice sounded weak. I took a step back into the house. "Just go away."

He looked uncertain, but then seemed to gather himself. "We need to talk," he said calmly. "I can see you're upset so now's not a good time, but we do need to talk." He touched my arm and I flinched. "Let's meet up away from your home. You won't be as nervous then."

"I don't want to meet up at all."

"I know you don't. But we have to. We have to talk about this, Emma. Look, Harry's in London tonight, isn't he? He's not due back until tomorrow morning."

"How did you know that?"

"His staff need training," he said. "They'll just tell you anything."

I didn't reply. I knew from my own experience that that was the case. I pictured Sarah chatting away to him, telling him everything.

"I'll be at The Crown down the road tonight at eight o'clock. Come along then and we can talk."

Chapter 49

Emma

The first thing I noticed about Tom was that he was dressed as though he was going on a date. He was wearing a dark blue suit that brought out the colour of his eyes and a crisp cotton shirt. He looked pretty good and at first I thought he was meeting me for a quick drink before going on somewhere else. It wasn't long before I realised I was the main event.

I arrived at the pub a few minutes late. I didn't want to get there early and give him the satisfaction of thinking he'd kept me waiting, and I didn't want to bump into him in the car park, either.

The pub was busy that night. There was a sign outside advertising a pub quiz and large groups of people were sitting around tables, talking animatedly. I had been there only a few moments when Tom came racing up toward me.

"Emma!" He reached in for a kiss on the cheek and I stood very still, not wanting to give him the impression that I was happy with that. "I'm so glad you came. Come and sit down." He showed me to the corner of the room where there were a couple of chairs and a small round table. "Let me get you a drink. What would you like?"

"Sparkling water. Thanks."

"Of course." He smiled. "Won't be a minute."

He was back shortly with a couple of glasses and a large bottle of water. He said, "I'd better stay sober for this, I think."

In a flash I remembered the night we spent together and blushed. Without meeting his eyes I took the glass he offered me.

"How are you? How are you feeling?"

"All right," I said warily. "Thanks."

"Great. So I thought it would be a good idea to meet up and talk through all our options."

Instantly I was irritated, but I stayed quiet. I didn't know where to start.

"So." He seemed a bit unnerved and I saw a faint sheen of perspiration on his forehead. "Do you know the due date?"

"I'm not talking to you about it until I can show you proof that Harry is the father. And then there won't be any point in talking about it at all."

He ignored this. "He's not the father. I know it would be more convenient for you if he was, but he isn't. Come on, Emma. Think of the likelihood of that. You need to get used to the idea."

Now it was my turn to ignore what he said. Two could play at that game. "So I'm just here to say that I'll be getting a DNA test done to reassure you..."

He interrupted me. "When? When will you be having the test?"

I tried to keep my face impassive. I really didn't want him to know this. If the test showed he was the father, I needed time to decide what to do. "I don't know yet. I'll speak to my doctor."

"Because you can get tested now. I've been online..."

I interrupted him. "I'll get the test done after the baby's born. There's no argument about that. In the meantime I don't want to see you. I don't want you to hang around my house. I don't want to go for a coffee with you or to the pub. I don't want to be here now. I want you to leave me alone."

"You must be joking! Everything you do – every single thing you do – is my business now."

"What?"

"You're carrying my child and I need to make sure that you're keeping it healthy. I want to come to your hospital appointments with you. The scans. And when it's born, we are going to share the care of it."

I stared at him, unable to believe what I was hearing.

"I'm going for fifty-fifty custody, by the way," he said. "I should have done that when Belinda and I split up but it wasn't so common then. I'm not going to make that mistake again. I'm not having another man seeing more of my child than I do myself."

"No way. Don't even think about it."

"There's no point arguing." He leaned forward; he seemed excited, fired up with adrenaline. I swear he was getting off on the challenge. "Ruby and I own that house outright. When it's sold I'll have enough for a smaller house and I'll be able to work part-time, so I'll be able to do my share of childcare." I opened my mouth to object but he continued, "And I've got enough savings to stop work altogether for a few years if I need to. So if you want to work full-time, that's fine."

"Are you insane? You're not going to have my baby half of the time!"

"Once the first three months have passed, yes. It's our baby, Emma. You've got to stop being so selfish. It's our baby: yours and mine. You might be the person carrying it, but once it's born, it's no more yours than it is mine."

I knew that I'd never see Harry again if he heard what Tom was saying now. There was the slightest chance he'd stay with me if it was another man's child, but not if that man was going to demand fifty-fifty childcare. And not if that man was Tom. Why would he? My heart raced at the thought of losing Harry and seeing my baby only half of the week.

I picked up my bag. "There's no point to this conversation."

"But there is! I've told you; I've been through all this before, with Josh. I'm not losing another child. And when you give birth…"

"Don't even think you'll be there for that."

"I'm the child's father," he said calmly. "And if you think Harry will be there, you've got another think coming." He gave me a cheeky grin. "The one who's there at the conception should be the one who's there at the birth. Everyone knows that."

I jumped up so quickly I stumbled. A young couple at the next table turned to stare at me. I saw them glance quickly at our glasses to see what I'd been drinking. I picked up my bag and pushed past him. "Leave me alone," I hissed in his ear. "I don't want to see you again."

He stood up, too, and followed me out of the pub. "When you've calmed down, you'll know I'm right. In any case, I haven't said what I wanted to say."

I opened my car door and quickly climbed in.

Tom held the door so that I couldn't shut it. I started up the engine and shouted, "Let go of the door!"

A couple of men who were about to go into the pub stopped and stared at us.

Tom lowered his voice. "I was going to say that if you want to see the child all the time, there's an easy way around that."

My first thought was that he wanted money. Mostly I felt disgust, but quite honestly the rest of me just thought: *How much will it cost me to get rid of you and when do you want it?* "What? What are you talking about?"

"We could live together. You, me, and the baby."

Chapter 50

Ruby

I found it impossible to sleep. My heart was racing as I thought of the silver car. Had it really been following me? Had I just panicked and imagined it? My mind kept going back to the feeling I'd had that someone was watching me. I couldn't help feeling it was something to do with the calls I'd had. Was the driver one of those men? He couldn't have recognised me. That photo wasn't even of me. But I hadn't found the site until days after I started to get the calls. Had there been other photos of me that were put up and taken down without my knowledge? Or were there some on another site, too?

Before I went to bed, I left the lights on in every room and wedged a chair against my bedroom door. If anyone tried to get in I'd hear him. I put my phone under my pillow and left the lamp on. It took ages for my breathing to slow down and for me to feel safe. I lay in bed thinking about the mess I'd made of my life. I'd lost Harry and though I hated him now, I missed him, too. I'd lost my home and I knew that was my own fault but it was still a loss. No matter how good my and Josh's intentions were, I knew I wouldn't have the same relationship with him now. He'd move away to university next September and if I moved away, too, I'd hardly see him. I had no husband – or not really. We weren't divorced yet, but the marriage was over. That was my fault, I knew, but there's something about having a husband – it's a kind of anchor, and without it, I felt like I didn't belong anywhere. I'd been stupid to think that I would ever belong to Harry.

As soon as it was daylight I sent Sarah a text.

I'm so sorry, I know it's early, but I need to talk to you when you've got a minute.

My phone rang within seconds. It was Sarah, sounding bleary and tired. "What's up? Are you okay?"

"I think someone was following me last night."

I could hear her moving around now and when she spoke all sounds of tiredness had gone. "What, after we left McCullough's?"

"Yes. I was waiting ages for a taxi but nothing came. I ended up walking home."

"Oh no. You should have come back with me."

"It's not that far, not even a couple of miles, but my shoes were killing me. I shouldn't have worn heels. But then I hit Weston Road, you know, where the road gets narrower? I hadn't realised how dark it was down there. And then I started to feel weird. I know this sounds crazy, but I'm sure someone was circling the block and driving past me really slowly."

"Who was it? Did you see him?"

"No. I couldn't see who it was. And then they stopped the car and I just turned and ran."

"I doubt it was anything," she said. "It was probably a different car each time. You'd had a few drinks and you were probably confused." I knew then it had been a complete waste of time talking to her about it. "I get nervous when I walk home late at night on my own, too." She spoke with great authority but I couldn't help wondering when exactly it was that she'd last done that. "It's when the streets are empty that it gets creepy. And the lightbulbs used in the streetlamps are lower wattage now; I was reading about it the other day. It'll just be that."

"I suppose so," I said doubtfully. "I'm not usually nervous, though."

"Are you kidding?" She laughed. "What about that time the lift broke down at work? You were only stuck in it for five minutes and you freaked out."

I winced at the memory. "That was a bit different. I thought it was going to fall down the shaft."

She laughed again. "I remember Harry explaining it to you very, very slowly."

I couldn't help smiling. "Even then I didn't really get it. I said I did but only because I didn't want to sound like a complete idiot."

She ended the call with a promise to be in touch soon. "I'd better get going," she said. "I'm taking notes at a meeting this morning."

"On a Saturday?" I hadn't intended to say that and it came out sharper than usual. When I'd worked there I'd sometimes had to work on a Saturday, but Sarah's job had never involved that.

She hesitated. "Yes. It's the board meeting." Harry always held the board meetings on a Saturday, so that they wouldn't be disturbed by other staff. There was an awkward pause, then she went on, "I'm Harry's PA now. There's been a bit of a reshuffle. Sorry, I thought I'd told you." I heard her call out to her daughter, telling her not to spill her orange juice, then she said quickly, "I have to go. Speak soon." And then she was gone, leaving me dumbfounded. Why hadn't she told me that the night before? Had she spoken to Harry about me? She hadn't wanted to talk about work and I could understand that, but to not mention she was working directly with Harry now?

As I showered and dressed I thought of the days I'd worked with him, of seeing him through the glass partition as we worked in our separate rooms. Now Sarah would be at my desk with the same view of Harry that I'd had.

I swallowed. I'd been such an idiot. He and I should have just stayed friends. I would have been there now, taking notes for him, chatting to him when no one was around, exchanging little messages that would disappear into thin air at the end of the day, as long as we remembered to close our screens. I'd ruined it all now. We'd ruined it all.

Then my phone beeped with a message. I checked it warily; those men from the escort site had made me frightened of my own phone. It was an e-mail from Tom, forwarding some tickets. It was for a showing of *Star Wars* with a live orchestra at the Royal Albert Hall in London, the afternoon before Christmas Eve. It was just the sort of thing I loved to do. There were three tickets.

> Hi, Ruby,
> Hope you're having a good weekend. I saw these tickets advertised and knew they'd sell out fast so I thought I'd get some for you. You'll love it. Perhaps take Josh and a friend? I'm in Scotland this weekend visiting my brother. He sends his love.
> So do I.
> x

Chapter 51

Ruby

I didn't respond to Tom's message, but he gave me plenty to think about that day. Buying those tickets was the sort of thing he'd done when we first met. He loved to give me surprises. Whenever it was my birthday or Christmas or our anniversary he'd be grinning for weeks beforehand, excited to see what my reaction would be to his gifts. And his gifts were perfect, thoughtful. Usually something I didn't know I wanted until I saw it wrapped up for me. Last night I'd felt vulnerable and scared; Tom's gift this morning made me feel as though he still loved me. Still cared for me. I knew that if I called him to tell him what had happened he'd come rushing back from Scotland to help me. I knew, too, that if he did that I'd move back into my house. What I didn't know was whether that would make me happy. Whether he'd ever forgive me. Whether I could ever truly love him again.

I went out for a walk and found myself near the local railway station. On impulse I caught the train into Liverpool. I knew it would be crowded there. I was sick of solitude. But as I walked among the shoppers all I noticed were other couples. Families. Happy mums beaming at their children. Couples kissing. It was too much.

I went to the café in Waterstones bookshop and looked at the Booker Prize shortlist there, planning which books I'd buy when I got paid, then wandered down to John Lewis, a big department store at the heart of Liverpool ONE.

I hadn't intended to look at the baby clothes there. I hadn't done that for years, since I thought I had a chance of becoming pregnant. But that day I went up the escalator to the third floor as though I was in a trance, and headed straight for the baby section. Instantly my heart reacted. I wanted to reach out, to touch things. There were tiny white woollen hats and pink velvet dresses. Soft toys, giraffes and teddies and elephants, sat in the perfect little cribs. A little knitted rabbit in a pale-grey-and-white-striped sweater lay on a bright blue blanket. I could feel myself soften as I saw them. I knew I shouldn't buy anything. I'd learned my lesson from Captain Barker, the little toy dog that Tom had bought me. It was too painful. Pointless.

A member of staff was hanging up impossibly small sleepsuits and turned to me and smiled. "Can I help you with anything?"

"No," I said, a bit too sharply. "It's okay, thanks. I'm looking for a gift for a friend."

I turned to leave. I needed to get out. It was a mistake coming here. When I'd given that little toy dog to the local Oxfam shop I'd vowed not to put myself in this position again.

And then I saw her. Emma. Harry's wife. The woman he'd chosen to be with, the woman who was having his baby.

She was looking at some crib blankets, stroking them as though they were precious objects. She had a faraway look on her face that I recognised, that I knew I'd held myself when I'd thought there was a chance I'd be pregnant. She seemed to be comparing the colours: the pinks and blues and lilacs and yellows.

"Go for plain white," I wanted to tell her. "There's plenty of time for colour."

I stood transfixed as she lifted a blanket to her cheek, as though to test its softness. The same assistant who'd tried to help me hurried over to her and I saw them laughing together and then laying the blankets on the counter to compare them. I remembered what Sarah had said, that Harry was afraid of bankruptcy once Emma saw those baby things. I knew exactly how she felt. I would have wanted to buy everything in the shop.

I hurried away, my heart pounding. I couldn't bear to see what she bought. I didn't want to picture her showing them to Harry. I knew how his face would soften when he saw them. He would hug her. Kiss her. I forced myself to stop. I needed to keep away from specifics. My nights were haunted by dreams of him as it was.

As soon as I was home I went into my bedroom, drew the curtains shut, and lay on the bed with the duvet pulled up around me. So many bad emotions swirled around my head; I just needed to hide away.

I don't think I'd seen Emma as a real person before. I'd shut out every thought of her, and Harry rarely mentioned her. It wasn't one of those affairs I'd heard about where the wife was criticised nonstop by her own husband and his lover. I think we both preferred to pretend she and Tom didn't exist. I don't know which is worse, really.

After a while I grew sick of thinking about them. I got out of bed, determined to go for a walk before dinner, to get some fresh air and hopefully some positive thoughts. Before I set off, I went into the kitchen to get a bottle of water from the fridge to take with me and stopped dead.

There on the kitchen counter was a mug of coffee. It was my mug, my coffee. I stared at it. I was sure I hadn't had it that morning. Warily I touched the mug. It was room temperature. I held it to my nose. Definitely coffee. The jar was on the counter and a spoon was in the sink. Inside the fridge was a plastic bottle of milk I'd bought the day before. I hadn't opened that bottle. I knew I hadn't opened it. I twisted off the green cap and saw the seal had been removed. I checked the bin. I'd taken the bin bag to the outside bins the day before and there in the fresh bin bag was the little foil seal. I frowned. Had I done that? I closed my eyes to concentrate. I could almost swear I hadn't.

Chapter 52

Ruby

I came back from work on Monday feeling a lot better. The end was in sight with that job. I no longer cared that the others sat about eating chocolates and putting work on my desk whenever I went to the toilet. They meant nothing to me, and anyway, I like to be busy. My house was up for sale. Soon I could move on. I was still worried that I was forgetting things and thought I'd make an appointment to see my doctor if it carried on. I must have had coffee on Saturday morning. It was something I did every single morning. I hated to miss it and felt out of sorts and tired before I had it. I wouldn't have gone out shopping if I'd felt like that. Just that morning I'd found myself halfway through a slice of toast and could hardly remember making it. And there were times when I was living with Tom where I'd be stressed and unable to sleep until the early hours, then the next morning I'd find myself at work without remembering parts of the journey. Sometimes you do things on automatic pilot; that's what I must have done with the coffee. It was normal when you were tired.

I went straight out for a run after work that evening. I took a different route, through a road parallel to the river. At the top of the hill that led down to the promenade I stopped for a second and steadied myself on an old stone wall. The smell of the river, salty and fresh, filled my lungs. I plugged my headphones in and scrolled through my phone's playlist. Bob Marley's "One Love" resounded in my ears as I ran down the hill toward the river. The sun was still bright, the sky a vivid blue.

My heart lifted. As my body warmed up and my breathing became more measured, I felt a spark of happiness. There's something about running, when there's enough wind to cool my face and when my arms and legs are in synchrony, that means I can let myself go completely and forget everything, just for a while.

I ran back to my flat feeling as though something had changed in me. I was ready to leave my past behind and move on. And that wasn't a punishment, it wasn't a penance; it was something I was looking forward to.

I was too hungry to shower before I ate, so I quickly put together some chicken and salad for dinner and took it into the living room. An e-mail notification pinged on my phone; it was just something from the local beauty salon offering a discount on treatments. I deleted it. The e-mailed tickets from Tom were now top of the list. I reread it. They had cost nearly £400. He'd known how much I loved those live shows. We'd never been to the Royal Albert Hall and had always gone to smaller places in Liverpool and Manchester, but he would have known how much I'd love to go there. And three tickets. Did he think he and I would go there with Josh? The show was at Christmas. Did he think we'd be back together by then?

For the tenth time I read his message.

I was in Scotland this weekend visiting my brother.
He sends his love.
So do I.
x

The phone rang in my hand, making me jump. It was Tom: a video call. I panicked that by rereading his e-mail I'd conjured him up. Hastily I ran my hands over my hair, pushed my plate away, and straightened my back.

"Hi," he said. "Just wanted to check in on you, make sure you were okay."

"I'm fine." I don't know why I felt so nervous. "Thank you for the tickets. That was really kind of you."

"You're welcome. It should be a great night." Again, I wondered whether he thought he'd be there with me.

"Why are we on a video call?"

He smiled. "I just wanted to see you, honey."

"Honey? You haven't called me that for years."

He seemed nervous when he smiled and said, "I realise that, Ruby. I think I got a bit lost. Didn't appreciate you enough. Being here on my own is making me think about things."

I kept quiet; I wasn't used to this version of Tom.

"I haven't seen you for weeks," he added. "You look great."

In the corner of my screen I could see exactly what he could see. My hair was tangled and damp from running and I hadn't put any makeup on since early that morning. I didn't bother to answer him but realised at least I wasn't apologising for the way I looked.

"You've lost weight," he said, and smiled at me. "It suits you."

As soon as he complimented me I lit up. I couldn't help it; I always did it, like someone who was desperate for approval. He was right; I had lost quite a lot of weight over the past few weeks, though I wouldn't recommend the way I'd lost it to anyone.

On the other hand, Tom *was* looking great. He was all dressed up in a dark blue suit and a white shirt and I realised I didn't recognise them. He must have been shopping for clothes on his own. I had a vision of a personal shopper telling him he looked fab, boosting his ego, making him feel wonderful. He'd had his hair cut, too, and looked younger. Happier. The difference between us was marked and I cringed. The confidence I'd gained during my run was slipping away.

"You look nice," I said. "Are you going out?"

His face flushed with pleasure. "Yes, just to the pub. The Crown. You don't fancy coming along, do you? Get a taxi; I'll drop you back home."

"No, thanks." There was a silence so I added, "It would take me too long to get ready." I don't know why I said that. I could have kicked myself. It sounded as though I'd be up for it if there was more time. "Who are you meeting?"

His eyes flickered, then he said, "Oh, just some of the guys from the office."

I frowned, then stopped when I saw my reflection. It made me look even worse. I knew he was lying. There was no way he'd be meeting work friends on a Monday night. And then it dawned on me. Did he have a date? Surely not. Why would he ask me to be there if he did?

I glanced down at my watch. It was seven forty-five. For a moment I felt like jumping in the car and going to The Crown just to see whom he was meeting.

"I'd better go," he said. "Come along if you like. It would be great to see you." He smiled at me. "I miss you, Ruby." Suddenly it was as though the years between the time we met and now had shrunk. Disappeared. This was the man I'd fallen for. I looked at him and in that moment I couldn't remember why I had left him. For a split second I thought I could get ready and be there by nine. We could have a couple of drinks, talk about things.

Of course I didn't do that, but the memory of his smile, the words he'd spoken, stayed with me. They comforted me. Confused me.

Chapter 53

Ruby

The night I spoke to Tom I went to bed early. There was too much to think about. Did he really want us to get back together? I'd given up on ever seeing Harry again, but in my heart he was the one I wanted. I couldn't just go back to Tom as though nothing had happened. At least he knew nothing of Harry. I knew his reaction would have been very different if he had. I started to think that maybe it would be possible to go back to Tom, if he could always be the way he was now.

I went to sleep pretty quickly but just before two o'clock I jolted awake. I'd heard a noise.

I sat up straight and strained to listen. I thought the sound was from outside the flat. Was it just a cat down in the alleyway? Then there was a bang; not a loud one, not enough to waken the street. I gripped my phone and slid out of bed. The flat was dark and quiet. Using the light on my phone to guide me, I tiptoed into the living room and edged my way to the window, where I moved the curtain slightly to one side and peered out onto the street. There was no one in sight. Nothing moved. My car was exactly where I'd left it. It didn't look like it had been disturbed. I stood for a few minutes looking out into the desolate street. It was a windy night and a plastic bag blew up and down, knocking into parked cars, then lurching away as the wind changed.

I stood at the window for a long time. I heard the soft roar of a car in the distance and the wind as it rattled the panes, but there was no other sound. There were no lights on in the houses and flats nearby. All was quiet.

Chilled and nervous, I went back toward my bedroom. To reach it I had to walk past the stairs down to the little hallway and automatically I glanced down, flashing the torch on my phone. When I saw the white envelope lying on the mat just inside the front door, I froze.

Stealthily I crept down the stairs and picked up the envelope then ran back upstairs as though someone was after me. My heart pounding, I switched on the lamp in my bedroom and opened the envelope.

Inside was another card, the same size as the first. It was a photo of me sitting at my window at night. The curtains were drawn back, the window open, and I could be clearly seen at my table, typing something on my laptop. It looked as though the room was lit by candlelight. There was no date stamp on the photo. I tried to think when it was taken, but I couldn't see what I was wearing. It could have been any night. Slowly I turned over the card and read the message.

Still thinking of you.

I hardly slept for the rest of that night. My mind was racing with all the things that had happened. Who had invited me to the interview? That was obviously a hoax, but why would anyone do that? They had nothing to gain from it. That escort site had terrified me and now photos had been put through my front door in the middle of the night. It was horrible to think of myself sitting there, feeling vulnerable and alone, probably looking online for somewhere to live, a place where I could be safe, while someone stood outside, taking a photo that they knew would frighten me.

I couldn't cope with this on my own. I needed help. I almost called Tom a dozen times, my finger hovering over the Call button, wanting him to rescue me. I knew that he'd come to fetch me, drive me home, and I'd be back in my old life. I wasn't sure I was ready for that. Sarah was the only person I could think of. I wondered what she'd say if she knew Tom had told me he loved me, that he missed me. I thought she'd tell me to go back, to count myself lucky he knew nothing of Harry. And then I wondered: Had he talked to her? Her contact details were in our address book at home. Had he told her he wanted me to come back? Had she told him where I lived?

She would be awake at seven, but I couldn't contact her that early. She'd be running around, too busy to reply. And I should get going, too; I had to be at work at nine. I got to work early and sat in my car until I knew she'd be at her desk. I sent her a message:

Have you spoken to Tom since I left home?

She replied immediately. No, I'm not the one who goes after married men ☺

I ignored this barb. I had too much to think about. I thought of the photos I'd had with their cryptic messages, the phone calls, those disgusting men who didn't even know me who thought I'd have sex with them for money. My phone number was on that site; who had put it there?

I'd been followed home from the wine bar. I knew I had. At times I'd wondered whether I'd imagined it, but that was just wishful thinking. I knew someone had been following me. That silver car had driven past three times round and had stopped just yards from me. I'd known that if the driver had got out, I'd be in serious trouble. I hadn't taken it personally, though, until I saw the same car driving up and down my road later that night. After I'd run away from it I hadn't seen it again until I was in my flat. Nobody had followed me there. I felt a surge of panic. I hadn't thought of that before. They knew where I lived.

I swallowed my pride and called Sarah, but she didn't answer. I sent her a message:

Something weird has happened. Someone put a photo of me through my front door in the middle of the night. They must have been watching me.

There was no reply for a while and I sat in my car watching my colleagues go into the building. They stared at me and I waved, but got no response. Just before nine, when I was about to go in to work, she replied. I could tell she was exasperated with me:

Honestly, Ruby, every time I speak to you, you tell me something weird has happened. First it was the phone calls, then the mysterious interview, then someone following you, and now this.

Energised, I replied: I know! And that's the second time I've been sent a photo! Who could have done it?

She didn't reply for an hour. I was frantically typing my way through the office's workload when her message finally came through:

Oh for God's sake. I always think that if someone's going through too much drama, it's down to them. Something to think about?

My face was hot when I read that. And then I remembered I hadn't even told her about the half-empty mug of coffee. I was glad I hadn't then.

Chapter 54

Ruby

I started to become quite withdrawn. Sarah's messages had upset me and made me realise that if she didn't understand, nobody would. I hardly said a word at work, just saying "*Good morning*" and "*Good night*" to people who didn't respond. When I got home at night I did nothing, just sat on the sofa, watching movies on my laptop, trying to figure out how I'd got into this mess and how I could get out of it.

The pull toward Tom was becoming stronger. When I was at my worst ebb on Wednesday night – I hadn't spoken to anyone for two days by then – he sent me a message.

Hey, Ruby, are you watching The Bridge? It's rerunning on BBC. I'm watching it on my own and missing you – it was always great to talk through the plot together. You always saw things I didn't notice! Hope work's going well x

Quickly I switched off *The Bridge*; I had been watching it on my laptop. I realised that Tom didn't know where I was working, didn't know I'd lost my job. I'd been careful not to say anything about it to Josh, and Tom hadn't asked about work since I left.

Another message came through. Tom again.

Oh and have you started to read The Goldfinch? Why did we never read that at the time? I'm reading it now, hope you like it x

I didn't answer him. I was worried I'd call him and tell him I missed him. I *did* miss him. I missed the comfort and security of my home. I missed having someone to talk to. Someone to watch television with and go out with occasionally. And all those times he wasn't nice to me, well, I thought he was stressed. I'd often wondered whether he was suffering from depression. I knew he'd wanted another child. He found living apart from Josh very tough. Whenever Josh called round unexpectedly, Tom would be so happy, as though he was whole again. Now he was living completely alone and I guessed he'd find that really hard. But then the other night he looked great. He seemed happy to talk to me. He was like his old self, the man I'd fallen in love with.

–

Midnight was always my weak point. It seemed to be hardwired into my brain that if I wasn't asleep then, I wouldn't be able to sleep. I lay curled up in bed and reached under my pillow for my phone. I searched through my photos and found some of Tom throughout the years. I still reacted to those early shots, where he and I would be arm in arm and he'd be smiling at me as though he loved me. He had loved me; I knew he had. But then the later photos – there were fewer of them – they were different. There were stress lines on his face and it was clear he was unhappy. I wondered whether he'd been the same with Belinda, whether he'd grown more intolerant as time went on. I'd noticed the way she avoided him even now, years after they were together. Even in the early days she'd always had Josh ready and waiting, coat on, so that he could run out to Tom's car. I had thought she was just good at timekeeping; it was only now that I thought there might have been other reasons behind that. He was always so nice to me then, and I didn't think for a moment that he might have been to blame in his marriage to her. I shut down that folder. I didn't want to think about that, especially not late at night.

Then I searched online for a photo of Harry and found one in a local business magazine. The photo was taken when Sheridan's first opened. It was a few years before I met him, but he hadn't changed too much. He looked out at the camera, little realising that one day in the future a woman would call up this photo in the privacy of a grotty rented flat and lie in bed crying at the sight of him.

I reached out to my bedside cabinet. In the bottom drawer was a silk scarf that Harry had bought me. It had an abstract design in bright blues and pinks, and I loved it. My phone lit up that corner of the room and all I could see was the scarf and Harry's face on the screen.

Harry had bought me the scarf in Paris, the weekend we decided to live together. We were walking through the city late on Saturday afternoon, looking for a restaurant that was far enough away from the conference centre, so that we wouldn't bump into any of the other delegates. A row of silk scarves was on display in the window of a tiny boutique and we stopped to look at them. He stood behind me, really close. Every nerve in my body was awakened and he leaned forward and brushed my hair to one side and kissed my neck.

The owner of the shop had been arranging a cashmere wrap on the shelf next to the window and she looked over and smiled at us.

"Come on," said Harry. "I'll treat you."

Back home I told Tom that I'd gone out on my own to look at the shops because I didn't want to sit with all the people at the conference. I said I was sick of listening to them talk about work by then and had bought the scarf with my savings as a treat for working over the weekend. He hadn't taken much notice, hadn't said a word about wasting money. He'd been a bit preoccupied and I'd quickly changed the subject, relieved he wasn't going to cross-examine me.

Now I held the scarf to my face and breathed in the smell of Chanel's Gabrielle that I was wearing in Paris. I hadn't worn that perfume since. I'd wanted it to always be associated with that trip, and now in the dark, memories overlaid memories. Harry telling me he loved me. That he wanted to be with me forever. Harry standing behind me at the boutique window, close enough to touch but not quite touching. I'd thought I would faint with excitement. We'd raced back to bed afterwards.

I put the scarf on the pillow next to me so that I could touch it while I slept. At one o'clock I reached out for my Kindle on my bedside cabinet. It opened at the copy of *The Goldfinch* that Tom had bought for me. I didn't want to think of Harry while reading the same book as Tom. Instead I found my copy of *Rebecca*. I'd read it so many times that I could recite entire passages. It was so comforting. My life might be bad at the moment, but at least I wasn't the second Mrs. de Winter. Before long I was asleep.

I woke hours later. I can't tell you what disturbed me. My arm had come clear of the quilt; the night was warm, but still I liked to be covered and I pulled it back over me. My Kindle was facedown on the bed beside me. It had turned itself off.

And then I heard a click.

I sat up sharply and strained to hear. Was that the front door? My mind went into a free fall of panic. It sounded like the Yale lock as the door was pulled to. Was someone inside my flat?

For several minutes I sat like that, my body leaning forward so that I could hear better. I stayed absolutely still and could hear my breathing, my heart beating. There seemed to be no other sound in the flat. No footsteps. No whispering.

I grabbed my phone and dialled 999 but held back on pressing the Send button. Silently I tiptoed to the bedroom door. It was pulled to, but not shut tight. Wasn't it shut when I went to bed? I just couldn't remember. I opened the door an inch or two wider and peeked out, my heart racing. There was nothing in the little hallway except the coat hooks, with my jackets and a couple of handbags hanging from them. The doors to the kitchen and living room were open, and the light from the lamp post outside filtered through, giving an eerie air.

I didn't know what to do. Should I shout, *Hello?* or *Who's that?* One good thing about living with Tom had been that if anyone had broken into our house, he would have been on them like a rottweiler. I took a couple of steps forward and peeped down the staircase. The front door was shut. There was nothing on the doormat.

Two steps farther and I could see inside the bathroom. That was empty; there was no place to hide there. I held my breath and took a couple of steps farther on to the kitchen. The sliding door was pushed back, just as I'd left it.

I tried to take another deep breath but my lungs wouldn't do it. I started to feel light-headed, as though I needed to pant. I tiptoed into the doorway of the living room and flashed on the light. There was nobody there lurking in the shadows, nobody crouching behind the sofa or under the dining table, wielding a weapon or reaching out to grab me.

I turned quickly in case someone was behind me, but all was quiet. I went back through the flat, putting all the lights on. I didn't know what I'd heard. I kept replaying it again and again in my mind. I was sure I'd heard my front door click. Had I dreamed it? But I thought I'd been awake just before I heard that. What had woken me?

I left all the lights on in the other rooms and went back to bed, though I knew I wouldn't sleep now. I took out my phone and scrolled through Tom's texts, where he said he loved me. He missed me.

I wanted to feel safe again. I wanted to go home.

Chapter 55

Emma

Harry was staying in London overnight so after I met Tom in The Crown I went back to an empty house. I seethed all night. I had a hit list of people to blame: Harry for having an affair, Ruby for having one with him, Tom for hounding me. Ultimately I blamed myself, though. I couldn't see one reason why I'd slept with Tom unless it was a last hoorah from my hormones, which meant it was far more likely that Tom was the father.

I was pretty quiet at work the next day. I know Annie was worried. Mid-afternoon, after barely a word out of me all day, she said, "Right, come on. Let's go to the café and have some cake. Something's clearly bothering you."

Despite my protests I found myself outdoors and walking down the street to a café – not the one that Tom had taken me to, thank God – realising that all those years of child-rearing had turned Annie into someone who couldn't be messed with. I had a fleeting thought of my own child. Was that how I'd be in ten years' time? I had a horrible feeling that this baby might play me like a fiddle, just like her father did. Whoever her father was.

Annie ordered cake and I had a fruit salad and we sat outside under a parasol, enjoying the summer sun.

"What's up?" she asked. "Come on, you can tell me."

I felt terrible. How could I tell her that last Friday I'd had a DNA test on the foetus and that I was waiting to see who its father was? She'd be horrified. She was my best friend. We'd worked together for years. We shared every secret, every stupid thing we'd done. She used to say that whenever she did something embarrassing she'd think, *I can't wait to tell Emma about this*. But this was way, way beyond embarrassing. And maybe if the test results showed Harry was the father, I could tell her about it and we could both cringe, but not now.

So I just said, "I'm worried about the baby. Whether it will be okay," and she gave me a long look as though she knew that wasn't it, but talked kindly and firmly about why I shouldn't worry unless there was something to worry about.

"You're fit and healthy," she said. "You eat well. You don't drink too much." She gave a little cough. "Nowadays." We both laughed, remembering some parties we'd been to when we were young. "Just enjoy being pregnant. If there's something to worry about, the doctors will tell you soon enough. Don't anticipate problems."

"I don't remember you being like that," I said, remembering her reaction when she had eaten a cracker with Brie on it then realised it was on the forbidden list. "You worried all the time."

"We're not talking about me." She finished her coffee. "And while we're talking about you, who was that guy at your house yesterday?"

I'd known I wouldn't get away with that. Since she'd had children Annie was like a bloodhound, able to sniff out trouble a mile off.

"Oh, him." I thought quickly. "He lives down the road."

"What did he want? You didn't seem very happy to see him."

"He was at a barbecue we went to last summer and whenever I see him now he wants to chat. I don't like him though."

"Why did he call round?"

"Oh, he does that sometimes if he sees I'm working from home. He asks if I want a break. A coffee. He's irritating."

She sat back. "You've got a good-looking guy calling round when you're working from home and you haven't told me? Does Harry know?"

"Yeah, he knows he's a pain. I don't let him into the house, though."

From Annie's expression I could tell she had me sussed. She knew I was lying about something.

"Emma, don't take any risks," she said. "You've got a lovely husband. A happy marriage. Don't do anything to mess that up."

That was so unfair – and yet so spot-on – that I started to cry. I didn't know whether I was crying with anger or with guilt. I brushed Annie away when she tried to put her arm around me.

"I'm so sorry. I didn't mean to upset you."

"It's just my hormones," I said, drying my eyes. "They're all over the place. Don't worry, though, I'm not having an affair. That guy is just a bit of a nuisance, that's all."

We walked back to the office in silence. I knew she was mulling things over. I just hoped she didn't connect Tom with the baby I was expecting.

–

I got home at six that night. Harry's car was in the driveway and when I opened the front door he came to greet me from the kitchen.

"Hi, sweetheart." He hugged me and kissed my cheek. "Good day?"

"It was fine. Busy."

"Well, that's good. Why don't you sit in the garden and I'll bring dinner out to you?"

I went upstairs to change into shorts and a tank top then came back to the kitchen. Suddenly I was starving.

"Something smells good. What are we having?"

"Spaghetti." He passed me a little bowl of olives, slick with garlic and chilli. "Go and put your feet up outside. I'll only be a few minutes."

I reclined my chair, enjoying the sun on my body. I'd worked hard that day, mainly to avoid answering any more of Annie's questions. I caught her glancing over at me but just gave her a brief smile each time and focused on my work. That night with Tom had changed all of my relationships.

After dinner Harry and I stayed outside for a couple of hours. Harry had a glass of wine and was reading a book and I was following a group of mums on a forum who were talking about their recent childbirths. It was funny, really funny at times, but was making me squirm and cross my legs. It was just as I'd hoped pregnancy would be and I could feel myself start to relax.

Then as we were going into the house for the night, Harry said, "Oh, something came for you today." He went into the dining room and came back with a huge box. "I've no idea what it is, do you?"

"No. Are you sure it's for me?"

"Your name's on the box. Have you ordered anything for work?"

"No. I'd have it delivered there, anyway. There's always someone who can sign for it. When did it get here?"

"No idea. It was left with the guy next door. He was working from home and took it in. He brought it round when he saw my car tonight."

I opened up the box. I had to. Harry was standing next to me, wondering what was in it. His birthday wasn't for a long time; neither was mine. I just knew this wasn't going to be good but had no excuse for not opening it.

Inside was a huge white teddy bear with a tartan bow around its neck.

"Wow," said Harry, pulling it out. "That's nice." He put it on the table. "Who sent it?"

"I've no idea. Could it be your mum and dad?"

"No, they're coming to see us next week. They wouldn't send something like this through the post. They never buy anything online anyway. Isn't there a note to say who sent it?"

There was nothing in the box but on the outside there was a document, taped to the box. It was facing away from Harry.

"No," I said. "That's odd, I can't see anything. Oh well, someone will call soon and claim it." I picked up the box. "Harry, would you do me a favour and run a bath for me? And put some of that bath oil you gave me in it?" I gave him a winning smile. "I'm so tired."

"Of course!" He bounded upstairs and I ripped the delivery note off the box and shoved it into my handbag. Later in the bathroom with the door locked I opened the note. Attached to it was a card with a message typed on it. It said:

For our baby. T x

Chapter 56

Emma

I opened my eyes the next morning to find the white teddy bear staring me in the face. Harry was kneeling by the side of the bed, holding the bear up in front of him. He moved it toward me, to stroke my cheek with its nose. I jerked away, pushing it to the floor. He laughed when he saw my expression. "He just wanted to say good morning."

My stomach leaped. "Who did?"

"The bear." Harry sounded like I was the one that was mad. "Who did you think I meant?"

"Sorry. You startled me."

I went into the bathroom to get a bit of peace. I couldn't have that bear in the house, but how could I get rid of it? It was huge; I couldn't exactly lose it. Even if I persuaded Annie to bring her kids round and persuaded them that they wanted to adopt the bear, I'd still know it existed. That it was meant for me.

As soon as Harry left for work I called Tom.

"What the hell are you playing at?"

"Hello, Emma. How are you today?"

"How dare you send things to my house? And that message – well, Harry didn't see it, despite your efforts. And anything you send to me again will be sent back to you, unopened."

"I just thought it would be good to start buying things for the baby," he said calmly.

I wanted to scream at him, but I knew the power he held. He could come round to the house anytime and tell Harry what had happened. I know that Harry started all this with his and Ruby's affair, but I was the one who was pregnant. The more I thought about it the more I realised that Harry would simply deny any involvement with Ruby. She wasn't even working for him now. I was the only witness to their affair and I was pregnant after sleeping with another man.

At that moment I wished I could just go to the airport and pick a flight – any flight – and just disappear and leave the whole lot of them behind.

"If you don't leave me alone, I'll get a restraining order against you," I hissed.

"I don't think that's how it works, babe," he said. "All I did was buy you a soft toy for our baby. But okay, if you're superstitious, I won't buy anything else."

I breathed a sigh of relief.

"I'll save the money instead."

"Okay. You do that."

–

That night Harry and I were in bed, about to go to sleep, when his phone beeped.

"Sorry, honey," he said. "I'll just check this in case it's work."

He was always open with his phone and was always happy to let me use it. I knew his password. He thought he knew my password, but I'd changed it since I'd started getting messages from Tom. I'd turned off the notifications, too, so that Harry wouldn't see a message from him pop up on the screen. Honestly, I was living as though I was the one having an affair.

"That's odd," he said. "I've got a message from PayPal."

At that point I was thinking I needed to have my blood pressure checked. I was two days from my test results and every time I moved that stupid bear into another room Harry brought it back again. It didn't seem to bother him that he hadn't a clue who'd sent it to us. Right then it was sitting on the armchair staring at us both. I was trying to relax, ready for sleep, but my eyes kept meeting the bear's eyes. I panicked, wondering whether Tom had fitted it with a recording device, and went over to put it in the spare room.

"How strange," said Harry. "It says someone's sent me a hundred pounds through PayPal."

"It'll be a scam." I was half-asleep and just wanted him to switch the lamp off and shut up. "The newspapers are full of this sort of thing. Someone puts money into your account and says it was a mistake. You send it back but they've already withdrawn their money. Just ignore it."

"No." He sounded confused. "There's a message. It says, 'You might need this after the baby's born!'"

My eyes snapped open. "What?" I sat up and took his phone. The sender's name was simply *T*.

"Who do we know whose name begins with *T*?" asked Harry. Thankfully he'd turned the lamp off by then and couldn't see my face. I didn't answer and pretty soon he went to sleep.

I lay there for hours, thinking about Tom, just as he'd intended. I knew that he was going to keep going on and on until I snapped.

I didn't think he'd have long to wait.

Chapter 57

Ruby

The first thing I did that morning was to e-mail Gill, the letting agent, to ask whether she could have someone put a bolt on the front door. I told her I was concerned about security and was happy to pay for it. It was something I could have done myself but of course I didn't have any tools with me. I knew I could have asked Tom if I could use some of ours, but he'd insist on coming round to do it for me and I didn't want him to see where I was living. Gill replied quickly, saying she'd send someone around as soon as she could, but that I wasn't to do it myself, as per the rental agreement.

I got to work by nine o'clock as usual and found another woman sitting at my desk. She was very tanned and heavily made up, and her eyes were swollen and pink. I guessed she'd been crying. She looked me up and down and I knew she must be part of the gang that worked in the admin office.

"Hi." I smiled. "I'm Ruby Dean, the temp."

She scowled. "I'm here now," she said.

I stared at her, wanting a further explanation, but she said nothing, just took out her makeup bag and focused on her eyebrows.

Mike, our manager, came out and saw me standing there. He ushered me into his office. As I left the reception area I heard the woman yell, "What's this computer doing here?"

"I'm so sorry," Mike said. "I didn't realise she'd be back today."

"I thought she was on holiday for three weeks?"

"She was." He closed the office door and whispered, "She was meant to be getting married abroad. They got drunk and had a huge argument and got kicked out of their hotel, so they had to come back."

I bit my lip to stop myself from laughing. "So now that she's back, you don't need me?"

"You can stay if you like," he said. "You'd have to work in the admin office with the others, though."

We looked out of his office window into the admin office beyond. The woman from the reception desk was there now, telling her story to an avid crowd.

"I'll give that a miss, I think."

"I don't blame you." He shook my hand. "Thanks for all the work you've done. I really appreciate it. I'll call Lesley and make sure you're paid to the end of the week."

I raced out to my car, feeling giddy with relief that I was getting out of there.

—

I didn't know where I was going to when I set off, but found myself heading toward Nantwich, a little market town about forty miles from home. I hadn't been there for months and for a while I walked along the narrow streets, looking at the shops and wishing I had the money to buy something. I was happy to leave that job but I had to find something else now.

As I walked down the street toward the market square, I saw a café that I hadn't noticed before. At the front of the shop was a counter where customers could buy cakes and homemade bread, then there was a seating area beyond. The café area was pretty empty but looked warm and welcoming. There was a bookshop next door and I went in to buy the latest Kate Atkinson novel that I'd just seen reviewed in the papers, then returned to the café and sat at the back at a table on my own.

I sent Tom a message:

Any interest in the house?

He replied pretty quickly: There have been a few viewers over the last couple of days. I'll let you know how it goes, if you're sure you want to sell x

I wondered whether he wanted to sell. Whether he wanted me back. I could see the man I used to love now. If he stayed like that, I knew I could be happy with him.

Another text came through.

Are you OK for money? Let me know if you need anything x

I didn't know what to say. I didn't want him to know how little I had and how worried I was. I'd always been proud that I'd supported myself; now wasn't the time to lose my independence.

The waitress came over and I made my order, preoccupied with how to respond to Tom's message. Just as she turned away, the door opened and Harry walked in.

Chapter 58

Ruby

I couldn't take my eyes off him.

He stood making conversation with the woman behind the counter. He said something to her and she burst out laughing. He was like that. Everyone was charmed by him. I stayed still, not wanting to draw attention to myself. I was so aware of him it seemed as though my whole body was buzzing. Alert. For a moment I forgot how he'd treated me; all I could feel was relief that I'd seen him again, that he was alive and well. Then a surge of anger rose in me and I wanted to punch his lights out for what he'd done to me.

He seemed to be choosing boxes of cakes. I heard him say, "I need a couple of dozen. Mix them up but make sure there are a few éclairs or there'll be a fight," and his voice was so familiar that my throat ached.

I looked at my watch. It was just before two o'clock. And then I remembered that one of his suppliers was nearby. Had he had a lunch meeting with them this morning? Was he going back to the office and treating the staff to cakes, or was he taking twenty-four cakes home to his pregnant wife?

When he took out his wallet to pay, I looked away quickly and stared down at my book on the table. I opened it at a random place and tried to read what it said. I could hardly make out one word. I didn't want to talk to him. I couldn't think of one civil thing I might say.

And then the air seemed to shift and I knew he was there, standing over me. I hadn't heard him, hadn't seen him, but I knew. I kept my eyes fixed firmly on my book.

"Hello, Ruby." He sounded nervous, as he should. "What are you doing here?"

I had to look up then. I didn't know whether to slap him or kiss him. I pressed myself back in my seat to stop myself from doing either.

My mouth was suddenly dry and I had to swallow before I could speak. "Hello, Harry. I didn't see you there." It wasn't convincing, I knew. "I was just reading my book."

"Do you mind if I sit down?"

I shrugged.

He pulled a chair out opposite me and sat down, putting his boxes of cakes on the table next to us. "Oh, Kate Atkinson. I like her." He took the book out of my hands. It was open at the centre pages. He read a line or two, then looked at the cover. "What's it about?"

"No idea," I said abruptly.

He gave a nervous laugh; he'd never known me to be rude. "How have you been?"

"Fine. Everything's hunky-dory, thank you."

Just then the waitress arrived with my hot chocolate and coffee cake. "That looks good," he said. "Mind if I join you?"

I glared at him, but he turned to the waitress. "I'll have black coffee and the same cake, thanks."

We sat in silence until she returned with his order. I kept my head down. I didn't want to talk to him or even look at him. When the waitress was safely back in the kitchen, he reached out to touch my hand. I snatched it away.

"Ruby, I'm so sorry."

Suddenly my throat was swollen with tears and I couldn't say a word.

"I know we can't be friends," he said. "That would be too odd after all we went through, but surely we can chat if we bump into each other?"

"All *we* went through?" I couldn't believe it. "We? I'm the person without a job or a home, thanks to your bright idea that we should leave our partners. I don't think you've been through much at all, have you?" My heart was pounding. "Oh, wait. Are you suffering early labour pains?"

He winced. "I'm sorry I couldn't tell you about the baby face-to-face. I know it must have hurt you."

"And you think dumping me wouldn't hurt me?"

"I'm sorry," he said again. "I was stupid. And thoughtless. And cruel. But what do you mean, you're without a home?" I was silent and then it dawned on him. "You've left home? But when?"

"On the day we agreed," I snapped. "At the time we agreed. When do you think?"

"But I told you not to," he said. "Or not until you were ready to."

"What? Your last words to me were, '*I'll see you at around eight o'clock. Don't let me down!*'" Actually he'd told me he loved me then, too. I didn't repeat that, I just couldn't, though from the flush that stained his face, I saw he remembered it, too.

"But I e-mailed you," he said. "I told you not to leave that night."

Chapter 59

Ruby

I looked at him in confusion. "No, you didn't."

"I did! I sent you an e-mail before I left work that night. A really long e-mail. I told you about the baby, remember?" He reached out for my hand, but I moved away. "I asked you to forgive me."

"I knew about the baby from Sarah, on the Monday afterwards. I didn't get an e-mail."

"What? I sent it to your Gmail account; the one linked to your phone. Remember you told me the address one time?"

I certainly did remember. I was in bed with him at the time.

"I didn't get it and I've used it dozens of times since then. But why would you do that? We never sent e-mails to each other."

"I needed you to get it straightaway. I couldn't call you in case Tom was there, and if I'd sent it to your work address you wouldn't have got it until Monday." He was quiet for a while and drank his coffee. "When you didn't reply, I thought you were angry with me."

"I was. I was furious." I didn't need to add that I still was; he must have been able to tell. "I wrote to tell you that."

"You did?"

"Yes, I gave a letter to Sarah. She put it in your drawer."

"No, she didn't," he said firmly. "You think I wouldn't have seen it? Responded?"

"I didn't ask her whether you'd read it. I thought that would sound pathetic." I saw pity in his eyes and looked away. "Let me check."

I sent her a message:

Hi Sarah, just checking you remembered to put my letter into Harry's drawer at work. X

Within minutes she replied, Yes, of course I did. I told you I would.

She was *definitely* getting more annoyed with me.

Do you know if he read it? I asked.

Ruby, I'm supposed to be working! Yes, he opened it when he came back into work. I saw him through the window, reading it.

I showed this to Harry. "Did you read it?"

"No. I didn't see a letter from you." He reached over and touched my hand. I moved mine away, but could feel the warm pressure for ages afterwards. "I would have called you if I had."

"But that means she's been lying to me," I said. I sent another message: Did you see what he did with my letter?

She replied immediately. I'm really sorry, Ruby. He read it and then he threw it into the bin. I didn't want to tell you that.

His face was grim as he read the message. "I'll have a word with her. She's lying to you."

"But why would she do that? We're friends."

He looked awkward. "I know I should have told you this, but a couple of Christmases ago she made a pass at me. It was at the office party, just before you started working there."

"What? Sarah did?"

"Yes. She said we could be friends with benefits." He saw my expression and laughed. "I told her I wasn't interested and she cried. She asked me not to tell anyone."

"But she's married!"

There was silence then as we both realised we, too, were married.

I thought of Sarah's shock as she discovered I'd had an affair with Harry. I thought back to the things that had happened to me: Had Sarah had anything to do with them? And she'd

266

listened to me as I wailed about Harry; I'd told her everything, and she'd said nothing at all, just watched, prompted me to confide in her, then lied through her teeth when I asked if she'd given him my letter.

It was obvious that she was impatient with me now. Had she always felt like that about me?

Chapter 60

Ruby

"So you went to the hotel that night?" asked Harry.

I nodded, my face hot with shame. "I stayed there for a few nights. Nearly a week. I went home on Friday, told Tom, and left, just as we planned." My mouth trembled as I spoke. "I waited for you! I thought you meant it when you said you loved me."

"I did mean it," he said. "I did. Listen to me." He reached out and tentatively touched my hand again. This time I didn't move, but every bit of me yearned to hold him. "After you'd gone that night, Jane came to my office. You remember she's Emma's sister?"

I nodded.

"I'd had a meeting with Rick Brown and I was there longer than I'd planned. Jane was waiting for me. We were to have an exit meeting. And for whatever reason she decided to use my laptop while she was waiting. I'm not sure why. She didn't stop long enough to tell me. And she saw our messages from that afternoon." He grimaced. "They went further back, actually. I hadn't deleted them for months."

I felt my face go crimson. Throughout the day we'd use the company's instant messaging service, thinking we were safe. Once the conversation thread was closed, they were lost and there was no way anyone could retrieve them. I used to close mine down all the time, in case someone saw them, but I suppose Harry hadn't thought anyone would look at his laptop.

"How much did she see?"

"Enough to see that we planned to leave home that night."

"Oh God."

"Eleanor came in then and we did the handover with Jane. Then when Eleanor went back to her room, Jane really let me have it. She told me that Emma had just found out she was pregnant. I hadn't realised, of course. I hadn't even thought she might be. We assumed we couldn't have children." He looked down. "We were tested years ago and were told it was unexplained infertility. Anyway, you don't want to know about that. She told me that Emma was pregnant and that if I carried on seeing you, she would tell her everything. I knew Emma would leave me if she found out I was seeing you."

"But you wanted to leave her!"

"I did. I wanted to be with you. I just hadn't factored in a baby." His face was pink with emotion and he gripped my hand tightly. "Ruby, I have never fathered a child. It's something I'd always wanted. Longed for. I wanted a baby even more than Emma did. And I loved you. Of course I loved you. You're wonderful. But I had to make that decision."

"And you didn't think you'd bother telling me?" I couldn't help it. I knew I sounded bitter, but I *was* bitter. I was still furious with him, not so much for not leaving his wife, but for not telling me. For letting me down. "Why would you treat someone you loved like that?"

"I told you. I wrote to you. I couldn't call you: We had that rule, remember? I wouldn't do anything to make things difficult for you at home. And when I got to work after that week away, you weren't there."

"Sarah didn't tell you why I'd gone?"

He shook his head. "I assumed you'd left so that you wouldn't have to see me." He looked down and I knew he felt ashamed. "You have to understand, though, why I couldn't leave home. I couldn't leave Emma, not if she was pregnant. What sort of man would do that? And when I got home she bundled me into the car and took me away for a week. She said we should leave our phones behind." He swallowed and I steeled myself for what he'd say. "She said we needed to bond. That we'd been living separate lives. We had. I'd told you that; we talked about it a lot. She said we had to be a family now, that our child came first. I couldn't call you. She was with me the whole time. And when I got back to work, you'd gone and I knew I deserved that."

"I was fired," I said.

"What?"

"I got to work on Monday morning and was told they were terminating my contract."

"What? Who told you that?"

"Eleanor Jones."

He nodded, his face pale. "I hadn't realised she was in on this, too. Jane must have spoken to her before she left work that day. But why didn't you e-mail me?"

"Are you kidding? You didn't turn up. You didn't write. Then when I tried to call you, your phone was switched off. What kind of e-mail did you want, exactly?"

"But I did write!" He sounded so frustrated. "I don't understand why you didn't get it."

"What time did you send it?"

"About six o'clock. I remember looking at the time when I was writing it."

I thought back. "Tom sent a text from the train before that, and after I replied I turned the sound off on my phone in case he called me. I was so nervous that I knew he'd suspect something if he spoke to me."

"Does he know your password?"

"No. No, of course not."

"So he can't access your e-mail?"

I stopped short. "Oh no. He had my iPad that day. He took it to London, to use on the train. And if you click on Gmail my inbox would open automatically; the username and password are stored there. I don't use it for anything private. Just shopping, that sort of thing. But he doesn't use Gmail. Why would he even open it?"

Harry ignored this. We both knew why Tom would be checking my messages. "You have e-mail notifications on your phone, don't you?"

"Yes, but nothing came through. Just a second, I'm trying to think…" I sat quietly, thinking back to the day I'd left Tom. I'd muted my phone, not wanting to be distracted by messages. "I checked my phone while I was waiting for Tom to come home. There were no messages at all."

"But if he saw it first and deleted it, the notification would disappear off your phone," Harry said. "What if he read it on the train and deleted it straightaway?"

"But that would mean he knew I was leaving him."

–

The moment I said it, I knew it was true. Everything fell into place, the way Tom hadn't shouted at me, hadn't argued. And hadn't asked whether I was involved with anyone else.

He knew.

And since I'd left him, everything had gone wrong.

My mind raced as I thought back to the conversation that night. "I wondered why he didn't ask why I was leaving."

"Why did he think you were going?"

"I just told him I was unhappy. I was. He knew I was. I'd told him a hundred times."

"Didn't he seem surprised?"

I thought back to that day, the way Tom had reacted. "You know, he didn't. But I thought that was because he knew I was unhappy. And since then he's been lovely to me. I thought he'd learned a lesson when I left. That he missed me."

The thing was that I'd been so glad to get out of the house that I hadn't given his reaction another thought and then, as soon as I got to the hotel, all I could think about was Harry.

But now I remembered seeing the iPad in his briefcase before I left home. It was on show in his bag, like a huge red flag that was waving at me, and I hadn't understood the significance. He must have loved that.

And then I realised something else. If Tom had been reading my e-mails, he'd know about the jobs I'd applied for. I cringed. He would have seen the contract between the landlord and me; he would know where I lived, where I worked. He'd said nothing.

I looked at Harry. I really wanted to talk to him, to tell him about the things that had happened since I'd left home. I wanted his help. But how could I trust him now?

I believed him when he said he'd e-mailed me. I should have realised he'd do that. And I could understand why he'd stayed with Emma, hard though that was to accept. But ultimately he'd let me down. He wasn't the man I'd thought he was.

Chapter 61

Ruby

The next morning I woke just after six. The early-morning sun was pouring through my windows and the room was already warm. I kept my eyes closed tightly, not ready to face the day. I'd slept heavily and seemed to have stayed in one position all night. My limbs were stiff and aching, but I was too tired to move. I lay on one side and for a moment it felt as though there was a weight on the bed, as though someone was lying behind me, just inches away. In that half sleep I thought of Harry and how I'd slept in his arms that weekend we were in Paris. I'd never slept so well. Now in the dark warmth of my bed I moved just an inch backward, desperate to find him there. As I pushed back I felt something blocking me and my eyes snapped open. I sat up with a lurch. The pillows from the other side of the bed had moved down while I was sleeping and had been pressing against my back.

In the pale light I saw the door was shut tight, a dining chair wedged under the handle. It was just as I'd left it the night before, when I was too frightened to sleep without protection. I tiptoed out of the bedroom and peered over the banister at the hallway below. There was another chair pressed against the front door. Last night I had been determined that nobody would get in without disturbing me. I felt stupid now. Paranoid.

I was so grateful I didn't have to go in to work and took a mug of coffee back to bed. As I sipped my drink I thought of Harry and wondered whether he was doing the same thing right now. I knew he'd be thinking of me, feeling guilty that I hadn't known he was staying with Emma. I knew, too, that as he saw her that morning, saw her belly start to swell with their new life, he'd have no real regrets. Unlike me.

I reached for my phone and signed up to Instagram again. I wanted to see the photos that Emma had posted of her home. Their home. I saw their kitchen; they'd had it remodelled last year and she'd posted before-and-after photos. The kitchen table stood near their patio windows and I guessed he'd be sitting there right now, looking out at their garden. He might well be tormented but I bet he was there all the same, eating toast from the toaster I could see on the counter, drinking coffee from the French press that was almost out of shot. I scrolled and scrolled through those pictures until I wanted to cry and then I came to my senses and deleted the app yet again. Just like last time, I vowed I wouldn't use it again. This was like heroin to me. I had to stop.

After breakfast I couldn't bear to be in my flat anymore. I didn't feel safe there. Outside the sun was bright and full of promise for a long, hot day. I set off to walk along the river. It was pretty deserted down there at that time of the morning, with just the odd dog walker around, and I kept my head down and walked and walked for miles.

I should have known Harry would have tried to warn me he wasn't turning up that night. I should have known he wouldn't let me down like that. I forced myself to think about whether I still loved him. I knew I had. Then I remembered something he'd said, shortly before he left the café.

"*Just because it didn't last between us,*" he'd said, holding my hand tightly. He and I both knew that this was the last time we'd touch each other. "*Just because it didn't last, it doesn't mean it meant nothing to me. It meant everything, Ruby. For all those months you were the world to me.*"

I rubbed my eyes, determined not to cry again. I'd doubted him for so long. All those nights I'd spent after I'd left home, it was Harry who'd been on my mind. When I met him a year and a half ago I'd felt as though a light had come on in me and, when he didn't turn up that night, I thought it had died. Now I wasn't sure.

But I didn't want a man who could leave his pregnant wife. I knew that. We shouldn't have had an affair, but I knew that I wouldn't have gone near him if he'd had children. Envy shot through me. I wanted Emma's life.

Normally I would have called Sarah to chat to her but those days were gone. Then I thought of Oliver. He was a good friend. I would talk to him, tell him everything, and ask for his advice. I sent him a message:

Hi, are you free tonight? x

He replied immediately. Sorry, I'm off to Ibiza for ten days this afternoon. I'll be in touch when I get back x

My heart sank. I couldn't talk to Sarah; I couldn't forgive her for lying to me. I had to tackle Tom, but needed someone behind me, someone to back me up.

Oliver sent another message: I'm free for an hour now, if you like? Where are you?

I answered: I'm walking down by the river, near the lighthouse. I felt so weak right then. Can you come?

Wait there, he wrote. I won't be long.

Minutes later his car pulled up. He jumped out. "Oh, Ruby, you look awful. What's the matter?"

He sat next to me on the bench and hugged me. It felt so comfortable and warm, so welcoming, and I burst into tears.

He touched my arm. "What is it?"

"I don't know where to start," I said.

"Start at the beginning. What's happened?"

I took a deep breath. "You remember I told you I thought I'd met someone?"

"Harry?"

I stared at him. "Did I tell you his name?"

275

"You mentioned it, but I was out in Liverpool last night and bumped into Sarah and her husband."

"I'd forgotten you knew her."

"They were at Tom's birthday party last year, remember? She seemed angry with you. She told me you'd left home to be with your boss, but he'd dumped you."

"He didn't dump me!"

"He didn't turn up and you never heard from him again. That sounds like you were dumped."

"Well," I said, my face smarting. "I saw him by chance yesterday and do you know what he said?"

Oliver frowned. "Oh God, you're not going back to him, are you?"

"No. No, of course not. His wife's having a baby. That's why he stayed with her."

"And they say romance is dead." He shook his head. "You can do better than that, Ruby."

I didn't think I could, that was the trouble.

"He told me that he'd e-mailed me to tell me he couldn't leave his wife," I said. "I didn't get the message. Tom had my iPad that day. I think he read Harry's e-mail and deleted it before I could see it."

"So Tom knew that you were being dumped?" He saw my face. "Sorry, I mean he knew that the guy you were seeing wasn't going to leave home that night and yet he let you leave home without knowing that?"

"Yes, exactly that. He didn't say a word. I noticed that he hadn't asked whether I was leaving for someone else. I was glad at the time, of course, but afterwards, when I thought about it, it did seem strange."

"Do you wish you hadn't left home?"

I thought about it for a while. "No," I said slowly. "I wasn't happy with Tom. And just when things were really bad, I met Harry. I knew that I needed to leave Tom. That was true whether Harry stayed with me or not."

"Wow. I didn't know any of that was going on." He took a deep breath. "I always thought you'd leave Tom one day. I just didn't think it would be like that."

"You did?" I wondered whether he'd noticed the moods, the way I smiled less when I was with Tom, the way I'd tense up and find it hard to breathe at times. The way I came to life when I met Harry.

"Yes. I hoped you would." When I looked at him, surprised, his face was pink. "To be honest, I thought we might get together sometime." He must have seen my confusion. "You and me."

I felt a moment of utter panic. I'd never thought of Oliver as anything more than a friend, but if I rejected him now, I'd be left with no one.

"I don't know," I said. "I've never thought about it."

"We get on really well, Ruby. We could take things slowly. See how it goes."

He leaned toward me and I thought he was going to kiss me. Just then my phone beeped. Automatically I glanced over at it.

"Okay," he said. "I get it." He jumped up. "Are you still hoping Harry will come back to you? You're wasting your time." He got into his car and drove off without another word. I stared after him. He had now joined that growing band of people to avoid.

I looked down at my phone. It was a message from Sarah.

Thanks very much for that, Ruby. Harry has told me there isn't a future for me at Sheridan's.

Immediately I was hot with anger. I replied, Don't blame me! You lied to me. You said you'd given him my letter.

Within seconds another message appeared. You think he wanted your stupid letter? I told you, he read it and threw it in the bin.

I smarted at the thought of this and knew I'd never know the truth. Was Sarah lying to me, to hurt me? Or had Harry read the letter and just discarded it now that I wasn't any use to him?

277

Sarah must have been really fired up because another message came through.

And who do you think fired you? Eleanor? Really? Harry's her boss; she couldn't just fire his PA. Eleanor told me yesterday that as soon as he found out Emma was pregnant, he told her to terminate your contract. He told her that you hadn't worked there long enough to have any rights and when she said you could sue, he said he knew you wouldn't do that. Don't you get it? He doesn't want you, Ruby.

Chapter 62

Ruby

For a moment I thought my heart had stopped, then it banged hard in my chest and I made a noise as though the air had been knocked out of me. I felt so ashamed then, so humiliated. I went back to my flat, my eyes lowered and my shoulders hunched. I didn't want to meet anyone's eye, to talk to anyone. I needed to be alone, to lick my wounds in private.

Harry had never said a word to me about firing me. He'd sat there in the café, and yes, I'd noticed he was pale when I told him I was fired, but I thought that was because he was angry. Was his response guilt instead? Or fear?

Had he told me in the e-mail he'd sent that evening that I'd have to leave my job, or had he left it to Eleanor to deal with? Had he thought of me that Monday morning, turning up at work only to be fired? I found it so hard to reconcile that with the way he was with me. There had been no apology from him in the café. No excuses. He must have been so relieved that I'd been stupid enough to think Eleanor had done that herself. I'd always known I was a good liar, that I could fake reactions, keep an impassive face. I hadn't realised that Harry was the same.

I wanted to get away. I couldn't cope. I was just about to phone my dad in Australia, to plead with him to let me stay in his house for a while, just to get away from here, when I heard a bang on the front door. I leaped to my feet.

I ran to the top of the stairs and looked down, expecting yet another envelope through my door. There was nothing there. I looked out of the kitchen window, which was above the front door, and saw a small white van parked by the side of the road. A man dressed in overalls was standing beside it, looking up at my flat. When I went down, he introduced himself as Sean.

"Gill's asked me to call round," he said. "You want a bolt for your front door?"

"Yes, yes. Thank you. Could you change the locks while you're here?"

"Lost your keys? I'll have to charge for that."

"No," I said. "I think someone's been coming into my flat."

"That's odd. I change the locks after every tenant leaves so that they can't get back in. I was here just a few weeks ago. Is that when you moved in?"

"Yes. I've not been here long."

"Phone Gill while I put the lock on," he said. "If she agrees, I'll do it and won't charge."

"My phone's upstairs," I said. "Won't be a minute."

I called Gill from my bedroom. "Sean's here to put a bolt on the front door," I said. "Thanks for sending him over. I've asked him to change the locks as well but he said I had to check with you. I'm happy to pay."

"Has something happened?" she asked. "First it was a bolt, now the locks. Are you okay?"

"I thought someone was in my flat on Wednesday night. I woke up and heard the front door click."

She took a deep breath. "Oh my God, that's my worst nightmare. Of course you can get the locks changed."

"Thanks. It's hard, living on my own. If there's someone with you, you've got backup. It's terrifying when you're on your own."

"Wasn't your boyfriend there then?"

"I don't have a boyfriend."

"But you said…" She sounded confused. "You asked for a spare key for your boyfriend."

"What?"

"You e-mailed me. Hold on, let me check." She was quiet for a few moments. "Here it is. On June twenty-seventh. Wasn't that the day you moved in? You sent an e-mail asking for a spare key for your boyfriend."

I remembered that day. It was the day I'd gone to Manchester on that wild-goose chase and come home to find my dresses hanging up.

"Are you there?" she said. "Ruby, are you still there?"

I tried to pull myself together. "I didn't send that e-mail. Did you see the person who picked up the key?"

"No, I wasn't here then. I'll have to ask around." She sounded panicky now, exactly how I felt. "I'm really sorry, Ruby. The message was sent from your e-mail address. I had no reason to believe it wasn't from you."

"I know. Don't worry." I just wanted to get her off the phone now. "I'll sort it out."

"Was anything taken?" she asked. "Have you noticed anything's missing?"

"I don't know." But as I spoke my eyes rested on my bed, on the pillows. The scarf I'd been holding that night, that I'd put on the pillow beside me before I slept, had gone.

–

I ended the call quickly, wanting time to think, and then Sean banged on the door to ask whether Gill had agreed to the locks. All the while I behaved like usual and thanked him when he'd finished. As soon as he got into his van, I bolted the front door and hurried up the stairs to my flat. I checked every room. I didn't feel safe. I didn't think I ever would again.

Despite the heat of the day I was cold and shivering. I lit the gas fire in the living room and crouched beside it, my mind in free fall.

Tom had been in my flat. I knew that now. He'd got himself a key and come into my home. He'd moved my clothes and made coffee, knowing it would drive me crazy. I shuddered.

281

He'd been there in the middle of the night. He'd come into my bedroom. He'd taken my scarf, taken it from my pillow. What would he have done if I'd woken?

I took out my phone and scrolled through the blocked numbers. There were so many of them. Calls asking for sex. Shaming me. Was Tom behind that, too? He'd never admit it. I knew now he hated me. I think I knew that even when we were together. He must have been furious that I'd left him. And he'd sent messages again and again, lovely messages, as though he cared for me, while I was getting those calls from strangers. I was so glad I hadn't told him about them, so glad he'd never known how much they'd upset me.

I had no one to talk to. No one to confide in. Tom's work was done. He'd isolated me from people, made me think I was going mad. He told me he loved me but did everything he could to hurt me.

I found his number on my Recent Calls list. I couldn't trust myself to speak to him, so sent him a message.

Tom, are you working from home today? I need to talk to you.

I hesitated, then added a kiss at the end of my message.

Chapter 63

Emma

The next night, Harry came home later than usual. I was sitting at the table typing an e-mail to a client and he leaned over and gave me a quick kiss.

"What are you up to?" he asked.

"Oh, nothing. Just confirming a finish date."

Quickly I closed the laptop lid and stood up. It would be just my luck to get a message from the DNA clinic while Harry was sitting next to me.

"I was driving back from Birmingham this morning when I had a call from Henry Mathers in Nantwich," he said. "He asked if I'd call in for a chat. His office is in the market square right next to a cake shop so I bought some cakes for people at work." He put a box tied up with ribbons on the kitchen table. "And I couldn't miss you out."

"You wouldn't dare." Eagerly I opened the box and looked down at the beautifully glazed strawberry tart, the perfect pastel macarons, and the chocolate éclair with fresh cream spilling from it, but instead of my mouth watering with anticipation, I turned from them.

"I thought they were the ones you liked," said Harry.

"They are." I pushed the box away from me. "They look gorgeous. Thanks for bringing them. It's just this sickness. I can't wait for it to stop." I couldn't tell him that now I felt sick because I was being bullied by Ruby's husband.

I got up from the table to pour some water from the fridge. Iced water seemed to be the only thing that helped the nausea.

283

Harry stood, too, and wrapped his arms around me. I breathed in the safe familiar smell of his cologne, felt his heart beating against mine. He kissed me on the cheek but somehow it seemed automatic. I pulled back to look at him. His face was pale and strained and he looked distracted. It reminded me so much of how he was before I discovered I was pregnant, and my heart fell. Was his recent change of mood over? I couldn't bear to go back to the way we were.

"Are you all right?" I asked anxiously. "Everything okay at work?"

"I'm fine." He stretched out his arms and sighed. "It was just a busy day. All I want to do is to relax."

"Come and sit down. Fancy a beer?"

We sat at the kitchen table and he had a beer and I had water while he ate one of my cakes. That was inevitable. All I could think of was my phone, on vibrate in my jeans pocket, as I waited for an e-mail to come through about the DNA of my baby. I knew it was too late for them to contact me but I couldn't turn it off just in case. I had to know the very second there was news.

When my phone did vibrate I nearly collapsed.

"Is that your phone?" asked Harry. He took another beer from the fridge. He had no clue what that message would mean for us.

I kept my face as still as I could and took the phone from my pocket. It was a message from Tom. Immediately I switched off my phone.

"Just work stuff," I said. "I don't want to think about it now."

He gave me a quizzical look because I'd never shown such a lack of interest in work and would always answer messages in the evening.

"I'm tired," I said. "It can wait."

When Harry was in the shower later on, I took out my phone and stealthily checked the message. Tom had sent so many that I'd ignored: He wanted to come to the scan with me, he would be at the birth. He sent me links to cots and buggies and clothes and teddies, asking what I liked. He wanted to share everything with me.

He told me that I didn't have to worry, he'd always be by my side.

Chapter 64

Emma

My eyes snapped open when Harry's alarm went off the next morning. Today was the fifth working day after I'd been tested and I knew the results could be in that day. Though our backs were to each other, I felt him reach out to turn off the alarm. He'd changed the alarm ringtone so it played a new song every day and there was always a reference to babies. This morning it was "Baby Love" and he laughed as he heard it and rolled over to hug me. I wanted to shake him off, to warn him not to get too excited, that the baby might not be his, but how could I? I might as well let him have this one last morning of ignorance. So I lay still, pretending to be asleep, and he edged away quietly and crept out of the room, leaving me to have a bit more time to myself.

As soon as I heard the bathroom door shut, I scrabbled for my phone and checked my e-mails. Of course there was nothing. Nobody would be at work for a couple of hours at least. I wondered about the staff who worked in a clinic like that. If they sent back DNA results to say that the alleged father wasn't the father, did they wince as they e-mailed the results, knowing the damage it could cause? Were they totally unsympathetic, thinking the woman had brought it on herself?

At that thought I hastily got up and pulled on my dressing gown. I couldn't lie there thinking about anonymous people judging me. There would be enough people I knew doing that soon enough. Downstairs I put the radio on and started to make coffee and toast for Harry. At last I wasn't feeling sick at the smell, though I wouldn't be able to touch it myself. He seemed preoccupied, too, and sat at the kitchen table in silence while I made a pretence of gathering everything I needed for work. I needed to go to work early today. I knew that once I had the results I would be fit for nothing.

Harry hugged me as he said good-bye and kissed my cheek. I moved to kiss him, but stopped short. The last thing I wanted him to remember was my traitorous kiss. So I hugged him hard and told him I loved him. I do. I always have. And then I watched him go out to his car and drive away, knowing that the next time I saw him, everything would be different.

–

The e-mail came through just before two o'clock that afternoon. I'd been deep in work, forcing myself not to think about it. This was the earliest day I could expect a result; I might have to wait for a few days longer. Annie was on the phone to a client and I was busying myself with e-mails when a notification slid up from the bottom of my screen. It slid down again, but not before I'd seen the words *Paternity Test* in the heading.

My heart banged so hard I thought Annie would hear it, but when I turned to look at her, she was still deep in conversation, making notes as she talked. She wasn't taking any notice of me. Clumsily I picked up my phone. I couldn't read the message here. I needed to go somewhere private. I picked up my car keys. I would read the e-mail in the privacy of my car.

Annie glanced up at me. She put her hand over her phone and whispered, "Don't forget I'm going home in a minute. It's the last day of term and the kids are finishing early."

I nodded and waved. I walked downstairs instead of waiting for the lift, feeling dizzy with fear. This was the moment. Now I would know.

I got into my car and opened the e-mail tab. The message appeared at the top of my inbox. I took a deep breath. I wanted to delete it without reading it, to stick my head back in the sand and act as though none of this was happening. I wanted to drive to Harry and hold him tight and tell him everything. I wanted him to say it didn't matter, it really didn't matter who the father was. He would be the baby's real father.

But I couldn't do that. I couldn't do it to him.

I saw Annie hurry from the building and drive her car out of the car park. I knew that one day I'd be doing that, racing to pick up my child, and I'd be doing it no matter what the results of this test said. That gave me the courage to open the e-mail. I quickly scrolled down the screen, desperately trying to understand what it said. It seemed as though it was written in a foreign language; then I realised it was written in a way that might be used against someone. In court.

I read the e-mail three times. I don't know how long I sat there before I understood what it said. I went back to the office to pick up my bag.

I needed to talk to Tom.

Chapter 65

Ruby

Through habit I parked in my usual place by the side of the road. Tom's car was on the driveway. Just as I reached the front door, a black BMW pulled up onto the drive, blocking in Tom's car.

A man in his fifties jumped out and opened the doors for a younger couple who were sitting in the backseat. I had no idea who any of them were.

"Can I help you?" I asked.

Just then the front door opened and Tom came outside. He was smartly dressed in a suit and tie and beamed at the visitors. "Hello, John, it's good to see you again. Is this Mr. and Mrs. Sampson?" He shook their hands. "Nice to meet you. Come on in."

I stood there like a fool while all of them backslapped one another, then the couple turned to me, as though wondering why on earth I was there.

"I'm Ruby Dean," I said.

They did a double take, then turned as one to Tom for verification.

He came over to me and kissed my cheek. "This is my wife," he said to them.

Then there were effusive hellos in my direction and they trooped into the house.

"I wasn't expecting them to get here this early," Tom whispered to me. He smiled. "I'll show them round and then we can talk."

It seemed he thought we were going to have quite a different kind of chat.

"Let's start with the kitchen," said Tom to the potential buyers.

I couldn't bear it. The kitchen had been my domain. My home, really. I'd bought every single thing in it; everything was the way I wanted it. I couldn't stand to see someone else go into it and judge it.

"I'll wait in the living room," I said. "You don't want too many people around." I stood in the doorway and looked around. Everything in this room was Tom's: The cameras and books on photography. The pictures he'd bought and put up without any thought of consultation. I liked some of them, but that was irrelevant. I'd learned not to tell him if I liked something; I'd known it to disappear. Whenever I said I liked something there'd be a silence or worse, laughter. "You shouldn't take it personally," he'd said. "It's not a reflection on you that you don't have good taste." I thought that's exactly what it was.

While they wandered the house I sat down in my usual place on the sofa by the window and I listened to the murmurs of approval and exclamations of delight, and the soothing sounds of the estate agent and Tom, who seemed to be in harmony with each other as they showed Mr. and Mrs. Sampson around my home. Meanwhile my stomach was tight and knotted and all I could think was, *You have tried to destroy me*.

By the time they left, I felt as though I was ready to explode.

Chapter 66

Ruby

The front door shut behind them with a click. Tom shouted that he was just going upstairs to get changed, and within a couple of minutes I heard him back in the kitchen.

I was on full alert and strained to hear what he was up to. I heard the kettle being filled with water, then a click as it was switched on. I heard mugs being placed on the counter, a spoon taken from its drawer. The noises were so familiar; they were the soundtrack to my life there. I could picture Tom as he moved about, staring into the garden while he waited for the kettle to boil, his back straight, his hands on the edge of the counter.

And then I heard something else and leaned forward to hear better. It was the sound of a cupboard door opening in the utility room. I knew it was the cupboard where we kept our drinks. There was the clink of a glass on the granite counter and then a glugging sound. The glass was lifted for a couple of seconds, then put down again. The sounds were repeated. Then the dishwasher door opened and shut.

I frowned. Was he drinking alcohol at this time of day? We kept the wine in the fridge or on the wine rack. I hadn't heard the click and hiss of a bottle or can opening; he couldn't be drinking beer. That cupboard held the spirits and liqueurs. What was he drinking? My mind flashed back: Had he always drunk like that, sneakily, without my knowing? It was as though the veil was slowly being lifted, as though I was seeing him for what he truly was.

I guessed he was wondering why I was there. Did he think his little romantic messages had done the trick? Did he think I'd fallen for his charms, unable to resist him? I used to think he thought I was stupid; now I knew he did.

–

When he came into the living room I saw he'd changed into his old grey T-shirt and jeans. He was barefoot and looked happy and carefree. He carried a tray in with the coffee. He'd used the better crockery, the stuff we kept for guests. I supposed I was one now. On the tray was a plate of biscuits and I realised he was trying to impress, as though a well-presented tea tray would make up for trying to drive me crazy.

He poured coffee from the French press and passed me a mug, then sat down on the sofa opposite me.

"It's good to see you, Ruby," he said, as though he was used to me dropping by. As though we had no history between us. As though we weren't at war. "How're things?"

I said nothing. I took the coffee, more for something to do, and sipped it. He could never make a good cup of coffee, and this was no different. I would have been better off with the vodka, or whatever it was he'd been fortifying himself with. But I was glad of the warmth and wrapped my hands around the mug. I hadn't realised until then how cold my hands were.

I wanted to say something, to accuse him, but I was frightened of breaking down.

"John seems to think that couple will make an offer," said Tom.

Distracted, I said, "Who's John?"

"That guy who was here just now. The estate agent. Mind you, he's said that before."

I tried hard to keep my tone civil. "Have many people shown an interest in the house?"

He shrugged. "A few. Some were time-wasters. Others wanted to knock too much off the price. The Sampsons have just come back from living in South Africa and they're cash buyers." He took a biscuit and drank some coffee; he looked like he was enjoying it and I resented every mouthful he took. "If they offer a reduced price, what do you think? Shall we just go for it? How far should we go? Five percent?"

I nodded. The sooner it sold, the sooner I could get away from here. The way I felt at the moment I would have sold it for half the price.

He finished his coffee and I noticed when he put his mug down on the tray, his hands were shaking. I wondered whether that was the drink or whether he was nervous. And then he leaned forward and said in his most sincere voice, "Is this what you really want, Ruby?"

I spoke carefully, trying to control myself. "Yes. Let's just sell up and call it a day."

"It doesn't have to be like this, babe," he said. "Can we talk about it? Can we try again? We're both at fault, really. Can't we patch things up? What do you think?"

For twelve years I'd managed to hide my feelings, but that moment was an exception. He saw my reaction and flushed a dark red. He started to speak, but then his phone rang and he picked it up, his eyes still on me.

"Hi, Gary." I knew this was his boss at work. "Yeah, all good, thanks." There was a pause, then he said, "Sure, do you want to go through it now?"

He reached out to grab a pen and paper from the coffee table, and I stood up and left the room. I could feel his eyes on me as I left. I could hear Tom talking and thought he'd be busy for a while. His boss wasn't one for short conversations and it sounded as though Tom was going through some sales figures with him.

I had so many questions to ask him that I didn't know where to start. I wanted to talk about him deleting Harry's e-mail, to ask why he had hidden that from me. I wanted to ask him how he'd felt when he saw me drive off with my car full of bags, knowing I'd end up homeless. But really, that wasn't what was important.

The thing I really wanted was to talk about him coming into my home. Trying to make me lose my mind. And then coming in at night, into my bedroom. Taking my scarf from my pillow as I slept. At the thought of that I felt breathless and faint. I wanted to confront him but I knew I shouldn't. I was too angry.

While he chatted away to his boss, as though he hadn't a care in the world, I went upstairs. I needed to calm down. To make myself think rationally. While I was here, I should take some more of my things. It would be autumn in a couple of months. I didn't want to come back here until it was time to empty the house completely and that could be ages away.

I heard Tom move to the bottom of the stairs, clearly frustrated that he couldn't tell me to get back downstairs.

I went into my bedroom. My old bedroom. Now it was Tom's, of course. The suit he'd been wearing was on a wooden hanger on the back of the door and his black leather shoes were kicked into a corner. I avoided looking at the bed and went straight over to my section of the fitted wardrobes. Nothing of mine was there. Tom had taken over some of it, but the rest lay empty. I frowned. What had happened to the rest of my things? I opened the drawers I'd used since we'd had the house. I'd had to leave some clothes there when I left home. Now the drawers were all empty.

I went into the spare room, thinking he might have packed the clothes up, ready for me to take. I knew he shouldn't have to do that, but maybe he'd thought he was being useful. My heart sank as I saw the bookcase was empty and there was no sign of any of my books. I must have had an inkling that something like this would happen as I'd photographed the shelves before I left, just in case. I could replace them, but new copies just wouldn't be the same. I looked inside the suitcases that stood by the side of the wardrobe. They were empty. I checked under the bed. Nothing.

And then I felt a dull thud in my stomach; I knew what was going to happen now. I threw open the wardrobe doors and thrust my hand to the back of the top shelf, past the spare pillows and the woollen throw, trying to find the box. It wasn't there.

My memory box was made of ruby red leather and bought for me when I was born by my aunt. I'd loved her and lost her to cancer years ago. My name was embossed on the box in gold lettering, and I'd used it all my life for the things that were precious to me. In it had been photos from my childhood, of my parents when they were young. A narrow silver bracelet that my first boyfriend had bought me; my first mobile phone, long defunct. Letters from my school friends when we all went off to different universities. My diaries in which I'd kept count of my menstrual cycle, so that I could work out my fertile periods. A tiny white velvet sleepsuit that I'd bought on the day we first decided to try for a baby. I used to hold it to me to imagine what it would be like to hold a child. And, tucked away in a little envelope, with nothing but the date written on it, was the scan photo of my baby, my only child, the one I'd lost when I was eighteen.

Panic surged through me. I pulled out the pillows and threw them onto the bed. I checked at the foot of the wardrobe but there was just his snorkelling gear and old running shoes.

I turned to leave the spare room, to check whether it was in Josh's room, but Tom was standing in the doorway.

"Where is it?" I asked. "What have you done with it?"

Chapter 67

Ruby

For a second he looked as though he was going to carry on pretending he didn't know what I was talking about, but then he said calmly, "Oh, it probably went out with the trash last week."

"What?"

"You're the one who wanted to sell the house. I didn't see you dealing with it. I was just getting rid of things so that there wouldn't be too much to do at the end."

I walked toward him. I felt as though my head was about to burst. All I could feel was buzzing and tingling and I think he must have seen he'd gone too far, because he took a step back onto the landing to avoid me.

"You've thrown it out?" I knew my voice sounded weird. I was trying hard to breathe properly and when I spoke my voice was high-pitched and breathy.

He shrugged. "I've thrown a lot of stuff out."

He had. And it was all my stuff.

By now my head was swimming. I took another step toward him. "But it wasn't *stuff*. It was important to me. Private."

"You never looked at it anyway." He took another step backward. "It was just taking up space."

For a moment I closed my eyes. I thought of the house and how, apart from the kitchen, you would never have known I lived there. This was something of mine and it was hidden from view, as were all my things. That box held my memories. He'd destroyed it, just as he'd tried to destroy me.

I had to say something. I had to. I'd been quiet for too long.

"I know you deleted my e-mail," I said.

Shock flashed across his face. "Which e-mail?"

He wasn't fooling me. "You know which one I mean." I said nothing more but let the silence lay heavily in the air.

Then his face changed, became ugly and dark. All of his flattery disappeared and I could see what he really thought of me. I recoiled.

"Oh, Harry's e-mail." He mimicked Harry, then: "*I'm so sorry, Ruby, but I can't leave Emma. She's pregnant and all I've ever wanted was a family.* Yeah, I probably shouldn't have deleted that." He laughed. "Oh, and…"

"What?"

He shook his head, smiling at me. "You'll find out soon enough."

My heart pounded. I thought of him reading my e-mails, following my search for jobs, reading my draft e-mails to Harry that I'd never sent, telling him I loved him and needed him and would always be there for him. But that wasn't what concerned me now.

My blood started to simmer. "That's not all though, is it?"

He shrugged. "I don't know what you're talking about."

"You came into my flat, didn't you?"

He raised his eyebrows. "Are you having delusions again?"

"What? What do you mean?"

"Like all those times you thought you were pregnant." Now he imitated me, his face twisted and hateful. "*I know I've said this before, Tom, but I really think I am pregnant this time.*"

I felt my face collapse and saw his glee. I realised then just how deep his hatred of me was.

"So you think I came into your flat? What did I do there?"

I bit my lip, frustrated. How could I say, *You made a cup of coffee* or *You hung up my dresses* or *You took the scarf my lover gave me*? I knew what he'd say in response.

"It doesn't matter," I said. "I know it was you."

He smirked. "Really? *Really?*"

"Are you mocking me?" In that moment I just lost it. "You thought you could control me!" He jumped. I'd probably only shouted a couple of times throughout our marriage. "You thought you could run my life!"

"Do you really think I'm that interested in you?" he sneered. "You think I waste any time thinking about you? I've got other things to think about. You're nothing. Absolutely nothing."

And I knew that was true. I couldn't help myself. I reached out to strike him.

He reared back, out of the bedroom. Now we were both on the landing. "Hey!" he said. "Don't do that."

"Don't do that." Now it was my turn to mimic. "Do this, do that. Live like this." I stopped and roared, "Stop telling me what to do. And stop following me."

"What are you talking about? You're mad."

"You know exactly what I'm talking about." I'd stopped yelling now. "And stop putting my phone number on those sites."

"I was doing you a favour! I thought you might like some company, now that you're all on your own."

"Just leave me alone." All I felt was weariness. "You try to control me with every breath you take."

He laughed. "Are you kidding? You're the one who left."

"Because I couldn't stand it anymore."

"No. You left so that you could sleep with another man. Own it, Ruby."

And then I realised. That wasn't why I left. I thought I'd left to be with Harry, but actually I'd left to get away from Tom. I didn't even really know Harry. We'd spent only two nights together. We'd never had a fight, never disagreed, even. We'd taken that to be a sign of compatibility, rather than a sign we didn't really know each other that well.

I stopped still at that thought. All I could hear was the sound of us panting. "So why were you sending me all those messages?" There was still a part of me that wanted to believe Tom had loved me once. "Why did you say you loved me and missed me?"

"You idiot. Did you really believe I meant that?" He laughed. "You think I want you?" He shook his head. "Unbelievable." He leaned toward me. "Every little message I sent you brought you closer to me."

"But why? Why would you do that?"

"Do you really think you get to say when this marriage ends? That you can just leave whenever you like?" He spoke as though I was stupid. A fool. "That's not your decision, Ruby. It never has been. I get to decide whether you stay or go."

"I did leave, though," I said. "And do you want to know why I left?" I reached out and pushed his shoulder.

He jumped backward. "Stop it!"

"I left because I didn't want to be with you anymore. You and your lies and your control. Telling me what to do all the time. What to think." I stopped, sickened. "I couldn't stand it anymore."

"Well, you've made such a success of being on your own, Ruby. All you've got is a man who won't leave his wife for you. Obviously you're too boring for him, too. Did you wait a long time that night? When did you realise he wasn't going to show? That was so funny, watching you go off with your little bags. Did you really think I wouldn't notice your car was full of all your things? I just wish I could have seen your face when you realised he wasn't going to turn up."

I screamed, "You bastard!"

He laughed. He pushed his face into mine and I smelled the alcohol, sour on his breath. "You are crazy," he said. Spittle landed on my face and I scrubbed my skin with my hand, repulsed. "You've always been crazy."

I'd had enough. I couldn't stand to see him anymore. I could feel the blood coursing through my veins. I was struggling and knew I should leave, but I just wanted to have the last word.

"Not any longer," I said, and reached out. I didn't want to touch him. I just wanted some space between us.

He leaned back, holding on to the handrail at the top of the stairs. Now, later, I realise that he was on the top step, but I didn't understand the significance then.

He seemed to swell with rage, to tower over me, terrifying me.

He said, "Why would I want you when I've got someone else?" His eyes were wild. "Someone beautiful. Clever. Funny. It's such a nice change." He reached out and jabbed me in the chest, hard. I found a bruise as dark as an olive there later. "And guess what?" He looked triumphant. "She's pregnant."

"What?" I couldn't believe it. "Pregnant?"

"Yes. She's pregnant with my child. I knew it was your fault we couldn't have a baby." He mimicked me again: "*It'll be so lovely to have a baby in the house.*" He laughed. "Well, now I'll have that. Unlike you, on your own in your cheap lousy flat."

I swear I didn't think about where he was standing, at the top of the stairs. All I could think of was that he would have what I wanted most. That he'd ruined my life and would be happy. He was right – I had nothing now. I felt a red mist rising and I swung my hand up to slap him. I wanted to slap him so hard. He could tell, and jerked back before I could touch him.

His hand loosened on the banister rail and I saw him try to grab it again. He took another step back but his foot couldn't find the step. I saw him stagger back, his arms windmilling. His eyes were wild and he reached out toward me.

I could have grabbed him. I really could have.

But I didn't.

Chapter 68

Ruby

It seemed to take an age before he reached the bottom of the stairs. There was a tremendous crack as he hit his head on the tiled floor. His body twisted in response.

All I could see was him. Nothing else.

I crouched by the side of him. The colour had drained from his face and his eyes were closed. I was going to move him, to see if he'd come to, but one glance at his twisted body told me not to. If I moved him, I might make things worse.

I saw blood seeping from his ear and my heart beat fast in a panicky tattoo. What should I do? I knew I should call for an ambulance, but it might be too late.

And then I thought: *I should take his pulse.* I touched the inside of his wrist. My hands were clammy with sweat and my fingers slid on his skin. I couldn't feel anything. I didn't know whether I was doing it right so I felt again. Nothing. His other hand lay under him.

Panic rose in me. I thought the emergency services would want to know if he had a pulse. He looked like he was asleep. Okay, he'd clearly done some damage to his head, and his back looked so wrong, but surely that wouldn't stop me finding a pulse? Desperately I tried to remember the training I'd had in first aid when I was in school; I remembered the teacher talking about the carotid artery but I couldn't remember where she said it was. I pressed my fingers on the side of his neck. There was no pulse, no sensation under my fingers. I couldn't feel anything except his cool skin.

Frantically I thought maybe I was touching the wrong side of his neck; maybe I should check the other side. I moved back and just then the light in the room changed. Suddenly it was darker.

My back was to the door. I looked up, into the long mirror that hung on the wall in the hallway.

I froze.

Someone was looking through the pane of glass by the front door.

She'd seen everything.

And I knew who she was.

Chapter 69

Emma

I was just about to knock on Tom's front door when I heard them. A woman was yelling at a man. All the windows were shut but the glass in the hallway was the original stained glass: it was beautiful, but not soundproof. I don't suppose they'd considered that when they moved in.

The shouting seemed to come from upstairs. I pressed closer to the window, all the better to hear. I could hear a woman yell, "You bastard!" and I thought, *Oh, that sounds interesting*. I could hear him try to answer back but she wasn't having it. She was livid.

And then I saw Tom standing at the top of the stairs. His back was to me, but it was him, all right. He had a grey T-shirt on that I remembered him wearing the night we met, and a pair of jeans. He was barefoot and just before it happened, I saw the legs of his jeans were just that bit too long.

He put out his hand to whoever he was fighting with. I couldn't see who it was. He reached over and held the rail, then let go of it and thrust his hand out again. A woman's hand batted it away and he moved to one side. Her voice was low now; I couldn't hear what she said, but I could get the gist of it. The tone was not nice.

This time when he tried to hold the rail he couldn't reach it. I don't know whether she thought he was reaching out for her because she knocked his hand away harder this time. He took a step back. And then it was like slow motion, where I could see his foot on the edge of the stairs, could see his jeans were too long. He turned to grab the rail and his jeans caught under his foot. His foot reached out for a step that wasn't there. And then he twisted and fell. He crashed down those stairs, his arms and legs flailing, and there was a loud crack as he hit his head on the tiled floor.

I held my breath. I knew I should call the police, the ambulance. Someone. But I couldn't move.

Then I saw her. It was Ruby. Tom's ex-wife. Harry's ex-lover. Hopefully. I'd thought it would be someone else, thought she'd moved out. I recognised her from the airport, where she was kissing my husband, the night I slept with her husband. She walked downstairs, her face pale and determined. She looked shocked, but she didn't look upset. She crouched beside him and felt for his pulse, in his wrist first, then on the side of his neck. It was clear she hadn't a clue what she was doing.

And as she knelt there, doing her amateur diagnosis, my first thought was: *I could ruin your life, Ruby Dean. Only you and I know what happened just now, and who would believe you? Tom's a bully and you're a cheat. Now he's unconscious at the bottom of your stairs. Who would believe that was an accident?*

Ruby's whole body trembled as she tried to find a pulse. With a shock I saw how thin she was now, much thinner than when I saw her at the airport with Harry, and how scared she looked as she touched Tom, as though he'd rear up and hit her. I winced. I'd seen myself as Tom's victim; I hadn't realised she was, too. I should have known. I really should have known.

When I looked at Ruby and Tom together, my overwhelming feeling was of relief that all this had ended. For a moment I didn't know whether to turn Ruby in and hope she spent the rest of her days in solitary confinement, or to shake her hand. And then I felt the strangest sensation, as though my baby was making its presence felt. It was still too small for me to feel movements, but in that split second when I held Ruby's future in my hands, I knew I needed to do the right thing. It was time for this war to end.

As I moved to get a better view, she looked up into the mirror that was on the hallway wall. She saw my face through the glass and she jerked back.

I tapped on the window.

Chapter 70

Ruby

"Let me in," she said, as though we were friends. As though this was a preplanned visit for a glass of wine or a book group, maybe. This was my lover's wife and she'd tracked me down!

I didn't know what to do. I backed away and flattened myself against the wall, away from Tom and away from her.

She tapped again.

"Ruby, it's me. Emma."

I knew who she was, all right. That was why I wasn't going to let her in.

"Let me in. I want to help you."

I stared at her through the glass. *Help me?*

She nodded. "Hurry!"

I hesitated, then went over to the door. I turned the latch and opened the door wide. She came in and quickly shut the door behind her.

She looked down at Tom's body, then back at me. "Is he breathing?" she asked briskly.

I shook my head, unable to speak.

She took a little cosmetic mirror from her bag and knelt beside him. She held the mirror to his mouth for a few seconds, then looked at it. There was no mist on it.

"That's how you check for breathing," she said. "I read about it in a book." She spoke as though I might find this information useful another day. Then she pressed her fingers on his neck.

She felt again and again, then tried his wrist. She shook her head, but her face gave nothing away.

She stood with an "Oomph" and took out her phone.

I stood frozen as she said, "Ambulance, please. It's an emergency. There's been an accident." She gave my address, then said, "My friend's husband's just tripped and fallen downstairs. He tripped on his jeans. He's banged his head and there's blood coming out of his ear. His back's all twisted. I think it's broken. I've checked for a pulse but I can't feel anything." She gave a gulp as though she was crying, but her eyes were dry. "I think he's dead."

At that I started to cry. Huge choking sobs overcame me. I kept reliving that moment where I could have grabbed his hand. I don't know what I'd thought would happen but I hadn't expected this. And yet I knew in that moment I was so furious I probably would have thought, *Good!* if someone had told me he'd die if I didn't hold on to him. I went into the kitchen and sat at the table there, sobbing for everything I'd lost. I could hear Emma in the hallway, still on the phone.

She called to me, "They're on their way, Ruby. Don't worry, they won't be long." She ended the call and came into the kitchen. "I'll put the kettle on. You must be in shock. Tea or coffee?"

I could still taste the coffee that Tom had made and thought I was going to be sick.

"I don't want a drink," I said.

"I'll make one anyway."

She passed me a box of tissues and I took a handful, then she moved about the kitchen as though she owned it, finding tea bags and mugs and milk. I edged away, still scared of her. Why was she here? Had she found out about Harry and me?

While the kettle boiled she pulled out a chair from its place by the dining table and said, "Now I need you to listen to me."

I stared at her, terrified.

"You were in the living room," she said. "Tom was upstairs. You were waiting for him to come downstairs to talk about whether to reduce the house price or not. And then you heard the crash. The living room door was half-closed. You didn't see him fall. When you heard the crash you went into the hall, saw him on the floor, and then you saw me through the glass, just as it happened. Exactly as it happened, remember? You had felt his pulse and were crouching down and that's when you noticed me. But I'd seen everything. I saw him fall downstairs and saw you come out of the living room."

I couldn't make sense of it.

"Let's go into the living room now." She guided me in there. I was shaking so hard it was difficult to walk. "Now sit in your usual place."

I collapsed onto the sofa.

"Look at the door. That's how it was when he fell. You can't see the hallway from there. And that's where you were sitting when you heard him fall."

I thought she was trying to trick me. I started to speak, to object, but she interrupted me.

"And there's coffee here. Did you have a drink with Tom?"

I nodded. I actually thought she was crazy at this point. "He was showing some people around the house and then he got changed out of his suit and made me a cup of coffee."

"So why had he gone upstairs? Think!" she urged. "What could he have been looking for upstairs?"

I knew now what she meant but I couldn't think straight. I pointed to my iPad on the windowsill, behind the curtain. "He was looking for the iPad. We were going to look at other houses online, to compare prices."

"That's great. Perfect. And he couldn't find it and he was in a hurry and fell downstairs." She gave me an encouraging smile. "Now listen to me carefully. You and I met in a yoga class in Liverpool."

It took a moment for this to register. "What?"

She repeated it. "We met in a yoga class in Liverpool."

I was trying to get my head around Tom lying on the hallway floor and Harry's wife sitting in my living room, talking about yoga. I snapped, "I don't do yoga!"

She sighed. "You don't get it. Listen to me. We went to yoga in Matthew Street. I can't remember the name of the studio and neither can you. We used to pay in cash. The instructor went off to India. To Goa, I think." She spoke so confidently I thought it must have happened. Had I really met her before? "Her name was Janie. I gave you a lift home a couple of times and that's how I knew where you lived."

"How *did* you know where I lived?"

"I told you," she said. "I gave you a lift home from yoga. And today I was out and drove past your house and saw the *For Sale* sign. I'm having a baby." She gave me a sidelong glance and I flushed scarlet. "As you know. I'm looking for a new house. And I saw your car outside so I thought I'd pop in and ask for a look around."

I stared at her. "You want to live here?"

"No, of course I don't!" She sighed as though I was stupid. "That's what I'll tell them."

I could hear the sound of a siren; it sounded as though it was a way away, but it was hard to tell. Panic was rising in me and I felt like I wanted to run on the spot.

She said, "Tell me how we know each other."

I was terrified; would I have to tell her I'd driven past her house and seen her kissing Harry? "I didn't mean to..."

"Forget that," she said urgently. "Tell me what I said."

"We went to yoga."

"That's right. Good. It was a beginners' class. We were useless and stopped going. It was ten pounds an hour. In Matthew Street. Two or three years ago. We didn't know each other beforehand. We haven't seen each other since."

Finally I got it. I nodded.

"And tell me where you were when Tom fell downstairs."

"I was here," I said, slowly. I'd stopped crying by now. I knew how vital this was. "He was showing people around the house; they seemed to like it. After they left he popped up to his office to look for his iPad. We wanted to check what other houses in the street had sold for. I was waiting for him to come downstairs. And I also wanted to talk to him about Josh's eighteenth birthday. I wanted to ask Tom what I could buy him."

I stopped dead in my tracks, realising that Josh had just lost his father. All the breath seemed to leave my body and I could feel my eyes bulging. Emma jumped up and put my head in my lap, telling me to breathe, that everything would be all right. I knew it wouldn't, though. Not for Josh.

"What happened then?" she whispered in my ear. "What are you going to say happened then?"

It took a huge effort to lift my head up. She was giving me an encouraging look, her face pale but resolute.

"I heard a crash and a shout," I said, remembering my lines. "I rushed out into the hallway."

"I know," she said. "I saw you."

"He was at the bottom of the stairs." At last this part was true. I started to cry. "His body was twisted and his eyes were shut and his ear was bleeding."

"And then?"

"I took his pulse. I remembered how to from school."

"Actually you didn't," she said. "But never mind that."

The siren grew louder and I knew it was near my street.

"It's just as it happened, but you were in the living room. You and Tom were getting on well. You were in the living room, heard him fall, saw me at the front door. Remember?"

I could hardly concentrate. I didn't know what she was doing there. When I saw her I thought she'd hunted me down, intending to hurt me, but now she was helping me. "Why are you doing this for me?" I asked.

For a moment I saw pity on her face, then her eyes hardened. "Don't flatter yourself, Ruby. Your husband tried to destroy me. You've just done me a huge favour. I'm hardly going to turn you in."

"But you don't even know him!"

"Oh yes, I do." She fumbled in her handbag and brought out an envelope. Inside it were two sheets of paper, one scrawled on, one typed. She handed me the typed copy. "Read it."

Honestly, I had no idea what was going to be on it. No idea at all. I opened the sheet of paper and stared blankly at it.

On the paper was a table of figures. I saw *DNA* and *99.99%*. I blinked. I didn't have a clue what I was looking at. Then I saw the word: *Mother*. Next to it was: *Emma Sheridan*. It seemed to take a long time for my eyes to find the words *Biological Father*. There it said, *Harry Sheridan*.

I looked up at her. It was too late to pretend we didn't know each other.

"Why do you think I was here?" she said gently.

Still I didn't get it. And the ambulance was roaring up the street with its sirens blaring. Blue lights flashed through the window as it parked on the path behind Tom's car.

Slowly she put the document and the envelope into her bag and turned to look me straight in the eyes. "You're not the only one who can sleep with someone's husband," she said.

Chapter 71

Emma

They bought it. Totally and utterly bought it. After all, I was an independent witness who said Ruby was in the living room at the time Tom accidentally fell downstairs. Why would I lie about that? Even I wasn't always sure why I had. Not really.

She stayed in the kitchen while the ambulance crew was there. She was crying so hard by then. Well, we both were. I don't know whether her tears were from losing him or from the shock of being responsible. Which she was, really.

For me, it was his T-shirt, I think, that started me off. It was the same one he'd worn the night I'd slept with him. As he lay on the hallway floor I had a sudden memory of him lying on their spare-room bed. I'd pushed his T-shirt up and was kissing his chest. I knew how that T-shirt felt. I knew how his skin felt beneath it. I'd felt his heart beat hard against my mouth and had known he was excited and terrified. It was the same for me. And now I knew it wouldn't beat again. That's what made me cry.

The police were so nice to us. Much nicer than we deserved. The ambulance crew disappeared as soon as the police arrived. They'd established Tom was dead; he'd died immediately when his head had hit the tiled floor. They told us over a thousand people in the UK die from falling down stairs every year. Many of them are drunk, and they said they could smell alcohol on Tom's breath. Ruby told them that she thought she'd heard him in the kitchen, having a sneaky drink while he made some

312

coffee, and the police officer found vodka in a glass in the dishwasher.

The police called the duty undertaker and then called in a crime scene manager, who secured the house. A photographer arrived to take photos of the scene before Tom was taken away, but I was in the living room and Ruby in the kitchen by then, giving brief statements. I told the officer I was pregnant and he hurried to make me some hot, sweet tea. I had to force myself to drink it and when I was sick they thought it was because Tom had died.

Ruby looked to be in shock when she came back into the living room; her face was so pale I thought she'd faint. She looked at me as though she hardly recognised me, which wasn't surprising, really, but while we waited for the undertaker to arrive she let me sit next to her and hold her. After Tom was taken away, the police locked up the house and kept the keys. They said she could have them back in a few days and she seemed too stunned to respond. We stood outside the house afterwards. Our cars were parked next to each other and we sat in her car for a while, neither of us knowing what to do. We swapped numbers, just as though we were normal people, as though we didn't have this history between us. As though we hadn't slept with each other's husbands and covered up the death of hers. She was going back to her flat, she said. It seemed like she had no one she could call on. Nobody she could talk to. It was exactly the same for me.

It was two weeks before I heard from her again.

—

She sent me a message early one Friday morning, two weeks after Tom died. I was taking a long weekend so I was at home on my own; Harry had gone in to work. Had she known that? I was just trying on my new yoga pants; there was a pregnancy yoga session on at the gym in town that morning and I thought I'd give it a go. I had every intention of being one of those lithe and relaxed yummy mummies that you see on adverts. And yes, when I put them on I thought of Ruby and me in our fictional yoga class, but then she was always on my mind.

When I saw the message: Hi, it's me. Are you free for a chat? my knees were suddenly so weak I had to sit down on the bed. Had something happened? Was she going to warn me that the police would call?

I took a deep breath. If they were going to contact me, I needed to know. I started to type Has anyone suspected anything? and realised how that might look if our messages were ever seen, so changed it to a chatty, Hi, how are you?

She must have assumed I was being friendly. Immediately she replied: Fine, thanks. Just thought a coffee would be good.

Oh, decisions, decisions. I could bend my tired body into downward dog while awaiting the treat of a wheatgrass smoothie. On the other hand I could face my husband's mistress – or was that my lover's widow? – and talk about how we'd collaborated in concealing the way he died. It was a hard choice but eventually I replied:

I'll be at the Oval Café at 11.

Chapter 72

Emma

I got there early and sat with a glass of water in the corner at the back of the café. There were just enough people there so that we wouldn't be noticed, but not enough that anyone would have to sit near us. The French windows were open and most people had spilled outside onto the small terrace. At the counter there was a wide array of cakes and normally I would've made the most of them, but that day my stomach was clenched and I couldn't have eaten a thing. I saw a little black car drive up the street, then slow down and park. I recognised it immediately. It had been parked outside their house that afternoon, two weeks ago.

My stomach tightened further as she climbed out of the car. It was as though I was seeing her for the first time. My competitor. The woman who'd been having an affair with my husband. She looked younger than I remembered, more like the old photo I'd seen on their mantelpiece, the one where Tom's son was young. Her hair was wavy now and I could see highlights there, glinting as she walked across the road.

She walked into the café and looked around. I waved half-heartedly, wondering why on earth I was there.

"Hi," she said. She blushed bright red and I thought, *Good, so you should*. I had to quell the thought that I wasn't exactly an innocent here. "Can I get you a drink?"

"No, thanks. I'm fine."

She ordered coffee at the counter and waited for it before coming back to my table. She sat down next to me; I knew she'd sat there so that we could both check out the room that way, see if we were noticed together. Nobody was looking at us, though. We just seemed like a couple of friends having a drink together. Appearances can be so deceptive.

Ruby stirred her coffee until I wanted to grab the spoon from her. She looked up and saw my expression and put the spoon down swiftly. "I've got something to tell you," she said.

My heart thumped hard in my chest. "Did they look at his phone?"

She looked confused. "No, why?"

"Are you sure? Absolutely certain?"

Every night since Tom died I'd woken at about three o'clock and lain in bed worrying about his phone. I hadn't thought about it on the day itself, there was too much to think about, but I'd thought of little else since. I knew it would be password protected, but the police could get beyond that, couldn't they? And once they'd examined it, they'd say, *Hold on, isn't this person he's sending threatening messages to the same woman who said she'd witnessed his accident?* Then they'd arrest me. Each night I panicked at the thought that I'd have my baby in prison and Harry would have to take care of it. We'd never get past that, and when I left prison the baby would stay with him.

"Yes. I took it with me." She flushed. "Actually I smashed it that night, down by the river, and threw the pieces away. Don't worry, nobody will find anything now."

I was overwhelmed with relief. "Oh, thank God. I wish you'd told me."

"I'm sorry. I should have. I just didn't think. I was waiting for the postmortem results."

I saw telltale shadows under her eyes and knew she'd spent her nights the same way I had. My mouth was dry. "Do you know the results now?"

She nodded. "Accidental death."

I was careful not to meet her eyes. We both knew the truth about that.

"The funeral will be on Monday," she said. "We had to wait for the results to come in before they'd release the body." I saw her swallow. "Tom died from the bang on his head, when he hit it on the tiles. There was a laceration at the back of his scalp where it had hit the floor and his skull was fractured." She stopped suddenly and looked down at her drink. I kept quiet. "He'd broken some ribs in the fall, too, and a couple of vertebrae were shattered in his lower back." She took out a tissue and rubbed her eyes. "There was a lot of alcohol in his bloodstream. Three times the drunk-driving limit. He must have been drinking all day."

I thought back to that afternoon when I'd kneeled next to him to see whether he was alive. I hadn't consciously noticed it at that point but late that night Harry had slipped into bed beside me when he got back from London. He'd had a couple of drinks on the train with one of the guys from work, and when he leaned over to kiss me, his breath had smelled just the same as Tom's had. I'd jumped out of bed and run to the bathroom. I shuddered at the memory. "Did he normally drink a lot?"

"He did, yeah. He said it relaxed him. It didn't relax me, though. I'd be on tenterhooks wondering what fresh argument he'd come up with."

I saw a look on her face then as she remembered. For a moment I forgot what she'd done to me and reached out to touch her arm. "Did he hurt you? Was he violent?"

She was quiet for a long time. Her face was pale, her eyes lowered. "When I lived with Tom there was always a threat in the air that was horrible to live with. He never hit me, but he hurt me in every other way you can hurt someone."

I winced.

"It left me not trusting people. Anyone. I became hypervigilant. And" – her voice faltered – "not quite whole. For a while I felt as though I didn't exist."

I knew, I just knew what had rescued her. Who had rescued her. I had to change the subject fast. "Did you realise he'd drunk so much that day?"

"I hadn't even thought of it when I went to the house. He was supposed to be working from home and I don't think he ever drank when he was working." She frowned, as if that thought just explained something from the past. "When I first got there he was really friendly. I didn't even think he might be drinking. But then I heard him in the kitchen when the viewers had gone and I thought he was pouring a drink. Two, actually. The police officer checked the glass, remember? And when I…" She faltered. "When he was shouting at me, his face was right up next to mine." She moved her hand so that the palm was an inch away from her face. "I could smell alcohol then."

Involuntarily I winced. "That must have been so scary."

She shrugged but I could see her eyes had filled with tears. "I was used to it." She was quiet for a moment, then she said, "I thought he was coping. I thought he was okay now." She dabbed her eyes again. "You know, he'd been lovely to me since I left. Really lovely. Supportive. Helpful. He was just like he used to be, years ago. I thought he wanted me to come back to him. I even thought I might. I could feel myself relenting. I was so lonely on my own. But then I realised what he was doing."

"What do you mean?"

"He was pulling me in so that he could dump me. He wanted to be the one to end things. He told me that his girlfriend was pregnant." She faltered. "I hadn't realised he meant you."

"I wasn't his girlfriend," I said firmly.

She ignored that, as though she didn't care whether I was or not. "And when I left him, things started to happen to me. I thought someone was coming into my flat. I couldn't see how that could happen and they didn't do anything much, but I just had a feeling." She swallowed. "One night when I was asleep, too. And I found he'd got hold of the spare key by pretending to be my boyfriend."

I drew in my breath. "That must have been terrifying."

"It was. It was part of the reason I thought of going back to him. For safety. Over the last few weeks, I'd thought he was my friend." Her voice rose. "Why did I think that, when he hadn't been my friend for years?"

Maybe I shouldn't have said anything, but I couldn't stop myself. "Ruby, for weeks he was telling me that he wanted to be with me. As a family, with the baby. He was convinced it was his."

We sat in silence.

Eventually, she said, "And the baby's definitely Harry's?"

I nodded. "Thank God it is."

"I didn't realise you were still sleeping with him." She looked completely crushed. "Harry said you weren't."

My eyes rolled nearly to the back of my head. "Of course we were. Weren't you? With Tom?"

She was quiet, then she said, "It hadn't happened with Tom in a long time. I think the fact we were trying to have a baby didn't help. He saw it as a sign of failure in the end. And I learned that if I wanted him, he'd turn me down. Every single time." She shook her head as if she wanted to get rid of that thought. "And then one day, he said something. He was so cruel."

"What did he say?"

She shook her head, her eyes glossy with tears. "Sorry, I can't stand to think about it."

"Get it out into the open," I said. "Don't let it fester. He can't hurt you now."

She took a deep breath. "We were having a row at Christmas, the year before last. He always found it stressful. And afterwards, I wanted to make up with him. I didn't want a horrible atmosphere, especially not at Christmas. So I approached him, you know…" She faltered. "In bed. And he flinched. Actually flinched. It was automatic, he didn't think about it, he just looked disgusted. He told me that I simply didn't do it for him anymore. That I had, when I was younger. And that it wasn't my looks, so much, though it was that, obviously. It was my personality. He said he'd lost all respect for me, that if he'd

319

known this is how I'd turn out, he wouldn't have married me. Wouldn't have dated me. Wouldn't have even spoken to me on the night we met."

"Funnily enough," I said, "that's exactly how I felt about him."

She stared at me, open-mouthed, and then she started to laugh but within a minute she was in tears. She picked up her bag and went over to the toilet. When she returned, her face was red and her makeup had been washed away. I thought she wouldn't say anything more but she drank her coffee, then carried on.

"I went on the pill after that. I knew I didn't want to have a baby with him. I didn't tell him. I was so unhappy, but I just couldn't pluck up the courage to leave. I remember thinking I was disappearing. That one day I'd look in the mirror and all I'd see was a ghost." She looked up at me and I swear in that moment she had forgotten I was Harry's wife. "And when I got involved with Harry, well, he brought me back to life."

I couldn't help myself. "Well, that's great," I said, "but it was at my expense."

Her face crumpled. I jumped up and went up to the counter to order us another drink. I had to get away from her. I was horrified at what she'd said about Tom, but didn't want to weaken. *She's not your friend*, I kept saying to myself. *She was having an affair with Harry. Don't go feeling sorry for her now.* But when I turned at the counter and saw her looking so frail, destroyed, really, it wasn't hard to understand how she'd fallen for Harry. He's a nice guy. A sympathetic listener. Easy on the eyes. I think that's when it dawned on me that she had a reason for the affair; Harry hadn't.

When I sat back down she wrapped her hands around the coffee mug, as though its warmth comforted her. "Does Harry know what happened to Tom?" she asked.

"I haven't told him." I added sharply, "Have you?"

She shook her head. "Of course not."

"He hasn't said anything to me. I kept the newspapers away from him." There had been only a short piece in the local press about Tom, not even a photo. It said he'd died by falling down stairs when he was drunk, and warned readers to be careful. My name wasn't mentioned; it just said that a family friend had seen him fall. That wasn't exactly how I would have described myself. "I wondered whether he might have heard about it from someone at work, but I don't think so."

Ruby drew a breath and I could see she was trying to pluck up her courage. "I need to ask you something. Something personal."

"Go ahead."

"When did you sleep with Tom?"

I wasn't expecting that one. "Remember when you went to Paris with Harry?" I said eventually. "I saw you at the airport with him. Kissing him." I was glad to see guilt suffuse her face. "I'd suspected for a while, but when I saw you together... well, it was pretty obvious what was going on. I went round to Tom's to tell him you and Harry were having an affair." I gave her my famous brazen look. "And we slept together."

There was a dead silence, then she said, "I left home a few weeks after that trip. So you knew all that time ago?"

"I guessed before then," I said. "I'm not stupid, Ruby."

"And Tom knew, too. I didn't realise."

"He only knew because I told him." I felt a surge of shame but quickly curbed it. "I don't think he had a clue beforehand. I'm sorry, but if you were having an affair with my husband, was I meant to just take it?"

"No, of course not." She brushed her hand across her eyes. "Why should you?" I could see her trying to control herself. "And now you're pregnant. Why did you have the DNA report with you?"

"I'd come round to prove to Tom that Harry was the father. I didn't want to talk to him; I printed out the e-mail and was just going to put it through his door. Tom wouldn't leave me alone.

He was convinced it was his baby. He wanted to tell Harry that he wasn't the father and watch him suffer, but it was more than that. He wanted to share custody of the baby. He seemed determined not to lose another child, as he felt he'd lost Josh. I would have had to have contact with him all of my life and I was terrified of that. When the results came in, I came straight over with a note telling him to keep away from me.".

I thought of those early days of my pregnancy, of having my blood taken and collecting Harry's nail clippings from the bathroom bin, terrified that the result would show the baby was Tom's. I still felt light with relief when I thought of the result. It dawned on me the night Tom died, when I couldn't sleep, that he could have still paid Harry a visit and told him I'd slept with him. He could have given the copy of the DNA test as proof that I was worried about the baby's parentage. But even if he had, and even if I'd had to admit to sleeping with Tom, then at least the child was Harry's. Still, I'd had a lucky escape; I knew that.

"How did you find out that Tom knew about you and Harry?" I asked.

She didn't speak for ages and I had to stare at her quite hard to make her notice. Then she said in a quiet voice, "The day before... Well, the day before I saw you, I bumped into Harry in a café in Nantwich. We hadn't planned to meet; it was just chance. He'd had a meeting with a client and was buying cakes to take back to the office. We had a talk. A coffee. We cleared the air. We won't be seeing each other again."

I breathed a sigh of relief, remembering that night and how I'd felt the distance between us. So that was why Harry had seemed to have something on his mind. "I'm glad you told me."

"I was an idiot," she said. "I think I wanted to get out of my marriage and saw him as my saviour."

I raised an eyebrow at her.

"I know. And I'm sorry. I'm so sorry."

"I just don't understand," I said. "Okay, so you bumped into Harry, but why did that make you realise that Tom knew about your affair?" Suddenly Ruby looked like a rabbit caught in the headlights and my stomach dropped. I knew she was going to say something really bad. "It doesn't matter," I backtracked, but she interrupted me.

"No. You need to know. Harry and I were going to live together."

"What?"

Her voice was unsteady. "I'm so sorry. It was a fantasy, on my part, at least. I was crazy to think I knew him well enough to do that. I got completely carried away." There was a long pause, then she said, "I am so sorry I did that to you. I'm ashamed of myself."

I forced my face to be impassive. I didn't want her to see the hurt that I felt inside. I said, "When was this?" but I knew. I still made her answer.

"It was June twenty-first," she whispered.

She didn't need to say it was the day that I found out I was pregnant. The day Harry came home late, with a huge bouquet of peonies. I'd been such a fool, thinking he'd bought them especially for me. I hadn't talked to Jane until five o'clock that afternoon and all the florists around here would be shut at that time of day. That bouquet wasn't for me at all; he must have bought it earlier in the day, before he knew I was pregnant. I felt a surge of anger. He'd bought my favourite flowers for Ruby, to celebrate leaving me.

I looked at Ruby. She was scarlet, wringing her hands, the lot.

I had to ask, but I really didn't want to know the answer. "How long were you and he together?" I asked. I remembered last Christmas when he was distant, remembered a holiday we'd had in the spring, when he seemed to spend a lot of time on the phone "*to the office*." And I remembered myself doing the pick-me dance again and again throughout our marriage, thinking he was a prize. What I deserved. He really wasn't.

323

She swallowed hard and I gripped my hands together. "Eighteen months," she said.

My mind was frantic as I tried to calculate. "Wasn't that when you started working for him?"

She lowered her eyes, her face a picture of guilt. "Yes. It started almost the moment we met."

And, just like that, the light went out in my marriage.

Chapter 73

Emma

I left Ruby pretty soon after that. I could hardly bear to look at her. My whole body was hurting as though I'd been punched in the gut.

Eighteen months of lies and deceit. It had started the moment they met.

And I'd known. I'd *known* he had a crush on her. I'd actually acknowledged that. And looking at her today and how vulnerable she still was – you could see her flinch if there was a sudden noise, see the desperation to be liked, as though we could ever be friends now – and I knew that Harry had needed that. He'd told me once in an argument that got out of hand, years ago, that I was too strong. I hadn't understood, hadn't thought a woman could be too strong. I'd built up my strength, thinking it was an asset, but now I knew he must have loved being needed by Ruby. He'd always known I could manage without him: I wouldn't want to, but I could.

He was right.

In our bedroom I saw the tangled sheets from the hours we'd spent making love the night before and suddenly everything was clear. When I first saw Harry with Ruby at the airport, all I'd wanted was revenge on her. But why her? He was the one who'd betrayed me. That night with Tom, both of us wanting revenge against our partners, coming together in an ugly mix of solace and revenge, it was Ruby I'd fixated on.

I was wrong.

And since then I'd thought that it was obvious Harry and I were destined to be together. We couldn't keep our hands off each other. I'd rewarded him for his betrayal with love and affection and more sex than we'd had in years.

On the dresser were my new yoga clothes, bright and soft and hopeful. I pulled them to me, held them to my belly. I could feel the difference there now. Almost see the difference. In a few weeks' time I would feel the first stirrings. A flutter. Harry and I had been reading my books on pregnancy and just last night when we lay in bed and talked about the future, he pushed up my pyjama top and brushed his eyelashes against my skin.

"That's what it'll feel like," he'd said. "I can't wait."

And, like a fool, I'd rolled over and kissed him, and made love to him as though he was something special. Precious. I was so relieved to have him back that I hadn't realised that when something precious breaks, no matter how much you want to, you just can't put it together again without noticing the difference. It'll never be the same. You will always see the tiny fine lines that shoot out from the damage; they will deepen and spread and can't be repaired.

–

I was sitting in the living room, waiting for him when he came home from work. I'd had a busy day. When I left Ruby I'd called my sister, Jane, from my car. She came straight to my house and I told her everything. Almost everything. She winced when I told her about Harry's affair with Ruby. I was gratified by her response when I told her I'd slept with Tom. I didn't tell her that I thought at the very last minute Ruby could have saved Tom. I still didn't know what I thought about that. Now Jane was waiting at her home for me. I'd told her I wouldn't be long.

My car was full of suitcases. We'd crammed in everything we thought I'd need. My clothes, my shoes, my hair dryer. My new yoga clothes and my pregnancy books. My NutriBullet blender for those wheatgrass smoothies. One of my positive pregnancy tests. I'd shredded the DNA results I'd taken to show Tom; there was no need for them now.

I'd opened a new bank account and transferred half of our savings to it. I wasn't taking any risks. In a folder I had all the documents I'd need: My birth certificate. Our marriage certificate. Mortgage details. Insurance. Passport. All those things that you need when you're leaving your husband.

Harry's car pulled onto the driveway. I couldn't have moved then to save my life. I heard his key turn in the lock, heard him call my name. There was a pause and I knew he would be wondering why I hadn't answered. He opened the living room door and saw me sitting there on the sofa by the window.

"Emma?" He came into the room and knelt beside me. "Are you okay, sweetheart?"

Despite everything, my eyes prickled. He sounded so concerned. As though he loved me. I looked at his face, at the man I'd thought I'd grow old with. The man I'd trusted with every cell in my body.

"Is the baby all right?" he asked.

And I knew that if there was no baby, he wouldn't be here. He'd be with another woman, planning a baby with her. If there was no baby I'd be here alone right now, and he'd had no qualms about that. I knew my worth in his eyes then.

"Harry," I said. It was hard to speak, my mouth was so dry. I picked up the glass of water I'd known I'd need and took a sip. "Harry, this isn't working out for me."

Chapter 74

Ruby

I didn't go back to my house until the day of the funeral, after everyone had left the reception. I hadn't been there since Tom died. I stayed at my flat and, oddly enough, nothing happened to scare me in all that time. At first nobody was allowed into our house and then I couldn't face going there. I was too superstitious. It was only after the cremation that I could believe he was truly gone.

–

I was the last to leave the hotel after the funeral reception. There'd been quite a crowd and I was exhausted and aching after talking to so many people, many of whom I didn't know. Tom's brother was there with his wife; they were kind to me but didn't seem to know what to say, and I wondered what Tom had told them about me after I left. They hadn't been in touch since I moved out, and I assumed I wouldn't see them again. They talked to Josh and to a few distant cousins but didn't stay long as they were travelling back to Scotland that afternoon. I heard them arrange for Josh to drive up there in early September and was glad they'd be there for him. There were a couple of neighbours and some of Tom's colleagues, too, who were singing his praises as though he'd died a martyr for his cause.

Perhaps he had.

Tom's ex-wife, Belinda, was there with her husband, Martin; her eyes were as dry as mine. And Josh. His weren't, and my heart broke as I saw him go from table to table to talk to people about his father. He avoided me and I wondered whether he was frightened of breaking down or whether he'd guessed that I wasn't actually mourning. I still hadn't spoken to him about Tom's death; I'd called Belinda the day it happened and she'd told him. She called a few days later to see how I was and told me that Josh had taken it badly. That was a very tough day.

Tom's funeral really hit home how few friends I had. Most of them had disappeared over the years. Tom would complain about them, especially if they wanted to see me alone. If they called me he'd be cold afterwards and say it wouldn't bother him if it was someone else, but that particular person should be off-limits. My best friend from my university days, Chris, had said when Tom and I first got together that he was isolating me. I couldn't believe it and after a while I didn't see her again. Perhaps now I could find the courage to write to her, to tell her that she was right.

My dad was there. I called him when I got back to my flat that day. I didn't know what else to do. I'd held it together through the drive home. I'd said hello to the lady who owned the florist's shop and agreed with her that it was lovely to have a sunny day. She told me I looked a bit peaky and I smiled but couldn't answer. I hurried upstairs and called my dad in Melbourne. It was three in the morning their time and I heard my mother's outrage first, then my dad's soft, familiar voice, asking if I was all right. Once I started to cry I couldn't stop. The problem was that I had to stick to the story that Emma and I had agreed on. I couldn't tell him about the fight I'd had with Tom, or about Harry, or how I knew Emma. I could never tell anyone the truth about what had happened.

He talked to me for hours that night until it was dark here and light there. He stayed on the phone until I slept and when I woke the next morning there was a message waiting for me, telling me he was already on a flight home. My mum stayed in Australia as planned; my dad told me she'd be back in a month, as though this was a promise, not a threat. Apparently she needed my sister's support to cope with Tom's death. Fiona told me that if she didn't leave soon there'd be another funeral on the cards.

When he arrived home he invited me to stay with him at their house, but I wanted to be alone then and went back to my flat. I couldn't trust myself not to tell him everything.

He was a godsend at the funeral reception, talking to people about Tom, just as though he'd liked him. He took me to one side once everyone had arrived at the reception and had been greeted and offered drinks.

"Just get through this," he said, "then it'll all be over."

I knew what he meant: He wasn't just talking about the funeral, but my marriage, too. I knew what he thought of Tom. Unlike my mum, who still thought Tom was marvellous, my dad seemed to go off him after the first couple of years. We always visited them; my mum didn't come to my house. I think she felt it reduced her status as matriarch if she had to visit me, though if we had a party she always wanted to be there. She hated to miss out on anything.

At the start my dad seemed happy to spend time with Tom, but after a few years I noticed that he'd find an excuse to go out into the garden and do something out there. He'd come back in shortly before we left and say good-bye with a troubled look on his face. One day when I was there on my own, I'd tackled him about it.

"Don't you like Tom?"

My dad's eyes had shifted nervously. "Of course I do."

"You don't seem to like talking to him nowadays."

"I do!"

I stared him down. "You leave the room as soon as you can. He's always friendly to you. Why can't you talk to him?"

"I do like him," he said again. "It's just…"

I waited, knowing he would hate that silence between us.

Eventually he said, "He seems a bit bossy. I don't like that, love." I know now that he was talking about his own marriage.

"He is not!" I'd said, hot with injustice. "He's very clever, yes, but he doesn't boss anyone around!"

"He likes things done his way," my dad had said quietly.

Red with embarrassment and wishing I'd never mentioned it in the first place, I said, "Well, don't we all?"

"You don't have things your way, though, do you?" he said.

My mum had come into the room and heard what my dad had said. "Are you kidding?" she'd said. "She has everything she could ever want. Look at the house they've got!" My mother had been furious about my house from the beginning because her sister had left me some money in her will, which I'd used to help pay for it. She'd left sentimental items for my mum, who couldn't care less about anything like that. My mother was an early advocate of eBay and had had those trinkets on sale before her sister was in her grave. "And her car. I'd say she has everything her own way." She gave me a hard look and, remembering that now, I realised she'd been jealous of the life I was leading. A life I became desperate to escape. "I'd say she's not as daft as she looks. She's the one in control there!"

But I wasn't. I never was. Even when *he* told me I was, I wasn't.

–

All afternoon at the reception I had to keep up the pretence that Tom was a great guy. "We had our differences, but I'm so sorry to lose him," I said again and again. I'd planned this well in advance, knowing I'd struggle with what to say. "Yes, it was a terrible shock" and "It's such a tragedy when someone dies so young." And then I'd move on with, "Will you excuse me? I should speak to his relations." And off I'd go until someone else approached me.

Oliver came to the funeral. He'd been away for a couple of weeks and didn't know Tom had died until another neighbour told him on his return. He'd called me immediately and offered to help with the funeral arrangements. He'd clearly moved past our conversation on the riverfront and told me about a woman he'd met on holiday whom he'd be meeting up with soon. It sounded as though they'd got along really well and he was hopeful something would come of it. He was polite at first but soon relaxed into being the friend I'd had for so long.

Sarah didn't show up. When we had a quiet moment, Oliver told me that when he checked his work e-mails after his holiday, he found a message from her, telling him she'd walked out of Sheridan's. She wanted to know whether there were any jobs going at his place. I asked him if they'd talked about Tom's death, but he said he hadn't had time to talk to her and that she hadn't mentioned it in her message. It didn't sound as though he'd be rushing to call her anytime soon, though that might have been wishful thinking on my part. I really didn't want Sarah to cast a critical eye over what happened that day.

He rescued me a few times at the reception. "I can't believe someone you've never met has just asked you to tell them *exactly* what happened, as though your life's some sort of soap opera and they've missed an episode," he whispered as we left someone who'd worked with Tom for only a few months but who seemed desperate to know the gruesome details of his death. "How come you're not angry?"

"I just keep reminding myself I'll never have to see them again."

"Is your friend here?"

"Which one?"

"Emma. The woman who was there when he fell downstairs." Oliver put his arm around my shoulders and I turned to him just for a moment, for comfort. "It must have been horrible."

"It was." I thought of seeing Emma at the front door and how I'd panicked, thinking she'd tracked me down. "I've never been more frightened. She wasn't able to come today." I hadn't even thought of asking her; I knew she wouldn't have wanted to come.

"She sounds like a good friend."

"She was the best friend I could have had," I said, thinking of what she'd done for me. And what I'd done to her.

"I haven't heard you mention her before. How do you know her?"

Without a moment's hesitation I gave him my practiced speech. "Oh, we met at a yoga class." I thought of Emma's face, pink and earnest as she'd told me what to say. She was so insistent that there was some part of me that thought that really was how we met. "We weren't any good, though, so we stopped going."

Oliver looked sceptical. I've never exactly been the yoga type. "What will you do now?" he asked. "Now that it's all over."

"I don't know."

Suddenly all those dreams I'd had for my life seemed to crumple and die. I just couldn't imagine what I would do. I felt I'd be travelling the world looking for salvation, or I'd live in another place and it would be just the same as this, in every significant way. I couldn't envisage a happy time ahead, where I'd meet Josh again and talk to him about his dad without guilt overwhelming me. I couldn't imagine I'd ever fall for anyone again. How could I trust them? And I knew that if I met someone nice, a decent guy, I should keep away from him, too. I wasn't fit to be with anyone.

Soon people started to drift away. I noticed they went to Josh before they left rather than to me, and I was glad for him, and grateful for the reprieve. His face was red and his eyes damp; he stood in the doorway, hugging and kissing everyone as they left. It seemed that he'd become a man overnight, and had had to learn how to do that without his father's help.

I couldn't bear to look at him, at his grief. I went to find the manager to settle the bill, and when I returned, Josh had gone. I went out to the car park and saw Belinda driving off, Josh by her side. I wasn't sure whether they'd seen me or not, but neither turned as I waved.

My dad came up behind me and tapped my arm. "Everything okay?"

I frowned. "It's Josh. He's gone off without saying goodbye."

He looked a bit awkward. "It's hard for him, you know. He knows you were divorcing his dad. Maybe he thinks you weren't bothered by his death."

I winced. If only he knew.

"He'll be okay," he said. "Just give him time."

"Thank you so much for coming." I hugged my dad hard. I meant it, too. He might be under my mum's thumb but he was great in a crisis. "I couldn't have done this without you."

He squeezed me tightly. "Do you want to come home with me? You're very welcome to."

I shook my head. "I need to go back home." For a moment I didn't know whether I meant the house I'd shared with Tom or my flat, then made up my mind. "I'll go back to my house."

"Shall I come with you?"

I shook my head. "It's okay, thanks. I need to do it on my own."

Chapter 75

Ruby

When I left I drove round aimlessly for an hour or so, deep in thought. Finally I stopped at the car park by the lighthouse and sat outside on a bench, looking at the river. The sun was high and the wind turbines were turning. It was a peaceful scene but I'd never felt so conflicted. Seeing Josh cry had brought home to me just what I'd done. And though I'd gone over it again and again, each time I thought of the way Tom had fallen, I knew that in that moment of fury I'd wanted him to fall. Not necessarily to die, but to learn his lesson. He couldn't treat me like that. He just couldn't. And to goad me about the baby. He'd always known what would hurt me the most.

Enough. I had to stop this.

I took a deep breath. Suddenly I had the courage to go back and reclaim my house. It was as much mine as his. I was glad now that we hadn't filed for divorce. I hadn't been able to afford it and Tom was playing a different game. It made things easier now; something he would have hated if he'd known.

On the way back I had to buy petrol. Since I'd left home I'd worried every time I'd had to do that, panicking in case one day soon I'd be flat broke. Now the opposite had happened. Since Tom died I'd found he'd had substantial savings that he'd kept hidden from me, and because we were still married and hadn't changed our wills, that money became mine. His boss at work had called to tell me that his life insurance would pay out a large lump sum and he put me in touch with their pensions officer, too. I thought how I'd struggled financially even when we were together, how he made me feel guilty if I spent anything, but made me contribute half of all bills, even though I earned a fraction of his income. Often I'd go overdrawn and he'd bail me out. I always had to pay him back.

In Paris I'd tried to talk to Harry about it, when I had to explain why I'd be broke for a while. We'd been talking about putting a deposit down on a rental flat and I wanted to pay my share.

"I'll have the money from the house," I'd said, "but that'll take a few months to come in. I just can't afford to put much down for a deposit."

"It doesn't matter," he'd said. "Honestly, honey. That's the one thing that I'm not worried about." He'd looked at me with concern. "But what do you mean, he has savings and you don't? That's not right. You're married; everything should be shared."

I didn't know where to start. I'd hinted at things that were wrong in my marriage but the problem was that I'd thought Harry knew nothing about control and possessive behaviour. In his personal life he didn't mix with people who were manipulative and who told him something was true when he knew in his heart that it wasn't. And he didn't know how over time it was easy to get ground down, so that it was impossible to know what was right or wrong, what was real or fake. Or that's what I'd thought.

Of course the reality was that he was cheating on his wife. He told lies easily, without guilt. He'd lied to Emma every day of our affair. He'd lied to me about sleeping with her, about his longing for a child. He'd lied, too, when he said he couldn't live without me.

After I filled up with petrol I got back into my car, feeling brave and determined, and drove through the familiar streets, feeling free for the first time in years. Since university, in fact. Since the day before my twenty-third birthday, when I first met Tom in a bar. I'd immediately fallen in love with him. I'd learned to blame myself at my mother's knee; Tom had merely taken over the baton. It had taken years before I realised what he was really like. I knew that journey of discovery wasn't going to end just because he was dead.

This time I parked on the driveway. Tom's car was still there, so I had to park behind it, but still. I can't begin to tell you how significant that was. The last time I'd parked up there had been the day I'd left Tom, but before then... well, I couldn't remember a day when I'd been allowed to do it.

When I got out of the car, it was as though a weight had lifted from me. I felt lighter. Hopeful. The sun was shining brightly and I lifted my face to the rays. It was the beginning of August and the day was hot and sunny. It was a perfect summer's day. Perfect in all sorts of ways. I thought I might sit outside for an hour or two with a gin and tonic and a book, and enjoy my garden again. Count my blessings.

I opened the door and let myself in. I leaned back against the front door and looked at my home. *My* home. I looked at the top of the stairs, where we'd had that fight, and then at the black-and-white tiles where traces of his blood still lay. I turned away and saw the mirror where I'd seen Emma's face, then hastily looked away from that, too. The coat stand held only Tom's coats. I took off my jacket and slung it on a hook, then stopped.

Something in the air was different. When I breathed in I sensed the change. I could feel it on my skin, too. I rubbed my arms vigorously, but my skin prickled again immediately. I held my breath and stayed very still. I could see nothing wrong. I could hear nothing at all except the drumming of my own heart.

But I knew. I just knew.

Someone was here.

Chapter 76

Ruby

Slowly I took my phone out of my bag and gripped it tightly. I picked up my car keys, too, so that I could get away if I needed to.

I stepped into the kitchen and glanced around. There wasn't anyone there. The back door was shut and everything looked the same as it had when I was here last. The coffee cups were still on the drainer and I knew Tom had touched them, had drunk from one of them. I closed my eyes. I'd have to get rid of them. I couldn't cope with having them there as a reminder.

Quietly, I turned to the adjacent dining room. Its door was open wide. I tried to think back to the last time I'd been here, the day Tom had died, but I couldn't remember how I'd left it. The room was filled with sunlight, and dust motes hung in the air. The patio windows were tightly shut and I could see from the position of the handles that they were locked. Nobody was there.

I craned my neck to look up the stairs. If someone was in one of the bedrooms, I didn't want to be up there with them. I listened so hard I thought my eardrums would burst, but couldn't hear anything at all.

My mind raced as I tried to think why I had thought there was someone here. And then I realised there was a faint smell in the air. The roses that had been in the hallway that day were there still, their petals dry and brown at the edges, their leaves crisp. And nobody had emptied the kitchen bin or washed up the dishes in weeks. When I'd last been here, stunned after Tom had died, I hadn't thought of clearing out the kitchen. It had been the last thing on my mind.

I breathed a sigh of relief. That was the difference. I just needed to clean the house and open all the windows to let some fresh air in. Soon it would feel like mine again. I opened the living room door then stopped dead in my tracks.

Josh was sitting on the sofa.

–

"Josh! You scared me!" I went over to him and kissed him. "What are you doing here?"

He smiled at me. He was looking relaxed, sprawled out on the sofa, his phone, as usual, firmly clamped in his hand.

"I wanted to see you," he said. "I didn't get the chance to talk to you at the funeral." His eyes were red and I guessed that he had worried about breaking down if we'd spoken.

"It wasn't the place for a real conversation, was it?" I sat down on the other sofa. "I didn't realise you had a key."

Either Tom or I would pick him up and take him home; there'd never been a need for him to have a key here. If he wanted a late night out with one of his friends he would stay over at their house.

"Yeah, Dad gave me one to put on my car keys."

I grinned. I guessed every conversation would involve a mention of his driving. "I'd forgotten you were driving now. But how did you know I'd be here?"

"I knew you'd come back," he said. "This is your house now. I thought I'd wait for you. How've you been?"

"I'm tired, but I'm fine. No need to worry. I'm glad you're here. I wanted to talk to you."

Immediately he looked shifty. "What about?"

"About your dad's car."

He stood up and looked out of the window at Tom's car on the driveway. "What about it?"

"I thought you might like to have it," I said. "I doubt you could drive it because the insurance would be sky high, but you could sell it if you wanted. Put the money toward university or a gap year, if you fancied that."

"Isn't it yours, though?"

"Technically, because our money was shared." Well, my money was shared. "But I don't want it. It's too big for me to drive." It wasn't that, though. I knew at such close quarters I'd feel Tom's presence and suffocate with the stress. "You should have it."

"Really?"

I nodded. "And in his will, because we weren't divorced, I'm left the house and savings, and his life insurance is split between you and me," I said. "But I don't think that's fair." He shot around to stare at me. "I'm going to split everything between the two of us. You still won't be able to touch your share until you're twenty-one, but you'll get interest off the investment. Your mum will take care of that. And tell her that she'll carry on getting child support payments until you leave university."

His voice was unsteady as he asked, "Are you sure?"

"Of course. You're his son."

He started to cry then. His back was still to me and I stood behind him and wrapped my arms around him. He felt unfamiliar in his suit; I was used to him in school uniform or jeans or a rugby kit covered in mud; despite his height he seemed like a boy wearing adult clothes.

"It'll be okay," I said again and again. "Everything's going to be all right."

Eventually he calmed down. His phone beeped with a message.

"It's Mum." He rubbed his hands across his eyes. "I'd better go. I'll talk to you later." At the front door he stopped. "Oh, I nearly forgot." He reached into his jacket pocket and brought out a candy-striped paper bag.

"Here," he said. "This is for you."

I reached inside the bag and pulled out my scarf, my blue and pink scarf with its wild abstract patterns and its soft, tender touch. The one Harry had bought me because he loved me. The scarf Tom had taken from me in the middle of the night because I loved Harry.

I could barely speak, my mouth was so dry. "Where did you get that?"

"Dad gave it to me," he said. "I told him I'd been to your flat and he asked me to give it to you the next time I saw you. You forgot to take it when you left home; he knew you loved it."

I breathed out. I knew I hadn't left it here. Tom had known that, too.

Chapter 77

Ruby

Oliver came out of his house as Josh was leaving. He gave the boy a hug and they stood talking for a moment. I didn't go out there to join them; I worried that Josh would get upset again.

I went upstairs to the study and stood to the side of the window, so that I could look down at them unnoticed. Oliver said something and Josh laughed. I held my scarf to my face and breathed in. I could smell the perfume I'd worn in Paris, the weekend Harry and I decided to be together.

Oliver and Josh talked for a while, then Josh pointed toward the road. Together they walked down the drive and I guessed they were going to look at Josh's car.

As they walked I noticed that from behind Josh looked just like Tom. He walked like him. They were the same height now, the same build, though Tom had filled out a bit over the years. But now, looking at Josh as he walked away I saw how alike they were. It was odd I hadn't noticed it before. I wondered which was his car; I hadn't seen it when he came to my flat. I would have thought he'd have parked on our driveway, enjoying showing me how he'd managed to reverse in without bashing the fender on the low brick wall.

They crossed the road. Just beyond Oliver's house, on the bend of the road, was a car. Josh held out his key fob and the lights on the car flashed.

I held my breath. I'd seen that car before. It looked like the one that had driven past me that night when I was walking home from the wine bar, the night when I was sure I was being followed. It had stopped just in front of me, on the darkest part of the road, and I'd been terrified. I'd known that something bad would happen if the driver got out.

I had to be sure. I searched frantically through Tom's desk until I found his binoculars. I'd bought them for him one Christmas when I was stuck for something to buy. He'd brought it up every Christmas afterwards, as a sign I didn't know him. He was right. I didn't, and now I never would.

I dragged a chair over to the window and, balancing precariously on it, I focused the lens on the back of the silver car.

Slowly the registration plate came into focus and I saw the letters *MW*. I held my breath and moved the binoculars down a little. There it was, the dual exhaust.

It was as though my brain couldn't compute what my eyes had seen. I stood staring for a few minutes, watched as Oliver clapped Josh on the back and turned to come back to his own house. I watched as Josh started his car and drove off carefully. Once Oliver was in his own house I went downstairs and into the garden and put the scarf into the bin outside. I didn't want to see it again. I'd thought it was bought with love – well, look how that turned out. And it was touched, taken, by someone who hated me.

When I came back into the house I was cold and shivering, though the day was still warm. I sat in the kitchen, the only room I'd really felt at home in, my arms around my chest, and thought about the car. Had Tom borrowed it from Josh, or had it been Josh who'd followed me that night? And then I thought: Who had been in my house? Had Tom really given Josh my scarf to give to me, or had Josh taken it from me in the middle of the night?

How could I know? I could never ask Josh without sounding as though I was crazy, and in any case I knew I would never completely trust his answer.

Tom would love that. He could rest in peace; I couldn't.

Chapter 78

Ruby

It took almost a week to get the house sorted out, and while I scrubbed floors and paintwork and deep-cleaned carpets and curtains, all I could do was think about Tom and how he'd got hold of a key to my flat and how he'd tormented me there, and Josh and his car.

When everything was sorted I sent Josh a message, asking him to come and take whatever he wanted. He'd already taken his dad's car; I came home from the shops the day after I'd said he could have it to find it gone. He'd left a note saying he was going to sell it and use the money for a gap year. In my message I said it might be a good idea to get his stepdad, Martin, to come with him in case there was anything heavy to lift. I didn't want to be alone with Josh. I had never considered before now that even a fraction of doubt in someone means you can never really trust them.

Martin arrived first, parking his huge Land Rover behind my car. I went out to greet him and he kissed me on the cheek, something he'd never done before.

"How are you coping?" he asked, a sympathetic look on his face.

Now, that was a hard question to answer truthfully.

"Oh, you know." I shrugged. "Is Josh coming?"

"Yes, I thought he'd be here by now," he said. "There won't be room for him on the drive, though. He'll have to park on the street."

I wondered whether that was deliberate, whether he'd chosen to arrive later so that he wouldn't have to park near the house. In case I looked closely at his car. In case I challenged him. But when Josh came bounding up the driveway, tanned after a few days in Brighton with his friends, that thought seemed impossible.

"I stopped off to get these," he said, thrusting some flowers into my hand. He leaned down to kiss me. I stood very still, unable to put my arms around him as I usually would.

"Thanks." I had no intention of keeping those flowers in my home. "I'll find a vase."

"Are you sure you don't want the electronics?" asked Josh.

"I don't want anything," I said. "Take whatever you want. Anything that's left is going to charity."

He looked confused.

"I'm having a fresh start," I said.

He nodded slowly, then went into the living room.

Martin and I stood in the hallway for a couple of moments. "I know what he was like," he said gently. "Tom, I mean. Belinda told me all about him. She said she felt claustrophobic at the end of their marriage, as though she was locked in a very small room."

I shuddered. I'd felt the same way at times.

"And I saw the way you were when he was there. At Josh's birthday parties and at drop-offs. You were so different when we saw you on your own. You never seemed relaxed when you were together. Or not for the last few years, anyway. Belinda saw it as well. She was worried about you, and when you left him, well, we weren't surprised."

Tears swelled in my throat. "Can I speak to you?" I whispered. The door between the hallway and the living room was ajar and I couldn't risk Josh overhearing.

Martin glanced at the door, then back at me. "Mind if I look around the garden?" he asked. "I might take some of those plants on the patio back with me if you don't want them."

We went outside and shut the kitchen door behind us. We sat on the bench on the patio, safe from anyone overhearing us.

"What is it?" he asked.

I gripped my hands tightly. I couldn't tell him what had happened, how I felt responsible for Tom's death but didn't regret what I'd done. What did that make me?

Instead, I said, "It was nice of Tom to buy Josh a car. I hadn't realised he'd passed his test until he came to see me at my flat."

Martin looked confused. "Yes, he's really enjoyed the freedom of being able to go wherever he wants."

"I bet he never lets it out of his sight, does he?"

Martin laughed then. "He spends most of his spare time in it. Either driving around or polishing it."

"I don't suppose…" I grimaced. This was going to sound so odd. "I don't suppose Tom ever borrowed it, did he?"

"Tom? Why would he borrow Josh's car?"

I shook my head. "I just need to know whether he did."

"Can't you ask Josh?"

"No. I don't want to do that."

He looked surprised. "I'll ask Belinda. She might know." He pulled his phone from his pocket and moved a few yards away to speak to her. I heard him say, "I don't know" a couple of times and then he looked at me and nodded. When the call ended he said, "I'd forgotten about that. Josh was away in London for a few days and Tom took it to the garage for a service. I was really busy with end-of-term stuff and hardly noticed Josh was away."

"Do you remember exactly when he took it?"

"It was about a month ago. The middle of July. My school finished on the twentieth and it was before then. Josh's school finished about ten days before."

I breathed a huge sigh of relief. I'd been followed home on the twelfth. That must have been when Tom had the car. Suddenly I felt guilty that I'd suspected Josh.

346

"So it was Tom," I said. "That car followed me home one night." I saw Martin's confusion. "Josh's car, I mean."

"What? And you think it was Tom?" Then it dawned on him. "Oh no, you thought it might be Josh? He wouldn't do that. He loves you."

"I know." And I did know Josh loved me. I'd always known. "I recognised the car, though, and couldn't work out why Josh would've done that."

"You must have been terrified."

"I was so frightened."

"That bastard," he said. "Belinda said he was really insistent he had the car; she thought Josh should have taken it for a service himself so that he could find out what was involved."

There was a moment then when I think Martin realised that the man whom I'd left, the man who'd followed me at night, frightening me, was also the man who'd died when I was in the house. There was a split second where I saw him abandon that idea.

"Come on," he said. "Let's get this house emptied and you can start again. You deserve that."

"You won't say anything to Josh, will you?"

"No. I won't say anything to anyone. Tom's dead now. There's no point raking over the past. Josh loved his dad; let's just leave him with good memories of him." He stood up. "Now, what do you want me to do? Josh is taking his dad's cameras and electronics. What were you going to do with his clothes?"

I shuddered. I couldn't bear to think of seeing them again.

"Why don't I take them to a charity shop?" he asked. "I can do that now, if you like. What will you do with everything else?"

"I've contacted a women's shelter and they said they'd take everything I didn't want. The furniture. All the kitchen stuff. They can sell what they don't need. They're sending a couple of guys over first thing tomorrow with a removal van."

"You're not keeping anything at all?"

I shook my head. "No. I don't want any reminders."

"I don't blame you," he said briskly. "And that's a great idea, to give everything to a shelter. They need all the help they can get. I'll get those clothes sorted, then."

I stayed in the kitchen, packing everything into the boxes I'd brought with me. After an hour, Josh came into the room.

"I'm off now," he said. "Thanks for letting me take those things."

I found it hard to look at him. I felt ashamed that I'd doubted him. I went over to him and gave him a hug. "Don't be silly. They're yours. It's what your dad would have wanted."

"And for the money."

"It's yours," I said again.

"You didn't mind me taking Dad's car, did you? One of our neighbours said they were interested in buying it."

"Of course not," I said. I'd been relieved it had gone. Every night before I left home I'd see his car come up the drive and my heart would sink. I'd learned to be supersensitive and to be able to know what mood he was in as soon as he got out of the car. I was glad I'd never have to see it again. "How long will you be away for?" he asked.

"I've no idea."

"But you'll be in touch?"

Now I wasn't acting. I could be my true self. "Of course I will," I said. "I love you, Josh."

Chapter 79

Ruby

The guys that the women's shelter had hired to pack and move everything arrived early the next morning and by midday the house was empty. I sat outside on the low patio wall and wrote a good-bye card for Oliver while they carried boxes and furniture out to the vans. I couldn't bear to see the dismantling of my home. I didn't want those memories. When they called to tell me they'd finished, I went to see them off, put the card through Oliver's door, then went back into the house.

It was empty now; even the curtains had gone. Nothing of ours remained. I took one last walk around the house. Everything looked light and bright, bearing no marks of our life together. I thought of the day we'd come to view the house and the hopes and dreams I'd had for our future. It was our first home together; we'd bought it after we'd been together a year, and we married just before we moved in. Tom had held my hand as we walked around and we'd talked about which room would be ours, which would be Josh's. Those early days were lovely and even now I don't know whether that was his true self or whether the man he became was the man he'd always been, deep down.

I called a taxi, then opened the door to the shed and saw my handbag and suitcase standing there just as I'd left them early that morning so that the removal guys wouldn't take them by mistake. The sun shone in, flooding the little room with light, and instantly I was taken back to the day I'd left Tom. So much had happened in those few months; I wasn't that woman anymore. I didn't know who I was, that was the trouble, and when I found out, I wasn't sure how much of myself I could reveal to anyone I met.

I put my bags by the front door and locked the shed and the front door and put the keys into an envelope. All I had with me now were some clothes and my passport and purse. A box of papers was at my parents' house. Nothing else mattered.

There was a beep of a car horn. The taxi had arrived. My car was gone, sold to my local garage, but when I looked up and saw the black taxi, parked at the side of the road in the spot I'd always had to park in, it reminded me so much of those years living with Tom that I leaped up, ready to get as far away as possible. The taxi driver came to pick up my suitcase.

"Going on holiday?" he asked.

I didn't know what to say. I didn't know where I was going or how long I'd be there. "Yes," I said in the end. "I'm going away for a while."

–

Before we headed to the airport I asked the driver to stop at the estate agent's so that I could hand over the keys to my house. They were handling the sale for me. He had to double-park and warned me to be quick, so I ran into the little office. Outside the sun was bright and when I entered the dim, cool reception area it took a moment for my eyes to adjust. In that moment I heard a familiar voice say, "How soon can the *For Sale* board go up? I really want a quick sale." I stopped in my tracks.

Sitting at a desk, chatting to one of the estate agents, was a woman I recognised. A woman I'd betrayed and who'd rescued me when I needed it most. Her face looked strained and pale. Her hands rested on her belly; it still looked flat but I knew that would change soon. My face burned with embarrassment. She lifted her chin and gave me a cool nod, then turned away.

I tried to smile, but I couldn't, and handed over the envelope to the woman behind the other desk. I hurried from the office to the taxi as though Emma might chase after me.

"Okay, love?" asked the driver. "Manchester airport now?"

I nodded. "Yes. Thanks."

"What time's your flight?"

"Oh, I've got a few hours."

I pretended I was sleeping on the journey to the airport so that the driver didn't talk to me. I couldn't stop thinking about what I'd overheard. Emma was selling their house. Were she and Harry having a fresh start, too?

We drew up at the airport ninety minutes later. I climbed out and paid the driver and took my bags into the terminal.

I was just looking at the flights leaving that afternoon, trying to decide where to go to, when my phone rang in my bag. I couldn't think of one person I wanted to speak to right then. By the time I found it, deep in my shoulder bag, it was silent again.

On the screen was a number I recognised. It was a number I'd said over and again to myself on the day I left home. Why was Harry calling me? And then there was a beep. I had a voicemail message.

As soon as I heard his voice I felt my knees shake and found a seat nearby.

Ruby, it's me. I'm so sorry, sweetheart. I made the biggest mistake when I let you go. Please, please will you forgive me? Can we meet up today? I have so much to tell you. I just want to be with you. His voice softened and automatically my body responded. *When I saw you in the café that day, I knew I couldn't let you go. I must have been crazy to lose you. I love you, Ruby. Call me. Please.*

I listened to the message again and again, remembering his voice as he talked to me in the dark in our bed in Paris about his plans for our life together. All the promises we made. For a moment I felt as I always had, that Harry was a prize that was just out of reach, and felt a jolt of disappointment that I couldn't be with him.

But then I remembered the humiliation of being fired and how I hadn't even considered he'd had anything to do with it. I'd trusted him. Yet he had. I knew that now. I think I'd known it before Sarah told me. It had been his decision; he wanted to get me out of his life. Then when he realised I hadn't received his e-mail, he'd lied to me and pretended he knew nothing about it, to save his own skin. I couldn't trust him now.

And I thought of Emma's face in the estate agent's office, brave and proud and so sad, and the way she was devastated when I told her how long my affair with her husband had lasted. She'd stood by me. I could never forget that. I would never betray her again.

I started to tap out a message to explain, to tell Harry that he'd hurt me too much. It could never happen. But as my finger hovered over the Send button, I knew I had to stop thinking of him as my friend. He really wasn't. I remembered how I'd waited for him to turn up at the hotel that night. He'd written one e-mail and hadn't even waited for a reply. He hadn't given me another thought.

I knew the torture of waiting, of not knowing what was happening, what my future held, and so I deleted his voicemail message and blocked his number and switched off my phone. Then I turned back to the departures board to decide where I should go.

Acknowledgments

Huge thanks go to my terrific editor, Danielle Perez, for her insight and editorial advice, and to my wonderful agent, Kate Burke, for all her encouragement and support. You have both made such a difference to my work, and it's always a pleasure working with you.

For each of my books the writer Fiona Collins has been my first reader and I can't thank her enough for her friendship and her critical eye. She's just the person any writer needs, both when times are tough and when everything's going well. She makes working from home so much fun.

Thanks to Caz Finlay for being such a great friend. She is at the start of her publication journey and I know she's going to make a huge success of it.

Thanks to Richard Hill for all his support and for discussing plots night after night.

Thank you, too, to Kourtney O'Dwyer, who was at Bouchercon in Toronto, and was kind enough to bid to have her name in my novel.

Finally, thank you so much to Rosie and Louis for all your love and encouragement. You mean so much to me.

Discussion Questions

1. On the night Ruby left home, Harry wrote to tell her not to leave and explained why. If Ruby had read the e-mail in time, do you think she would have stayed with Tom?

2. When Jane confronted Harry about his affair, he told her he would dump Ruby immediately. Should Jane have told Emma what was going on, or do you agree with her that it would have been better for Emma if she remained in ignorance? Would you answer differently if Emma hadn't been pregnant?

3. Emma and Tom slept together after discovering that their spouses were having an affair. Would you still consider this infidelity on their part? Or was this revenge, or something else?

4. What do you think Tom's intentions were toward Emma and her baby? Did he sincerely believe he was the father and simply want to be involved, or did he just want to control Emma? How much did his divorce, which led to him living apart from his son, affect the way he behaved with Emma?

5. If Emma hadn't realised Harry was having an affair and hadn't got pregnant, do you think Ruby and Harry would have had a happy life together, given how their relationship started?

6. What should parents do if they realise their adult children are involved with a controlling partner?

7. Do you think Tom's controlling behaviour will have any effect on Josh's adult relationships in the future?

8. Do you think Sarah was telling the truth when she said that Harry threw away the letter from Ruby? Might Sarah have had other reasons for the way she responded to Ruby?

9. Do you think Tom thought he was happily married? If not, why do you think he didn't leave Ruby?

10. If Ruby and Tom had had a child a few years earlier, do you think they would have been happy together or do you think Tom would have always ended up trying to control her?

11. Do you think Emma would have still protected Ruby if she'd seen her actually push Tom?

12. Who do you think has the best chance of a happy relationship with a new partner now: Ruby, Emma, or Harry? Why?

About the Author

Mary Torjussen has an MA in Creative Writing from Liverpool John Moores University and worked for several years as a teacher. She is the author of three novels, *Gone Without a Trace*, *The Girl I Used to Be* and *The Closer You Get*. She writes dark, gripping thrillers and her debut novel, published in several international territories, has been optioned for television by Ecosse Productions.